"By election day, America is going to be reaching a condition of maximum fear. Fear about its future, fear about its safety, fear about its economy. Winter will be setting in, and that means that every unemployed worker will be wondering how to put a turkey on the table at Christmas, and how to scrape together enough money to buy gifts for the kids. Old people are going to be worried about the cold, the cost of heating and lighting, and the prohibitive cost of medical treatment. The young graduates who left college in the summer and who still haven't found a job are going to be facing their first winter on the executive breadline. Fear, Greta, that's what it's all about. Absolute fear. And that's where I come in."

CONDOR

Look for these other TOR books by Graham Masterton

GRAHAM MASTERTON
CONDOR

TOR

A TOM DOHERTY ASSOCIATES BOOK

CONDOR

Copyright © 1983 by Graham Masterton

Reprinted by arrangement with Wiescka Masterton

A TOR Book

Published by Tom Doherty Associates
8-10 West 36 Street
New York, N.Y. 10018

First TOR printing: July 1985

ISBN: 0-812-52195-1
CAN. ED.: 0-812-52196-X

Printed in the United States of America

Du musst herrschen und gewinnen
Oder dienen und verlieren,
Leiden oder triumphieren,
Amoss oder Hammer sein.

You must either conquer and rule
Or serve and lose,
Suffer or triumph,
Be the anvil or the hammer.

—Goethe

ONE

s best friend Bernie had to go to a piano lesson that
ternoon, and so he spent nearly an hour throwing a ball
against the back of the garage until his mother put her
ad out the kitchen window and told him for heaven's
ke to find something *useful* to do, like rake the lawn or
ean his bicycle. So he decided to take his BB gun and
plore the woods on the far side of Conant's Acre, like
diana Jones in *Raiders of the Lost Ark*.

He left his bicycle propped up against the split-rail fence
at divided Webster Crescent and its neat, new, three-
droomed homes from the down-sloping wilderness of
onant's Acre; then he walked in his rubbers across the
owed-up clay—a nine-year-old boy with unruly blond
air, a snub nose just like his mother's, and exactly his
ther's way of squinching up his eyes when he looked
to the distance.

He could have been alone on the whole wide planet.
here was nothing to the south but fields and trees, noth-
g to the northwest but the windblown grazing land of the
elly estate, of which Conant's Acre was the southern-

most part. Ahead, to the east, were the woods, tangled a
dark, which Bernie had solemnly sworn were haunted.

"There's ghosts in those woods, and witches and devils
Bernie had told him. "If you ever go in there, they'll s⟩
you alive and throw you out on the Acre for the vultu⟩
and the hyenas to eat."

He had protested to Bernie that there were no vultures
hyenas in New Hampshire, but Bernie had not been deterr⟩
he had read every horror novel that ever was, and when⟩
came to witches and devils, Bernie knew it all. Bernie w⟩
ten.

It took him almost ten minutes to cross the field. In t⟩
spring it was usually planted for barley, but now it w⟩
furrowed and crusty and difficult to walk over. Above h⟩
a flock of crows suddenly soared upward, alarming hi⟩
They swung around and flew away to the west under a s⟩
that was already pale with the approach of winter. ⟩
watched them for a while and then walked on, snifflir⟩
from time to time because the air was so cold.

The woods were very still and even more overgrov⟩
with briers than he had imagined. He stood in the fiel⟩
staring into them intently, his BB rifle pumped up a⟩
ready to fire. There was a rustling in the weeds at th⟩
border of the woods, but it was probably nothing mo⟩
than a mouse or a shrew. He looked back across the fiel⟩
and saw the safe and tidy rooftops of the Crescent. For
moment he considered turning back. But then he though⟩
what am I going to tell Bernie? That I walked across th⟩
field and looked at the woods and didn't go in? I coul⟩
pretend that I *had* gone in. Or I could say I did somethin⟩
else this afternoon, like cycled down to the Winant Mal⟩
But he knew that he always told Bernie the truth, eve⟩
when it was embarrassing or hurtful. Bernie was his be⟩
friend and they didn't keep anything secret from eac⟩
other.

He took an unbalanced step over the weedy undergrowth

shed aside a dense array of brambles with the stock of
s rifle and then hopped-skipped-jumped into the shadow
the woods themselves. He stood silent, listening, but
ere was only the sound of the wind and the birds and the
cking of dry leaves, and he thought to himself: there's
othing to be afraid of. Witches and devils are only stories
books. At least I *hope* they're only stories.

Taking out his penknife, he blazed a mark on a nearby
ee. A triangle with a circle in the middle. He and Bernie
lazed marks wherever they went, even in the corridors at
chool. He had read in the Children's Section in the *Concord
ournal* that a good tracker always blazes marks. He snif-
led and then took another few steps forward.

It was so quiet in the woods. Outside it had been windy
nd wild. In here it was almost like church. He blazed
nother mark and then moved deeper into the silence. He
ept his rifle raised though, just in case there was some-
hing around worth shooting at—like a witch or a devil.

"Okay, men," he whispered when he was twenty or
hirty paces into the woods. "We'll stop here for rations."

He hunkered down, propping his BB rifle against a tree,
nd took a pack of gum from his jacket pocket, wrenching
a piece out of the wrapper with his gritted teeth as though
he were biting pemmican. "It looks like the Japs have
gone. Maybe we should turn around and start back to
HQ."

While he chewed the sugar out of the gum, he carved
his initials on the side of a tree so he would be able to
bring Bernie back to the same spot and prove that he had
ventured into the unknown completely by himself. Bernie
might be ten but he had never ventured into the unknown
completely by himself, let alone cut his initials on a tree to
prove it.

He stood up and as he did so, there was a flickering,
fluttering sound right behind him. He knew that it couldn't
be anything really terrible, but it scared him all the same

and he swung around and snapped off a BB shot betwee
the dark trunks of the trees. Even though it was only a bi
or a squirrel, he frantically pumped up the air in his rif
again and slid the action backward and forward to chamb
another pellet. His heart pounded against his ribs.

He waited, listening. He was pleased with the quicknes
with which he had reloaded his rifle. He was an expe
hunter, no doubt about it. Slowly he backed up, retracin
his steps, keeping his rifle raised, his eyes squinched u
and his face as mean as possible. One look at that face an
any ghost would know he meant business.

He was still walking backward when his foot slippe
and the leafy ground seemed to fall right from under him
He twisted around to recover his balance, but it was too
late. A large piece of earth collapsed, and he was tumble
into a hole in the ground nearly three feet deep. He wa
followed by a shower of leaf mold and twigs, and some o
it fell into his face. He coughed and snorted, struggling to
get back to his feet. His first nervous response was to pick
up his rifle and look around quickly in case this was a
mantrap. If he wasn't careful, he'd be porcupine-quilled
with native spears before he could loose even a single shot.

"All clear, men," he said. He threw his rifle over to the
edge of the hole and prepared to hoist himself out. But as
his feet scrabbled against the clay, he heard a hollow
sound, as though he were kicking a pipe or a tin box.

Frowning, hesitating, he stared down into the hole. He
found a long stick and poked around the sides of it.
Treasure? A boxful of gold? It could be. There had been
plenty of wealthy people around here in Colonial days, and
plenty of highway robbers too. Maybe he had accidentally
come across a hidden cache of gold sovereigns. He could
buy his father a silver Cadillac and have it driven right up
to the front door and nonchalantly say, "There you are,
Daddy, it's yours," and hand him the keys. And his
mother could have a white fur coat.

He leaned down and started scraping away. Soon he had
uncovered a large, bare curve of metal, like the side of a
trash can or something except that it had a row of rivet
heads on it. It looked as though it had once been painted
gray or green, but there was hardly any paint left at all.
Maybe it was an old water heater.

As he dug more of the clay and leaf mold away, he soon
began to realize that what was under the ground wasn't a
trash can at all, or a water heater. It was *enormous*. He
dug with his stick as far as he could, down through the tree
roots that clung around it, as far as he could in each
direction, panting a little. Even after nearly half an hour of
digging, he still couldn't find the beginning or the end of
it. It was cylindrical and metallic, and the rivets were
arranged in long rows along the top and down the sides.

Wow, he thought, it's like a rocket ship. Maybe it
arrived from Mars one night and crashed into the ground
and nobody ever knew. Or maybe it's a secret tunnel that
leads under the woods. Or maybe it's an airplane.

But how would an airplane get buried in the woods? Who
would have wanted to bury it, and why? And most puz-
zling of all, *how* had they buried it? The roots of the trees
had virtually grown around it. Some of the finer root hairs
had even clung under the rivet heads, so it must have been
here for years and years and years.

He thought he heard a branch snap and he stood up
straight and listened, his nose smudged with mud, his face
flushed from all that digging. But it was nothing: just the
crackling of the woods. He wondered what he ought to do,
whether he ought to tell Bernie about what he had found,
and nobody else, or whether he ought to tell his father. If
somebody had *really* buried an airplane here, the police
would want to know about it, wouldn't they?

He dug a little farther, and it was then that he discovered a muddy, milked-over window. He tried to rub it with
his handkerchief, but it had become so discolored that he

was unable to see anything through it. There was another
window next to it, and when he dug a little farther with the
point of his stick, yet another. They were arranged in a
curve, like the pilot's windows in an old-fashioned plane
a Dakota maybe, or a Lockheed Electra. All the windows
were opaque. They reminded him of Mr. Ferris, who used
to run the newsstand by the Concord depot—Mr. Ferris
and his blind white eyes. He used to reach out and ruffle
Michael's hair and say to Michael's father, "Fine boy
you've got there, fine boy."

He was growing tired now, and the temperature was
beginning to drop. Twilight was thickening the shadows.
Maybe he should come back tomorrow with Bernie so that
they could break open the windows and see what was
inside. But then the secret would be Bernie's secret too;
the great discovery would have to be shared. And for this
secret he wanted *all* the glory, *all* the attention, because he
alone had braved the witches and the devils. He alone had
discovered where the airplane was buried, and he alone
had dug it up.

He craned his neck backward and looked up at the sky
above the treetops. It wasn't as dark outside as it appeared
to be from the woods. Four o'clock maybe, not later. He
still had time to break into the plane and explore around
inside it before darkness began to fall in earnest and the
real ghosties and gremlins started to scurry through the
trees. Daytime was one thing; he could scorn such things
in the daytime. But everybody knew that the night was
dangerous; even grown-ups knew that.

Not far away from the trench he had dug around the
plane's windows he found a heavy piece of stratified rock.
Cautiously he lifted it, and he was right to be cautious for
underneath it the soil was alive with centipedes, a whole
nest of them. He rolled the rock to one side and waited
until the centipedes had scurried away under the surrounding leaves, and then he brushed the stone off with the

sleeve of his jacket. It was almost too heavy for him to carry but somehow he managed to heft the rock right to the very brink of the trench and rest it there, forty pounds of good New Hampshire sandstone.

He spat out his bubble gum and bit off a fresh piece. He sat chewing for a while, getting his breath back. Then he hopped down into the hole beside the fuselage and grasped the rock in both hands. All he had to do now was to pitch himself forward, keeping the rock upraised so it would smash straight through the plane's window.

However, he hesitated. Supposing there were people inside? Skeletons. If the plane had crashed here years and years ago, supposing the pilot and the crew had died inside of it and were sitting there now, trapped behind these blind and muddy windows, just waiting for a boy like him to break open the cockpit and let them out, their bony fingers as tenacious as the roots that clung around their craft.

Bernie would know what to do. Bernie would have finished his piano lesson by now. He let go of the rock and stood there in the hole, biting his lip, thinking of Bernie. Good old Bernie. Maybe he should run back across the Acre, climb on his bicycle and go fetch him, and then at least they could break into this airplane together.

But something impetuous inside him, a sudden madness he had inherited from his mother's side of the family, led him to seize the rock again and think, what the heck? I'm going to do it. I'm going to smash this rock straight into the window.

At first it wouldn't break. But he smashed at it again, and then again, and at last it splintered and blistered until he had actually made a hole in it, triangular-shaped and ragged. He put the rock down and bent forward cautiously, peering into the hole as though he expected to see Satan himself peering back at him. But there was nothing: only darkness and a curious smell, like very stale sheepskin jackets. He pushed the point of his stick into the hole, widening it until at last the whole window was open.

He peered into the cockpit again, but it was still too dark to be able to make anything out. If only he had brought his bicycle with him: he could have used the front lamp to illuminate the inside of the plane and maybe he could have used the pedals like a winch to haul out the treasure—if there was any. Well, even if there wasn't any treasure, there had to be *something* interesting in there.

He cleared away the second window and broke that too. It was still dark inside the cockpit, but if he kept his head to the side, he could just make out a row of reflected half-moons—dials, they must be, on the instrument panel. And there was something dark and ragged, like an inciner-ated scarecrow; something in a soft helmet with earflaps, and he knew—with a silent scream that jangled his spine— that this was the pilot. The pilot was still actually there, sitting in his seat.

''God!'' he said aloud and sat back on his heels. He was shaking and breathless, and somehow not so much scared as dreadfully excited. He had seen only one dead body before: his grandfather, lying in his coffin, waxey-faced and as pink as a prawn—not his grandfather at all but a puffed-up joke grandfather from a carnival store. This scarecrow pilot, though, was *death*. Real, undisguised *death*. Looking back into the cockpit, he could make out a gloved hand resting on the throttle levers and a wrist that gleamed with knobby bones.

He knew that he wasn't going to be brave enough to squeeze through the cockpit window. Supposing the corpse suddenly turned around and snatched him? He was tough and courageous, but he wasn't an airbrain. He would have to come back with Bernie so that Bernie could cover him with his BB rifle while he scrambled inside. He wouldn't mind Bernie knowing about the airplane now—not since he himself had thoroughly discovered it and broken into it and seen the pilot.

Still, he would have to take some kind of evidence to prove his story. It was no good climbing to the top of Everest if you didn't come back with something to show that you'd actually been there; you could have been hiding behind a snowdrift for all anyone else knew. And now that he'd dug up the relic, maybe somebody else would stumble across it and claim that it was theirs, and unless he had a souvenir, he wouldn't be able to prove that the wreck was his. There could even be a reward for finding it. It was obviously an airliner; it was huge. It must have been missing years and years ago and nobody had ever found out what had happened to it. It was probably still full of people, all sitting in their seats like the pilot was—rows and rows of skeletons in ragged clothes with all their luggage and bags and hats and coats.

He shivered at the thought of it. He had no idea of how an entire airliner could have ended up underground, under the woods off Conant's Acre; but here it was, he had discovered it on his own, and he was going to take something back home with him to prove it.

Taking a deep breath, he reached down inside the broken window of the cockpit and felt around. There were some switches and levers that he didn't recognize. Then his fingertips touched the edge of a steel-and-canvas seat and a loose seat belt. The copilot's seat was empty. Either the copilot had managed to bail out before the plane crashed or he had gone into the cabin to reassure the passengers.

He tugged at the seat belt, trying to loosen the buckle from the rotting webbing, but he couldn't break the stitches. There had to be *something* loose in there, something he could take back to show Bernie. He reached in right up to his shoulder, praying that the pilot wouldn't suddenly decide to come alive and sink his teeth into his arm. He groped cautiously around the copilot's seat, first around the front, next around the space behind it.

It was then that he touched a leather strap like the handle of an old-fashioned camera case. He touched it again and managed to hook the tips of his fingers around it. Grunting with effort, he gently lifted the case out from behind the copilot's seat and at last brought it out into daylight.

At first he thought that it *was* a camera. It was an oblong of hard brown hide with a corroded metal clasp on one side and a lid that flapped up. There was no label on it, no initials, no brand name—nothing to indicate what might be inside. He sniffed it but it just smelled old, like the leather suitcase his grandmother kept on top of her wardrobe.

The clasp was very stiff; he took out his penknife and gradually eased it open. He didn't want to break it; the case might be valuable. He lifted the lid and looked inside.

It certainly had nothing to do with a camera. Inside, the case was divided into six green cardboard compartments, and in each of these compartments was a small glass bottle with a glass stopper. Each stopper had been sealed with something that looked like white candle wax.

He lifted out one of the bottles. There was no label on it, no instructions, nothing at all. It was made of clear glass, and inside there was about a teaspoonful of clear liquid, slightly oily, like his parents' gin or Russian vodka. He shook it but it didn't bubble or fizz.

Perhaps it was some kind of chemical that old-time airline pilots had needed; perhaps it was the copilot's medicine. But the leather case had summoned such strong associations with a camera case that he felt pretty sure the fluid had something to do with photography. Developing fluid, hypo, something like that. His older cousin Nat did his own film developing and sometimes let him sit on a stool in the darkroom and watch. He was always fascinated to see the smiling faces gradually appear on the bottom of the developing tray.

He picked away the candle wax, first with his fingernail and then with his penknife blade. He wasn't so dumb that he would drink any of the fluid. There weren't any signs on the bottle but it could still be poisonous. All he wanted to do was to sniff it to find out if he was right. He tugged at the stopper and with a grinding pop, it was open.

Carefully he leaned forward and sniffed it.

It had a very faint odor, not altogether unpleasant, like sugar water or boiled candy. He sniffed it again, trying to think of what it reminded him. He dabbed a tiny spot of it on his finger and touched it with the tip of his tongue. It didn't *taste* poisonous. It didn't burn or anything. And after he sat there for five minutes waiting for any peculiar side effects and none materialized, he decided that whatever the liquid was, it was nothing particularly dangerous. He stoppered the bottle again, put the bottle back in the case and closed the lid.

It had grown quite dark now. The wind was beginning to stir through the woods; not far away he heard the call of an owl. He brushed himself off, knocked the worst of the clay off his rubbers and started to climb out of the hole.

As he did so, however, he heard a rattling, collapsing noise from inside the cockpit. He turned around in shock, his breathing halted. The dead pilot had dropped sideways in his seat and was now staring at him out of the broken window, smiling in a bizarre and half-mummified grimace. His skin was yellow and leathery but it was still intact, stretched across the angles of his skull like half-roasted chicken skin, and although his blond mustache was scraggly and bleached by all his years of burial, it somehow gave him a hideous look of being alive.

Slowly, whimpering, taking as much care as he could not to disturb the sides of the hole, the boy climbed away from the airliner, still clutching the case, picked up his BB

rifle and crept away through the woods with all the frozen
caution of a rabbit that can sense wolf but knows the
consequences of making a sudden break for it. At last he
was out to the knee-high brambles and the sneezeweed,
and then into the open Acre, and he ran across the plowed-up
furrows with his head thrown back and his arms pumping
and his breath rasping in his throat.

He climbed over the split-rail fence, jumped onto his
bicycle and tore off home, the leather case swinging from
his handlebars. As soon as he reached the house, he
skidded into the open garage, leaped off the bike and stood
there with his hands on his hips, gasping for breath. He'd
made it. All the way home without the skeletons catching
him. All the way home, and safe.

He walked up and down in the garage for a while until
he had stopped panting. Then he picked up the leather case
and took it down to the far end of the garage where his
father's tool shelves were. He cleared aside a heap of
greasy rags and cans of polish and trays of screws. Carefully he pried out a loose cement brick, and here in the
cavity was his secret treasure trove: a dollar in change, a
live .22 bullet that he had once found and a notepad
containing the secret code that he and Bernie were trying
to learn so they could communicate without anybody knowing what they were saying. He managed to just fit the
leather case into the hole; then he replaced the brick and
covered it up again with rags and cans of polish.

His mother wasn't home, although she had left the back
door open. There was a note on the kitchen table that read:
"Shopping at Winant Mall. Help yourself to Coke and
cookies." He went to the refrigerator, poked around for
anything interesting, squeezed out a little canned whipped
cream and licked it for the fun of it, and eventually
discovered a container of cream cheese. He made himself
a thick and messy sandwich, leaving crumbs all over the
table, opened up a root beer and went into the living room,

where he slung his legs over the arms of his father's chair
and watched the rest of *Star Trek*.

His mother came home from Winant Mall a few minutes
after five o'clock. She set her shopping bags down on the
kitchen table and shook her head when she saw the chaos
he had left. She called, "Michael? I'm home."

There was no answer but that wasn't unusual. She took
off her red-leather jacket and hung it over the back of a
chair. She said, "Ferdie was down at the Mall. It's his
birthday next week. His mom was looking for one of those
E.T. wristwatches for him. You know, the digital kind?"

There was still no answer. Only Mr. Spock saying,
"The Zarans are unlikely to attack. . . ."

She frowned and walked through to the living room,
picking up a discarded sneaker as she went, the automatic
genuflection of all mothers. Michael was still sitting in his
father's chair, but his can of root beer was spilled across
the beige-colored rug and his half-eaten sandwich was
lying on his chest. His eyes were wide open and his lips
were blue, and even before she could speak his name, she
knew he was dead.

TWO

It was the kind of triumphant coincidence that could have almost led Humphrey to admit that there *was* a God after all. Not that he had ever been allowed to question it, at least not openly. Even in those tiresome years after the war, when he had doubted everything—religion, rationing, sex, the meaning of socialism, even his own reality—he had been shepherded along by his sister every Sunday morning to St. Botolph's Church, well-supplied with mints to suck during the sermon and five shillings for the collection bag; and he been obliged to sing at the top of his inaccurate voice "O God Our Help in Ages Past" and "Lead, Kindly Light."

Every Sunday for fifty-three years to St. Botolph's Church—except for the war years (those blessed war years!)—looking for a sign from the Lord.

And here it was: the sign. Not at St. Botolph's at all but here, out on this sidewalk café in Stockholm on a chilly late-September afternoon, with the sun already falling behind the reddish facade of the Sheraton Hotel and gilding his glass of Pripps Fatöl as though it were the Holy Grail. Perhaps it wasn't as spectacular a sign as a burning bush or

20

shower of locusts, but for Humphrey it was nearly as
~od. He had come out of the café with his sandwich and
~s beer and then realized after he had made himself
~mfortable that he was sitting opposite the most wanted
~erman war criminal since Joseph Mengele.

It was coincidence, of course. Humphrey had never
~en to Sweden before, and this was the first holiday he
~d taken in nearly six years. But he thought there was
~mething wonderfully *appropriate* about it that smacked
~f Christian destiny. He continued to drink his beer and eat
~s prawn-and-dillweed sandwich, his legs crossed, glanc-
~g from time to time at the seventyish man opposite him
~ his dark-brown reindeer overcoat as though he were any
~ther tourist like himself—just another old buffer come to
~isit Sweden for the saunas and the adding-machine exhib-
~s and the sex shows, and the temporary reassurance that
~erhaps he wasn't so geriatric after all.

The afternoon was sharp, sharp as a scalpel, and ten
~inutes earlier Humphrey had recognized the man as Klaus
~lermann, alias Klaus Schreiber, the so-called "Vampire
~f Herbstwald," wanted in seven countries for the murder
~n the autumn of 1943 of more than three thousand men,
~vomen and children at the Herbstwald concentration camp,
~ear Hoyerswerda.

Humphrey glanced across at Hermann with curiosity
~ather than distaste. The man looked older than he would
~ave expected him to be. White-haired, stooped, with that
~ind of liver-sausage complexion that only Germans seem to
~ake on when they age. Yet he seemed quite animated. He
~poke briskly and laughed a lot, loud enough for Hum-
~hrey to hear, and every now and then he would lean
~forward and say something to his middle-aged female
~companion with a suggestive smile, a touch on the shoul-
~der and—once—a quick kiss on the cheek.

It gave Humphrey an extraordinary feeling of achievement to have recognized a Nazi of such notoriety. He

could hardly have felt more pleased had he discover
Hitler sitting at the next table, or Martin Bormann. The
had been few triumphs in Humphrey's life, particular
since his retirement.

During the war he had worked in South London f
BDG7, known as "the Budgies," a small team of leg
clerks whose task it had been to prepare for the eventu
prosecution of hundreds of minor Nazi war criminal
using information brought back by escaped POWs an
reports from the Resistance. Humphrey had enjoyed th
work more than almost anything he had ever done. He ha
learned to identify by sight two to three hundred Nazis b
snatched photographs or by artists' impressions alone; an
he had also trained himself to recognize the same face
when they were disguised with beards, false hairpieces
spectacles or surgically modified noses.

He was quite surprised that Hermann had done nothin
to alter his appearance. He had grown older of course, an
that had made him fleshier and more wrinkled; and tim
had changed his jet-black, swept-back hair to iron gray
But the distinctive cleft-tipped nose was just the same, an
so was the horselike jawline, and those close-set eyes tha
had always made him look excited to the point of mania
All his life Hermann had had the stereotyped face of
"Nazi butcher," and now, over forty years later, he hadn'
changed.

Perhaps Hermann felt that in Sweden no one woulc
recognize him and that the war was too long past. Perhaps
he was relying on the fact that most concentration-camp
victims had been too traumatized to want to recall the
faces of their captors: they could pass them in the street as
though they didn't even exist. For every victim who could
never forget, there were a thousand others who would do
anything to prevent themselves from remembering. Hermann's face in particular was a face no former internee at
Herbstwald could ever think about with any degree of

almness or sanity. His title, "The Vampire," was well-
earned. In 1947 Humphrey had interviewed a woman in
Ennelager whose three children had been killed by
Hermann. When Humphrey had routinely shown her a
photograph of the man, she had collapsed on the floor of
the interview room and gagged uncontrollably. It had been
on a March afternoon, and he had never forgotten it. A man
whose very likeness could make people physically sick.

Humphrey finished his beer and wiped his mouth with
his paper napkin. It looked as though Hermann was preparing to leave. He kept opening and closing a gray leather
briefcase that was propped up against the white tubular
legs of his chair. The woman leaned forward and kissed
him, and for a moment they held hands on top of the table,
one brown-leather glove on top of one rainbow-colored
knitted glove, the sort of Lappish knitwear you could buy
in Ahlens or any of the tourist stores.

Humphrey went back inside the café and paid his bill.
The place was quite crowded, and several people stared at
him openly. The Swedes were unabashed starers, and
Humphrey sometimes wondered whether the purpose of
his holiday was for him to look at the Swedes or for the
Swedes to look at him. He didn't much care for staring at
people directly; if you genuinely liked a person, you didn't
have to keep inspecting him to make sure you did, and if
you *didn't* like a person, there wasn't much point in
looking at him anyway. His mother had always snapped,
"Humphrey, don't *stare!*" But as the girl behind the
register counted out his change, he did allow himself the
luxury of inspecting himself in the mirror behind the counter.
A stockily built man peered back through shelves of
rollmops, salted sild, prawns and bright-yellow cheeses.
Not bad, he thought, for his mid-sixties: ruddy-faced,
clean-collared, well turned out. Rather like James Mason,
only with a bigger nose. Sensitive, even cultured. And
nobody could fault the shine on those brown oxford shoes.

Through the picture window Humphrey saw Herman get up from his chair, take the woman's arm and slowl begin to walk up toward Lilla Nygatan, the narrow shop ping street at the back of the café. They hesitated at th corner, where Hermann leaned close to the woman an whispered something in her ear and they both laughe Then, quite abruptly, they separated.

Humphrey had never "tailed" anybody before. Follow ing Klaus Hermann through rush-hour Stockholm was quit a challenge. Now that the sun had dropped behind th skyline of the city center, the streets became chilly and th buildings were suffused in a strange, brick-colored hal light. Saabs and Volvos sped this way and that across th bridges that connected Stockholm's fourteen islands, the lights teeming past like a steady meteor shower. Hum phrey fastened the top two buttons of his coat and the followed Hermann down the narrow sidewalk of Lill Nygatan to Kornhamnstorget, where he stood right behin him at the curb as he waited to cross. A young ma beside him sniffled noisily and hawked. That was anothe Swedish habit Humphrey found difficult to get used to.

Across the square the waters of Lake Mälaren were th same eerie, chilled color as the sky. A train that woul take its passengers home to the suburbs of Södermalm an Hammarby rattled across the sloping bridge, its lighte windows reflected in the water. Humphrey stayed clos behind Hermann, feeling cold and overexcited but also extremely professional. Hermann coughed and cleared his throat, and Humphrey coughed too, feeling rather daring.

Hermann swung his briefcase in short, mechanical swings as he walked up the unevenly cobbled slope of Fünkens Grand to take a shortcut through to Skeppsbrön, where the ships from Finland and the USSR tied up. Incongruously on this cold September evening, soap bubbles floated all around them from a bubble machine outside a boutique.

Hermann looked neither to left nor right but walked like a man who came this way often.

Not far away a busker with a disturbing resemblance to Bjorn Borg was playing a folk violin, and a group of teenagers in blue-and-yellow quilted anoraks were hooting and laughing and kicking a Coke can around on the cobbles. It was only five o'clock but already the restaurants had switched on their lights, and there was a Christmasy atmosphere that didn't usually reach Derbyshire until the middle of December, sometimes later if the snow stayed away. Humphrey watched Hermann walk around the fountain in the middle of the small square at the top of Fünkens Grand and then continue up the narrow sidewalk of Osterlanggatan. To their right the tall, old-fashioned houses and tenements were divided by a series of dark little streets that led downhill to Skeppsbrön, and as they passed each one, Humphrey could see the pale, cold water of Saltsjön, the inlet from the Baltic. High above, sometimes seven or eight stories up, gulls perched on the sharply pitched rooftops and screamed like discontented eunuchs.

Hermann suddenly took a right turn down one of the narrowest and smelliest of the side streets and then stopped at a shadowy doorway and scrambled around in the pocket of his coat for his keys. Humphrey waited at the end of the street, pretending to read a poster for cheap travel to Denmark. He saw Hermann go inside and heard the door bang shut behind him. Cautiously he walked down the sloping street and stopped outside the house into which Hermann had disappeared. No. 17, Pilogatan. He looked up, and after a minute or two he saw a light go on in the third-floor window, and a pair of beige-linen drapes were drawn abruptly.

Well, thought Humphrey, if Hermann has a key, quite obviously he lives here. There was the usual row of nameplates beside the front doorbell, but only two had cards in them; Lars Wahlöö, Gynokologisten, and somebody called

Gösta Mokvist. Humphrey stepped back to the opposite
side of the street and stared up at the building's facade. It
was cracked and grimy, and streaked with the marks left
by decades of thawing snow. A rusty rainwater gutter hung
out from under the eaves and clanked in the evening
breeze. Not the sort of building he would have expected a
Nazi-in-hiding to live in. But he remembered that the blonde
guide who had shown him around the Gamla Stan on
Monday had told him that many of the older tenements
had been expensively converted on the inside, sometimes
at a cost of millions of kroner. Perhaps behind this dingy
Strindbergian exterior Klaus Hermann lived a life of bright
Scandinavian luxury.

Humphrey waited outside in the street until his feet
began to feel numb. Then he walked back up to Osterlanggatan, turned left and made his way along Stora Nygatan
to the bridge called Vasabrön, which took him over to the
main railroad station and back to his hotel. It was farther
than he usually liked to walk, and he was sweating and
chilled when he arrived.

The Lantona Hotel was a featureless 1940s building that
had somehow escaped demolition when the developers
were erecting the Stockholm-Sheraton on one side and the
"Elegant-80" Swedish furniture store on the other. It
stood between the two like a dowdy old grandmother
among her chic young children. Inside its noisy swinging
doors there was an oval lobby with a red marble floor and
an overhead light that gave the room all the qualities of an
incipient migraine. The old woman with white-cropped
hair who muttered and sniffled behind the front desk handed
Humphrey his key. He went up in the rattling elevator and
let himself into his room.

The strange loneliness of foreign cities at going-home
time descended on him. He wasn't quite sure of what he
ought to do now. Perhaps he should call the British Embassy and tell them what he suspected. Perhaps, on the

other hand, he had made a mistake and the man wasn't
Klaus Hermann at all but simply an innocent Swedish
businessman who happened to look like Hermann. Supposing the British Embassy wasn't interested—what could he
do then? Call the Israelis? They must have contacts with
accredited Nazi hunters, people like Simon Wiesenthal,
who would know how to arrest a man like Hermann and
how to arrange to have him deported. Humphrey knew that
he himself certainly wouldn't be able to tackle Hermann
on his own, despite the fact that he was at least five years
younger. It was entirely possible that if Hermann *were*
Hermann, he would have a gun and shoot anyone who
looked as though he might have uncovered his identity.
What would one more matter when he had already slaughtered three thousand?

Humphrey took off his coat and jacket and hung them in
the cramped built-in wardrobe beside the washbasin. He
switched on the light and inspected his face in the mirror.
If Hermann *were* Hermann, it wasn't beyond the bounds of
possibility that Humphrey would now become moderately
famous, with his picture in the papers and perhaps on
television too. The quiet man who brought a vicious Nazi
killer to justice. "Derbyshire Law Clerk in Nazi Arrest
Drama." He pushed up the end of his nose with his finger
to make sure no extra-long hairs were protruding from his
nostrils. He had always associated that with senility and
regularly plucked them, no matter how painful.

He loosened his necktie and sat down on the edge of the
bed. Below his bedroom window two buses for Arlanda
Airport drew up with a burst of diesel noise and idled their
engines while they waited to pick up more passengers.
Humphrey sat where he was, thinking, listening to the
sound of the buses as though for important advice.

Perhaps he ought to confront Hermann himself. Wait for
him outside his apartment and then simply say, *"Hermann!
Ich weiss wer Sie sind!"* But of course if Hermann *were*

Hermann, such a confrontation would alert him and he might very well escape. It might even be dangerous. And if he *weren't* Hermann, Humphrey would look extremely foolish.

And, when it came down to it, what duty did Humphrey actually have to pursue Hermann after all these years? Did he have any duty at all? The war had been over for more than four decades, and if this gray-haired old man had survived until today, who was Humphrey to report him and send him to inevitable execution? Why not let evil old memories lie? And in any case, what was the point of hanging a man who had already escaped the consequences of his crimes for more than a lifetime? Humphrey sympathized with the Jews, but he had no racial or religious ax to grind.

Humphrey had been a Budgie, of course, but none of the Budgies had associated all those years of identification and compilation with *real* men and women. They had jokingly referred to all the war criminals as "WCs" and even had nicknames for some of them. It seemed rather tasteless now, but in wartime, attitudes had been different; if you hadn't been flippant, you would have been a mental case.

The truth was, the notion of being the only person who knew where Hermann was rather appealed to Humphrey. Every day that he kept the secret to himself he would be exercising over Hermann an almost Godlike power. He could say in years to come, "I once saved a Nazi war criminal's life," and what a story that would be.

Mind you, his sister would disapprove rather a lot. His sister disapproved of Britain's being in the Common Market because it meant association with the Huns.

Humphrey looked over at the color photograph hanging above the head of his bed. It was a view of the Gruvon pulp mills on Lake Vanern, and when he had first set eyes on it, he had decided it was by far the most boring photograph he had ever seen.

Suddenly he picked up the telephone beside the bed and jiggled the cradle.

"Jes?" asked the old woman at the desk.

"I wish to make a call to Cricklewood, in England."

"Jes?"

"Can you give me a line?"

"You want to make a telephone call?"

"Yes, to Cricklewood, in England."

"Krickelvo?"

"No, no, Cricklewood. Near Dollis Hill."

There was a crackle, then a dialing noise and then a very long silence. Humphrey waited for a while before jiggling the cradle again and saying, "Hello? Hello?" but there was no reply. He couldn't get through to the desk again and so he sat with the receiver pressed to his ear, hoping the woman would eventually answer.

He was sitting like this when there was a quiet, modest knock at his door. He said "Hello?" once more into the phone, and when there was no reply, he put the receiver on the bed and went to the door.

"Yes?" he called. But whoever was standing outside was either deaf or disinclined to answer. "Yes?" he said again; the only response was another discreet knock.

He unlocked the door and opened it. Standing there in the corridor, wearing a wide-brimmed hat so that his face was almost completely concealed, was the man whom Humphrey had recognized as Klaus Hermann. He raised his hat, smiled and stepped past Humphrey straight into the room. Then he turned around, gestured toward the door and said, "You may close it now." Then, "Please."

Humphrey looked at the door, then down at his hand on the doorknob. His brain suddenly made the connection that one could be used to some effect on the other, and he closed the door and stood staring at the notorious Klaus Hermann in apprehension.

Hermann inspected the room, his hat in his hand, and at last said, "Not luxury, is it, Mr. Browne?"

"You know who I am?"

Hermann smiled again. "You know who *I* am. Or you seem to think you do."

"I—er, I don't know. I'm not at all sure. But I'd really like to know what you're doing here. This is my room. Private."

"Yes," said Hermann. "But you are not in England now, you know. You must remember that Sweden was neutral during the war, during *both* wars. So if you choose to make a commotion in Stockholm, it will not have quite the same effect as it might if you chose to make it in, shall we say, Cricklewood."

Humphrey felt his heart tighten, and he began to think that if ever in his life he were likely to have a coronary, it was going to be just about now. He said breathily, "I must sit down. Please."

"My dear Mr. Browne, it's your room. You may do as you wish."

Humphrey sat down on the bed and suddenly realized that the telephone was still off the hook. He picked up the receiver and was about to tell the old lady at the desk to call the police when Hermann indicated with a wave of his hat that he should replace it. Hermann sat down next to him, rather too close, and Humphrey could smell the tanning on his sleek reindeer-skin coat. That and sweet, peppery Jacomo after-shave.

"You must first of all understand that there have been several others before you," said Hermann. "I am not in Sweden too much these days. Most of my time is spent in the Soviet Union. But they let me have a little pied-à-terre here so I can keep in touch with the latest developments from the West and—most important of all—so I can see my dear Angelika. They understand the importance of morale, the Russians, even for a man of my advanced years.''

Hermann put an arm around Humphrey's shoulders and hugged him with unexpected strength. ''You will never be a spy, my friend. The second rule that any spy must learn is that even the watchers have watchers. The first rule is never to go to bed with a Bolivian woman. One day you will understand that. Or perhaps not. Do you think I did not notice you staring at me in that café? Do you think I do not occasionally glance out my apartment window to see who might be loitering outside? An elderly gentleman like yourself, shuffling about outside my front door for over an hour? Well, I had to be suspicious. Wouldn't it have made *you* suspicious had you been me?''

Humphrey said, ''I have to blow my nose.''

''Please,'' said Hermann expansively as though he were the grand dispenser of permission to blow noses. ''This is your room, do what you wish. You must tell me though, how did you find this hotel?''

''It was recommended to me.''

''Recommended? By whom? Surely nobody dislikes you so much!''

Humphrey unfolded his initialed handkerchief, blew his nose in puffy and discreet snorts and then said, ''My vicar. He stayed here once in nineteen fifty-five during an ecclesiastical conference.''

Hermann nodded. ''I see. Well, let us forgive him. The hotel was probably different in nineteen fifty-five.''

Humphrey said, ''Is it true then? Who you are?''

''Is it true who I am? What an odd question. Yes, of course it's true. I am who I am; and who I am is nobody at all, nobody who concerns *you*, Mr. Browne. Well, that of course is why I came here, to say to you most emphatically that whatever you think, you are quite wrong and that I strongly suggest you refrain from leaping to peculiar conclusions. The eye can be deceived, you know, not just by time, but by emotion. We see what we dearly hope we will see. How our eyes trick us!''

Humphrey's mouth was dry. He said, as steadily as he could manage, ''I believe that you are Klaus Hermann, a wartime associate of Dr. Joseph Mengele and the camp doctor at Ravensbrück, and then at Herbstwald.''

Hermann placed his hand over his mouth and sat there thoughtfully for a long time. At last he looked up at Humphrey and smiled. ''You are quite mistaken of course. But then anybody is allowed one mistake.''

He stood up and busily reshaped his hat. Those close-set eyes were quite extraordinary; when he looked at you, you couldn't be sure of whether he was going to burst out laughing or hit you in the head with an ax. He said, ''I am sorry you were put to such trouble, such inconvenience, out in the cold there in Pilogatan, and only this place to return to. It's noisy, isn't it, right opposite the Centralstationen? Well, well, I'd better be off.''

''I have been considering reporting you,'' said Humphrey.

Hermann kept on smiling. ''That would make *two* mistakes. First, to mistake an identity. Second, to report it. If I were you, I would consider carefully and then decide not to make any mistakes at all.''

''But you *are* Klaus Hermann,'' Humphrey protested, a little bolder now he could see that Hermann wasn't going to shoot him, beat him up or have him abducted.

Hermann stared at him. ''You truly believe I am Klaus Hermann? How much do you believe I am Klaus Hermann?''

''Emphatically. I worked for the Budgies during the war. You know, war-crimes arraignments.''

''Aha, so that is your interest. A one-time lawyer.''

''Lawyer's clerk, actually,'' Humphrey corrected him.

''So,'' said Hermann and gripped Humphrey's arm. ''You believe emphatically I am Klaus Hermann. How emphatically? Emphatically enough to lay money on it?''

Humphrey nodded, unsure of what the man meant.

"Emphatic enough to protest that it is true under torture?" asked Hermann.

"Look here," said Humphrey, "there's no point in making threats. All that you can do is to make things worse."

"But you said you were emphatic."

"I am. Absolutely emphatic."

Hermann leaned close and Humphrey could smell tobacco on his breath. "Absolutely emphatic enough to *die* for what you believe to be true?"

Humphrey felt chilled. Hermann remained close for a moment, his large face looming at him. Then he smiled quite suddenly, put on his hat and opened the door.

"I will say ta-ta for now," he said. "But perhaps we may see each other again."

He closed the door quietly, as though Humphrey were an invalid not to be disturbed. Humphrey heard his footsteps retreat down the hallway and then the rattling of the elevator. He went to the window and looked down into the street to see if he could watch Hermann leave the hotel. Had the man left a car parked outside, or had he come by taxi? But the hotel's canopy obscured the sidewalk below, and the blue fluorescent light that said *Lantona* made it difficult to see.

Humphrey let the drapes fall back and returned to his bed just as the telephone rang. He looked at it for a second or two and then picked up the receiver.

"You will eat in the hotel tonight, Mr. Browne?"

"Yes, thank you. About eight o'clock if that's not inconvenient."

"Jaha."

He put the phone down and immediately picked it up again.

"Jes?"

"That call to London. Can you give me a line?"

The old woman didn't reply but connected him through

so that he heard a dial tone. He hadn't called the number in eleven years but he still remembered it without difficulty, the way he had still remembered Klaus Hermann's face. An orderly, clerklike memory. The code for Britain was 44; the code for Cricklewood was 208.

It seemed like whole minutes before the telephone was answered by a rather testy English voice. "Milner." Then even more snappily, *"Milner."*

Humphrey said. "Major Milner? I'm sorry if I've called at an inconvenient time. It's Humphrey Browne."

There was a digestive silence. Then, *"Humphrey!* Well, this is a surprise. It must be . . . what . . . well, years. My dear fellow!"

"Something rather peculiar has just come up," said Humphrey. He glanced toward the door; it suddenly occurred to him that perhaps Hermann hadn't left the hotel after all but had tiptoed back to see what he would do. Perhaps he was out there now, listening.

"You sound frightfully far away," said Major Milner. "Where are you calling from? Not all the way from Derbyshire?"

"I'm in Stockholm, actually."

"Stockholm? My dear fellow! What in the world are you doing in Stockholm? This call must be costing you a fortune."

"Actually, Major, I think I've run into something rather important. Something to do with the shop."

"Oh, yes? Good God, Stockholm! Well, you're very *clear,* considering it's Stockholm."

"Major," insisted Humphrey, "I saw a man today who answers the description of Klaus Hermann."

"Who?" There was another silence as the information was absorbed. Then, "Hermann? You're sure?"

"As sure as I can be. I've even spoken to him. Well, he's spoken to me. He didn't admit he was Hermann, but he made it clear that he would make things unpleasant for

me if I suggested to anyone else that he might be. While
he didn't say so exactly, he suggested that he would have
me done away with, if you know what I mean.''

"I can't believe that it really *is* Hermann," said Major
Milner. "After all these years. And what's he doing in
Stockholm? The last we heard of him, he was on his way
to Ecuador. Was it Ecuador? Or Nicaragua?''

"Major, I promise you. I might have made some
legal mistakes, but I never mistook a WC's face. Not
once. You know that. Everybody in the shop knew that.''

"Hmm,'' said Major Milner. Humphrey could just imagine him puffing out his upper lip so that his mustache
bristled like a small hedgehog.

"What do you think I ought to do?'' asked Humphrey.
"I don't want to be done away with, for goodness' sake.''

"Oh, I don't think there's any danger of that. If I were
you, I'd forget about the whole thing. The fellow's probably someone quite innocent, someone who just happens to
be unfortunate enough to look like Hermann. All krauts
look the same to me; don't know how you ever told the
difference. You say he spoke to you?''

"That's right. I followed him home, but then he followed me back to my hotel.''

"Where does he live?''

"Major Milner, if you don't think it is Hermann, where
he lives isn't really important, is it?''

The major cleared his throat. "You're not baiting me,
are you, Humphrey?''

"No, Major, but—''

"Always had a bit of snideness in you, didn't you,
Humphrey? Well, never mind. If I were you, I'd forget the
whole thing. Get on with your holiday; have a good time.''

"I'm worried, Major. Supposing he decides I'm too
much of a risk? At least I thought you could have—''

"Could have what? I can't do anything these days,
Humphrey. I'm retired. We don't have reunions for the

department—still too hush-hush, even today—so I don't have the contacts anymore. They put you out to pasture and they close the gate behind you, that's what they do. All I have now is my garden and the telly. Do you ever watch 'Coronation Street?' Dammed good program, of its kind.''

"Major—"

"Did you say where he lived? Hermann?" Major Milner interrupted.

"No," Humphrey replied.

"Ah," said the major. "Well, mustn't keep you. This must be costing you a fortune."

Humphrey hesitated. Major Milner said nothing. The long-distance telephone wires warbled their secret and plaintive songs, like messages from distant galaxies—untranslatable and infinitely sad.

"Number Seventeen, Pilogatan, third floor," said Humphrey and put the phone down.

THREE

He was waiting for her when she drove her scarlet Ferrari up to the front steps. He stiffly raised one hand in greeting and walked around the front of the car to open the door for her. She kept him waiting while she collected her pocketbook, her sunglasses and her scarf and slipped on her shoes. Then she gave him a smile like a squeezed lime and said, "Hello, Reynard. You've put on weight."

Reynard stooped to kiss her cheek but she turned her head away. He said, "I always eat too much when I'm lonesome. You remember that time when I had to stay in Brussels?"

"Everybody eats too much in Brussels," she countered. "There's nothing else to do there. And I can hardly believe you've been *lonesome*. Not with Chiffon Trent around."

Reynard followed her across the futura-stone driveway and up the semicircular marble steps. Dick Elmwood was waiting for them at the open doors, and as Greta stalked past him, he nodded to her and then made a quick grimace at Reynard.

Reynard told him, "You can put Madame's automobile

away for me, please, Dick. That's if Madame has really decided to stay."

"Madame has simply come to negotiate," Greta retorted from the hallway. "You can leave the car where it is."

Reynard hesitated for a second, then shrugged and said, "Okay, Dick. Leave it where it is."

Inside the grand domed hallway, with its pale Adam-green walls and elegant white marble fireplace, Greta was looking around, her hands perched on the hips of her six-hundred-fifty-dollar Geoffrey Beene pantsuit, her nose raised in the air.

"The place hasn't changed any, has it?" she remarked. "Still the same old smell of death."

"Some can smell it and some can't," replied Reynard, trying to sound amused but feeling instead as though he had grit between his teeth. "Was it Carl who told you about Chiffon Trent?"

"Carl?" Greta asked obliquely and walked across to the living room without answering.

"Don't tell me you had Nathan's Discreet Inquiries onto me again," he said.

"Nathan's Discreet Inquiries accept inquiries only into affairs that are discreet." She looked back at him with a mixture of sharpness and overplayed pity. "You and Chiffon Trent have been so damned public you might as well have published a picture in *People*."

"We're dinner companions, that's all," said Reynard. "Come on, Greta, it was *you* who left *me*. You can hardly complain if I find it socially necessary to have a lady on my arm from time to time."

"Lady!" she said scornfully. Then, "You've moved the Troy. What on earth is it doing over there?"

The Troy was an oil cartoon for *Esther Fainting in Front of Ahasuerus* by Jean François de Troy, the final painting of which was hanging in the Maurice Segoura

Gallery in New York. Reynard had moved it from its usual
spot over the fireplace to a shadowy corner by the window
seat. "I moved it because it reminds me of you. A beautiful woman in a synthetic swoon."

Greta sat down and crossed her legs. She opened her
pocketbook and took out a gold cigarette case. Reynard
offered her a light and she glanced up at him as she
inhaled.

"You've changed, you know," she told him, blowing
out smoke. "There's definitely something coarser about
you. Or perhaps you always were coarse and I never
noticed. Even your *pores* are coarse."

"My pores?" he said. He put down the heavy Dupont
table lighter and sat down opposite her. "Well, that's bad
news. Who's going to vote for me if my pores are coarse?"

"Oh, don't worry, people will vote for you by the
millions." Greta smiled. "American voters have always
been irresistibly drawn toward the vulgar and the overblown.
If you're really lucky, they'll not only see that your pores
are coarse, they'll remember that you were one of Lyndon
Johnson's favorite spitting partners."

Reynard drummed his fingers on the gilded arm of his
chair. "What about a glass of wine?" he asked. "Are you
still drinking Sancerre?"

He was trying so hard to be controlled that the muscles
in his face were rigid when he spoke. His attorney had
warned, "Be patient, that's all I can say to you. Don't
commit yourself. And *don't* get angry." He wished Maurice were here this afternoon, if only to ward off Greta's
needles and barbs and relentless sarcasm, but Greta had
insisted on a completely private discussion—no lawyers,
no toadies, no men-at-arms. She had always loathed his
political entourage, his publicity managers, his male secre-
taries and his adenoidal accountants. She had collectively
called them "the Snake Pit." She also believed that when
Reynard was alone she could hurt him more, even if she

couldn't outwit him. Pain was important to Greta, both her own and Reynard's. Most of their married life had been pain.

They had been apart for nearly ten months now, although no one knew their separation was permanent except their children, their close friends and their respective attorneys. Greta was living in Newport, in the white summer home that Reynard's grandfather Leonard had built in 1884, when he had first made his fortune in railroads. The children were at school in England. Reynard spent most of his time in Washington or New York, and the weekends when he was able to come back to the family seat in New Hampshire were increasingly rare. This was his first visit to Concord for three months, and as it was, he was going to have to fly back to Washington at first light in the morning.

Both Greta and Reynard were wealthy, well-connected and good-looking, regardless of Greta's gibes about Reynard's lack of refinement. By all the normal laws of nature and American high society, their marriage should have been idyllic and stable. Greta was a Verrier, second daughter of the Pasquiset Verriers. She was small and blonde, with a face as perfect as a piece of Dresden and blue eyes that could have chipped diamonds. Reynard, of course, was the oldest of the three Kelly brothers, the social and political princes of New Hampshire. He was physically bigger than his siblings John and Lincoln; since he had chaired the Ways and Means Committee, his hair had grown wirier and whiter. But he was still young looking for a man in his sixties; there was a *Saturday Evening Post* openness about his face, something American, wholesome and fresh. He could jog for two miles without losing his wind and swim thirty lengths like a professional. He was by far the most charismatic of the northern Democrats, although time and time again his flirtations with the presidential primaries had ended in confusion and withdrawal. In 1984 his name had been connected by *The Washington Post* with an unsavory toxic-dump scandal; unfairly, as it later turned out, but too late to salvage his bid for the presidency. In 1980 he had been linked with Ellen Wangerin, the one-time girlfriend of Sydney "The Pig" Mandello, and that little item of dirty laundry had obliged him to withdraw from the race on grounds of "discretion" and to make a public announcement on network television that he and Greta had been through "temporary marital difficulties, the same kind of husband-and-wife fighting that eighty percent of all Americans go through." He had added, however, that his marriage to Greta was now "stronger than ever."

The Kelly name had been glittering enough to carry Reynard through both of these scandals, and more, with only a slight tarnishing of his shining armor. But his appetite for pretty girls remained insatiable, and his addiction to roulette meant that he was always in the company of men whose reputations were less than honorable, men who were quite happy to provide him with all the creature comforts he could ask for—sexual, gastronomic or sensational. He was not a corrupt man but he enjoyed the pleasures of power too much to be absolutely honest.

Now, however, he wanted to be president. His aides had weighed all the political chances and checked every last closet for skeletons. He was ready, as ready as he was ever likely to be. He was at a warm and fatherly age—ripe for his next move. He was a Democrat, with policies that touched on nuclear disarmament, social welfare and a revolutionary new system of low-cost medical aid. And he was the kind of man who could be presented as the caring champion of the unemployed, a tough and benevolent hero with a legendary name to match.

There was only one immediate drawback: Greta. If Reynard were going to run for president, he needed her. That was why he had asked her to come up to the Colonnades

and talk to him. He wanted to be president, and a presiden
required a First Lady. He was prepared to talk money; h
was prepared to talk houses and yachts and racehorses. H
was prepared to talk anything that would guarantee tha
Greta would play the part of his adoring and supportiv
wife, at least for as long as he was sitting behind that des
in the Oval Office.

He knew that Greta found the idea of the White Hous
alluring; otherwise she would not have come here today
But he was still not sure of what she was going to exac
from him in return for her performance. She was not a
forgiving woman, none of the Verriers ever had been, and
she had already taken him for a house, a car and an annual
allowance of nearly half a million dollars. "My *pour-
boire*," she called that allowance. "My tip."

So here they were in the living room at the Colonnades,
two wealthy and suspicious people surrounded by satin-
wood antiques, priceless rugs and pale-blue velvet drapes
with swags and tails and silken cords. Outside on this
chilly and restless day, the estate stretched for 326 acres,
as far as Oak Hill to the north and Conant's Acre to the
south. Trees, pastures and rough grazing. Fields of Indian
corn, red-speckled and whispering in the wind. And beyond,
a view of the Highlands Ski Area and the White Mountains.

Two wealthy and suspicious people, on whose agree-
ment the entire political and social future of the United
States might depend.

Greta said, "You'll have to give up Chiffon Trent of
course."

"Is there any need for that? Nobody has to know. And
I'd hate to hurt her feelings."

"Girls who are rash enough to have affairs with you
deserve everything that's coming to them," said Greta
caustically. "You don't feel sorry for the lady lion-tamer,
do you, if the lion happens to bite her head off? It's her

wn fault for sticking her head in its mouth to begin
ith."

"Chiffon's . . . different," Reynard protested. "She
nderstands me. Nobody ever understood me the way
hiffon does."

"Is Chiffon her *real* name?"

"Sure it's her real name. What difference does that
ake anyway?"

"I don't know. I just thought any girl who went out
ith you would more likely be called Percale, or Sacking."

Reynard pursed his lips. "You're a bitch, you know
at?" he told her. "Once a bitch, always a bitch."

"Why should you worry? You've got Chiffon. *Chiffon*
nderstands you."

"Can we get down to business?" he demanded.

"Well, of course," said Greta. "Much as I enjoy talk-
ng to you, Reynard, I didn't drive all the way from Newport
ust to share pleasantries. I gather from what you told me
n the telephone that you're thinking of running again."

"The political conditions are perfect."

"You mean that America has been swept by an over-
vhelming urge to drag itself out of the Slough of Despond
nd hurl itself into the Chasm of Infinite Crassness."

"You know something?" Reynard snapped back. "There
sed to be a time when you respected my politics."

"One has to respect the man to respect his politics,"
said Greta.

"But you're still a Democrat? You'd still want to see a
Democratic president in the White House?"

"Even if it were *you*, you mean? Well, I suppose so.
But I don't think your chances of winning the nomination
are very good, do you? You've got two strikes against you
already. You're the man who made toxic dumps famous."

"You know I was innocent of that."

"I know you were *shown* to be innocent of that."

Reynard stood up and walked to the French windows.

He looked out across the hewn-stone patio, where flowe
less potted geraniums were shuddering in the mid-afternoc
wind.

"By next November, election day, America is going
be reaching a condition of maximum fear. Fear about i
future, fear about its safety, fear about its economy. Wint
will be setting in and that means every unemployed worke
will be wondering how to put a turkey on the table
Christmas. Old people are going to be worried about th
high cost of heating. A lot of young college graduates ar
going to be facing their first winter staring at the executiv
breadline. Fear, Greta, that's what it's all about. Absolut
fear. And that's where I come in."

Greta crushed out her cigarette, half-smoked. "Yo
mean that you're going to *frighten* the electorate int
voting for you rather than entice it? I shouldn't think you'
have much difficulty in doing that. My mother always use
to say that you would have scared the pants off Lo
Chaney, not to mention Lon Chaney, Jr. Your *eyes*, sh
said. Never trust a man with eyes that bore holes in you."

"Your mother was an aristocratic basket case."

"My mother was good enough to give you her only
daughter."

"Give? Your mother never gave anything. That scar
your father liked so much? She sold him that. *Sold* him.
for seventeen dollars. He told me about it once when
we were having a drink together. And look at what *you*
cost. An arm and a leg and a sprained back."

Greta said nothing. Reynard looked at her for a long
while and then said, "I'm going for the presidential
nomination, Greta, and this time I'm going to make it. The
people in this country are afraid, and I'm going to be
offering them freedom from fear. Do you know what that
means? Freedom from unemployment, freedom from outra-
geous medical costs, freedom from crime and mugging

nd urban decay. What I'm offering is what every single
oter most desperately wants."

"You're obviously expecting a landslide then?" asked
Greta. "Don't you think you ought to win the nomination
irst? After all, you're going to be up against tough compet-
tors with cleaner records than yours." Then she added
rritably, "Did you call for that glass of wine?"

"Whether I'm nominated or not is up to the party," said
Reynard. "And whether I'm elected to the presidency or
not, and by how much, is up to the people. I don't expect
anything more than plain and honest support for plain and
honest measures."

"Plain, I'll give you," said Greta. "Honest, I'm not so
sure."

Reynard came back from the window and sat down.
"Greta, this country has to start living like a family again;
the only way we can do that is to start taking care of our
weak and our sick and our defenseless, the way all families have to. I'm running on a ticket that includes an
enormously expanded program of government spending,
vastly improved medical care, new building projects, new
highways, new handouts for the destitute and the unemployed."

"All funded by higher taxes, I suppose?" asked Greta.

Reynard looked at her steadily and said, "Government is
there to help and to serve the people, but for their part the
people have to accept all the responsibility, both moral and
financial, that a really caring administration requires. The
present administration has been founded on selfishness.
Bread for the rich, stones for the poor. But good government begins and ends with truly human behavior—true
kindness if you like. I am going to be nominated, and I am
going to win the presidency, because I am prepared to
come up front and say I care about every single member of
this family that calls itself the United States: rich, poor,

middle class, blue collar, drunkard, dropout, addict, whore or pimp.''

"You care about *pimps?*"

"I care about everybody equally."

"I see," said Greta. "It's a pity you didn't demonstrate it to your wife and your children. But I guess when you care equally for over two hundred million people, you have to spread yourself pretty thin."

"Greta—"

"Oh, forget it," she said. "I know you care for them in your own idiosyncratic way. Well, I think you do. Where's this wine?"

There was a knock almost immediately at the living-room door, and in walked a pretty black girl with cornrowed hair and a maid's black-and-white uniform. Her starched apron was stretched tight across extravagantly large breasts, and as she carried her silver tray across the room, her hips moved in a rhythmic glide that had Greta staring in elaborately feigned astonishment.

"This is, uh, Eunice," said Reynard as the girl bunny-dipped to put down the silver cooler of Sancerre and two Waterford crystal goblets.

"Pleased to know you, madame," smiled Eunice, all teeth and twinkly eyes.

"Eunice is Mama Rice's little girl. Well, not so little now," Reynard said smoothly.

"Quite," Greta pronounced. And then, when Eunice had closed the door behind her, "You didn't tell me you were doing research into racial attitudes. Not firsthand research at least."

Reynard's hand trembled slightly as he poured Greta a glass of wine. "Most connoisseurs describe the flavor of this wine as 'catty,' " he said as he handed it to her.

"*À votre santé,*" smiled Greta.

Reynard said, "You know why I asked you to come here."

"I do," she nodded. "But I would love to hear you wriggle and squirm as you try to explain it."

Reynard sipped his wine and then set his glass on the table beside him. He didn't like dry white wine very much; he was a burgundy drinker. The only problem was, burgundy always gave him a crashing headache. So did Greta. He could feel the nagging pain in his left eyebrow already.

"I won't be able to seek nomination for the presidency as a separated man," he said. "A president with liberal policies like mine has to be seen as a national father figure, with a happy family of his own. The family that lives at the White House is the nation itself in microcosm; that means I have to bring the children back from England and also that I have to ask you to come back and live with me as my First Lady."

"Perhaps you should have thought of that when you took such a fancy to Katherine," said Greta. It had been Reynard's affair with the swan-necked Mrs. Katherine T. Welsh that had finally driven Greta to pack her trunks and leave the Colonnades for good. Mrs. Welsh—syrupy-voiced, achingly beautiful—had been a college friend of Greta's, and of *all* people, Greta had been unable to tolerate Reynard's going to bed with *her*. It had been like having her past violated as well as her future.

"I'm putting this whole thing to you as a business proposition," said Reynard, rotating his hands as though he were working a Rubik's Cube. "I'm offering you a job, a four-year contract. Would-be president requires would-be First Lady, with a view to prestigious live-in position at nation's most fashionable address. Plenty of social duties, extensive charity work, constant smiling."

"And the salary?" asked Greta.

"Well, it depends on whether or not you're interested."

"Give me an idea."

"A great deal of money, obviously. And at the end of the four years, a selection of prime stocks."

"You're seriously intending to rent your estranged wife' services so you can put up a fraudulent political front?"

"Fraudulent is the wrong word," Reynard retorted. "The word is 'stable.' A stable sociopolitical image. Just be cause you and I can't personally get on with each othe: doesn't mean that we can't present ourselves as an idea couple in order to give millions of Americans the example and the inspiration they so sorely need. For God's sake. Robert Wagner and Stephanie Powers aren't married—fo: all I know, they don't even like each other—but nobody accuses 'Hart to Hart' of being fraudulent."

"Reynard, if you can't tell the difference between 'Hart to Hart' and the presidency of the United States, I don't think you're *fit* to be president."

"Of course I can damn well tell the difference!" he snapped. Then, with enormous restraint, he said, "Of course I can tell the difference. I'm simply using 'Hart to Hart' as a metaphor. If Mr. Wagner and Miss Powers can be convincing as a happily married couple in a fictional context, there isn't any reason we can't be equally convincing in a political context. Both fiction and politics are perceived by the general public through the same media; the same devices can be used."

Greta took a small mouthful of wine and held it against her tongue for a moment before swallowing it. Then she said, "I think you're making one false assumption."

"What's that?"

"You're assuming that I'm going to say yes. You're also assuming that I'm going to say yes under conditions you find acceptable."

Reynard said, "I'm talking in the area of three to three and a half million dollars in scheduled payments according to the progress of the contract."

"What do you mean by 'the progress of the contract'?"

"For three and a half million, Greta, I expect a First Lady who *acts* like a First Lady."

"Oh," she said. "You mean that if I don't kiss you frequently enough or keep referring to you as The Most Unforgettable Husband I Ever Had, you won't continue to pay me regularly?"

Reynard looked at his glass of wine and decided not to drink any more. "All you have to do is to agree in principle. Once you've agreed in principle, our lawyers can work out the rest. You can have the whole thing down in writing."

Greta watched him for seconds on end and then said, "You realize what a highly explosive document this contract is going to be. How do you know I won't use it to blackmail you for the rest of your days?"

"For two reasons," he replied. "The first is that a mandatory condition of the contract will state that, once fulfilled, all copies of it will be destroyed. What's more, neither of us will actually be permitted to keep a copy of it, but two copies will be lodged with a disinterested third party. A bank, for instance, or a Supreme Court judge."

"But if I tell?"

"I've already discussed that possibility with Maurice. This won't be written down anywhere of course, but you can take it from me that if you attempt to use this arrangement to threaten me in any way, or to extort money, then, well, you will be dealt with."

"Dealt with? You mean *murdered?*" Greta laughed, her voice high and harsh. "Poor Reynard, I think you should have been a television detective instead of a politician. Can't you just imagine it, 'Reynard's Law,' eight o'clock, Central and Mountain. 'If you attempt to use this arrangement to threaten me, Greta, you will be *dealt with*.' God, you're pathetic sometimes. Worse than pathetic. You're infantile."

"But?" said Reynard, inclining his head to one side. She could call him whatever she liked, even though it irritated him into controlled fury, but she could never accuse him of lacking in perception.

"But?" she echoed.

"But you'll accept the contract," he coaxed her.

Greta lifted her head. That was the trouble with Reynard. He knew her just a little too well: her ploys and her vulnerabilities. In spite of his apparent naiveté, in spite of his pomposity, he was always so perfectly dressed: light-gray mohair suit, socks without a single wrinkle, shirt with white embroidered monogram. And this immaculate attire was the outward evidence that he was so wealthy he could afford to be naive, he could afford to be mawkish. He could even afford to be wrong. He was so untroubled by financial pressures of any kind—so detached from the violent anxieties that daily assailed the American family of which he spoke so sympathetically—that he could smile and say he cared about whores and pimps. That was his strength. Very few politicians could afford to be so crass.

He could say he cared about *whores,* damn it, when decent, hardworking men in Milwaukee and Seattle and Detroit were standing in interminable lines for the chance of a three-hundred-fifty-a-week job and respectable middle-class families were having to shop in thrift stores. Yet those same decent and respectable people would vote for Reynard as enthusiastically as though he were an old friend—and in exactly the same way Greta would eventually say yes to his offer of a rented First Ladyship. She knew it and she hated herself for it—and him. But he was a Kelly, and the Kellys had always been irresistible.

"You'll have to give me some time to think about it."

"Of course."

"You're a shit, you know," she said and sipped fiercely at her Sancerre.

Reynard shrugged. He wondered how his feelings toward her could be so ambivalent; she aroused him and he loved her cutting classiness, yet at the same time she could

annoy him to screaming pitch. She was the only thing in
the whole world, animal, vegetable or mineral, that could
ruffle him. Perhaps they should never have married. Perhaps they should never have split up. Perhaps—and this
was probably the most accurate thought of all—perhaps
they should never have been born on the same planet. Or
at least not in the same century.

"I have several conditions," said Greta.

"I imagined you would," he told her. "Is there anything special, or can we leave it all to the lawyers?"

"There's one thing," said Greta. "I want you to promise me that you'll find a senior position on your election
staff for a friend of mine. An *effective* position, not a
sinecure. And if you're elected, I want you to promise me
that you'll appoint him to the government post he wants."

"Now, Greta—"

"You *know* him," she interrupted. "He's not a fool; in
fact, in many ways he's wiser than you could ever hope to
be. He also happens to be a Democrat, so I'm not asking
you to appoint a man who's going to give you any political
trouble. Walt Seabrook."

"*Doctor* Walt Seabrook? That gynecologist you've been
fooling around with? He's like George McGovern in a
white coat."

"He happens to be a very sensitive and politically ori-
ented person. He's also very good at mah-jong. You have
to be sensitive to be good at mah-jong."

"*Mah-jong?*" asked Reynard, incredulous.

Greta said, "You can pour me some more wine." Then,
when he hesitated, she raised her empty glass and said
sharply, "Please?"

"Where am I going to find a place on my staff for a
technicolor charlatan like Walt Seabrook?" Reynard
demanded. "Quite apart from the fact that he's your current stud."

"Can't you *ever* resist the temptation to be vulgar?" she

demanded. "Walt Seabrook is very special. The fact that we happen to relate to each other both physically and mentally is completely irrelevant. I mean *politically* irrelevant. He wants to be Assistant Secretary for Health, and you know as well as I do that he's absolutely perfect for the job."

"Greta," Reynard protested, "Walt Seabrook is twenty years behind the times. He's a political hippie. When I talk about medical aid, I mean improved tax concessions for the building of private health centers and government subsidies for unusual and expensive medical treatment. I don't mean free Band-Aids for all comers, with a lid of grass thrown in."

"Walt Seabrook is just the man you need," insisted Greta. "Have you ever seen him on television? He was on that CBS special about fallopian disorders. He was so *warm*. He could talk about inflamed tubes and really make you feel he *cared*. You could see that he lived that pain right along with the women who were suffering it, and that he lived their childlessness too."

"Are you serious?"

"You're asking me if I'm serious? Walt Seabrook is a human being."

"The implication being that I'm not?"

"Reynard, this is a condition of my signing that contract. Either you say yes or it's no go."

Reynard looked across the room toward the window, as though he wished he were outside walking in the fresh air instead of discussing the sordid details of a political contract. But after a while he said, "I suppose you'll want to go on seeing him."

"What? Of course. You're not going to ask me to give him up, are you?"

"You asked me to give up Chiffon."

"Reynard," Greta complained, "Chiffon is nothing but

one of your two-week flirtations. Walt is *real*. There's a strong possibility that he and I might eventually marry."

"Suppose somebody sees you canoodling with the Assistant Secretary for Health? The First Lady making time with him? The whole thing could collapse in ruins, and the country with it."

"Well, what are you asking? You're asking me to stay celibate for four years? That's ridiculous. Apart from being ridiculous, I won't do it."

"All I'm saying is that you're going to have to be discreet. I mean discreet to the point of invisibility. Because if I hear one rumor that the First Lady has been fornicating with her one-time doctor, just one word in the *National Enquirer,* then believe you me, you're going to die. And so is Walt."

"You're jealous," Greta provoked him.

"Am I? Maybe I am. I'm only human."

"You're *jealous,*" she repeated. Her eyes were bright with caustic delight. "You're deeply, painfully jealous."

"So?" asked Reynard.

"So I'm beginning to wonder if you're running for the presidential nomination for the sake of your political convictions or simply as a means of getting me back."

"You think I care about that *putz* Seabrook?"

"You must, otherwise it wouldn't upset you whenever I mention his name."

"He doesn't upset me."

"He does too."

"Listen, Greta!" Reynard shouted. "He does not upset me! Believe me, whatever you do these days, it's your own affair. Walt Seabrook—I beg your pardon, *Doctor* Walt Seabrook—is your own affair. You're a free agent."

"Then you won't have any trouble in saying yes."

Reynard stared at her. His eyes protruded with anger. "You mean yes, Walt Seabrook can work on my staff?"

"That's right. And yes, he can expect to be appointed Assistant Secretary for Health."

Reynard rubbed his face. At last he looked over at her through his fingertips and said, "Every time I meet you, I remember why I cheated on you."

"No, you don't," she smiled. "You don't even remember what you ate for lunch yesterday. You cheat because you're an incurable cheat, because it's your nature. This plan of yours for winning yourself the presidency—don't you think that's cheating? You're a cheat by nature, Reynard Kelly, and that's all there is to it."

Reynard thought for a while in silence. Greta finished her second glass of wine and took out another cigarette. The sunlight crossing the floor began to fade; outside, the New Hampshire landscape took on a threatening appearance—black metallic sky, menacing trees, ominous gusts of wind.

At last Reynard said, "All right. Walt Seabrook can have what he wants. *You* can have what you want. As long as you promise to keep yourselves silent. Not only you, Walt Seabrook too."

"Or you'll kill us," said Greta, lighting her cigarette and breathing out twin tusks of smoke.

"Yes," he said, in the flat voice of someone who has given in a long time ago.

FOUR

He held Michael's body in his arms as tenderly as though the boy were his own son and still alive. He looked down at the white, sculptured face, the breathless nostrils, the blue-veined eyelids, and then he laid him down on the sofa, the head propped up by a cushion, and slowly he drew the plaid blanket up to the neck. He didn't cover the face.

"Was there anything I could have done, anything at all?" Michael's mother asked. Her expression was blurred with grief. Behind her, Michael's father stood tall and silent and stunned. He had moved here to New Hampshire, changed his engineering job, changed his life, just to give Michael a healthier environment in which to grow up.

Edmond unclipped his stethoscope. "I'm sorry, Mrs. Osman, nothing." He looked down at Michael again. "I don't quite understand how he died, or how it could have been so sudden. The coroner will obviously want to make a thorough check of his own. As far as I can make out, he just stopped breathing."

"Nobody just stops breathing," protested Mr. Osman. He stared at Edmond with a despair that verged on a peculiar kind of fury. "I mean—nobody just stops breathing." He paused. "*Do* they?"

Edmond shrugged, not dismissively but helplessly. "Mr. Osman, I simply don't have any answers. Not at the moment. Michael was feeling quite well the last time your wife saw him, wasn't he? No sudden temperature? No complaints about stiffness or weakness in his arms and legs?"

Mrs. Osman bit her lips. "He was never healthier," she answered, her voice congested with tears. "Running, playing with his friends, laughing."

Michael's body lay on the sofa like an alabaster statue. For some reason Edmond felt for a moment as though the boy might be playing a practical joke and that suddenly he might open one eye, grin at them and run out of the house and off down the street, laughing. But there was to be no more running for Michael, no more laughing. Nothing but a medical examiner's knife, a fall funeral and a few color photographs—in which he would never grow old—on top of the television.

Mrs. Osman shuddered with the pain of it, with the sudden and devastating absence of her only child.

Edmond said, "The reason I asked about fever is because what appears to have happened here is a paralysis of the intercostal muscles, the muscles the body uses to breathe with. The same thing can happen in—" He hesitated, then said, "I know that Michael was vaccinated. But there are some remarkable similarities to polio here that I can't ignore."

"Polio doesn't strike as quickly as this, surely?" asked Mr. Osman. He kept staring at Edmond so he wouldn't have to look at his son.

"Well, not usually," Edmond told him. "The symptoms are usually gradual and very noticeable. Fever, aches and pains, stiffness. I don't know. Maybe I'm all wrong. I don't have the facilities here to make an expert judgment. But the pathologist will certainly find out what happened."

He felt desperately inadequate, standing here in front of the Osmans and having to tell them he didn't know what had killed their son. But what else could he do? The boy had simply stopped breathing. His intercostal muscles were in a state of paralysis, a condition Edmond would normally have associated with poliomyelitis. Yet how could such a severe paralysis have attacked so swiftly? What had happened to Michael appeared to be something ferociously different. A mad-dog virus that killed as soon as it struck.

Mrs. Osman took hold of Edmond's arm and clutched it so tightly she pinched his skin through his jacket. "They won't—cut him up or anything?"

Edmond said softly, "No. They'll have to take a sample of spinal fluid but all they need for that is a needle. And they'll probably take a thin slice of skin so they can examine it under the microscope. They have to see if Michael had an excess of cells in his spinal fluid, or an excess of protein, and those could be indicative that he had polio."

"Polio," whispered Mr. Osman. "Who'd have believed it?"

"Well, we don't know for sure," said Edmond. He went across to the table and opened his bag, tucking away his stethoscope. On the wall in front of him hung a reproduction of William Ranney's famous painting, *The Pioneers:* a woman on a horse, a man walking beside her with a musket over his shoulder. Maybe, in some curious way, that was how the Osmans viewed themselves, lone pioneers in a lonely landscape. Outside, he could hear the whooping of a siren as the ambulance came around the corner of Eddy Drive. No sirens necessary, he thought. For Michael Osman, sirens are too late.

The ambulance drew up before the house, and right behind it was the khaki-colored station wagon driven by

Oscar Ford, the pathologist. Oscar tramped red-faced up
the sloping garden path and was just raising his hand to jab
at the bell when Edmond opened the door for him.

"How are you keeping, E.C.?" Oscar asked. He grasped
Edmond's hand so tightly that he crushed Edmond's wed-
ding band against his knuckle. "Didn't see you over at the
Motz place last week."

"I was held up at the pediatric clinic."

Oscar slapped Edmond's shoulder. "You work too hard,
you know that? Joe Sullivan says you're building yourself
quite a reputation for conscientiousness. You must remember that this is the boonies, E.C. The pace of life is slower
here; not many of us know how to *pronounce* conscientiousness, let alone get ourselves a reputation for it. Joe said
you're becoming the Albert Schweitzer of Concord."

"I hope he meant it kindly."

"Joe never means anything kindly. Hey, by the way,
Judy ran into Christy at the market last week."

Edmond gave Oscar an impatient grimace. "Yes. Christy
said she'd seen her."

"Judy said Christy was buying favors for your birthday
party next week," said Oscar. Then suddenly, melodramat-
ically, he clapped his hand to his mouth. "Hey—oops,
I'm *sorry*. E.C., I'm really sorry. Now I guess it's no
surprise."

Edmond stared at him glumly. He had suspected that
Christy was planning a party but he hadn't known for sure.
He said, "You're all class, Oscar. You know that?"

"I probably saved your life," Oscar told him, winking.
"Surprise parties are the biggest single cause of cardiac
arrest after balling your secretary. You remember that
mass homicide over at Laconia? That was a surprise party.
The wife shouted 'Surprise!' and the husband took out his
shotgun and shouted 'Surprise to you too, old girl!' and
blew away his wife, his Borzoi dog *and* four of his guests,
including his broker, before anybody could stop him. It

as stress, you see. The human nervous system is not designed to take surprises like that. Now, where are the remains?''

"The dead boy," said Edmond emphatically, "is in the living room."

"The parents?"

"They're with him."

"Get them out."

"Oscar—"

"I said, *get* them out, not throw them out. I'm not totally lacking in sensitivity, whatever you think. You know I'm going to have to do things to that boy they won't want to see."

"I'll get them out," said Edmond, "but let's get one thing straight. These people have just lost their only child. Are you listening?"

"You don't think I know how to be tactful?" Oscar demanded.

"I think you sometimes forget that dead people aren't a selection of cold cuts and that they are still very dear to the people who loved them, that's all."

"E.C.," said Oscar harshly, "I've cradled more weeping widows on my shoulder than you'll ever count. Now let's get this on the road, before the boy starts decomposing on us."

Edmond went back to the living room. Mr. and Mrs. Osman were kneeling on the rug beside the sofa, both of them saying a prayer over their son's body. The last light of day faded around them, and in the twilight Michael's face appeared almost luminous.

When the Osmans had finished their prayer, Oscar said *"Amen."* Edmond glanced at him but Oscar remained impassive. Short and ruddy-cheeked, he looked more like an Irish boatman than a pathologist.

Edmond spoke quietly to Mr. and Mrs. Osman and then ushered them out of the room. Before he left, Mr. Osman said in a voice that trembled, "You'll treat him with respec⋅ won't you?"

Oscar nodded almost imperceptibly. "Sure thing, M⋅ Osman," and he almost managed to sound as though h⋅ meant it.

When the Osmans had gone, Oscar brought over ⋅ lamp, lifted off the shade and switched on the naked bul⋅ so it shone over the dead boy. He tugged off the blanke⋅ that covered the body and expertly stripped off the boy'⋅ clothes. Edmond stood in the background, watching hin⋅ silently.

"Any conclusions?" asked Oscar as he tapped a⋅ Michael's chest and then directed a light into the boy'⋅ mouth, lighting his cheeks in eerie scarlet.

"Any conclusions about what?"

"Cause of death, what else? You have come to *some* conclusions?"

"I made a cursory examination in case it was anything infectious I should know about."

"Covering your tracks, huh?"

"Protecting the neighborhood."

"Oh, I'm sorry. I forgot you were a D.S.A."

"What the hell's a D.S.A.?"

Oscar wiped his hands and smiled. "Doctor in Shining Armor."

"Is that another one of Joe Sullivan's gibes?"

"Tell me what conclusions, that's all."

Edmond was silent for a moment or two. Then he said, as logically as he could manage, "I'm not at all sure. But it appears to me that Michael died from asphyxia caused by paralysis or a traumatic spasm of the respiratory muscles. Without having taken samples of spinal fluid, I would guess that he might have died from an unusually sudden attack of poliomyelitis."

"Was he sick? Feverish?"

"No symptons whatever as far as the parents can recall."

"Hmm," said Oscar. He closed Michael's mouth and drew the blanket over the boy's head. "Did the parents have any idea of where he might have picked up anything like poliomyelitis in the past few weeks?"

"No."

"Where was he today?"

"Out on his bicycle."

"Do the parents know where?"

Edmond shook his head. "They said his best friend was having a music lesson, so Michael went out on his own."

"Make sure you check the best friend," said Oscar. "Preferably today."

"I've already called his parents. His name's Bernie Mayer, and he lives two blocks to the northwest in Strafford Circle. I've arranged to see him this evening."

Oscar lifted Michael's buttocks and matter of factly pushed a rectal thermometer into his anus. Then he turned the body this way and that, inspecting the bruiselike marks caused by blood pooling in the lower parts. This would help him to corroborate Mrs. Osman's estimate of the time of death.

"You've talked to the parents about the autopsy?" Oscar asked.

"Sure. They seem to accept that it has to be done. Just no hacking, that's all."

Oscar looked up at Edmond with immediate hostility and then realized that Edmond was getting back at him for spoiling the surprise of Christy's party. "All right," he said. "No hacking." He inspected the dead boy's fingernails. "I do the neatest job in the business and you know it. One slice around the middle of the head to get at the brain, one slice down the middle of the abdomen to get at the guts. Divide the sternum. That's all. And always perfect. *Art*, you know what I mean?" He sniffed and then said, "Hacking, for Christ's sake."

They stood together and looked down at the dead boy in

silence. Each felt unsettled by the death. Not because Michael was a child who should have had all his life in front of him—they had seen too many juvenile fatalities for that—but because the sickness that killed him had attacked so quickly and so uncharacteristically. To be asphyxiated by polio in a matter of minutes was unheard of, and nothing in their years of medical experience had prepared them for it.

"It *looks* like polio," said Edmond.

"It has all the characteristics," Oscar admitted. "From what I've seen so far, death seems to have been caused by a virally induced paralysis of the intercostal muscles. But, well, you know what they say about first impressions."

"What do they say about first impressions?" Edmond had the feeling that Oscar was trying to tell him something.

Oscar withdrew the rectal thermometer and peered at it carefully. "The same thing they say about country doctors who used to be city doctors. Don't trust them."

"Oh, yes?"

Oscar wiped his hands. "They usually say no one moves up to New Hampshire unless he has to. Especially when he's been running a wealthy practice in midtown Manhattan."

"You're trying to impart some delicate information, is that it?" asked Edmond. The trouble was, he already had half an inkling of what Oscar was going to say. It had been bound to come out sooner or later. He hadn't expected it so soon.

Oscar went over to the living-room window and beckoned to the ambulance crew outside. Then he turned back to Edmond, thrust his hands in his pockets, sniffed and looked down at Michael's body again. "I like you, for some stupid reason. I think you're good, although I wouldn't normally admit it. Probably too good for Concord. But something happened to you in Manhattan that you know about and the Concord Board of Health knows about and that is now becoming the subject of some pretty bizarre rumors down at the hospital, and over at the ambulance station too—not to mention the Concord Country Club.''

"What rumors?"

"You really want to know what rumors?"

"I think I have a *right* to know."

"Well, I don't know whether it's true or not, but the rumors are that you had to leave New York because you tried to perform an impromptu tracheotomy—using only a carving knife—on a woman who was choking. And the rumor is that you weren't too steady and you weren't too sober and you ended up cutting her throat. And the rumor says that you got away with it only because that woman was the wife of your senior partner and if the scandal had gotten out, his whole practice would have been sunk.''

Edmond was silent for a long time before he turned to Oscar. "You believe this stuff?"

Oscar made a face. "It doesn't matter whether I believe it or not, does it? The point is, the rumor's going around.''

"And?"

"And I'm just trying to warn you to keep a low profile, both politically and medically.''

Edmond said nothing, but just as Mrs. Osman let the ambulance crew in through the front door, Oscar said, "It's election year next year. Somebody on the Board of Health approved your appointment and said you were fit to practice here in spite of whatever it was you are rumored to have done. You get what I'm saying? Next year that somebody is going to be very vulnerable because of you. So you can bet that the local sharks are going to start circling and that whatever you did or did not do that caused you to leave Manhattan so promptly is going to be the bleeding meat that brings them in.''

"You have an inimitable way of putting things."

Oscar shrugged. "I'm not saying anything, E.C. I'm just passing on rumors. But if you hear that a storm's coming, what do you do? You go out and buy yourself a lightning rod, you understand me? Forewarned is forearmed."

"Listen—" said Edmond.

"A friendly caution, that's all. Me, I don't care what you've done or where you came from or why. I judge only by results. But this is election season and there are people who *do* care."

The ambulance crew brought the gurney into the hall-way outside, pushed open the door and asked, "Where is he? In here?"

"That's right," said Oscar, standing up. "Treat him gentle, will you? Edmond—I'll catch up with you tomorrow. Maybe we should have a drink."

"Sure," said Edmond flatly, picking up his bag and leaving.

He drove the long way back to his home in East Concord, just off Shawmot Street, even though it was dark and beginning to rain. The radio was playing soft and sentimental jazz, the kind that always made him feel lonely. But he had to think things over before he went back to Christy. He had to think of what he was going to tell her and, most critical of all, he had to think of how he was going to cope with his entangled past, a past that never seemed to let him forget. He had somehow hoped that once they were settled in New Hampshire, he would be able to lead a new life—Edmond Chandler, M.D., private physician and pediatric consultant to the Merrimack County Clinic.

But his life was still too crowded with memories, and the memories refused to be shut away.

The most complicated memory of all, of course, was Arabelle Thorne. Dead now for three and a half years but yet as vividly alive in his mind as the day he had first made love to her. He could still imagine her standing in that pale summer dress by that open window in East Hampton, the breeze billowing the curtains, her head half-turned toward him, her lips slightly parted, and Beethoven's *Emperor Concerto* filling the room like bars of sunshine. Arabelle: dead now, and gone. Yet hopelessly unforgettable.

She had said to him once, "Midnight shakes the memory, as a madman shakes a dead geranium." And she had pursed her lips, her eyes bright with amusement, waiting for him to say *"What?"*

"T.S. Eliot," she had whispered, kissing him unexpectedly on the sensitive spot of his wrist. And then she had switched off the light.

Now, on the road between Sugar Ball and East Concord, in the rain, he drew his Camaro over to the verge, pushed on the parking brake and sat there with the windshield wipers squeaking against the glass while Gil Evans and his orchestra played "Hotel-Me" as though it were a personal message from Edmond's past.

If you hear that a storm's coming, what do you do? You go out and buy yourself a lightning rod. Oscar Ford's words rang in his ears.

Edmond Chandler was forty-one years old, although not many people he met believed it and he could hardly believe it himself. Right up until the evening before his fortieth birthday he had thought: not me, not forty. It can't be. I'm fresh out of med school; I've only just begun my career. Thirty-five maybe; thirty-six at most. Not *forty*. But the day had arrived and the birthday cards had given malicious proof that his life was already more than half-lived. And ever since then something inside him had slipped and he couldn't find it within himself to care so much anymore.

He had stopped exercising, although he still played a desultory game of squash and he hadn't yet lost his leanness. He had brown, brushed-back, Clint Eastwood-styled hair, but his face was less angular than Eastwood's and his eyebrows were thicker. When he read or wrote out prescriptions, he wore thick-rimmed tortoise-shell glasses;

when he drove a car, he wore a permanent frown as though he were trying to determine whether he saw a caravan on the horizon or only a mirage.

He was both fascinated and alarmed by the gradual process of falling apart that seemed to be attacking his body and mind. He couldn't understand how a man of his age and condition could still be so fiercely in love with the girl he had killed . . . and still be so deeply dependent on the wife who had seen him through it.

He had never really grasped that Arabelle was dead, or that Christy had stuck with him. Perhaps he had never been worthy of either of them—the living wife or the dead lover. He had analyzed himself so many times he felt as though he were wrapped in self-examination, tight as a mummy in bandages, and that now he could no longer move or think. All he could do was to sit here in the rain—tired, defeated and ceaselessly troubled—listening to the rubbery complaints of the windshield wipers.

At last he released the parking brake, flicked down the directional and pulled out onto the highway to drive home, which appeared all too promptly—no sooner driven toward than arrived at: a large, modern, split-level house with a shingled roof, a line of miniature trees beside the driveway and a sloping front lawn that shone unnaturally green in his headlights.

All the lights in the house were on. Edmond could see into the living room, where the television was flickering, where potted yuccas flourished and where his medical certificates were hanging, tastefully framed in gold, on the tasteful natural-stone wall. It wasn't East 85th Street, but then what was, except East 85th Street? In the window Christy appeared briefly, then turned and walked back toward the hallway. Perhaps she had heard his car coming. She was wearing her scarlet housedress, the one he liked. He turned the Camaro into the angled driveway and stopped. He was still sitting in the car when Christy opened the front door and raised her hand, not to wave but to shield her eyes from the bright porch light.

He sat in the car for so long that at last she came out into the rain and tapped on the glass. He put down the window and the rainy breeze blew her Arpège perfume into the car. "Edmond?" she asked, "what's the matter? What are you sitting here for? Come on in. Supper's ready."

He gave her a small, pursed grin and nodded. "Tired, that's all," he told her as though that were explanation enough. He closed the window, removed the key and climbed out.

Halfway back to the house she turned and looked at him. "Come on. Edmond?"

Inside the door he took off his coat and hung it on the ornate hatstand that used to grace their hallway in New York. It looked pretentious here in Concord, but then so did almost everything else they owned—clothes, cars, furniture, paintings. Their living room was furnished with elegant Italian chairs and tables they had bought at Acapellas on Fifth Avenue; there were three splashy de Koonings on the corridor wall as well as two Richard Lindners and an Andrew Stevovich. The suburban proportions of the house made them all look absurd.

Christy said, "Something's wrong. You look pale. My God, Edmond, you look *white*."

He sat down and unlaced his shoes. "Hard day, that's all."

"Would you like a drink?"

"Yes, I think I would."

She made a move toward the lacquered Chinese dry bar, then hesitated. "Edmond," she said, "something's *wrong*."

He looked up at her. For a split second his temper almost erupted. Then he took a deep breath to steady himself and attempted a smile.

"A boy died today. Nine years old. I guess it upset me."

"Lara told me you were called out on an emergency," said Christy. "Somewhere over by Conant's Acre?"

"Webster Crescent. The boy was dead by the time I got there."

"Anyone I know?"

"I don't think so. The Osmans. Nice couple. Haven't been living in New Hampshire for long. Newcomers, like us. They took it pretty hard, as you can imagine. The only reason they moved here was to give their son some fresh air and open fields."

"What was it?" asked Christy.

"What killed him? I don't know. Well, polio I think. But not the usual kind of polio. This morning he was fine; this afternoon he was dead."

Christy opened the bar and poured Edmond a stiff three fingers of bourbon. He rarely drank these days; he didn't trust himself. But every now and then he needed a short, hard belt, and this was one of those moments.

Edmond watched her as she recapped the bottle. She seemed more serene since they had relocated to New Hampshire. She was slim, wide-shouldered and stylish, especially fitted for a community like this, where most of the women wore jeans. Even the casual housedress she was wearing looked fashionable. But she conducted herself with far greater confidence these days, and they both drank less and had fewer prickly arguments. Maybe she was growing older gracefully. Maybe the countryside had a settling effect on her with its trees, forests and dark, reflective lakes.

And although this was one thought he usually didn't permit himself—maybe she was calmer because Arabelle was dead and because she knew that he wouldn't dare entangle himself in another affair if he wanted to remain in practice. Harold Bunyan had warned him when he first recommended his appointment that all his outstanding favors had now been repaid and if there was ever one whisper of scandal, one suggestion of misconduct, Edmond would be out on his own, and probably out of medicine too.

Christy asked, "It's not catching, is it?"

"The polio? Well, I don't know. It's usually transmitted by contaminated feces. I won't be able to tell for sure until Oscar makes all his tests. Even *then* he probably won't tell me the whole story. Oh—he told me one thing though."

"What was that?"

"Judy saw you at the market, shopping."

"So?"

"He told me what you were shopping for."

Christy opened and closed her mouth in exasperation. "He *told* you? He told you about the—?"

Edmond nodded. "The surprise party, yes. I'm sorry. It's just Oscar's way of trying to be funny."

"Well, ha-ha. Oh, Edmond, I'm *sick* about that. I've gotten so much ready."

Edmond swallowed bourbon and coughed. "It's okay. I didn't want to be forty-two anyway."

"Thank you for nothing. Why on earth did Oscar have to tell you? And why did Judy have to tell Oscar? Oh, I'm so damned annoyed."

"Have you invited many people?" asked Edmond.

"Forty."

"Well, maybe I could pretend to be surprised. I don't want to spoil *their* fun."

"It's not the same," Christy protested. "The whole point about a surprise party is that you're really surprised."

"Who's coming? Anyone from New York?"

Christy went over to the bar and poured herself a gin-and-tonic. Then she knelt down on the carpet beside him and rested an elbow on his knee. He bent forward and kissed her forehead. Her eyes were the color of pasque-flowers, almost violet. Her housedress was slightly open and he could see the full bulge of her breasts. For a moment there was no sound but the faint noise of effervescence in her drink.

"I'll probably cancel it," she said.

"You didn't invite the Forbes, did you?"

"I did, as a matter of fact."

"Who else?"

She shook his hand and stroked it with gentle absentmindedness. "I invited your brother."

"Malcolm?"

"You only have one brother, haven't you?"

"I really don't believe you sometimes," Edmond told her. "I haven't spoken to Malcolm for three years and I don't intend to start now. What the hell kind of party were you planning? The New Hampshire Chain-Saw Massacre?"

Christy sat up straighter and flushed. "I thought it was time that you two made up. He's your brother, Edmond. You can't ostracize him for the rest of your life."

"For what he did to me, I think I'm entitled to blood."

Christy could easily have made the sharp remark that drawing blood was something at which he excelled, but she pursed her lips, and looked away and said nothing.

"I'm sorry," he said. "But none of my family has ever been particularly close and I don't feel much like cozying up to Malcolm now."

"Well then," said Christy, "I suppose it was just as well that Oscar told you about the party. It obviously would have been a resounding flop."

"Christy—"

"For Christ's sake, Edmond," she said tiredly. "You can never take things as they come, can you? You never like anything I do for you, no matter how hard I try to please you. The trouble is, you're not even a perfectionist. You just have to do things your own way."

Edmond held her shoulder, touched her neck with his fingertips. "Listen," he said, "let's have the party anyway. Just as a normal party."

"I don't know. It seems like it's spoiled now."

"Well, think about it. But I'd like to have it. I'll even ry to unclench my teeth to speak to Malcolm."

Christy finished her drink and stood up. "I'm not sure. I'll think it over. Do you want anything to eat?"

"Let me take you out. I have to go back to Webster Crescent in any case to take a look at the dead boy's friend. You know, just to make sure there's no infection. We could stop by at the Penacook Lodge."

"I'm not dressed," said Christy.

Edmond put down his glass and stood up beside her. He unfastened the four small flower-shaped buttons on the front of her housedress and then slipped his hand inside, cupping a bare breast. She stared into his eyes for what seemed a long time. Then she said "Hmmm," and turned away. Edmond stood and watched her as she walked out of the living room and up the stairs.

At the landing, with only her ankles and her red-thonged sandals in view, she paused, turned and said, "Aren't you coming?"

As Edmond was following Christy upstairs, young Bernie Mayer was cycling around Webster Crescent on his way to see Michael. He skidded to a stop outside the Osman house, surprised to see the garage open and empty and all the windows dark.

He laid his bicycle down on the lawn, went to the front door and pushed the bell. He heard it chime but there was no reply. He pressed it again—still no reply. That was weird. Double weird. He went into the garage to see if Michael's bicycle was there. It was, parked against the wall. Bernie pressed the button that was supposed to activate the bicycle's siren but the battery must have gone dead.

Oh, well, maybe Michael had gone out with his parents for a hamburger. He hadn't *said* they were going, but maybe they'd just decided to on the spur of the moment. It wasn't really fair though. They had known he was coming back later, and they might have waited. It wasn't *his* fault he had to go to his stupid old music lesson.

He went to the back of the garage. Maybe he should take out the dollar in change they always kept in the treasure trove in case of emergencies. This was a sort of emergency, after all. Well, if not an actual emergency, it was the kind of situation that could definitely be improved by a few bars of candy.

He moved aside the rags and cans of polish and dislodged the loose brick. It was dark down at that end of the garage but he didn't want to put on the light in case any of the neighbors saw him poking around. Nevertheless, as soon as he put his hand inside the cavity and groped toward the back of it, he found the leather case. *Treble* weird, he thought. Michael's found a new treasure, something I've never even seen before, and he's hidden it.

He drew out the case and held it up, gently shaking it. Bottles, definitely. But bottles of what? And why was Michael hiding them?

Well, there was only one way to find out: open them up and take a look. *That* would teach Michael for going out for a hamburger without even waiting for his best friend. That would show him he couldn't pull a fast one on Bernie Mayer. I mean, who did Michael think he was?

FIVE

He was stalking like M. Hulot around the cold courtyard of the Swedish Royal Palace, erratically taking photographs of the gray, uncompromising buildings and the oddly long-haired sentries in their white-painted helmets, when he became aware, quite acutely, that he was being watched. A tall young blond-haired man in a putty-colored windbreaker was leaning against one of the palace walls, his arms folded, making no attempt to disguise the fact that he was staring at Humphrey with all the avidity of a wolf. The young man was tanned and extremely handsome in a ski-instructor kind of way, and Humphrey's first thought was: Oh, no. A homosexual.

Humphrey put away his filters and his Nikon and carefully fastened the cases. Then he briskly walked away from the palace walls, his shoes tapping sharply on the cold cobblestones. I must resist the temptation to turn around, he thought. That would look like a come-on. I must keep my back to the man and leave the palace promptly but unhurriedly.

Humphrey was not a homosexual himself, although he sometimes wondered if his celibate life with his sister had led some of his friends and neighbors to believe he was. He had loved a girl once. Her name was Marjorie, and she had been perky and pretty, with bubbly curls. He had caught her bus every morning and one time he had taken her out for tea. They had kissed by the park gates. But of course she had been hopelessly unsuitable. His sister had said, "Not really our type, dear," although in some ways she had been quite nice about what she had always referred to afterward as "Humphrey's little spot of wild-oats sowing."

In every memory of those postwar years it seemed to Humphrey that it had always been August and that he had always been desperately hot in a Fair Isle sweater, floundering in wool. These days he felt the cold, relentlessly and to the bone.

He reached Stortorget, the old square, where he was surrounded on all sides by flat-faced medieval buildings. He turned, and to his alarm the tall young man was only a few paces away from him and, worse, he was *smiling*.

"Mr. Browne?" the young man asked in an American accent.

Humphrey stood where he was, feeling the wind at his back. The young man appeared even taller seen close up, and by the way he walked, he was evidently something of an athlete. A jock, wasn't that what the Americans called it? The word *jock* had terrible connotations with *straps*. Humphrey sniffed but said nothing. He didn't know what to say that wouldn't sound either vixenish or coy.

"You *are* Mr. Browne?" the young man asked, smiling to show Humphrey his even white teeth.

"What's it to you?" asked Humphrey and immediately regretted it.

"My name is Bill Bennett," the other told him. He held out his hand. "I've been watching you for most of the afternoon."

Humphrey ignored the outstretched hand. My God, he

thought, how bold could a homosexual be? He let out a peculiar laugh, more from nerves than anything else, and said, "I'm not interested, you know. Just because I'm English, it doesn't mean—"

"I don't think you understand," interrupted Bill Bennett, frowning. "I was sent here to talk to you because of something you said to Major Milliner."

"Milner," Humphrey corrected him. Then, more slowly, "You were sent here? By whom? You were sent here because of something I said to Major Milner?"

Bill Bennett glanced around the square. On a bench in the far corner four old Stockholm winos were drinking vodka from bottles in brown paper bags and having what sounded like a hawking contest. "Listen," he said, "maybe I can buy you a drink."

Humphrey hesitated. "I was intending to go back to my hotel for a rest."

"You're right next door to the Sheraton, aren't you? That's where I'm staying. Go take a rest and then meet me in the bar at seven. How's that?"

"Well," said Humphrey, feeling dreadfully uncertain, "all right. But I wish you'd give me some idea of what this is all about."

Bill Bennett smiled. "Do you play tennis?"

"Tennis? What has tennis got to do with it?"

"Nothing. But I like to keep my game up, even when I'm working."

Humphrey took a taxi back to the Lantona, locked his door, undressed and took a hot bath. Afterward, crimson, he sat on the bed in his bathrobe and wondered whether he ought to call Major Milner to find out if "Bill Bennett" were genuine. Yet for some reason he felt reluctant to do so. How could "Bill Bennett" be anything *but* genuine, especially since Major Milner was the only person who knew that Humphrey had identified Hermann? Except, of course, Hermann himself. And if Hermann had known

Humphrey was calling Cricklewood, he must have been
told as much by the old woman at the reception desk. That
meant she could just as easily have listened to his long-
distance call and told Hermann all about it.

Humphrey gnawed at his thumbnail. He didn't like this
spy stuff at all. At least in John le Carré novels everybody
played out a dreamlike but infinitely controlled existence.
This business with Hermann was all too random, and
frightening too. It was quite possible that a fellow might
get killed and who would ever know about it? Only his
sister, and what would she do then? Nothing, except sit in
church and suck mints while the Reverend Johnson talked
about death as "a mist of darkness forever."

Sod that, he thought, surprised at his own vulgarity. He
picked up the phone and asked for a line, then dialed
Major Milner's number. The phone rang and rang but
there was no reply. The major was probably down at the
Three Tuns, drinking Bell's-and-water and telling everybody what a jolly nice chap he was. Humphrey was annoyed,
but also vaguely relieved.

Bill Bennett was waiting for him on one of the black-
leather bar stools in the Sheraton Hotel. There was soft
Muzak playing in the background and the rustle of travelers
arriving and leaving on the polished concourse below.

"Lager, please," said Humphrey as he awkwardly
perched on the neighboring bar stool. In front of Bill Bennett
stood a large glass of Perrier water with a slice of lemon in
it.

"You don't drink?" asked Humphrey as the girl brought
him a Pripps.

"Not while on duty."

"You're not a policeman?"

"No."

"Then I suppose you're a spy. A secret agent."

"Hardly. I work for the U.S. Information Service. Mostly in Central and South America."

Humphrey drank a little of his beer and patted his mouth with his handkerchief. "It seems curious that they should have sent someone from South America."

"Not really," said Bill Bennett. "I also happen to be familiar with identifying one-time Nazis. When you're working in South America, it's part of the job. I spotted Barbie originally, although I didn't get the credit for it."

"Well, that's interesting," Humphrey commented. "I used to work for BDG-Seven during the war. 'The Budgies' they called us. I spent years training myself to identify Nazi war criminals. I could have picked out Martin Bormann in a crowd, even if he were wearing a Chaplin mustache. I pride myself that I still could—well, if he were alive today."

"You saw Hermann." Bill Bennett smiled at him. "Leastways you thought you did."

"Oh, I saw him all right, and spoke to him too. No doubt at all that it was him. Very nasty piece of work, Hermann."

"Major Milner—Milner, is it?—he said you were always one of the best. Cream of the team, he called you."

"Well, that's a compliment," said Humphrey. He was suddenly beginning to warm to this young Bill Bennett, especially now that it was quite clear he wasn't going to make a pass. "It takes a special sort of eye, you know. Not everyone's got it. You have to look for the shape of the head, and the ears, and particularly that point between the eyes where the nose and the eyes and the forehead all conjoin. That single square inch is the most distinctive part of a person's features. Even if he dyes his hair and undergoes rhinoplasty, he can never change the appearance of that central spot. I was once thinking of writing a treatise on it: 'Browne's Law of Criminal Identification.' But, well, you know how it is. Other things press. Time goes by."

Bill Bennett watched Humphrey carefully as he spoke. "Why did you call Major Milner?" he asked.

Humphrey shrugged. He didn't quite know why himself. "Sense of duty, I suppose," he suggested. "Showing off perhaps. Quite a feat, don't you know, recognizing a man after forty-four some years, especially when you've never seen him in the flesh. Three photographs we had, and a drawing made by an inmate in one of the camps. But there's no doubt that it's him. Not in my mind. And why would he act in such a threatening way if it *wasn't* him? Tell me that."

"The apartment at Seventeen Pilogatan is a rental," said Bennett. "It belongs to a Swedish trading company called Södertälje Exports. It deals mainly with the Soviet Union. Electronics, plastics, pharmaceutical goods, things like that. Hermann—if it *is* Hermann—is renting it under the name of Rangström."

"Have you been 'round there?" asked Humphrey. He was surprised and a little alarmed that the Americans should have taken such a sudden and enthusiastic interest in his discovery. He took another swallow of beer and realized he had finished it long before he meant to.

"Give Mr. Browne another one," Bill Bennett told the barmaid. When Humphrey started to demur, he said, "Go on. You deserve it."

"Well, if you put it that way. . . . But I must go to the men's room in a moment. This Swedish beer goes right through me."

"The reason I've contacted you," Bennett continued, "is because we want to make an absolutely positive identification."

"You're going to arrest him?"

"It depends."

"I see. Then you might want me to stand up in court, point him out and suchlike?"

"That's right. The main thing is to ensure that we can make the identification stick."

"I see," Humphrey repeated. Then, suddenly, "I was thinking in bed last night, you know—or the night before last, I mean—I was thinking of how unusual it is for a Nazi war criminal to have fled to Russia. Most of them went to South America, didn't they? Barbie and Mengele and Eichmann. It was very unusual for Hermann to go to Russia. I'm surprised they didn't tear him to pieces."

"Hermann had something the Russians wanted. He was the medical equivalent of Wernher von Braun, if you understand what I mean. He and Mengele had been working for years on all kinds of medical experiments, and of course they made tremendous progress because they had all those Jews to work on. Living human subjects, not rats or guinea pigs or white mice. For instance, Mengele found out as long ago as nineteen forty-one—from the work he did on concentration-camp inmates—that saccharin was carcinogenic, but of course his report was discredited because he was a Nazi war criminal and also because the big U.S. pharmaceutical companies had a vested interest in keeping his medical records under wraps."

"Is that really true?"

Bennett nodded. "It's true, Mr. Browne, and it's only the tip of the iceberg. Think about it. For at least ten years the Nazi doctors could do anything they wished to anyone they wished. Any serious research scientist worth his sauerkraut couldn't have failed to make enormous steps forward, given those facilities. The Nazi work on genetics stands as one of the great sociomedical achievements of the twentieth century, although nobody is actually allowed to say so. But who else could have cut open living people to see how their organs worked? Who else could have injected human beings with any poison or virus they wanted—sometimes two or three thousand people at a time? If it hadn't been for the Nazis, we would never have heard of the double helix or test-tube babies, and we still wouldn't have heard of alpha-phthalimidoglutarimide.''

"I'm not sure I've heard of it yet,'' said Humphrey.

"Thalidomide,'' said Bennett. "A colleague of Hermann's by the name of Mietzner was working on the synthesis of a similar drug for the specific purpose of shortening the limbs of 'inferior' races so they could be employed in tunneling and mining work. Sounds bizarre today, doesn't it? But it happened. Of course the German chemists who synthesized thalidomide in nineteen fifty-three had no access to Mietzner's records, so they couldn't have known what was going to happen.''

Humphrey was silent for a long time. Bennett kept watching him and kept on smiling. At last Humphrey said somewhat heavily, "You're an expert on this, aren't you? I mean, you're an expert on Hermann?''

"No one can be an expert on someone who hasn't been seen for over forty years. If anyone's an expert, *you* are.''

Humphrey shook his head. "All I know is what the man looks like. You know all about him. You know what he *means*.''

"Well, I guess so,'' said Bennett cheerfully. "But I was trained to. It's my work.''

"He means a lot to America then? He must or they wouldn't have trained you so carefully.''

"Shrewd point, Mr. Browne.''

"You may, if you wish, call me Humphrey.''

Bennett held out his hand for the second time. "You can certainly call me Bill.''

Humphrey asked, "Does Hermann still represent some kind of threat to America? I mean in the same way that Wernher von Braun must have represented quite a threat to the Russians when he was helping you to build your missiles?''

Bill put down his drink. "Hermann *does* represent a danger, yes, in a certain sense. He helped the Soviets build up their chemical-warfare arsenal and as far as we know, he's still improving it, if you can use that word. He was the first person to develop a method of spreading rabies by missile, and one of his greatest achievements was to breed and develop a psittacosis virus that could be added to a nation's water supply. He's also done work on poliomyelitis and smallpox, although we've never been able to locate his wartime records so we don't know how far he got. Yes, he's a dangerous man, even at his age. There's no age limit on treachery, is there?"

"I suppose not," Humphrey replied, although he didn't quite understand what the young American meant.

Bill poked at his lemon wedge. "The amount of freedom the Soviet regime allows its citizens is in direct proportion to their loyalty and usefulness to the state. If Hermann is being allowed to travel to Stockholm and to keep an apartment of his own, then all I can say is that the Soviets must trust him a very great deal, and value him too."

"So you're really more interested in what he's doing now than what he did during the war?" asked Humphrey.

"The two are closely related," said Bill. "But, yes, you could say that."

"So what do you want *me* to do?"

"We don't want you to do anything."

"But you must; otherwise you wouldn't have told me any of this. You're trying to recruit me, aren't you? I'm not a fool, you know. I had to do it once or twice myself during the war. It's an old technique. The trouble is that I'm rather too old to go along with it—at least until I know what it is you want and what you might be offering."

"I didn't say I was offering anything," said Bill offhandedly.

"Then you expect me to help you out of the goodness of my heart?"

Bill Bennett was about to say something in reply, but then he caught himself, shook his head and smiled. "All right,'' he said. "We need your help. That is, we would very much appreciate it if you could see your way clear to assisting us. That's a good evasive British way of asking, isn't it?''

Humphrey said, "You mustn't take too much for granted, you know.'' It sounded prissy but he couldn't help it.

"I'm not taking anything for granted. I'm asking you to help us simply because you're the best at what you do. I can recognize Nazis like Vogel and Kress; I even picked out Hörlich once, although the Argentinian police had to let him go on a technicality. But I'm not at all sure about Hermann and people like that. I need you to finger him for me.''

"Supposing I'm not interested in fingering him?'' asked Humphrey. The beer may have been passing through his kidneys quickly but it was also going to his head just as fast. He felt lightheaded and a little sick. "Supposing I refuse to identify him, whether he's Hermann or not?''

"You're not making any sense,'' said Bill tensely.

"I wasn't aware that I was obliged to,'' Humphrey retorted. "You follow me about—on my holiday—and then tell me you need my help in identifying Klaus Hermann. Well, what are you going to do then? Arrest him, kill him, or what? And what are you going to do with me? You've probably told me too much already.''

Bill said, "Everything I've told you has already been openly reported in the *International Journal of Biology*. There's no secret about it.''

"Still,'' protested Humphrey petulantly, "I don't see why I should do it.''

"You were pleased that you identified him; why are you backing out now?'' He paused. "Come on, have another drink.''

"No, no thank you. Well, just a small one. Half-liter.''

Bill beckoned to the barmaid. "Give this gentleman a small beer, and I'll have another Perrier.'' Then he laid his

hand on Humphrey's arm, leaned forward and said in a
confidential voice, "You'll still get the credit."

"What credit?"

"You know what credit. The credit for finding Hermann.
That's what you're worried about, isn't it? You're worried
that if I take over, the media will attribute Hermann's
capture to me."

Humphrey looked down at Bill Bennett's hand and then
turned away. The American was disturbingly right. The
whole thrill in recognizing Hermann was that he, Humphrey,
had done it alone; it had given him the first opportunity in
his whole life to seek a little personal glory, the first
chance to exercise power and influence over another human being. He shouldn't have called Major Milner; he
knew that now. At the time, of course, he had been
prompted by a mixture of pride and fright, but the call had
obviously been a mistake. Now his achievement had already been taken out of his hands by this tall, tanned,
intelligent and unbearably good-looking American, and he
would get nothing for it, not even the satisfaction of seeing
his name in print.

Bill said, "Let me tell you something, Humphrey. You'll
get the credit. I promise you. In fact, I don't even want my
name to be mentioned."

Humphrey glanced at him, then looked away.

"Just tell me you'll help us, that's all," Bill urged him.
"Then you can have the kudos for the whole damn thing."

"What exactly do you want me to do?" It was more a
statement than a question.

"You have to identify Hermann, nothing more. Point
him out. I'll do the rest. But I have to be absolutely
one-hundred-and-eight-percent sure that it's him."

Humphrey politely lifted Bill Bennett's hand off his
sleeve, nodded toward his beer to indicate that he wasn't
offended by the personal contact—although he was—and
that he simply wanted to free his arm to have a drink.

"I'm really not too sure," he said. "I mean, I haven't seen your credentials, have I?"

"Humphrey, my credentials are that I know what you said to Major Milner."

"Well. . . ."

"I'll tell you what we'll do. We'll drive over to Pilogatan and say hi to Hermann and make sure it's him. What do you say to that? After that I'll buy you dinner at the Opera-Kallaren, and then we can go to the Chat-Noir for the sex show."

Humphrey said nothing. This all sounded terribly wrong and terribly complicated, yet he didn't know how to back away from it without losing his dignity.

"I must go to the loo first," he said.

SIX

Bill Bennett waited for Humphrey with the patience of a
man who is used to waiting. He ate one or two olives from
the dish on the bar and stared at the traffic outside the
window, but his eyes and his mind were blank.

He disliked Stockholm. He found the Swedes boorish
and provincial; their preoccupation with alcohol reminded
him of his father's sweaty, loud-voiced associates in
Mankato, Minnesota, where he himself had been born and
raised. He was thirty-four now, and he had spent his entire
adult life striving hard not to be like his father. He had
studied relentlessly in high school, and at the first opportunity he had joined the army. The army had disciplined
him, trained him, hardened his body and straightened his
mind. By the time he had left the service at the age of
twenty-nine, he had grown into a tough and capable young
captain.

For a year after his discharge, Bill Bennett had worked
for a security corporation in San Diego. He had used that
year to teach himself some of the finer ways of the world:
to appreciate wine and music and good food and, most of

all, to appreciate other people. He was a far more cultured and sensitive man than when he was in the army.

One of his girlfriends, Yvonne, had called him "a male stereotype of a male stereotype," although she hadn't meant it unkindly. He knew the difference between a Volnay and a Vouvray, a châteaubriand and a Châteauneuf-du-Pape. He also knew the finer techniques of arousing a woman. But there was more to him than that. Beneath that captain's crispness and that playboy's statistical savoir-faire there was a man of considerable sentiment and emotional strength.

He was a better man, in fact, than he believed himself to be. And that was probably why Army Intelligence had contacted him only seven months after he left the service and suggested he help them. They were looking for prominent Nazis whose wartime activities might have been, well, embarrassing. They might have compromised some of today's more respected citizens. It was a good, worthwhile, patriotic task. Besides that, it paid sixty-eight thousand a year, which was more than most three-star generals were entitled to.

Bill had just broken up with the most intense love of his life, Karen Windom. It had been easier to say yes than no, and within a week he had been sent to Omaha for training in identifying those Nazis who were still thought to be in hiding in Central and South America. Scores of them: Adler, August, Berthold, Bergen—one hundred and ninety-six altogether, and only four positively identified.

He had sat at his desk in Omaha overlooking Fontenelle Park, trying to picture these men in his mind's eye as they might be today. But he had been able to conjure up only a quorum of wrinkled, white-haired old monstrosities, warped by their past atrocities and hysterical about their future. He hadn't really been able to believe they were still alive or that it made any difference to the United States whether

they were caught and tried or allowed to go free. The war
had begun and ended before he was born. He had been a
toddler during Korea. Sometimes he felt as though he had
been sent to look for Bismarck. Who cared about Hermann
or Barbie and how many they had killed? They were so old
they were scarcely worth hunting down, and they weren't
the men they used to be, for sure.

But, well-paid, with a fat expense account, he had sat in
the bar of the Hotel Concepcíon in Managua, his eyes
shaded by the brim of his white straw hat, watching while
three former SS officers toasted each other with apricot
juleps and talked about Munich before the war; and he had
sweated his way on the back of a mule up the side of the
Cerro Gaitál in Panama to a small, steaming community
they call El Valle, just to talk to a shuddering old man
with Parkinson's disease who had once crushed living
children under the wheels of railroad cars.

He had done these things because he had been ordered
to and because he valued the experience; and for much the
same reasons he was here in Stockholm, making contact
with Humphrey Browne.

He found Humphrey tiresome and too British to be
anything other than socially awkward. But he believed
himself sufficiently professional to know how to handle
him, and he'd learned that Englishmen are deceptively
strong in their personal relationships, both male and female.
Somehow his own relationships with women seemed to
have become oddly fractured, like boxes full of hopelessly
mixed-up jigsaw puzzles. After Karen not very much had
made sense; but then, had it ever?

They left the bar when Humphrey came back from the
men's room. Bill's car was parked in the basement; it was
a rather shabby Grand Prix that belonged to the U.S.
Embassy. "I could have rented a Volvo," he said as they
pulled out of the exit ramp on squealing tires, "but, you
know, a *Volvo?*"

"I always thought Volvos were rather splendid," said Humphrey. "Very safe, I understood."

Bill glanced at him as they drove across Vasabrön toward the old part of town. "Real men don't drive Volvos," he said. The Grand Prix's suspension clunked as they hit the cobbles of Stora Nygatan. "Shocks are shot, that's all," he explained.

They parked outside the Enskilda Banken on Kornhamn-storget and walked the rest of the way to Pilogatan. The night was cold and Humphrey turned up the collar of his coat. For no clear reason he felt quite afraid, more afraid of Bill Bennett than he was of Klaus Hermann.

At last they reached the dark, smelly canyon of Pilogatan and stood outside No. 17. Up on the third floor the lights were shining through the blinds, and occasionally someone's shadow moved across a window like in an Indonesian puppet theater. Bill fumbled in his pocket and produced a selection of lock picks and then quite openly began to ease back the tumblers of the front-door lock.

Humphrey watched him dubiously. "We won't get arrested for this?" he asked.

"Arrested?" asked Bill, pushing the front door open so it groaned softly on its hinges. "Come on, all you have to do is to take a look at him and tell me you're sure he's Hermann."

"I'm not sure I like this," said Humphrey.

"You're not sure?" Bill retorted.

"Well, I have to think of my sister."

There was no elevator; the building was too old for that. They mounted the winding stone steps, passing private and tightly closed doors from behind which they could hear the faint strains of music or the clipped sounds of the Swedish television news.

They reached Hermann's door. There was a small brass slot on the front of it bearing a neatly penned card that read: A. Rangström. Bill looked back at Humphrey and smiled. "All you have to do is say 'That's him' and we can get this over with."

"Very well," said Humphrey, although he felt just the opposite.

Bill selected another of his lock picks and delved into the keyhole, whistling between his teeth. He had enjoyed his lock-picking course at Omaha more than any other: there was something extraordinarily exhilarating in knowing that he could walk into practically any house or office undetected and that he could steal almost any car.

The apartment door opened. Inside there was light and music and fragrant warmth, almost like a sauna. Pale beige walls and a shaggy cream carpet. Just in view, a black-and-white etching of dancing satyrs.

"Shouldn't we announce ourselves?" Humphrey suggested. "I mean, ring the doorbell or something?"

Bill put his finger to his lips and then turned back his putty-colored windbreaker to lift out a nickel-plated Smith & Wesson .38. Humphrey said, "That's it. I'm going. You didn't tell me there was going to be guns."

Bill snatched out with his left arm and caught Humphrey's shoulder. "You stay where you are. I need you."

"What are you doing?" Humphrey protested, flailing feebly. He fell back, stumbled on the stone steps and thumped his back against the curving wall.

"For Christ's sake, stay calm," Bill hissed at him. Then he beckoned with the gun and ordered, "Get back up here."

Humphrey stayed where he was. Bill snapped at him, "Get back up here, do you hear me?"

At that moment a voice inside the apartment said, "Who's there? Birgitta, the door's open!"

The sound of music suddenly blared, then softened. Humphrey pressed himself back against the wall and stared at Bill in fright. A woman's voice, very Swedish, said, "I locked it. Don't be ridiculous."

Again the man's voice called, "Who's there?"

"Nobody," laughed the woman. "Go and close it and then come back here."

Humphrey whispered, "That's not him. That's not him at all. His accent—quite different—very German."

"You couldn't have locked it," the man said as his voice came closer. Bill eased back from the doorway and stood just out of sight, the revolver raised with both hands. Humphrey repeated in a scared whisper, "It's not—" but Bill's concentration was total and he didn't even hear him.

A hairy, naked, bald-headed man suddenly stuck his head out of the lighted doorway and stared straight at Humphrey in complete disbelief.

"What the hell is happening?" he demanded, his eyes wide. But at that moment Bill snatched him around the neck and pushed the nuzzle of the revolver hard against his temple. The man sagged, tried to struggle and then knocked his shoulder against the door jamb. "What are you doing? What the hell are you doing?"

"Is this him?" Bill asked Humphrey in an off-key, over excited whisper.

"Of course not," said Humphrey. "Hermann's old, over seventy years old. This man can't be more than forty-five."

"Get that gun away from my head," the man protested. Bill kept it where it was, pressing so hard that the man's skin was ridged.

Humphrey said, "It's not Hermann. Hermann's old, really old."

"Get inside," Bill ordered the man and twisted him back into the open doorway. "Humphrey, come along. Close the door behind you."

"Bill, I'm not really sure that I—"

"Get in here and close the door behind you before I blow this idiot's brains out!" Bill barked at him. The "idiot" turned around and pleaded with Humphrey. "Come, will you, for God's sake."

Silently, biting his lip, Humphrey followed them into the apartment and closed the door. Bill shoved the naked man into the living room, and the first thing Humphrey heard was a woman's scream, then Bill saying, "Keep quiet and nobody's going to get hurt. Do you hear me?"

Humphrey came into the room and found that it was as white and modern inside as the hallway outside was dark and forbidding. The walls were an off-white, the carpet was as pure as snow. There were Swedish-style lamps on glass-and-wooden furniture, and overlit pieces of Boda and Orrefors crystal. All the furniture was upholstered in white hide.

In the corner of the sofa sat a very ample, dark-haired woman with a mouth as purple as smashed raspberries. She was wearing a black laced-up basque over which her breasts bulged, black garters, black fishnet stockings and black-patent stiletto-heeled shoes. Something protruded between her thighs, and it took Humphrey two or three discreet but mesmerized glances to understand that it was a vibrator. He was shocked and looked away, unable to bring himself to look back.

The naked man said, "What is this? A robbery? You want money? I don't have any money. You want my American Express card? Take it."

"Sit down," said Bill; then, turning to the woman, "You want to cover yourself up?"

Humphrey said, "I'll, er, get you a . . ." and walked erratically across the living room to the bedroom. The bedroom walls were mirrored and he could see himself tugging a blanket off the bed. Back in the living room, he handed it to the woman at arm's length, and tried not to be aware of her as she reached for it.

Bill had ordered the naked man to sit on a small leather hassock, where he now perched knock-kneed, his hands clutched between his thighs and looking extremely unhappy.

"You're going to have to tell me your name," Bill told him. He waved the revolver at the woman. "You too."

"This is very embarrassing," the man said.

"Well, of course it's embarrassing," said Bill. "But I might have killed you, and *that* would have really been embarrassing."

"You have no right," the woman suddenly said in her strong Swedish accent. "What are you, robbers?"

"I want to know your names," insisted Bill.

Humphrey cleared his throat. "It really would be better if you told him." He smiled nervously at the woman. She didn't smile back.

The man said, "This is an outrage. An absolute outrage."

"All right, it's an outrage," Bill agreed. "But I have the gun and you don't, and I want you to tell me your name."

The man closed his eyes for a moment, either in anger or in prayer. Then he said, "My name is Vojtech Mňačko. I am the Czech commercial deputy. This woman is Birgitta Gillsäter, from the St. Eriksplan Theatre Group."

"Neither of you is called Rangström?"

"No," said Mňačko.

"This apartment is registered in the name of Rangström."

"Yes."

"So what are you doing here?" Bill demanded.

"I would have thought it quite obvious," said Mňačko. "Miss Gillsäter and I have been friends for many years. You have interrupted one of our rare opportunities to spend an evening together in private."

"If this is Mr. Rangström's apartment, where is Mr. Rangström?" asked Bill.

"You mean *Miss* Rangström," put in Birgitta Gillsäter sharply.

"I do? *Miss* Rangström?"

"Miss Angelika Rangström. She also is a member of the St. Eriksplan Theatre Group. If you knew anything about Stockholm of course, you would have been aware of that already. She is considered one of Sweden's most talented actresses. Last season her *Hedda Gabler* won her the Valhalla Award."

"And Miss Rangström's male friend?" asked Humphrey.

"What about him?" asked Mňačko.

But Birgitta Gillsäter said, "She has no man friend. She used to, but no longer."

Bill reached into his inside pocket and produced an artist's sketch of Klaus Hermann. Humphrey leaned forward and looked at it; although the artist had assumed that Hermann would have lost his hair after forty-four some odd years, it was a remarkably accurate impression.

"Is this the man?" Bill asked Birgitta Gillsäter.

"She has no man friend."

"Look at the picture."

Reluctantly Birgitta Gillsäter lowered her eyes and examined the drawing. But then she slowly shook her head. "I don't know this man. I never saw him before. He is a stranger."

Bill showed the picture to Vojtech Mňačko. "You know this man? Ever seen him before?"

Mňačko defiantly raised his head and refused even to look at it.

Bill tucked the picture away. "I have to tell you that you people have created a serious difficulty, being here tonight like this."

"I think it is you who has created the difficulty," replied Mňačko.

Bill thought for a while without saying anything; the others sat and watched him. Humphrey nodded toward Birgitta Gillsäter as though to reassure her that everything would be all right, but the actress looked away from him coldly. It seemed remarkable to Humphrey that a woman whom he had caught in such an intimate and peculiar sexual act should treat him so haughtily. No shame at all. But of course this was Sweden, the home of legalized pornography, and Humphrey supposed it must have some effect on the manners and morals of the native Swedes.

Mňačko asked, "What will you do now? We can't sit here all night."

"Well, I'm trying to decide," said Bill. "I think that on the whole the best thing would be to tie you up."

"Tie us up? What is the use of that?" Mňačko demanded.

"Let me decide what the use of it is. Let's do it in the bedroom, where we can tear up some sheets."

"You can't do that," Birgitta Gillsäter protested. "This is not our apartment. Angelika will be furious."

Bill raised the revolver. "The gun says I can do what I want. Primitive, I know. Just what you'd expect from an American. But there we are."

He prodded Mňačko up from the hassock and through the bedroom door. "Go lie facedown on the floor," he ordered. Then he beckoned to Birgitta Gillsäter to follow him into the bedroom. "Take off the blanket," he ordered.

"Bill, that's not necessary," said Humphrey.

Bill turned and smiled at him. "Will you keep an eye on the door, please?"

Humphrey hesitated, but there was something about that smile that made him retreat and say, "Yes. All right. The door."

Once Humphrey had gone to the hallway, Bill closed the bedroom door and locked it. Mňačko was lying facedown on the rug, his hands crossed palms-upward over the small of his hairy back. Birgitta Gillsäter was spread out beside him, her wide bottom matching the off-white walls. Bill laid the revolver on the bedside table and said, "I warn you. Any attempt to get up and I can go for that gun so fast you won't even know what happened. If you want to keep your brains inside your head, do as you're told."

Using his penknife, he quickly ripped two bedsheets into ribbons. Then, with all the speed and expertise they had taught him in the service, he tugged Mňačko's hands up behind his back and bound his wrists. Mňačko complained, "That's too tight," but Bill didn't answer him. He took two more lengths of sheeting and lashed together Mňačko's knees and ankles. Finally he gagged him.

The door handle rattled; then there was a knock. Humphrey said, "Is everything all right in there, Bill?"

"Fine," Bill called back. His breathing was forced, his pulse rate was around a hundred. "Go back and watch the door. I'm nearly finished here."

Birgitta Gillsäter looked up from the floor and stared at him. "You're going to kill us, aren't you?" Her voice was shocked.

"Yes," answered Bill.

At this Mňačko tried to raise his head and speak, but Bill placed his foot on the back of his neck and pushed his face into the rug.

Birgitta Gillsäter stayed where she was. Her lipstick had made a red smear on the white pile of the carpet. She said suddenly, "I don't want to die. Please, not like this."

"You don't have any choice."

"Do you want to know about Angelika's friend?"

Bill stared down at her, expressionless. "Well?" he asked.

"If you spare me, I will tell you where he is."

Bill took out the artist's impression again and held it only inches from her nose. "This man? You know where he is?"

She nodded

"You can take me to him personally?"

She nodded again.

Bill thought about that and then said, "All right. You can take me to him tonight?"

"He is in Uppsala. Only an hour's drive."

"All right," Bill repeated—as though agreeing to accompany her to a rather uninteresting little restaurant just down the street.

"What will you do with Vojtech?"

"You get yourself dressed. Vojtech and I are going to have a little talk." He bent forward and said loudly, "Isn't that right, Vojtech? A few minutes of relevant conversation."

"Grrrgg," said Mňačko.

Birgitta Gillsäter collected her salmon-colored woolen suit from where she had first abandoned it by the side of the bed; Bill unlocked the bedroom door for her and nudged her back out into the living room. "Humphrey!" he called. "Miss Gillsäter's getting herself dressed. Keep an eye on her."

"Yes, very well," said Humphrey, looking uncomfortable where he stood by the door. Bill went through to the kitchen and switched on the overhead light. He drummed his fingers on the white counter top and then reached up and opened one of the cabinets. There were only cups in it. He opened another, then another, and at last he found what he was looking for. Plastic trash bags. He went back into the bedroom without speaking either to Humphrey or Birgitta Gillsäter. He locked the bedroom door behind him.

Without a word he opened the white plastic bag he had brought from the kitchen and tugged it over Mňačko's head. Mňačko twisted and writhed but Bill pushed his knee into the middle of the man's back. When the bag was firmly over Mňačko's head, Bill twisted the neck of it so it was an airtight fit.

The bag was sucked in against Mňačko's features as he tried to breathe. Through the plastic Bill could see the contours of his wide-open eyes, the gaping muscles of his cheeks—a living death mask in white. He checked his watch. Even the fittest human being was unable to hold his breath for much longer than two minutes. The bag suddenly blew out and then sucked in again. Mňačko jerked and shuddered, and Bill pressed his knee into his back once more.

The bag half-inflated again: carbon dioxide. And then the same carbon dioxide was breathed back in. Then again, and again, and again. At last, after four minutes, the bag relaxed with a soft crackling sound and Mňačko lay still.

Bill stood up and holstered his revolver. He looked around the bedroom to make sure everything was arranged the way he wanted it; then he stepped out and locked the door. Humphrey was waiting for him in the living room and Birgitta Gillsäter was now dressed.

"Very fetching," Bill remarked of the salmon-colored woolen suit. Birgitta refused to smile.

"Mňačko's all right?" asked Humphrey.

"Oh, sure," said Bill. "Are we ready to go?"

"I cannot say good-bye to Vojtech?" asked Birgitta.

Bill shook his head. "He's all right. As soon as we've located Miss Rangström's friend, you can come back and cut him loose."

"That sounds like something out of a cowboy film," Humphrey remarked, although he was unsettled by the unusual deadness in Bill's voice.

They left the apartment and clattered down the stone stairs to the street. A freezing east wind was blowing across Skeppsbrön and whistling up Pilogatan like a bevy of malevolent trolls. Humphrey looked up at the window of the apartment and saw that it was still brightly lit. He felt quite sorry for Vojtech Mňačko, tied up and helpless on the bedroom rug. What a way to spend an evening, he thought; it was almost funny. He gave a small, half-suppressed snicker and Birgitta stared at him over the collar of her sheepskin coat.

"It's not so cold yet," she said. "You wait until winter."

SEVEN

Chiffon Trent was quite intimately preoccupied when the doorbell rang. It was a soft, bland chime, but it was enough to destroy the whole afternoon—the lunch at the Oyster Bar, the arm-in-arm walk in the park, the kisses and the champagne. The young Asian-looking man rose from the sheets and said, "Who is that? Not that jerk in the three-piece suit. Not now."

Chiffon touched a finger to her lips and rolled off the bed. At once she reached for her sheer silk dressing gown with the ruffled collar; she had always thought of herself as a lady, even in the throes of passion. She swirled across the room, pressed her tangled blonde curls against the door and called, "Who is it?"

"Dick Elmwood, Miss Trent. Just to tell you the senator's downstairs in the Palm Court and he'll expect you shortly."

"Is it four already?"

"It's three-forty-five, Miss Trent. The senator's a little ahead of time. Traffic from the airport was unusually light."

Chiffon made a face at the young man on the bed and mimicked Dick Elmwood's nasal intonation: "Traffic from the airport was unusually light, huh?'' The young man laughed and lay on his back, dark and slim and naked.

"Tell the senator he's going to have to give me a half-hour,'' called Chiffon. "Tell him I had a headache, you know? I'm only just over it.''

"I think he'd appreciate it if you hurried,'' said Elmwood. He waited for a reply and when none came, he noisily cleared his throat.

"All right,'' said Chiffon. "But I have to curl my hair. And my eyes, I have to bathe my eyes. Tell him a kissy-wissy on the tip of the nose, will you? And another kissy-wissy on the bum-bum.''

The young man on the bed snorted hysterically. Chiffon waved at him to keep quiet. "Did you get that?'' she asked.

Elmwood cleared his throat again. "I got it,'' he said flatly. "I'll tell him.''

Chiffon giggled and danced across the room, swirling her silk dressing gown, pale bare thighs flickering beneath transparent silk, breasts bouncing. She tossed back the curtains at the window and leaned forward on the sill with an exaggerated sigh of contentment.

"Ah,'' she said. "Isn't life perfect?''

The young man said uneasily. "You're coming back to bed?''

"I don't think so. I'm going to dress.''

"You're going to leave me lying here? Look at me! I was holding back for you. That's the only reason I was holding back.''

Chiffon turned to him and smiled, a beatific smile. "So you should. Gentlemen always finish last.''

"Last, yes. But at least they get to *finish*.''

"Oh, don't be so animalistic,'' Chiffon dismissed him. She pressed her nose to the window so her breath created a misted butterfly on the glass. Seven stories below, the taxi-infested traffic crawled slowly backward and forward along Central Park South and pedestrians hurried along the sidewalk, clutching their hats, their scarves flapping in semaphore. New York was right on the brink of fall, just as Chiffon had been right on the brink of her climax. The trees in the park were trembling and thrashing, and a snappy northeast wind was whipping up newspapers and candy wrappers across General Motors Plaza. Something exciting was happening; it was time for change.

The young man sulkily climbed off the bed and stood arms akimbo by the other window, still half-aroused, the curls on his stomach still drying. "You're like a child," he told her.

"Of course I am. If I weren't you wouldn't like me so much."

"You're going down to see him?"

"Certainly. He paid for the room. He pays for everything."

"He's a pig."

"I didn't say he wasn't, did I? But he's a rich pig. How do you say that in Russian?"

"Richski pigovich."

Chiffon giggled. She was twenty-three years old, a Pisces, and unnervingly pretty. Five-feet-four with wide green eyes, a straight, perfectly shaped nose and high cheekbones that could have been cut by Rodin. And she had skin and a figure to match: skin that glowed pink on white and big, buoyant breasts. When Chiffon walked into a restaurant wearing one of the white pleated décolleté evening gowns Reynard had brought her from Sabra, the entire place would hush and men would sit with their knives and forks frozen in their hands and silently rail against the god who created a girl like Chiffon without giving them a chance to make love to her. She created social waves, cultural eddies, just by being so stunning; it was one of the reasons it had been impossible for Reynard to keep his affair with her a secret. A current avant-garde artist had called Chiffon "the face of total today," and an

internationally famous author had once sent her a rose
across the room at The Four Seasons.

She was smart, and she could be funny; but the truth
about Chiffon was that she had been born to utterly ordinary parents in Cedar Lake, Indiana, and that she had been
nothing at all in school except a flirtatious, gum-cracking
teenager bored with class. She had lost her virginity the
day before her fourteenth birthday to a sullen boy named
Carl, and after that she had been neither particularly good
nor particularly bad, either in bed or out of it.

By the time Chiffon was noticed by Reynard at a private
party at Studio 54, she had done almost nothing of note
except a casual-wear commercial, a walk-on, giggle-off
part in a television series and some fashion spreads for
Seventeen. But her love affair with Reynard had immediately opened her horizons, and now she was making regular guest appearances on television and was featured on
every magazine cover from *Redbook* to *Secrets*. Reynard
had scores of sycophantic Hollywood connections and infinite supplies of money; everyone in the business knew that
if they wanted to make Reynard happy, they had to make
Chiffon happy too—especially since there was every likelihood that Reynard would be elected the next president of
the United States.

The media accepted Reynard's affair quite equably as
just another of his passing infatuations. None of them yet
knew that Reynard had permanently separated from Greta,
and because of that, none of them were aware that Chiffon
already saw herself as the next Mrs. Kelly and, ipso facto,
the next First Lady. Not even Reynard was aware of it.
But she did, despite the fact that he had made it quite clear
to her that he never wanted to marry again. Just as he
stipulated that she should never wear panties. It didn't
strike Chiffon as at all incongruous that the First Lady
should be forbidden to wear panties; after all, she hardly
ever wore them anyway.

She drank nothing but White Star champagne these days
and never went to sleep before three o'clock in the morning;
as far as she was concerned, life was wonderful. More
than wonderful. Ecstatic.

The young boy said, "You should tell the jerk what you
think of him. Have some courage."

"Hmm," said Chiffon haughtily. "What would *you*
know about courage?"

"Courage is being yourself."

"I *am* being myself. I'm the greediest little girl in town,
and that's my nature. Any complaints?"

"I don't know." The boy rubbed his forehead with the
back of his hand. "Maybe I don't like to think of him
sleeping with you."

"You're jealous?" asked Chiffon in disbelief. She let
the curtains fall back; they seemed to drop around her in
slow motion, a pale and slightly grimy shroud.

"I don't like to think of him sleeping with you, that's
all."

She came toward him with her arms outstretched. Her
breasts bounced rhythmically under the silk of her dressing
gown; pale nipples gleaming through transparent silk. She
reached for his mouth with her lips, pushing him backward
toward the bed. Then, all silk and soft flesh, she straddled
him, kissed him and nipped at him with her teeth.

"Jealousy is a *sin*," she giggled.

They tussled and struggled, but at last she grew
bored, rolled away and got up from the bed and began to
dress. He watched her sullenly as she donned her cream-
colored pleated dress and turned his face away when she
leaned forward to kiss him.

"Sulking is a sin too," she said, less amused.

"All Russians have black moods," he told her. "It's in
our nature. The vastness of our country weighs on our
shoulders like a heavy cloak we can never unfasten."

"Mmm?" she said, pursing her mouth before the mirror as she put on her lip liner.

"Well, you wouldn't understand."

"I'm not at all sure I'd want to. In any case, you know I have to go see him. I *like* him. And he's my meal ticket."

"Meal ticket," sniffed the boy disdainfully.

"Listen," said Chiffon when she was ready to leave. "I'll meet you at the Russian Tea Room at seven sharp, and I'll fill that sensual mouth of yours with the best caviar and finest vodka. Then we'll come back here and finish what we didn't manage to finish this afternoon. So don't say 'meal ticket' down your nose like you're suffering from some kind of allergy."

"I have rehearsal this evening," the boy sulked. "The big love scene, where Natasha finally surrenders."

" 'The big love scene, where Natasha finally surrenders,' " Chiffon mocked him. "Skip rehearsal. I'll see you at seven."

The boy said nothing but propped himself up on his elbows and stared rebelliously at the headboard. Chiffon blew him four or five kisses and left the room, closing the door noisily behind her.

The boy continued to stare at the headboard, pouting, until he was quite sure that Chiffon had gone and that she wouldn't come back to apologize or kiss him, or to collect the lipstick she had left on the dressing table. Then he got up, sat on the edge of the bed and lit a Winston, blowing out the smoke through his nostrils.

In a minor way the boy was famous in his own right. His name was Piotr Lissitzky, and two years earlier he had defected to the United States during a tour of the Moscow Youth Theater Ensemble. A rainy afternoon in Pittsburgh, a spontaneous escape down the back stairs of the Carlton House Hotel, a confused appeal at the local police station for political asylum. For one moment he had been so irritated by the desk sergeant, who had been far more interested in discussing last night's football game with his colleagues than in a stuttering young Russian, that he had almost walked back to the hotel again. But at last he had made them understand; and then his life had become a carousel of news reporters, intensive interrogations and endless visits by gimlet-eyed officials from the State Department. George Rosenbaum had offered him a part in *Days of Sadness* at the Shubert. Clive Barnes had said of Piotr's opening night on Broadway, "Lissitzky's theatrical credentials appear to be that he once saw a James Dean picture."

Piotr was still acting—mostly in off-Broadway Chekhov revivals and television commercials that required someone with a thick foreign accent. But these days he was more of a gigolo than anything else, moodily escorting minor starlets in and out of fashionable nightclubs, shopping with wealthy and frustrated widows, swimming, posing. His affair with Chiffon Trent was just eleven days old. Sometimes, like now, sitting on the edge of this wide, expensive bed in the Plaza Hotel, and smoking, he felt drained and old before his time.

He thought of his childhood in Moscow—the concrete apartment block, the yard where he used to play ball. He thought of the family he had left behind on that teeming day when he had crossed the street in Pittsburgh and entered that police station. His mother, lively and smiling; his tired father; his two sisters. He hadn't realized that when you defect from one ideology to another, you leave everything behind, including your own history. These days he felt as though he were nobody at all.

"Natasha," he said, quoting from the play in which he was about to appear, "you are nothing but a reflection in a mirror in an empty room."

Downstairs in the Palm Court, Reynard was sitting at his usual table—as far away from the piano as possible. He liked piano music but disliked having musicians leer at him as they played; music, as far as he was concerned, was a private experience, like sex. He was dressed in black, with a black-and-white spotted necktie and gleaming black shoes. He had to fly back to Washington on the seven-o'clock flight; there was an important late-night meeting with the Burns Committee at ten.

He drank tea with lemon and played with the spoon in his saucer. The Palm Court bustled with brittle tea-time conversation, and a constant stream of guests and visitors flowed around its perimeter. Reynard was beginning to wish he had chosen somewhere more private to meet. A white-haired woman in a garish suit of rainbow-colored silk had already waved saucily to him and several people had murmured, "There's Reynard Kelly," to each other as they passed. "You see there . . . don't look . . . you know who that is? Reynard Kelly."

Dick Elmwood was standing just outside the entrance to the Palm Court; he was accompanied by one of Reynard's private-security men—a tall, cultured-looking man named Pollock. Reynard turned around in his chair and grimaced at Dick, but all Dick could do was to tap his wristwatch and shrug.

Damn it, thought Reynard, I'm not waiting for this girl very much longer. One minute, no more.

But almost as he thought it, he could see Chiffon's curly blonde hair and the jiggle of her walk, and within a moment she was escorted over to his table, as delicious and tasty looking as one of the Plaza's cream cakes, soft and fragrant and still irresistible.

She kissed his cheek and he felt her breast against his wrist—as well as a sudden surge of desire. That annoyed him still more because he would have to sit down and talk with her, pretending to be polite, when he would like nothing more than to take her upstairs to bed.

"You look tired," she told him, opening her pocket-book and checking her lipstick in the mirror.

"Thank you. You look terrific."

She closed her purse with a snap and gave him a bright, mouth-closed smile as though she hadn't heard him.

"How was Washington?" she asked.

"Cold. Argumentative."

"Did you miss me?"

"Don't I always?" said Reynard.

The waiter came over and asked Chiffon what she would have. "A cup of hot water," she told him. "And do you have any of those plain crackers? The ones without the salt."

Reynard gave her a lopsided smile. "I don't know why you don't just suck your napkin. It's probably more nutritious."

"You want me fat?"

"Is that all you think about? Your weight."

"No," she said coyly. "Sometimes I think about you."

He recrossed his legs, looked down at his cup of tea and started playing with the spoon in his saucer again.

Chiffon asked, "What time are we flying back to Washington tomorrow?"

Reynard continued to play with his spoon. "Well," he said, "that's one of the things I want to talk to you about."

"What do you mean?"

"I mean—I'm going back to Washington this evening."

"This evening? But the whole point of my staying in New York was so we could have lunch with Bergel tomorrow. I mean, that's the only reason I'm still here. What about that part? You know how much I want to do that part."

Reynard glanced up at her and then back at his cup. "The lunch with Bergel is canceled."

"Canceled? Or postponed? Reynard, you *promised* me!"

"There'll be other parts, all right? It's just that right now I have to draw in my personal and political horns a little. Everything's set up. I'm going to be running for the nomination in earnest. That means I have to be careful of any kind of irregularity, any kind of suggestion that I might be fixing things. And that includes parts in movies for my close friends."

Chiffon's cheeks were pink. "You're really serious? You're really going to run?"

"I'm really going to run," he nodded. "But don't say it too loud. It isn't official yet."

All her irritation had evaporated. She glowed. "Reynard, that's *marvelous*. I forgive you about the part. Just imagine it—Reynard Kelly, president of the United States. And Mrs. Kelly—First Lady. Really, I forgive you about the part. It was only some tacky street-crime movie anyway. Oh, I wish I could kiss you."

Reynard put down his spoon and laced his hands together tightly. It was a gesture of self-defense, but it also expressed the difficulty he was having in telling Chiffon what was on his mind.

"Reynard," smiled Chiffon, reaching out to hold his locked-together hands in hers. "Reynard, you're amazing. There are millions of men half your age who aren't as positive *or* as good-looking *or* as virile as you are. You're just *numero uno*, and that's all."

Reynard opened his mouth and then closed it. "Thank you," he said, a little more breathily than he'd meant to. Then, "Chiffon—"

"You don't have to say anything. I love you. That's all that counts."

The waiter brought Chiffon's hot water and a plate of plain crackers with a decoration of cucumber slices and cottage cheese.

Reynard stared at the cucumber as though he had expected it to be a message of reprieve. Then he said, "The

. . . er . . . the process of drawing in my horns—you know what I'm talking about? The . . . the *care* I now have to take to regulate my private and my public life in order to reassure the Democratic party and the electorate at large that I am a suitable candidate for the presidency of the United States . . . I mean, I have to regulate my gambling activities. . . ."

"Reynard," said Chiffon, "I'm a woman, not a Senate hearing on organized crime. *Talk* to me."

His cheek muscles tightened and his chin clenched. "I *am* talking to you, damn it, if you'd only listen to what I'm saying. Do you understand at all what I'm saying? Is the message getting through?"

Chiffon sat back in her chair and frowned at him. "*No*," she said, "it isn't."

"Well," he said, "it's like this. I want you to know here and now, right here, that I think a hell of a lot of you. Without question you're the most understanding girl I've ever met in my life. You're also one hell of a lover. But when a man decides to put himself up for the nation's highest office, as I have, he has to observe certain proprieties, at least until he's elected. So what I'm saying is, while the media may turn something of a blind eye to a senator who's seen around with a beautiful girl on his arm, they certainly wouldn't afford the same courtesy to a presidential nominee."

"Therefore?" said Chiffon, filling in the conjunction for him, her eyes wide, her face flushed.

"Therefore . . . we have to deactivate our relationship for a while. I'm sorry. I'll make sure you have plenty of funds to see you through . . . but the deal I've had to make to ensure that I have a fighting chance of winning the presidency . . . well, I'm very regretful that it can't include you."

Chiffon's eyes filled with tears; more from rage than unhappiness. "*Deactivate?*" she snapped at him. "Deactivate? You're not deactivating anything, you're throwing me over. Isn't that it? Come on. Talk straight, for Christ's sake.''

"Keep your voice down," Reynard ordered her.

"Why the hell should I? You promised me that one day you would be president, and you told me that when you were, I'd be your First Lady. Didn't you say that?''

"Chiffon, it's something I might have said in bed after a pretty wild party. . . .''

"Reynard, you *promised* me. One day, you said, we're going to be standing on the White House lawn, and the whole world's going to be looking at us, and it's going to be like the movies. Mrs. Chiffon Kelly, you said, First Lady of the United States of America.''

Reynard beckoned to the waiter to bring him the check. "Listen, Chiffon," he said quietly, "I'm not going to sit here and discuss a few fantastic things I might have said to you in bed; nor am I going to argue with you in public about the future of our relationship. I told you how I feel. I'm very fond of you; in fact, I adore you. But I have a duty to my country as well as a duty to myself, and I thought you'd understand that and accept it like a lady.''

"You rat," said Chiffon with such vehemence that the elderly ladies at the next table turned around in astonishment. "Do you think I would have stayed with you for one minute if you hadn't promised that I was going to be First Lady? Do you think I wanted *you*? Your *body*? You dried-up old geriatric! Why do you think a girl who looks like me spent her time with a man who looks like you? Did you think I was *crazy* or something?''

"Chiffon—" said Reynard.

"Don't you say another word," rapped Chiffon. "Don't you say one more word. I'm going to scream if you say another word.''

"There isn't any need to get hysterical," Reynard insisted. "We only need to break up temporarily, just until the election's over. Meanwhile you'll be living a life of complete luxury. Anything you want, just name it. If it's money—cars—you name it.''

"I want what you promised me. The White House."

"What are you so hot about? Being First Lady is a lot of work. You'd hate it. You'd have to spend all your time at charity dinners, visiting the handicapped, talking to the wives of African visitors, smiling your ass off. You'd detest it.''

"You promised me the White House," Chiffon repeated, her expression masklike.

"What did she say?" whispered one of the elderly ladies. "He promised her *what*?"

Chiffon said in a voice choked with disappointment and rage, "Do you know what I'm going to do? I'm going to walk out of here now. But let me tell you something. If I don't hear by this time tomorrow that you've changed your mind, I'm going to go straight to the media—television and newspapers—and I'm going to show you up for what you are."

Reynard said, "If I were you, darling, I wouldn't do anything rash."

"*Darling*," she spat at him. "You can make it sound like an insult."

"If I'd only known that you thought I was going to take you to the White House with me . . . I didn't realize for a moment that you took it so seriously. It just can't be, Chiffon. I adore you, and I'd love to keep you around, but Greta—"

"Greta? What does Greta have to do with it?"

"Well, obviously if I'm going to be running for the Democratic nomination, I have to do it as a family man. I'm not going to be running on my own; I have to have a wife beside me."

Chiffon stared at him. "After everything you said about Greta. What a bitch she was. How she never understood your deepest ambitions. How bad she was in bed. You liar. I don't think I ever met anybody in my whole life so *unprincipled*.''

The waiter brought the check. Reynard signed it with his firm, familiar squiggle and gave the man a ten-dollar tip.

''Thank *you*, Senator,'' said the waiter, looking uncertainly at Chiffon.

They walked out of the Palm Court amid an unusual hush. Heads turned. Reynard found himself obliged to nod to two or three people he knew, including Ken Gibbs of Standard Oil, who was smirking like a schoolboy.

''Don't bother to see me up to my room,'' said Chiffon; she stalked off across the wide-patterned carpet.

Dick Elmwood straightened his tie. ''She looks upset.''

''She is upset. I misjudged her.''

''What's she so mad about? Doesn't she understand that you're upset too?''

Reynard took a breath. ''She thought that when I ran for president, I'd be taking her along with me. She was under the impression that she was going to be First Lady.''

''Are you joking?'' asked Elmwood. ''You never told her that, did you?''

''I might have one night when I was feeling drunk and happy. But I never believed for a single moment she'd take it so seriously. I mean, it's more important to her than money or anything. She's really sore about it.''

''Hmm,'' said Elmwood. ''That could be embarrassing, to say the least. If she takes it into her head to talk to the media—''

''She's already taken it into her head to talk to the media. She says that if I don't change my mind by tomorrow afternoon, it's blow-the-whistle time.''

Dick Elmwood chewed at his lip and looked reflectively at Pollock. Pollock stood with his hands neatly parked in front of his genitals and didn't say a word. He spoke only when spoken to, and then monosyllabically.

"What do you want to do?" Elmwood asked.

"I don't think there's much we can do."

"She won't be persuaded? Bought off?"

"I don't believe so."

Elmwood thought for a while. Then he said, "I think you'd better leave her to me, sir."

Reynard waved and smiled at a passing acquaintance. With the smile fixed on his face, he said to Elmwood, "All right then, if you think that's the only way. But I don't want to know anything about it whatsoever, do you hear? Don't mention it to me again, ever."

"Pollock?" said Elmwood. "You understand what's going on here?"

"Yes, sir," replied Pollock. Although he was a handsome man, there was something peculiar in his expression; a terrible deadness that somehow made him seem asexual and utterly without emotion.

"Well, then," said Reynard uncomfortably, "I'll freshen up and see you a little later."

EIGHT

Edmond was having lunch with Dr. John Metcalf when Oscar Ford came over, laid a hand on his shoulder and said, "Can you spare a moment? Hi, J.M. Sorry to interrupt."

"Can it wait?" asked Edmond. He was halfway through his steak. Besides, Dr. Metcalf was a difficult man to persuade to come out to lunch and Edmond had been trying for almost two months now to talk to him about improved screening equipment at the clinic.

"I'm too pushed, I'm afraid," said Oscar, checking his watch, and flapping a blue-foldered autopsy report as though it were the final and conclusive proof of the theory of evolution.

"That's the Osman autopsy?"

Oscar nodded. "And believe me, you have to see it."

Edmond looked across the table at Dr. Metcalf. White-haired, elegantly spoken, Dr. Metcalf was still chewing his brochette of steak tips and had sipped only a little of his dry white wine. His face remained mild and unreadable, as though deliberately refusing to give Edmond any clues whatsoever as to whether or not he would be spoiling his chances for better equipment by leaving the table now and talking to Oscar.

Oscar stared urgently at Edmond and said, "Believe me, this is two-hundred-percent crucial."

"Dr. Metcalf, could you give me just a moment, please?" asked Edmond.

Dr. Metcalf closed and opened his eyes in the subtlest of acknowledgments. Edmond pushed back his chair and followed Oscar across the restaurant.

"I hope this isn't a put-on," he said as they made their way between the trees and plants of the restaurant. Oscar said nothing but sniffed and waved the autopsy report again, ushering Edmond outside to the glass-enclosed balcony. It was brilliantly sunny and oppressively hot out there, but at least it was quiet, away from the laughter and clatter of knives and forks and that restaurant sound that Arabelle always called, after a line in *Twelfth Night*, "the babbling gossip of the air."

"I'll give you a full copy of the report later," said Oscar, "but what you have to know right now is that whatever killed Michael Osman, it wasn't polio."

"If it wasn't, I'd sure as hell like to know what it was," said Edmond.

He had almost forgotten the Osman autopsy in the past two days, what with a sudden outbreak of measles at the Concord Union School on Rumford Street, and two cases of suspected malnutrition out near Snap Town. Malnutrition, in rural New Hampshire. They'd be having the Black Death next.

Oscar licked his thumb and leafed his way through the autopsy protocols until he came to the virologist's report. "It was a virus, all right. But it sure wasn't poliomyelitis, even though it had the same effect. Here, let me read it. 'A microscopic examination of the tissue sample from the intercostal muscles has revealed the presence of a virus that so far defies identification, although it has evidently been wholly or largely responsible for a polio-like paralysis of the respiratory system. The virus is not unusual in structure, consisting of the usual nucleic-acid genome surrounded by a protein coat. It measures eighty micrometers in diameter. A series of electron microscope pictures of the virus has been taken for the purpose of further identification and study.' "

Edmond peered at the report. "Who did this? Wilson?"

"No, Corning . . . and you know how damned unimaginative *he* is."

"What does he say down at the bottom there?"

"Ah," said Oscar, wagging a finger. "This is where we come to it. He adds a footnote to the effect that . . . here we are—'Early tests on this virus under limited conditions suggest that it has an unusual and dramatic rate of growth and replication.' Well, it gets very technical here, but then he says, 'Whereas viral infectivity can usually be destroyed by lipid solvents like ether or by ionizing X rays or non-ionizing ultraviolet. . . .' I'm going to skip some more of this. Now, here it is. 'The infectivity of this particular virus appears to be not only unaffected by lipid solvents and radiation, but actually to become more vigorous when attacked. Most viruses are readily destroyed by heat, but this virus measurably trebles its replicative process at high temperatures and, in common with other viruses, preserves its infectivity even at very low temperatures.' "

Oscar stopped reading and stared at Edmond steadily. It seemed to be even hotter out on the balcony than before, and there were obvious beads of sweat on Oscar's nose.

Edmond said, "Let me understand this. Corning is saying that you can't *kill* this virus?"

"That's what he's saying."

"Not only that, but that it spreads like wildfire?"

Oscar nodded.

Edmond shaded his eyes and looked out through the

window toward the parking lot and beyond, the sun-dancing curve of the Merrimack River. A virus, he mused, that replicates itself at high speed and can't be destroyed by conventional means. It was a doctor's nightmare, the kind of unnerving, vertiginous dream that woke Edmond up sweating in the small hours of the morning. That and his endlessly recurring dream of what had happened to Arabelle. It seemed ridiculous, impossible, especially on a bright day in early fall like this, with people talking and laughing all around them. And yet here it was in Dr. Corning's preliminary virology report; and here was the plain, ugly fact that Oscar was standing in front of him so worried that he couldn't even joke anymore.

"It's a—it could mean an epidemic," said Edmond. His mouth was dry.

"Well, so far Michael Osman is the only reported victim," said Oscar. "But, you know, we haven't yet found out where this came from—and what's worse, we don't know how it's carried. If it's anything like polio, it could even be carried by people who have been vaccinated against it."

Edmond licked his lips. "How long before Corning finishes his full tests?"

"He didn't say. He's sending some samples to Berkeley."

Edmond took a step sideways so he could glance back through the restaurant and make sure Dr. Metcalf wasn't growing too impatient.

Oscar asked, "Did you check up on Michael Osman's friend?"

"Young Bernie? Yes. I saw him the same night. Clean as a whistle."

"No reports since?"

"No."

"Well, maybe it's just a freak," Oscar suggested. "Maybe, for some reason, this one boy just happened to react to a regular polio virus in such a way that the virus mutated.''

"Do you really believe that?"

"No, I don't. To tell you the truth, I don't know *what* to believe. I'm just running every damned flag I can think of up the flagpole to see if it flies. I mean, look at it this way. There's a possibility that this virus is pathogenic only to particular types of people and Michael Osman just happened to be unlucky. It's so virulent that I can't imagine why his friend Bernie didn't pick it up, especially since they spent almost the whole day together, every day. You know what kids are like, sharing candy, sharing cans of Coke, not washing their hands. There was every opportunity for that virus to be passed on to Bernie, and yet it wasn't.''

Edmond took out his handkerchief and dabbed sweat from his forehead. "I'm going to have to get back to Dr. Metcalf," he said. "But give me some time to think this over. Have you told Bryce?"

"Not yet. You're the first, apart from the guys in the lab.''

"You don't think Bryce is going to like it?"

"Do *you* like it?"

"That's not what I meant.''

"I know what you meant," said Oscar. Dr. Bryce was the medical examiner for Merrimack County: a stiff-necked, conservative, hickory-hewn New Hampshire man. He was a member of the Sons of the American Revolution and busily active in about a dozen local organizations. His family had settled in Concord way back in the days of Nathaniel B. Baker, and as far as Bryce was concerned, Concord was the only righteous and upstanding city in the United States.

Boh Edmond and Oscar knew that Dr. Bryce would receive the autopsy on Michael Osman with more than his usual skepticism and querulous hostility. He regarded ev-

ery violent or unnatural death in the Concord district as a
personal slight, a deliberate and ill-bred slur on his fine
community. Oscar used to say that if Dr. Bryce had his
way, anyone who hadn't been courteous enough to die in
his sleep with a smile on his face would be smuggled by
night over the Belknap County line and dumped.

"You're going to have to tell someone else, in addition
to Bryce," said Edmond. "If you leave it up to him, he'll
file it under 'Review Next Year' and forget about it. By
that time half the population of Merrimack County could
be wiped out."

"Who do you suggest?" asked Oscar.

"Well, there's always Harold Bunyan."

"Is he your guardian angel on the Board of Health? I
thought he might be. He's about the only doctor on the
board with anything like your style."

"I did Harold a favor a long time ago in Manhattan,"
Edmond explained. "His son was convicted on a dope-
dealing charge. The boy was a heavy user too. I managed
to get him sprung on medical grounds."

Oscar's bright-red face remained expressionless. It was
obvious that he was waiting for Edmond to explain how an
ordinary doctor, no matter how wealthy and well-connected,
could have saved a drug dealer from serving a mandatory
minimum sentence.

"I was a very close friend of someone who was very
close to the assistant district attorney," Edmond added.

When Oscar still remained unmoved, he said, "His
wife."

"All right," said Oscar. "I'll file the report with Bryce;
after that I'll go tell Harold Bunyan."

"Can you get me a copy of the autopsy too?" asked
Edmond. "Then, when Harold's had a chance to read it, I
can go over it with him and fill him in with any other
details he needs to know. Personal case notes, stuff like
that."

Oscar said, "I just hope this thing doesn't backfire on us. If Bryce finds out that Harold Bunyan got ahold of the autopsy report at the same time he did . . . well, you know what he's like about protocol, apart from the fact that he can't stand the sight of Harold Bunyan's face."

"I'd better get back. Dr. Metcalf looks like he's about to get up and walk out on me."

"Okay," said Oscar. "I'll call you this evening and tell you what Bryce had to say about the report. He'll probably say, 'A freak, Dr. Ford, an aberration.' But I'll give it my best shot."

Edmond gripped his hand and turned to walk back to his table. But as he went, Oscar said, "One more thing, E.C."

"What is it?"

Oscar half-lifted the autopsy report in a gesture of apology. "I'm sorry about the surprise party, you know?"

Edmond shook his head. "Don't be. I think you've saved me a visit from my brother."

"You don't get along with your brother?"

"One day I'll tell you about it. But listen—I'll catch you later."

Dr. Metcalf was distinctly unamused by Edmond's extended absence. He had finished his brochette and was now drumming his fingers on the table and checking his watch.

"I'm sorry," said Edmond as he sat down again. "Dr. Ford had something of a crisis on his hands."

"I see," said Dr. Metcalf. "Well, I'm afraid it hasn't left us with very much time to talk about screening equipment, has it? I have to be back at the hospital by two."

"Dr. Metcalf, do I really have to sell you on the need for this equipment?" asked Edmond. "You know yourself how vital it is, and if the board reduced next year's

building budget by just one percent, it could allocate us all
the money we need.''

"Unfortunately you're not the only consultant who wants
to take one percent of the building budget,'' replied Dr.
Metcalf. "Dr. Abrahams wants a new therapy unit; Dr.
Krassner wants beds; Dr. Wollinsky needs a whole range
of laboratory equipment. If I give you one percent, what
am I going to say to them?''

The waitress came over and said, "Would either of you
two gentlemen care for apple pie? Or we have some
terrific Baked Alaska.''

Dr. Metcalf looked up at her and then at Edmond. "I
think I'll pass,'' he said. "And I'm afraid I'm going to
have to say the same about your screening equipment, Dr.
Chandler. Talk to me next year; maybe we'll have a little
more money then.''

Edmond didn't even try to smile.

Bernie had cried when they told him Michael was dead.
For days afterward he was pale and withdrawn, scarcely
eating, not speaking to anyone, sitting alone in his bedroom watching television or cycling out to the fields and
sitting with his arms folded tight as though trying to
protect himself from the cold wind of knowing that his
best friend would soon be buried.

Edmond had explained to Bernie's parents that there
would be weeks of grief and that Bernie should be allowed
to feel unhappy and abandoned. Part of his grief was the
irrational feeling that his dead friend had somehow betrayed
him, slipped away without saying where he was going, not
even leaving a note. Bernie's parents had been terrified
that Bernie might already have contracted the virus that
had so quickly killed Michael. But Edmond had examined
the boy closely, taking samples of blood and spinal fluid,
and it was soon clear that he had miraculously remained
free of infection.

"But if there's anything—even the trace of a sore throat or stiffness of the joints—call me immediately," Edmond had warned.

On the same afternoon that Edmond was having lunch with Dr. Metcalf, Bernie was sitting in his bedroom with Michael's leather case on his desk in front of him. He opened and closed it and then opened it again. He took out all six of the clear glass bottles and set them up in a line.

To Bernie the case was a complete mystery. Michael would never have hidden anything in their secret hiding place without telling him; Bernie couldn't think of a single time when Michael had kept any discovery to himself. And if Michael hadn't told him about it on the morning before Bernie had gone to his piano lesson, he must have come across it sometime that afternoon and had been planning to tell him about it later.

Bernie had already examined the leather case over and over again. It seemed pretty old and musty; there was even mold inside it. Five of the bottles were sealed with some kind of dried-up wax, although the sixth bottle had been opened. By Michael? Bernie didn't know. He had opened the bottle himself and sniffed at it, but it didn't seem to smell like anything at all. Maybe the stuff in it was just water.

Bernie wondered if he ought to show the case to his parents but he decided against it, at least for the time being. He and Michael had hidden things in the garage wall only if they were top secret, for their eyes alone, and Bernie felt that if he showed the case around, he would be letting Michael down. He felt the case had somehow been entrusted to him. It was Michael's last cryptic bequest, and until he understood what it was and why Michael had hidden it, he wanted to keep it to himself.

Mrs. Osman had said that Michael had gone out on his bicycle that afternoon. He hadn't gone to any of his friends' homes, and he hadn't gone to Winant Mall to find his

mother. He might have gone to Turtle Pond, but usually
they rode their bicycles through the mud around the pond's
perimeter and Bernie hadn't noticed any mud on Michael's
bicycle. He might have gone to Sugar Ball to see old Mr.
Keeler, who used to be their class teacher, but that was
unlikely. It was a long ride and most times they went
together and told their parents where they were going.

He might have gone to Conant's Acre, but how could he
have picked up a disease at Conant's Acre? And where had
he discovered this leather case? Right in the middle of the
fields?

Bernie slipped all the bottles back into the case and
closed it. Then, carefully, he lifted it up to his top shelf,
next to his model airplanes and his Star Wars figures, and
hid it behind a stack of comic books. Maybe he should
bicycle down to Conant's Acre and take a look around.
After all, it was the most likely place for Michael to have
gone. It wasn't too far away, and since they had still been
in the process of exploring it, it hadn't yet lost its fear and
excitement for them.

Apart from that, Bernie felt like being alone.

His mother waved to him from the kitchen window as
he cycled off down the road. It was a bright, sunny
afternoon but a sharp wind was blowing from the northeast;
Bernie had put on his green-and-yellow windbreaker and
his yellow baseball cap. Old Mrs. Rogers called from her
front lawn, "Hi, Bernie!" and he called back in his polit-
est voice, "Hi, Mrs. Rogers!"

He had to cycle around Webster Crescent on his way to
Conant's Acre, past Michael's house. The house looked
strange and forlorn. The downstairs drapes were drawn
and there was a plain wreath on the front door. It was
weird to think that he would never play in that house
again. It was double weird to think that Michael was dead,
lying with his eyes closed in his coffin, all ready for

Thursday's funeral. This time last week they had been playing together out on Appleton Street.

He reached Conant's Acre and dismounted, propping his bike up against the split-rail fence. He looked around for signs that Michael might have been here, but there was only the usual tangle of weeds and Coke cans and torn-up newspapers. The wind blew across Conant's Acre and roared softly in his ears. He sniffed and climbed over the fence, pausing for a moment on the top rail to shade his eyes and look around. Try to pretend you're Michael, he thought. You're on your own and you're playing a game. Try to think at what Michael would have done.

Across the field, in the distance, were the woods. Would Michael have gone to explore the woods? It didn't seem likely. They were both scared of the woods—Bernie more than he ever cared to admit. They reminded him of the woods in *Dracula*: the sort of woods in which vampires moved like tall, gray shadows and out of whose leafy soil zombies might rise, with wriggling red meat worms dangling out of their eye sockets.

There were times when Bernie wished he hadn't read quite so many horror stories. Even here, a few yards from the split-rail fence, the silence of the windy afternoon was frightening.

He heard a scurrying sound behind him and turned around in alarm. It was nothing but a rabbit, staring at him from the weeds along the fence. He said, "Here, rabbit; c'mon, rabbit," but the creature loped away up the field and disappeared into the hedgerow.

Maybe Michael had found the leather case just lying on the ground. Maybe somebody had dropped it and Michael had been planning to take it down to the police station as lost property after he had shown it to Bernie. Yet why hadn't he shown it to his parents? Maybe it had come from someplace special, someplace that Michael hadn't wanted his parents to know about either because he shouldn't really have been there or because it was a great and secret discovery. Maybe Michael had at last found a hideout. He and Bernie had been looking for a good hideout ever since Bernie's father had caught them lighting matches in the summerhouse at the end of Bernie's backyard and forbidden them to use it as a camp. They had tried a pup tent but it hadn't been the same.

Bernie walked halfway across the field and then paused, his hands on his hips, looking at the woods ahead. Surely Michael hadn't actually gone as far as the tree line? Not on his own; it was too scary. The woods were rustling and whispering as though they were alive; even on a bright day like this, they were shadowy and dark—a small forest of unexpressed fears.

Bernie turned around and began plodding back toward the split-rail fence. But after only a few paces he hesitated and looked at the woods again. They were scary, yes, but he almost felt as though they were beckoning to him. Had he been Michael, alone on that windy day, would *he* have gone into the woods? There was a chance that he might have. Think of what he could have said when he got back; think of how he could have boasted that alone he had dared to penetrate the one place neither of them had dared to go before. He and Michael had argued about who was the braver only two or three days earlier, and Bernie had forced Michael to admit that because he was ten and Michael only nine, he was a year braver by virtue of natural human development. As you grew older, you grew braver, and that was it.

Bernie headed for the woods again. He told himself there was no danger, not in the daytime because vampires and such come out only at night. The trouble was, it might be dark enough inside the woods to qualify as night, and then what? Perhaps Michael had met a vampire and been bitten and that was why he had died. Infected blood.

He had almost reached the edge of the woods when he

heard a whistling. He looked up the field to his left and saw a man walking toward him; he was dressed in a Norfolk jacket and wore rubbers and a soft tweed hat. The man took his time but at last he came up to Bernie and stood there with his hands in his pockets, half-grinning and half-grimacing at him.

"What's your name, son?"

"Bernie."

"Hmm," said the man. "You know this is private land here, Bernie? Private woods."

"No, sir." Of course Bernie knew it was.

"Well, I'm afraid it is," the man explained. "All of Conant's Acre—all of these woods, right down as far as Loudun Road—is private."

"Aren't people allowed to walk here?" asked Bernie.

The man slowly shook his head. "Question of insurance. Supposing you fell down on this land, broke your ankle or something. Mr. Kelly doesn't want anybody suing him for negligence or anything like that. He doesn't mean any offense, doesn't want to lose any friends, but he's a wealthy man, and wealthy men have to be careful. Three times children and winos have stepped out in front of his car just for the settlement money. You could be up to the same kind of trick. Not saying you are, but you could be."

In actual fact, Bernie was quite relieved to be turned away from the woods. Now he could retreat without feeling cowardly.

"You get along there," said the man. "And tell your friends too. Mr. Kelly's a good man, a good neighbor, but he asks you not to wander around his property."

Bernie took one last look at the woods—at the tangled briers and the nodding branches—and it was then that he glimpsed on one of the tree trunks a more-than-familiar mark. It was the secret blaze he and Michael had devised between them: a triangle with a circle in the center. He felt his heart bump and he glanced up at the man to make sure he hadn't noticed the mark too. Michael *had* been here! His guess had been right.

He ran quickly back across the field, his cheeks alight with excitement. He swung over the fence, collected his bicycle and began to pedal his way home. He was right, he was *right*! There *was* a mystery, and one of the clues was the leather case with the bottles in it. Somewhere in the woods he would find the answer; it was even possible that he would solve the riddle of Michael's death. The first thing he had to do was to go home and work out a plan. A plan was essential. Then he would have to find a way to slip into the woods undetected and trace Michael's trail.

It was a stiff pedal up Webster Crescent; after a few yards he dismounted and pushed his bicycle beside him. He was still on foot when he passed Michael's house. He stood outside it for a moment, staring at it, and suddenly the excitement of finding out what had happened to Michael seemed to evaporate. All he really wanted was Michael himself, his friend lost forever. His throat choked up and his eyes filled with tears.

"Don't ever be ashamed to cry," Dr. Chandler had told him, and remembering those words, he wept.

He took out a crumpled Kleenex and wiped his eyes. Then he started walking up the Crescent again. But as he did so, he saw the most extraordinary thing. In the front upstairs window of Michael's house there was a tonguelike flicker of orange, almost up to the ceiling. Bright, rippling orange, as though someone had thrown a vividly colored bedspread into the air. He paused, and then he saw it again. But this time it was quite clear that it wasn't a bedspread; it was a flicker of fire. And before he could even think of shouting out to anyone, he saw the bedroom drape catch alight and burn at the window like the draperies of hell.

"Fire!" he shouted.

A man washing his car two houses away raised his head

and stared at him. Bernie pointed toward the Osmans'
bedroom and shouted again. "Fire! The house is on fire!"

It was Edmond's afternoon off. He needed it after that
lunch with Dr. Metcalf. But he and Christy had only just
started a game of backgammon when the telephone rang.
He picked it up and said, "Dr. Chandler." Then, to
Christy, "Go ahead, you can throw if you like."

It was Oscar. His voice sounded distant because he was
patched through from the mobile phone in his car. "I'm
out at the Osman place on Webster Crescent."

"What are you doing there?"

"There's been a fire. A real bad one. The fire department has only just managed to get it under control. The
whole house is a shell."

"Jesus! What about the Osmans? Was anyone hurt?"

"They're both dead. They were up in the front bedroom
where the fire broke out."

"You want me to come over?"

"I think you'd better. Wear something warm. It's damned
cold out here."

"Give me ten minutes, okay?" said Edmond and hung
up.

Christy asked, "What's wrong?"

"The Osmans, the parents of that boy who died of
poliomyelitis. They've both been burned in a fire at their
place."

"Oh, my God."

Edmond went into the hall, opened the closet and took
out the fur-lined anorak he usually wore when he went
fishing. "Don't wait for me," he said. "Oscar's down
there and I'm not sure how long I'll be."

Christy kissed him. "Do you want a thermos of coffee
to take with you? It's almost perked."

He shook his head. "Jobs like this are better done on an
empty stomach."

He drove out to Webster Crescent with the radio playing Vivaldi's *Four Seasons*. Arabelle had adored Vivaldi. She had listened to *Four Seasons* with her head back, her eyes closed and one finger tracing and retracing the veins on the back of his hand, so gently it made him shiver. He could remember the room, the day, the time, the place. He could even remember the way she had smelled as he buried his face in her hair.

Webster Crescent was crowded with fire trucks, ambulances, rescue cars and pale-faced onlookers. Edmond was waved through by a policeman and he parked right behind Oscar's station wagon. Oscar was standing there with Dean Conran, the fire chief, and the assistant commissioner of the Department of Safety, Tom Simoneau.

"The house went up like a torch," Oscar said. "They didn't stand a chance."

Dean Conran said dryly, "It was one of those upper-story fires that build up to super heat. The downstairs windows were open so plenty of air was drawn into the lower part of the building and up the stairwell. Since the bedroom door was open too, there was nothing to keep the fire bottled up. The hotter it got, the more air it drew in, and that fueled it even more. The heat actually fused the victims' bones to their bedsprings."

"Any ideas on how it started?" Edmond asked.

"Hard to say. They were both upstairs in the bedroom, lying on the bed, so one of them might have been smoking. Maybe there was an electrical fault. It's impossible to tell until we go over the whole building with a fine-tooth comb."

"Is anything left of the bodies?" Edmond asked Oscar. "I mean, anything worth autopsying?"

"Come see for yourself," said Oscar. "We haven't moved them yet because the county investigators haven't finished taking pictures."

They crossed the road, which was running with sooty

water. Edmond wished he had worn his rubbers instead of his light-colored suede golfing shoes. They stepped over a tangle of hoses and then treaded over the black, crunchy ashes of the Osman house, past a skeletal couch resembling an incinerated horse, around a half-melted television set and over a strange array of surrealistically twisted candlesticks and cutlery.

The bedroom floor had collapsed into the living room, bringing with it the Osmans' fiery bed and what remained of the Osmans themselves. Two bland young men in ash-smeared safety helmets were taking photographs and making notes. They treated the bizarre spectacle in front of them as though it were no more shocking than a modern sculpture or an interesting tourist attraction.

The burned-out bed lay at an angle of forty-five degrees, its foot propped up in the air by a scaffold of charred flooring. The Osmans' bodies still clung to the mattress; the red-hot springs had literally been welded to their flesh and bones, and they were suspended like dead flies on a screen door.

Mr. Osman's body had been burned far worse than his wife's. It was blackened and half the size of the man Edmond had met a few days earlier—now only a shriveled-up mummy. His clublike hands were held against his chest and his legs were drawn into the air: the effect of intense heat on his sinews. His face was stretched into a tortured expression.

Mrs. Osman had been protected from the worst of the flames by a wardrobe door that had fallen across her body. She was already dead when this happened, and while her legs had been burned to the bone, her torso remained reasonably intact. Edmond couldn't look at her face.

Oscar said, ''At least I'll have some internal organs to work on. *Cooked* internal organs, but internal organs all the same.''

They trod back through the ashes. The fire chief said,

"What do you think, doc? Not a pretty sight, huh? And people tell you to mind your own business when you warn them against smoking in bed. The deaths I've seen, I can tell you."

Edmond took Oscar across the road. He bent over and brushed some of the clinging wet ash off his shoes while Oscar, his hands in his pockets, stared at the burned-out house. Edmond said, "There's one thing that doesn't seem to ring true."

Oscar nodded. "I thought of that. What were they doing in bed at four o'clock in the afternoon?"

"Unlikely they were making love, especially so soon after Michael's death."

"Resting?" suggested Oscar.

"Possibly. But if they were resting, would they have fallen asleep so soundly that they didn't wake up when the room caught fire? They obviously hadn't made any effort to escape."

"Maybe they were poisoned by toxic gas from the burning mattress," said Oscar. "Maybe they were overcome by smoke before they managed to wake up."

Both men were silent. An ambulance backed up to the sidewalk and three medics climbed out of the back carrying body bags. One of them raised a hand in greeting to Oscar and called, "Kind of late in the year for a barbecue."

"That Johnson has the sickest sense of humor," said Oscar.

Edmond said, "You know what I'm thinking, don't you?"

Oscar cleared his throat. "I feel like I had smoke for breakfast, smoke for lunch and smoke sandwiches for supper." He paused before replying, "Yes, I know what you're thinking. But we won't know for sure until I've run some tests."

"Did you see Bryce this afternoon?"

"I left the autopsy on his desk. He was stuck in some committee meeting."

"And Harold?"

"He's out of town until tomorrow afternoon."

Edmond said, "On the face of it, it makes a lot of sense, doesn't it? They didn't make an attempt to escape the fire because they were dead, or almost dead, already."

Oscar shrugged and looked away. "We'll see," he said.

The early evening wind scattered ashes across the road.

NINE

Bill Bennett insisted they drive to Uppsala at once, even though Humphrey protested that he was very tired, not as young as he used to be, and that, after all, he *was* supposed to be on his holidays. What responsibility did *he* have to find Klaus Hermann?

"You're the person best qualified to make a positive identification," Bill replied. They were driving around the monumental modern fountain at Sergels Torg before heading northwest up Sveavägen to join the E4 motorway leading to Uppsala Län. Bill drove the Grand Prix at a steady, unrelenting fifty miles per hour, as though the car had no brakes. The worn-down tires protested as they swerved around the square at the end of Sveavägen and dove under the railroad bridge.

Birgitta Gillsäter sat silently in the back seat smoking a cigarette, her face intermittently lit up by the passing sodium lamps. She appeared to be strangely resigned to this kidnapping, and even when Humphrey turned around in his seat to ask if she were all right, she did nothing more than shrug a shoulder and blow smoke out of her nostrils. Humphrey disliked cigarette smoke and opened his window an inch or two, until the wind grew too chilly.

Bill Bennett felt calmer now. He always felt calmer once an operation started to tick. He didn't particularly mind the waiting beforehand; after all, he had been trained to wait. But when you were waiting, you had time to think of all the things that might go wrong, some of them petty, some of them inconvenient, some of them disastrous—and some of them, particularly in an operation like this one, potentially fatal.

Dealing with old-time Nazi war criminals wasn't like dealing with modern-day spies. Most of the Nazis who successfully escaped at the end of the war had been able to do so because they were already well-connected; they had been given all the necessary facilities to disguise themselves behind layers of aliases and false credentials. It had been over forty years since the end of the war too, and in that time they had been able to establish themselves in highly influential positions—positions from which it could be diplomatically and economically impossible to dislodge them. How could American agents capture and arrest Hans von Trenck when he had financed and organized a major offshore oil survey in Mexico and was one of the most powerful figures in Mexican politics? The capture of Klaus Barbie, with which Bill himself had been directly involved, had caused explosions in the United States; and two other unnamed Nazis captured along with Barbie had been secretly released.

It was sometimes possible for Nazi hunters to exact vengeance on war criminals, and get away with it. Martin Bormann was the classic example. He had worked for years after the war as chief executive of the Brasilia Mineral Corporation AG under the name of Walter von Ischl. But he had been abducted one morning in 1971 by Israeli agents, killed at once and his body returned to Berlin. It had been "distressed" by forensic experts to give it the appearance of age. Then, later, it had been formally identified and the "mystery" of what had happened to Bormann had been officially cleared up.

The Brazilian government had been unable to protest. After all, how could it protest at the abduction of a man who had apparently never been to Brazil but had been lying dead in Berlin for thirty-five years?

Only a few agents, Bill included, were aware that the Israelis had been assisted in this effort by the CIA, as part of a larger foreign-policy deal in which Israel was to curtail a plan to invade parts of Egypt.

Sometimes Bill was convinced that the influence of the Third Reich really would endure for a thousand years, just as Hitler had promised.

They drove through the dark landscape; lakes appeared in the blackness like secret mirrors. It was so cold outside that Bill had to use the defroster to keep the car's windows clear. Birgitta Gillsäter stared out at nothing; Humphrey tried to doze but kept dreaming about his old headmaster and confusing him with Major Milner.

When he opened his eyes, he wasn't immediately sure of where he was or even of the year. Was the war still going on? It looked so dark outside, like a blackout. He glanced across at Bill, whose face was illuminated green by the dials on the instrument panel, and then he twisted around to look at Birgitta.

"Where are we?" he asked in a dry-mouthed voice.

"We just passed Rosersberg. In a minute we'll be driving past the airport. There, you can see the lights now. Over to your right."

"How much farther to Uppsala?"

"The airport's a little better than halfway."

"I could do with a cup of tea, you know."

Bill looked at him and smiled. "Didn't you know that apart from anything else, the Swedes make even worse tea than the Americans?"

"I've found that out already. However, I'm not particularly fussy at the moment. I just wish I hadn't come. I just wish I had never seen Klaus Hermann."

They drove in silence for another few kilometers, past the airport, up toward Knivsta. Several Saabs and Volvos overtook them at high speeds. A little farther on they had to slow down for a bad accident—emergency lights flashing, policemen in white caps waving them on. There was blood and broken glass, and a woman sitting by the side of the road, weeping. The first fine flakes of snow began to fall and Humphrey couldn't help but think of Christmas. How could anyone live in this peculiar land where it was nearly always Christmas?

After another ten minutes Birgitta leaned forward from the back seat and abruptly asked, "Why are you looking for him? Has he done something?"

Bill said, "Nothing too serious. It's a tax matter."

"For taxes you drive out in the night to find him? I don't believe you."

"Let's just say that we were involved in a little business together," said Bill.

"You're not thinking of doing anything . . ." she couldn't think of the word at first, but at last she said, ". . . wyolent?"

"Of course not. Do we look the wyolent type?"

Humphrey tried to smile at Birgitta reassuringly, but the trouble was that he wasn't at all happy about this business himself. If British and American Intelligence really wanted to arrest Hermann and deport him, why hadn't they sent a proper security team instead of this one man? He didn't like the idea of Bill's gun either. He had never been comfortable when guns were around.

Bill was aware that Humphrey was uncomfortable but there was nothing he could do about it. Hermann had to be fingered, and fingered accurately, mainly because Bill could not risk the legal and diplomatic rows that would follow if he made a mistake, and also because his career wouldn't stand it. If he performed this particular operation smoothly and efficiently, it could mean his passport back to headquarters in the United States and the end of all that sweaty field work in South America. But if he failed, they would probably send him out indefinitely to Argentina or Chile, or—even worse—Australia. There were only five major Nazi war criminals in Australia, and two of those were running an extremely popular bakery in Melbourne.

Birgitta said, "Is it because he lives in the Soviet Union?"

"Is *what* because he lives in the Soviet Union?" asked Bill, deliberately obtuse.

"Are you looking for him because of that? You think perhaps he's a spy?"

"A spy?" scoffed Bill. "Just because he happens to live in Russia? That doesn't make him a spy. No, no; we were in business together, that's all. A little import-export."

"He never mentioned you."

"Why should he?"

"I don't know," said Birgitta. "He's a very open man. He is not the sort of person who has secrets. They respect him in the Soviet Union, you know. He lives in Cerepovec for most of the year, in a beautiful house on the Rybinskoje Vodochranilisce. Did you know that?"

"Of course. He talks about it often. He even invited me to spend the summer with him once."

"Then you are lying," said Birgitta flatly. "He lives in Leningrad, and if you knew him at all, you would have known that."

Bill looked up at the rear-view mirror. His eyes were like an alien's eyes in a 1950s science-fiction movie. "You just be careful with me, lady," he said. "I didn't fly all the way over here to freeze my ass off and have someone like you make a fool out of me."

"You should let me go free," said Birgitta.

"You think so?"

"You have no right to hold me any longer."

Without a word Bill drew the Grand Prix over to the side of the road. He unlocked the doors, then reached behind and opened Birgitta's door. A freezing wind blew into the car with razorlike intensity. A few snowflakes whirled around, vanishing as they were touched by the warmth of the heater.

"You want to go, go," Bill told Birgitta.

There were no other cars on the highway, either behind or ahead. The night was howling and dark; towering pine trees thrashed and screamed in the wind. Birgitta hesitated for a moment, then reached forward and took Humphrey's shoulder.

"I don't understand what you want," she said.

"You don't have to understand," said Bill. "We're using you to help us in a specific operation. All you have to know is that we're going to require you to perform certain actions for us and that we'll be mortally upset if you don't. Why we're doing this doesn't concern you. So I suggest you close the door, keep your mouth shut and consider yourself lucky we're not looking for *you.*"

Humphrey said, "I do think we're rather overstepping ourselves, Bill. I mean, we don't actually have any right—"

"*Right*?" snorted Bill. "You're talking about Klaus Hermann here, and you think we don't have the *right*? Did Klaus Hermann think about rights back at Herbstwald?"

"Herbstwald?" asked Birgitta, frowning. "That was a concentration camp, wasn't it? Like Auschwitz and Bergen-Belsen. Surely he hadn't anything to do with that?"

"Let me tell you the truth then," said Bill. "Klaus Hermann was the camp doctor at Herbstwald between nineteen forty-one and nineteen forty-three. He was a close friend of Dr. Josef Mengele, whose name may be familiar to you. Hermann was a specialist in medical virology—the best of his day and still one of the best in the world."

Birgitta said, "I *know* him. I know him well, ever since

he first met Angelika. How could any of this be true? Why are you telling me this lie?''

"It's not a lie, my dear," put in Humphrey. "Klaus Hermann was indeed responsible for the deaths of more than three thousand men, women and children during the war. He used them for medical experiments, to develop new strains of virus and to find antidotes for existing viral infections. If you were to be completely cold-blooded, I suppose you could say he was a great man. A *very* great man. Certainly one of the greatest research biologists of his time. But unfortunately he cared only for science and research; he ignored the terrible suffering he inflicted on thousands of innocent people."

Birgitta looked from Humphrey to Bill and then back again. "This is a trick," she said, her voice desperate. "How can this be? He has always treated Angelika so well. He is such a gentleman."

Bill said, "Are you getting out or what? My ears are about to drop off."

Birgitta hesitated and then slammed the door. "I will stay. But I do not trust you."

"You're going to have to do as you're told," said Bill.

"I will do what I have to."

Bill glanced in the mirror and then pulled the Grand Prix back onto the highway. The snow began to fall more thickly now, and he was obliged to switch on the wipers.

"Nice country you have here," said Bill. "Remind me to stay in Uruguay next fall."

Humphrey said cautiously to Bill, "This won't change anything, will it?"

Bill said, "I don't know. It might."

"I mean, her knowing about Hermann," Humphrey persisted, nodding toward Birgitta. "It won't . . . jeopardize her in any way?"

"Why should it?" asked Bill.

"I'm not sure. But it already seems to me that knowing about Hermann is a great personal responsibility."

"*Jag vet inte var mina skyldigheter börjar och slutar,*" said Birgitta bitterly.

Bill looked up in the rear-view mirror again. "Well, neither do I, sweetie," he told her. "But that doesn't prevent me from doing my job."

Birgitta directed them off the E4 just before they drove into Uppsala itself and onto 282 east toward Funbo. Although the snow had died away, the road was still wet and the tires made a sizzling noise on the pavement. It was nearly eleven o'clock now; it was all Humphrey could do to stay awake, particularly since his normal defense in any situation he wasn't enjoying was to fall asleep. If his sister argued with him, he fell asleep. He quite often fell asleep at dinner parties.

"It's here," said Birgitta just as Humphrey was falling off another precipice.

Bill turned the car sharply off to the right, down a corduroy road made of logs. The car bucked and swayed; the suspension sounded like spanners falling into a trash can. On both sides, pine trees closed in until their boughs were scraping and squeaking at the windows. Humphrey woke up sharply and sat upright, staring into the dark tunnel ahead.

"I hope this is on the level," said Bill. "If this track winds up in a lake or a quarry, I warn you, you've had it. And I mean *had* it."

But after two or three minutes the trees widened out and the corduroy road abruptly gave way to a mud track. They found themselves driving out in the open, across a night blown field under a frigid sky magnificent with northern stars.

"Please turn off the lights," said Birgitta. "They will see us otherwise. The little house is over there now, to the

left, behind those rows of trees. You see the light? You
see the log pile?''

Bill turned the car into the shadow of a stand of pines
and switched off the engine.

"Aren't you going to drive all the way up to the house?"
asked Humphrey.

Bill shook his head. "No. We're going to walk the rest
of the way. And we're going to walk there quietly. You
understand me? You too, Miss Gillsäter. Any funny business and someone's going to get hurt. And we don't want
that to happen, do we? We want everybody to come out of
this smiling and cheerful. *Glada som lärkor.*''

"I will do as you ask," said Birgitta haughtily. "I have
already agreed—because of Angelika."

"Quite so," said Humphrey and then cleared his throat
and looked away when Bill stared at him disapprovingly.

Bill reached into his coat and took out his .38. Then he
matter-of-factly fumbled in his jacket pocket and produced
a silencer, which he quickly screwed onto the muzzle. He
did all this without taking his eyes off the house, which
gave Humphrey the feeling that he had certainly done this
kind of thing more than once.

Humphrey said, "The gun . . . it is only a precaution?"

"Oh, the gun?" asked Bill. He held it up and looked at
it as though this were the first time he had ever seen it.
"Oh, sure, a precaution. I mean, you never know. Hermann might get a little jumpy, and just about everybody
around this neck of the woods has a hunting rifle.''

"I'd rather there weren't any shooting," said Humphrey.

"*You'd* rather there weren't any shooting?" Bill retorted.
It was then that each realized for an instant what disparate
characters they were; and for both of them to be wandering
around a field in the middle of the night near a place called
Funbo seemed incongruous to the point of madness.

Birgitta climbed out of the car first and Bill promptly
followed her. Humphrey eased himself stiffly out of the

passenger seat, asking, "Is it all right if I relieve myself? The cold, you know."

Bill waved his gun impatiently out at the night. "There's the whole of Sweden out there. Go piss on it."

As he moved a little distance away, Humphrey wondered if it might not be a good idea to simply go walking off into the woods, leaving Bill to cope with Hermann on his own. The only trouble with *that*, however, was that Humphrey was older than he used to be; he felt the chill more readily, and furthermore, he didn't have a clue as to where he was. They would probably find his snow-covered body three weeks later and the Reverend Johnson would have yet another opportunity to talk about death as "a mist of darkness forever."

"Are you ready?" Bill demanded impatiently as Humphrey buttoned his pants.

"Quite ready, thank you. Well—as ready as I'm ever going to be, I suppose."

They set off across the field, tramping over dried bracken and tangled weeds. Birgitta walked in front, Bill a few steps behind and a little way off to her right. Humphrey puffed along behind them, wishing he'd remembered to bring his scarf. As they skirted a diagonal stand of pines, the house came into clear view—a small wooden cottage of varnished pine, with a veranda, an upstairs balcony and a stone chimney that was smoking furiously as though the fire had only recently been lit. The shutters were closed against the cold but bright chinks of light shone out, and above the low fluting of the wind, they could hear the sound of Bach, the saraband from *Partita in B-minor*.

"You can never fault these old Nazis for taste," whispered Bill. "They like good art, they like good music, and they like fine wine."

Humphrey said, "I don't think we should forget that they rather enjoyed killing people as well."

Bill didn't answer. They circled the right side of the

cottage until at last they crouched down behind a clump of bracken only twenty yards from the front door. Humphrey and Birgitta were shivering, but Bill seemed to be impervious to the cold.

"What do you actually plan to do?" asked Humphrey.

"Very simple. I kick the door in, you point Hermann out to me, and I hit him. Not more than fifteen seconds' work from start to finish."

"Yes, but what are we going to do with him afterward?" Humphrey wanted to know. "We don't have anything to tie him up with."

Bill looked puzzled. "What do you want to tie him up for?"

"Well . . ." said Humphrey, blushing a little, "supposing he tries to make a run for it? Or are you trying to tell me you don't think he will? He *is* rather past it, I suppose." He snickered, then stopped when he realized this wasn't at all funny. In fact, it was bewildering.

Bill said slowly, "He won't . . . 'make a run for it.' "

"As long as you're confident," said Humphrey, sobered.

"Of course he is confident," put in Birgitta. "Hermann will not try to escape because your American friend here intends to shoot him. Did you not understand that?"

Humphrey stared at Bill through the darkness. His teeth were chattering. "You're going to *shoot* him? Is that true?"

"Come on," said Bill. "You know who he is. You know what he's done."

"But he hasn't had a trial. Even Eichmann had a trial."

"There are plenty of Nazis who didn't. Let me tell you something, Humphrey—shooting is almost too good for this sadist. But that's beside the point. It's what I've been told to do."

"I won't allow it!" Humphrey hissed.

"I'm afraid you have no choice in the matter."

"I refuse to identify him. You can't shoot him unless I identify him."

"In that case, I'll shoot him anyway. Then see what you think about having an innocent man's death on your conscience."

Humphrey screamed: "You're mad!"

"For Christ's sake, keep your voice down. Do you want him to hear you?"

"It wouldn't be a bad idea."

"Well, make up your mind," Bill told him roughly. "Are you going to point him out for me? If you don't, I'm going to blow away whoever happens to be in there, so you'd better think about it quick."

Birgitta held on to Humphrey's sleeve. "Don't listen to him. He won't shoot anyone. He simply wants you to give this man away. But don't do it. Let him handle his own dirty work. I know this man you are calling Klaus Hermann, and he is not the man you want. How could he be? He is a gentleman!"

Humphrey turned to Bill. "Well?" he demanded hotly. He could feel his heart bumping painfully under his ribs. "What do you say to that?"

Bill gave him a quick, emotionless stare, then looked down at his wristwatch and said, "We're hitting the front door in exactly ten seconds. Make up your mind."

Humphrey said, "Really, Bill, I—"

But as he spoke, behind him Birgitta turned, rose to her feet and began to run. He heard her legs whipping through the long grass before he had the presence of mind to turn around; when he did, he was startled to see how far away she already was, almost to the trees. Because he turned to watch her, he failed to see Bill raise the .38, his left forearm lifted before him as a support, and he failed to understand how Bill could possibly stop her until he heard that peculiar sharp, sneezing noise right next to his ear—

and Birgitta began to roll over and over as though she were turning cartwheels.

For one second he thought: what an amazing woman, how acrobatic. But then he understood that Bill had actually shot her and that she was tumbling because the impact of the bullet had sent her flying forward. Because she was dead.

He stared at Bill open-mouthed. "You've shot her."

There was a lengthy silence. Birgitta fell into the grass by the trees with a soft thud. The wind blew hard, making the bracken whistle like wailing pipes.

Bill said, "You have to know something, Humphrey. I was going to take her out right from the very beginning, sooner or later. I would have preferred later."

"But you've *killed* her."

"I was told to kill anyone involved. It's very important that no one knows about this."

"But what about me?" asked Humphrey. "I know about it. I know *all* about it. In fact, I know more than you do. Are you going to kill me too?"

"Of course not."

"But suppose I threaten to call the police? Suppose I refuse to identify Hermann?"

"You won't do either of those things."

"But if I do?"

"You won't."

Humphrey looked at Bill through the darkness. It was almost impossible to make out the lines of his face. Only his eyes seemed visible, glittering, like beads of ice.

"I think I rather wish I had never telephoned Major Milner," he said.

"I don't know why," Bill told him. "They'll probably give you a medal for this when it's over."

"As long as it's not posthumous. My sister wouldn't care for that at all. She never liked medals. Only jugs."

"Jugs?" asked Bill, perplexed.

They heard a sigh and a rustle from the direction of the trees. Humphrey said, "Listen! Do you think she's still alive?"

Bill shook his head.

"But I heard a noise. I distinctly heard a noise."

"Come on, Humphrey. If she *is* still alive, she won't be for long. I took most of the side of her head off."

Humphrey swallowed. "I think I'm going back to the car. I think I've had enough of this for one night."

"Oh, no, Humphrey. We're going on. We have some urgent business with Herr Hermann, remember?"

"But you've killed her! She was quite innocent, and you've killed her. I won't stand for it!" For the first time the shock of what had actually happened penetrated Humphrey's consciousness. This wasn't a play; it wasn't the autumn production of the Baslow Dramatic Society. A girl had just been shot down and killed right in front of his eyes. But the calmness surrounding the event, the matter-of-fact way in which Bill Bennett had turned and aimed and fired at her, the promptness with which she had dropped into the grass—all this had deceived Humphrey into believing until now that her sudden death had been almost an ordinary occurrence.

Bill snapped, "For Christ's sake!"

"I'm going," said Humphrey. He clambered to his feet.

"If you go, I'll kill you."

"Like you did her? Just shoot me down, like a dog?"

Bill's eyes glittered. He raised his revolver and he wasn't smiling.

"You're a murderer," said Humphrey.

"Don't be so damned stupid," Bill retorted.

"You're a murderer. I saw you murder that girl. You just . . . shot her . . . for your own convenience."

"Will you pipe down?"

"I'll speak as loudly as I like. And as truthfully as I

like. I won't have it. I didn't come along to help you for this."

"What did you come along for? To add to your sister's jug collection?"

There was a moment of shared exasperation. Then Humphrey, losing his rage and his energy like a deflated balloon, sat down again and protested, "That was most unfair."

"Did I say I was going to be fair?"

"No, but . . . well, it was most unfair all the same." Humphrey looked in the direction in which Birgitta had fallen. There was no movement now, no sound. She had likely died at once and that rustling noise he had heard was probably nothing more than a rabbit, or a startled bird.

"This isn't easy, not any of it," said Bill. He kept his eyes fixed like studs on the veranda of the small wooden cottage. "It isn't easy physically, and it isn't easy psychologically, and it isn't *morally* easy either. The overriding principle they teach us is that of the Greater Good. That was why I killed that girl. More lives would have been harmed by letting her go than by killing her. On balance, I was serving the Greater Good."

"The Greater Good?" echoed Humphrey. He could hardly believe it. He began to feel that he had wandered into some peculiar parallel existence in which all the commonplace values of life were turned upside down. "You're going to shoot Hermann too, I suppose? Is that it? Is that why they sent you here? And that's why you have to have him so positively identified—in case you kill the wrong man?"

"Hermann is a murderer, Humphrey," said Bill. "A fanatical, cold-blooded murderer. He also happens, despite his age, to be helping the Soviets build up the most comprehensive arsenal of plagues and diseases you can imagine."

"So you *are* going to shoot him?"

"If you must know, yes."

"Without a trial?"

"We already know that he's the right man, don't we?"

"But even at Nuremberg—"

Bill let out a sharp, tight breath. "Humphrey," he said. "I'm not here to argue the rights and wrongs of killing war criminals without a trial. I'm here to do a job. You're going to help me do it, and that's all there is to it. Now will you keep quiet?"

At that moment one of the shutters on the left of the cottage was opened and a rhomboid of yellow lamplight fell across the veranda. Bill reached out and pressed Humphrey down, right into the grass, and said, "Quiet."

They heard a casement rattling, and the sound of voices talking in German. A man's voice said, *"Nein. Es war nur eine optische Täuschung. Das licht hat mir einen Streich gespielt."*

Then the casement closed again with a bang, and the shutter too.

Humphrey whispered, "What were they saying?"

"Something about an optical illusion. Maybe they saw us, or thought they did. We've got to be quick."

He stood up and beckoned Humphrey to follow him. When Humphrey hesitated, he turned and hissed at him, "Come on, will you? We don't have all night." Reluctantly Humphrey stood up and followed.

Bill said, "Will you try to make a little less noise? I mean, would you mind? Try *stalking*, like you did in the Boy Scouts."

"I didn't join the Scouts," said Humphrey. "My chest."

"Well, just try to walk more quietly. We have to take them by surprise."

They moved on, carefully approaching the cottage in a half-circle, Bill keeping his revolver raised high in both hands, crouching a little, Humphrey stepping high-footed behind him. They were fewer than ten feet from the veranda when the shutter suddenly banged open again and they found themselves face-to-face with an astonished-looking young man with a blond mustache.

Bill shouted to Humphrey, "Drop!" and as Humphrey awkwardly got down on his knees, Bill fired two shots in quick succession toward the window. Two quick sneezes. The young man fell out of sight. Bill seized Humphrey's sleeve and dragged him sideways out of the light with such force that Humphrey heard the lining of his jacket tear.

"My God!" he murmured.

"Down!" Bill shouted at him.

There was a rattling noise from the open window, and the grass and dirt in front of the cottage were peppered. Bill took aim but didn't fire again. "Come on," he told Humphrey. "Let's see if we can't hit 'em from around the side."

"This is quite ridiculous!" shouted Humphrey. His heart felt as though it had expanded to press against the inside of his ribs. He gasped and stumbled; then there was another burst of rattling, and the grass and stones were torn up all around his feet and something bit him sharply in the ankle. He cried out and his cry was met by a third rattle, and the air hummed and twanged and whistled around his ears.

Bill left him now. He was a liability to the Greater Good, Humphrey supposed. Running at a crouch, Bill skirted around the far end of the cottage, and disappeared.

There was silence for a while. Humphrey lay facedown on the ground, his eyes wide, panting for breath, unable to move. He prayed the people inside the cottage would understand that he was a noncombatant and that he was not involved in this grisly affair out of choice. His shoe felt as though it had been ripped open at the back, and he could feel dampness on his heel. He was quite sure he had been shot. He found that he was reciting under his breath a line from *The Ancient Mariner:* "The Nightmare Life-in-Death was she, that thicks man's blood with cold." It did, after all, seem quite possible, even *likely*, that he would die tonight, that his predictable life in Derbyshire would come to an abrupt and unpredictable finish in a freezing-cold field in Uppsala. If they were ever to draw a graph of his life, it would be one long, tedious line, with an odd hiccup at the end.

"Oh, God," he prayed.

There was another rattle of submachine-gun fire. It sounded somewhat hollow this time, as though the gun was being fired indoors. There was a short silence and then a scream, a woman's scream, and a lot of shouting in German. *"Das dürfen Sie nicht tun! Aufhören! Nicht schiessen!"*

The front door of the cottage was thrown open as though someone were trying to wrench it off its hinges. Two men hurtled out, crouching low, one in blue pajamas, the other wearing a white raincoat. The one in the white raincoat was obviously the younger of the two because he grasped his companion's arm and dragged him at full pelt toward the field, toward the trees where Birgitta had fallen. The one in pajamas kept shouting to him hoarsely to slow down.

Humphrey rolled over in the bracken and rose to his feet unsteadily just as Bill came hurtling through the door too, shouting: "Freeze, you bastards!" and raising his revolver.

"Bill!" shouted Humphrey. He limped rapidly up to the house, up the veranda steps, and threw himself heavily against the American as though he were embracing him after a long sea voyage. Both men teetered for a moment, staggered, then fell to the veranda floor with a bruising thud.

"Jesus Christ!" Bill screamed. "You stupid bastard! I could have hit him!"

Humphrey got to his hands and knees, panting. "I didn't *want* you to hit him."

"That was Hermann, you stupid bastard! I had him, and you let him get away!"

"I *wanted* him to get away."

"Are you crazy? That was Klaus Hermann!"

"I know," said Humphrey, trying to get his breath back. "But even the Vampire of Herbstwald deserves a trial. If we don't allow him a trial, we're just as bestial as he is."

Bill stood up and in frustration smacked his hand against one of the veranda posts. "Jesus," he repeated. "We won't even *get* him to trial now. We won't ever see him again. He'll be back in Russia before you can whistle 'The Red Flag.' "

"I'm sorry. But I have to do what I believe is right and proper, that's all."

"You meddling old man," snapped Bill. He looked away; the only visible clue Humphrey had to his high-voltage professional tension was the tightness of his grip on the veranda railing. After a moment, however, Bill turned around and said, "I'm sorry. I apologize. I shouldn't have called you that. You'd better come along inside and see what we've got."

"I think maybe I've got a bullet in my heel," said Humphrey.

Bill looked down, then crouched beside Humphrey and raised his left trouser leg. The back of Humphrey's shoe had been shot off and his green Wolsey sock was sticky with blood, but it was only a superficial graze, congealing already.

"You were lucky," said Bill, standing up again. "Couple of inches farther and you might have lost your foot. Peg-leg Humphrey Browne."

Humphrey twisted around to look at his heel and then gave Bill a self-deprecatory little smirk. "Wounded in the course of action," he said. "I expect it will leave something of a scar."

"Oh, yes, I'm sure," said Bill. "Now let's get inside. There's something I want to show you."

* * *

Angelika Rangström was sitting by the blue-and-white enameled stove, wrapped up tightly in a red dressing gown, smoking a cigarette with quick, anxious puffs. Humphrey recognized her at once as the woman who had been sitting with Klaus Hermann at the outdoor restaurant: a rather tired-looking, middle-aged blonde with pale blue eyes and perfect Swedish bone structure. Years ago she must have been ravishing, and she still had an extraordinary femininity about her that made Humphrey feel quite clumsy.

Bill Bennett leaned toward her, his nickel-plated revolver hanging loose in his hand, and said, "Your boyfriend got away. You can thank Mr. Browne here for that. Mr. Browne believes in trial by jury."

Angelika glanced up at him and then looked away. "You can believe about him whatever you like," she said in an English accent as cold as marble.

"We know who he is. It's no good trying to pretend."

"He is not what you think," she retorted.

Bill gave Humphrey a wink and a smile. "Gutsy, isn't she? Well, she must be, to be able to sleep with an aging old butcher like Klaus Hermann. Just think about it, lying next to a man who *personally* murdered three thousand people. Kissing a fellow who slaughtered innocent children in their hundreds. Very gutsy indeed."

Humphrey said, "I don't think I really understand." Then, "Do you mind if I sit down? My foot hurts."

"Help yourself," said Bill. He dragged over a chair and offered it up to Humphrey's descending bottom. The cottage was furnished and decorated in the style of Carl Larsson—carved tables, wooden walls of eggshell white with painted blue borders, rows of potted fuchsias on the windowsills and the Gothic-lettered words *Guds Fred* over the lintel.

Bill said to Angelika: "I suppose you did know who Klaus actually was when you first met him?"

She dragged at her cigarette and then said, "You have no authority here. How can you ask me such questions?"

"Your friend Birgitta is dead," Bill told her. He raised an eyebrow and stared at her hard to show he meant it.

Angelika raised her head as though she were acting. Humphrey found himself watching her like a theatergoer, wondering what she would say next. The painted room, the lamplight—it all seemed so Ibsenesque. Humphrey almost expected her to say, "Take the saving lie away from the average man, and you take away his happiness, too"—a line he remembered from *The Wild Duck*.

But instead she said, "Are you trying to tell me that you have killed her?"

Bill said, "She didn't cooperate."

"Cooperate? Cooperate with whom? With *you*? With this man here, with his bleeding foot? And now Klaus has had to run for his life. You understand that I may never see him again. That is what you have done to me. I don't think threats of death mean very much after this. Here," she said and bent her head forward so that her blonde hair parted from the white nape of her neck. "Shoot me if you wish. What difference does it make now?"

Bill sniffed. "There's a dead man in the kitchen."

"That was poor Vassili," she said without lifting her head.

"Were both of them Russian?"

"Yes. They met us here. Klaus was talking to Bendix— when was it, two days ago?—because he was afraid he had been recognized. Bendix told us to come here, at least until he could be sure there was no longer any danger. But of course there was. I told Klaus to go straight back to Leningrad. I told him over and over. What is a few weeks lost compared with a lifetime? But he wouldn't listen. Such a stubborn man. And now look at what has happened."

Bill walked around the room, his sneakers squeaking on the polished boards. He peered at a painted wooden bowl as though he were a connoisseur. Then he turned and stood over Angelika and said, "Klaus talked to Bendix?"

"Who is Bendix?" Humphrey wanted to know.

"It's a code name for the Soviet officer who deals with all the imports and exports that go through Stockholm," said Bill. "*Human* imports and exports, that is. It's not a secret. I think there was an article about him in *Time* magazine. He deals with defections, that kind of thing."

"He will not allow Klaus to return," said Angelika. "Not after this." She looked up now, her pale eyes sharp with tears. "I will never see Klaus again because of you."

"Listen, Frau Rangström, there were thousands of Jewish women who never got to see their husbands and lovers again because of your boyfriend," said Bill. "So don't get too sentimental about it."

"You killed Birgitta," she said. Her voice was completely expressionless.

Humphrey thought she was probably suffering from shock. He knew that *he* was. He said, "I must have a drink of water," and limped across the room and into the hallway.

The dead Russian agent was crumpled up in a corner. Bill's bullet had hit him on the bridge of the nose, and the dark wound was so large that parts of the brain were exposed. The wall above him was spattered with blood. Humphrey's mouth felt dry and he gave the body as wide a berth as he could, pressing himself against the opposite wall.

He stood in the darkened kitchen and drank a large glass of very cold water, one hand still resting on the pump handle as he drank.

When he returned to the living room, Angelika Rangström had left her chair and was standing on the far side of the room, smoking a fresh cigarette. She held the pack in the palm of her hand, a Swedish brand called Solna. The smoke in the room was bright blue and pungent. She was saying, "I suppose it fascinated me at first, what Klaus had done. I was going through a strange period of my life then. My first husband had been very cruel—physically very cruel. What he did to me, I cannot describe to you, but believe me, no man has ever humiliated a woman in the ways that he did me. Night after night, week after week, month after month, until I was completely subjugated. And still I had to pretend each day when I went to the theater that I was normal, happy and bright. I dreaded the nights at first, but then I grew to accept them. My family believed we were such a contented pair. Well, sometimes I think my father suspected. There was a look in his eyes whenever we met. But that was all. The experience changed me forever. I took drugs for a long time. I was still taking drugs when I met Klaus."

Humphrey was about to say something, baffled at this unexpected confession, but Bill shot him a quick look to silence him.

Angelika touched the rail of the chair on which Humphrey had been sitting and said, "How we poor mortals become caught up in larger events—swept along, thinking we control our own destiny. I would never have met Klaus if it hadn't been for the war."

Bill and Humphrey watched her without saying a word. Gradually, as she spoke, Humphrey began to realize what she was doing. She was acting out the part of a woman who had taken as her lover one of the most terrible butchers of all time and who for years had suffered a secret guilt that her lovemaking somehow implicated her in each of the murders he committed.

How many times, looking at her face in her dressing-table mirror, had she imagined she heard the voices of those three thousand crying from their mass graves? How many times had she promised herself that she would never see Klaus again? Yet, the fascination of his soft, manicured hands . . . the barbarism hiding in his eyes . . . .

"I met him in Prague," she said, "in nineteen fifty-one."

"Yes," said Bill.

"Prague is my favorite city. Do you know that it was once occupied by the Swedes? In the middle of the seventeenth century, I think. I was on tour there with the theater company. We were performing *A Doll's House*. 'In that moment it burst upon me that I had been living here these eight years with a strange man, and had borne him three children.' Do you know *A Doll's House*?"

"Yes," said Bill.

"Not exactly," said Humphrey.

"There was a party," she went on as though she hadn't heard either of them, "and Klaus appeared . . . materialized out of the crowd . . . smiling. He never told me why he was there. And, well, I suppose I saw in him the total masculinity my husband had exhibited, yet combined with courtesy and understanding. We went to bed together that same evening, and who can blame us?"

There was a long and difficult silence in the room. Angelika finished her cigarette and crushed it out impatiently. Bill said nothing but leaned back against the wall with his arms folded. Humphrey felt that he had a hundred questions to ask, but he didn't dare to break the atmosphere.

"Klaus took me for a long walk through Prague. It was late afternoon, in the summer, and the shadows were very long. He had visited Prague during the war because he used to be a friend of Heydrich. Such parties! he used to say. Wine, and roasted game, and women. All gone when the Third Reich collapsed. He took me to see the cathedral of St. Vitus, where all the kings of Bohemia were crowned, and then to the royal palace on Hradcany Hill. You cannot imagine a more beautiful place in which to fall in love, with the Vltava River flowing beneath us. . . ."

There was another long silence. Bill sniffed and looked

around the room; Humphrey sat on a chair and nursed his foot. It hadn't been as badly wounded as he had at first imagined, and he was quite concerned that he wouldn't even have a scar to show for his trouble.

Bill said, "They won't be able to get him back to the Soviet Union, you know. Not straightaway."

Angelika said, "I don't understand."

"Well, all the ports and airports are being watched, as well as the major highways. Nynashamn, Oxelosund, Saltsjobaden . . . I made sure that every one of them was alerted before we came out tonight. And Bromma and Arlanda Airports too. Bendix will know that he can't get him back to Leningrad, not yet."

Angelika took out another cigarette. "You must want Klaus very badly," she said, almost with pride.

"We want him, yes," said Bill. Humphrey, in an effort to show his neutrality, gave a spastic shrug.

"Well, I can tell you where Bendix will probably take him," said Angelika. "But I will do this only on the absolute understanding that you will not try to kill him. You will have to arrest him, won't you? But I do not want him shot. He is not a beast, whatever you may think. He is not to be exterminated. And I want your guarantee that I will be able to see him whenever I want to."

"You want conjugal rights?" asked Bill.

Angelika shook her head. "Don't you think we're both a little old for that? A little too dignified?"

Unexpectedly Bill said, "What do you think, Humphrey? Think we should play along? We don't have to. We could always let Hermann go. After all, what has he ever done to us? Only problem is, we'll have to take care of Angelika here; we can't have her squealing to the Swedish police."

"You're bluffing," said Humphrey in a disgruntled voice.

"You think so?" asked Bill.

"You mean you're going to shoot her? Right here, right in front of my eyes?"

"If necessary," said Bill. Then, without warning, he held up the revolver and fired off four shots, one after the other, four silenced sneezes; two plates on the wall shattered into shards, the cuckoo clock burst apart and a window dropped out of its frame. Bill smiled. The room was full of flat, powdery-smelling smoke.

Angelika said bravely, "Why don't you stop play-acting? You knew from the beginning that I would help you."

"Yes," said Bill, "I did."

"Well, then," she said, "they will probably take Klaus to Lingslätö. It's a little village on the Baltic coast south of Grisslehamn. I've been there only once. They call it their 'safe house.' You know, in case of emergency."

Bill flipped open the cylinder of his .38 and reloaded it with fresh shells. Then he tucked the revolver into his coat. "All right," he smiled. "Lingslätö it is. How's your foot, Humphrey?"

Humphrey pressed his thumb and his index finger to his eyelids. He felt shocked, old and impossibly tired. "How far is it?" he asked.

"Sixty kilometers," said Angelika. "It won't take long."

"You'd better get dressed then," Bill advised her.

When Angelika had gone into the bedroom for her clothes, Humphrey said to Bill dully, "I never imagined it was going to be like this."

"I know," said Bill. "I guess I ought to say I'm sorry."

"Sorry? Well, a little late for that now. Two people dead already."

"Klaus Hermann has to be caught, Humphrey. A lot of people in the United States and Britain want him silenced, believe me. Important people. Know what I mean?"

Humphrey didn't answer but closed his eyes and leaned back against the wall. He felt as though the inside of his head were a prison from which even the most sensible of actions would not release him. Who were these people in the United States and Britain who wanted Klaus Hermann silenced? Was their need so urgent that he had to stay up all night in Uppsala Län, tired beyond belief, with a neurotic Swedish actress and a trigger-happy young American who seemed to have been taking etiquette lessons from Genghis Khan?

He was due to fly back to England the day after tomorrow. Manchester Airport, rain, gray skies and the soft, green curves of the Derbyshire Dales. They all seemed so ordinary, and yet beyond achievement. Something had died inside him here in Sweden, and perhaps it was simply his faith in human nature and the sanctity of human life.

He said to Bill, "Why did she tell you where Hermann might be?"

Bill looked surprised. "Didn't you think she would?"

"But they're . . . *lovers*," said Humphrey.

Bill shook his head. "She's been dying to confess for years. All she needed was the opportunity. You wait. She'll spend the whole sixty-kilometer ride to Lingslätö telling us the full, gory story of what they did together and how often she felt like calling up Simon Wiesenthal. Women are all the same."

"If you say so," said Humphrey. He thought of his sister. He thought of the Reverend Johnson. He closed his eyes and thought of his heel.

TEN

Reynard flew back to Concord that weekend to make the announcement that he intended to run for the Democratic nomination. Already the newspapers were heatedly speculating "Kelly to Declare?" and rehashing the old toxic-dump scandal, as well as publishing saucy photographs of Ellen Wangerin, his one-time gangster girlfriend. Reynard pretended to find the press reports irritating, and as far as his campaign was concerned, they were. But he had always privately thought of himself as a swashbuckler, a man with red-blooded desires, both carnal and political, and secretly he found his notoriety exciting. Especially since Greta would be standing by his side when he sought election, forgiving and loving—every inch a First Lady.

The LearJet made its approach to Concord Airport from the southeast, whistling low over scattered lights. Next to him, Dick Elmwood began to gather his papers and screw the caps on his variously colored pens. Reynard said, "This is it, hey, Dick?"

"Yes, sir," Dick replied with a smile about as appealing as a plateful of ground oats.

Reynard said, "I want you to know that Mrs. Kelly has

to be treated just as respectfully and just as warmly as though everything were normal. I don't want any sharp remarks, if you understand what I mean. I want warmth.''

"Yes, sir.''

"Is Dean Farber coming up tomorrow?''

"Oh, I expect he'll be here tonight, sir. He has a lot of preparation to do.''

"Good. He's really keen, isn't he?''

"That's the impression he gives me, Senator. But I think I'm going to wait and see. I suppose I'm naturally conservative.''

"Hmm,'' said Reynard. "Once in a while, Dick, you ought to let yourself go. It's bad for the spirit, too much reserve. Once in a while you ought to get smashed and find yourself an accommodating broad.''

The LearJet nudged the runway, then touched down and roared its engines in reverse thrust. The headlights of a limousine detached themselves from the clustering lights around the airport terminal and moved swiftly toward the plane as it taxied around to park. Dick said, a little too brightly, "I get all the satisfaction I need out of my work, sir. Can you believe that?''

Reynard grunted. "If you say so, Dick. But don't let me catch you with any of those Kelly-for-President girls. Otherwise I'll start thinking you're getting tired of your job.''

They held on to their hats as they crossed the windy tarmac and climbed into the long, black Cadillac. Then they were swept almost silently out of the airport and out onto Loudon Road toward the Kelly estate.

Reynard said, for no particular reason, "I always feel wary at this time of year. I always get the feeling that something or somebody is going to die. Unsettling, isn't it? I always get the feeling that not all of us are going to survive the winter.''

"Pre-declaration nerves,'' suggested Dick.

Reynard shrugged and grunted, but secretly he thought: what a damned vapid thing to say.

Greta's red Ferrari was already drawn up in front of the house when they arrived. The limousine's headlights swept across the driveway and illuminated the twin rows of bay trees on either side of the entrance. As soon as the limousine crunched to a halt, two of the house staff came forward and opened the door.

"Welcome home, Senator."

"Good to have you back, sir."

They escorted Reynard up the steps and into the domed hallway. There he was greeted by Len Gieves and Natalia Vanspronsen, his leading publicity agents. Len was a snappy, aggressive man with gingery hair and a wild mustache; Natalia came from the efficient-immaculate division of the women's movement; she was beautiful, bespectacled and faultlessly groomed—and politically serious as all hell.

"I see my wife has arrived," said Reynard, handing his hat and coat to Eunice and his working papers to Dick Elmwood. "What kind of mood is she in?"

"Wavering between sardonic and acidulous," Natalia Vanspronsen replied. She, for one, had not been particularly enthused about the idea of promoting Reynard and Greta's family togetherness as a number-one campaign sales point, even though she was unaware that, up until now, they had decided to part permanently. Natalia had even argued at one meeting that Reynard should promise, if elected, to abolish the traditional title of "First Lady" since it imposed an overwhelming political-social stereotype on the female partner in the nation's most prominent marriage. "If the *president* treats his wife as a secondary human being, what is every other man in the country going to think?" Nevertheless, Reynard liked her. She was a very sharp operator.

Len Gieves said, "There's something you ought to know, sir. Doctor Walt Seabrook is here too."

"That ape? Who invited him? Well, of course, my wife did. Damn."

"He appears to be keeping a comparatively low profile, sir."

"The only comparatively low thing about Walt Seabrook is his brow," said Reynard. "I hope you searched him for dope before you let him in. We're going to have enough problems without playing host to coke-snorting simians with degrees in self-lobotomy."

"Don't worry," Len Gieves assured him. "I'll have a quiet word with him."

"Make sure it doesn't have too many syllables," said Reynard. "I do want him to understand what you're saying."

"Dean Farber called," put in Natalia. "He'll be here at ten. I'll send the limousine for him if I may."

Eunice said, "Your bath is ready for you, sir."

"I'll be right up. Dick, will you call Senator Hampton and ask him if he still has those papers on Green Mountain. That's one of the issues I want to raise tomorrow."

"We have some new material on that," said Len Gieves. "Maybe we can run through it later."

"I had Jack Pope from *Congress Special* on the phone too," said Natalia. "I think he's quite interested in a background piece on your whole conservation ethic."

"Do I have a conservation ethic?" asked Reynard. "I thought I just wanted to prevent people from turning New Hampshire's forests into paperback books."

"You *have* a conservation ethic," insisted Natalia, unmoved by Reynard's attempt at humor. "Your conservation program is one of the most important planks in your platform. Along with your Medicare ethic, that is; and your defense ethic."

Reynard said, "I think I'll go take my bath, if you don't mind."

"We have a presentation meeting at ten," said Len.

"Provided I've had my dinner and finished with Greta,

I'll be there," said Reynard. "Natalia, give Greta my compliments, will you, and make sure that Doctor Seabrook has enough to drink. I'd hate to find him intelligible when I come down."

"Yes, Senator," said Len and propelled Natalia back to the living room in spite of her obvious wrath. Reynard heard him saying, "You want to keep your job or don't you? Calm down, for Christ's sake."

Greta was in fine fettle, and Walt Seabrook had already helped himself to an over-generous glassful of Reynard's 1927 cognac. The fire in the drawing room was crackling and Reynard's Great Dane lay on the rug by the fire irons, looking sadly contemplative. Reynard walked in red-faced from his bath, smelling of Floris cologne, and bowed dramatically.

"Well, well," said Greta. "Nice of you to come."

"Hullo, Greta." Reynard nodded and walked across to kiss her hand. Then he turned to Walt Seabrook, looking him up and down. "Less hairy than usual, Dr. Seabrook. What happened to the beard?"

"I donated it to medical science," said Walt. "How are you keeping, Reynard?"

"I'm keeping my peace and I'm keeping my temper, and I'm keeping them well," Reynard told him. "You shouldn't have come up here today, Dr. Seabrook; you weren't invited. And if there's one kind of animal I dislike more than a gloater, it's an uninvited gloater."

"What do I have to gloat about? Besides, I *was* invited. Greta invited me."

"This is no longer Greta's house."

"Well, for your sake I just hope the press won't get wind of that," Walt retaliated.

"You know something? My mother once told me that some matches are made in heaven. All these years I didn't believe her—until now, looking at you two. The bitch and the blusterer.''

"I hope we're not going to have a fight here," said Walt. "I didn't come up here to start a scrap."

"I don't care why you came," Reynard told him. "This is my house, and if I want to tell you what I think of you, I will."

"Reynard, for God's sake, pour yourself a drink," said Greta. "Walt's been anxious enough about meeting you face-to-face as it is, without your actually living up to his worst fears."

Reynard looked at Walt Seabrook sharply. Then he nodded and walked over to the drinks table, where he selected the bottle of Jack Daniel's and poured himself a small glassful.

"So," he said. "Dr. Seabrook's anxious, is he?"

"Of course he is," said Greta. "He's a very sensitive person."

"Oh," said Reynard. "Sensitive. Well, that's something I never was. Acute sometimes. Understanding occasionally. But never sensitive. I congratulate you, Greta, on having found yourself somebody sensitive at last."

He went up close to Walt Seabrook with the sourest of smiles and added, "You're not *too* sensitive, though, right? I mean, anyone with real sensitivity couldn't stand Greta for more than a half-hour. Forty-five minutes at the outside."

Walt Seabrook said, "I'd prefer it if you'd take that back."

"Why?" Reynard demanded. "Because I'm talking about 'the woman you love?' "

"If you want to put it that way, yes."

"You know what you are?" Reynard said, and this time he was heated and serious. "You, Dr. Seabrook, are an opportunist—the worst possible kind of opportunist, a medical opportunist. You see Greta as a way of getting rich and setting yourself up as a big cheese in the medical profession.

Well, let me tell you something straight from the shoulder. I'm going to appoint you Assistant Secretary for Health because that's part of my deal with Greta. But the deal stops there. The job is all you get. Don't expect me to be nice to you, or generous to you, or polite to you, because I won't be.''

Reynard tipped back a little whiskey and then looked at Walt Seabrook as though he pitied him. "Sensitive," he mocked. "I've seen blocks of Barre granite more sensitive."

Greta watched Reynard as he walked across to the window, then come back and sit down. "You're a sore loser, you know that?" she told him. "I just wonder what kind of a *winner* you're going to be."

Reynard smiled and shrugged. It was almost unnatural to see them together, Greta and Dr. Seabrook. Greta, after all, was so elegant in her suede Polly Edwards tunic with handpainted fleur-de-lis, her nails painted like talons, flaunting her gold jewelry and her flawless skin; whereas Dr. Seabrook seemed totally blunt and unkempt. He was a heavily built man on the late side of forty-five, with thick, dark hair through which his scalp was beginning to gleam and that kind of rounded, snub-nosed face that Reynard could never take seriously. Reynard found it extremely difficult to imagine them in bed together. Who usually climbed on top? Samson or Delilah?

Dr. Seabrook said, "It seems to me, sir, that we have to work out some kind of modus vivendi."

"It seems to *you*," Reynard retorted.

Greta interrupted. "Are you two boys going to spend the whole afternoon squabbling? You're not being rational."

"Rational? With this Neanderthal?"

"I think you're jealous," Walt Seabrook commented. "Isn't that it? You can't stand the thought of my going to bed with Greta. You can't stand it."

Greta laughed, high and bright, sounding a bit hysterical. Both men looked at her in involuntary surprise. Then

Reynard said, quite soberly, "Perhaps you're right. Perhaps, on the other hand, I've grown out of jealousy. Grown up altogether. Perhaps I'm old enough and cold-blooded enough to be seeking the presidency because it's a job I know I can handle, and handle exceptionally well. And perhaps I'm occasionally prepared to put up with clowns like you, Dr. Seabrook, because you're going to help me win. But I don't want any illusions about it."

Walt Seabrook looked unhappy. "I'd better go. Really. It would be better for all of us."

"It would certainly be better for me," put in Reynard.

Greta said, "Don't go, Walt, darling. Don't let him get to you."

Walt Seabrook shook his head and then gave Greta a quick, dismissive smile. "I think I know what the problem is. I'll go, okay? I don't mind. Senator Kelly here is feeling crowded, and maybe a little inferior too; quite apart from the fact that he doesn't happen to like my breed of doctor. All right, I accept that. But he has to accept in return that I very much want that job with HEW and that I'll do anything at all to get it. Let's face it. It's the ultimate government health job, and suddenly I'm going to see all those surgeons and neurologists who snubbed me on the golf course crawling on their hands and knees in front of me just to make sure they get a few extra bucks' allocation. Well, I can live with Reynard Kelly for that, all things being equal. I'll keep my mouth shut and I'll enjoy my job. But let me say one thing: I won't take any insults toward Greta, or any bad treatment. She may be your phony First Lady, but I'm the guy who takes care of her, *really* takes care of her, and I want that understood."

Reynard could think of a dozen cutting things to say. But the soap-opera quality of Walt Seabrook's speech had quite tickled him. He lifted his glass and said, "You're a stout man, Dr. Seabrook, in every sense of the word.

Greta, I congratulate you. A stout man. Though, of course, sensitive."

"And *you're* running for president," said Greta in disgust.

"Oh, I'm not just running," said Reynard. "This time I'm going to win."

At that moment there was a knock at the living-room door. It was Eunice, wearing her evening uniform: a long, black dress with small, triangular sleeves and a buttoned bodice. Greta looked sharply at Reynard, but he ignored her and said, "Come in, Eunice."

"There's a telephone call for you, sir," she said. She looked over at Greta and quelled her stare as effectively as though she had thrown a damp blanket on a fire. "It's urgent, so the gentleman says, and private."

"Do we know who it is?"

"Mr. Eldridge, sir. Commissioner of Health and Welfare."

"Hmm," said Reynard. He finished his bourbon. Then he said, "Greta, Dr. Seabrook, perhaps you'll excuse me for a minute or two."

"I'm sure you're excused," said Greta.

Reynard went through to the library, closed the door tightly behind him and picked up the phone.

"Hello?" he said. "Reynard Kelly speaking."

"Senator Kelly? I'm very sorry to trouble you, sir, at this time of the evening. This is Jim Eldridge, New Hampshire Commissioner of Health and Welfare."

"How do you do, Mr. Eldridge. Do you want to tell me what your problem is? I'm a little pushed for time right now."

"Well, sir, I've just received a call from Dr. Carroll Bryce, the medical examiner for Merrimack County and an old friend of mine. Been to every one of my daughters' weddings, six in all. You wouldn't credit six daughters, would you?"

"Have we ever met?" asked Reynard patiently.

"Oh, yes, sir. Two or three times. We met at the Douglas Everett Ice Arena five years ago, and we sat four places away from each other at the Kidney Foundation dinner last fall."

"Ah, yes," lied Reynard. "Now I remember you. The dignified-looking gentleman."

"Well, good of you to say so, Senator. That's what my wife always says, but I guess it's just the gray hair."

"What's on your mind?" Reynard asked him. He sometimes wondered, probably blasphemously, whether Jesus had ever felt as bored when people came to Him with sores, madness and twisted limbs.

"Well, Senator, Carroll Bryce said that he was given the autopsy protocols on a boy who died in East Concord last week; it appears from the early tests they made that he was killed by some kind of virus. Like poliomyelitis, Bryce says, only quicker."

"Yes?" asked Reynard.

Eldridge was hesitant. "It's difficult to come to any conclusions, Senator, but it seems like we might have the makings of an epidemic on our hands. That's what Dr. Bryce said. You see, the trouble with this virus is that it doesn't respond to any of the usual treatments."

"You're talking about a polio epidemic?"

"That's right, Senator. And quite a bad one."

"Can't you organize a vaccination program? How much would that cost?"

"Senator, I'm trying to explain to you. This virus doesn't respond to any of the usual treatments."

Reynard frowned. "It's polio?"

"Kind of. Only much more virulent."

"How many people have caught it already?"

"As far as Dr. Bryce can make out, just the one, sir."

"Well, one person and you're predicting an epidemic? That doesn't make too much sense, does it?"

Eldridge was silent for a moment. Then he said, "Dr.

Bryce is an extremely conservative man, Senator. I have never known him to call me up the way he did today and raise the alarm. I have to tell you that he is *very* worried. He's seen the virology report and some early cultures, and he is *very* worried."

"Er, how, I mean, where—" began Reynard. "Where did this boy pick up this virus? He must have caught it somewhere. Are we talking about some kind of health hazard here?"

"We don't know, sir. There are very few available facts other than the autopsy protocols. The boy seemed to live a completely normal life. Up until the afternoon he died, he showed no symptoms of any illness, and during the afternoon he met none of his friends or anyone we can find who might have contracted it."

Reynard slowly rubbed his eyes. There was a knock at the library door; Dick Elmwood put his head in and mouthed something, but Reynard waved him away.

He said to Eldridge, "Listen—does anyone know where the boy lived?"

"East Concord, sir. Right on Webster Crescent, next to Conant's Acre."

"So presumably he picked it up somewhere around his home locale?"

"Well, presumably."

Reynard was silent again. But a dark voice inside his head recited, *What have you done? The voice of your brother's blood is crying to me from the ground. And now you are cursed from the ground, which has opened its mouth to receive your brother's blood from your hand.*

Eldridge said, "Senator Kelly? I did think you ought to know. We might meet some resistance here because of local interests. I don't think the commissioner of the Department of Safety is going to be too happy. In fact, I believe he's going to be downright hostile. And the Department of Resources and Economic Development is probably going to fight us all the way.''

Reynard said, ''Well . . . we need more facts, don't we? One boy dying of a freak virus. . . .''

Eldridge said, ''I had hoped for a more positive response, Senator Kelly. The way to stop epidemics is to nip them in the bud.''

''You have to understand that I can't do anything officially,'' said Reynard. ''Apart from that, I don't want to cause any unnecessary panic. The effects of panic might be more dangerous than the effects of the virus itself.''

Jim Eldridge took a deep breath. He was obviously a reserved man, unused to expressing himself firmly, let alone fighting his senior state senator one-to-one.

But he continued his argument quietly. ''I wouldn't have troubled you with any of this, Senator, not unless I believed it was serious. We're still waiting for more test results from Berkeley and Santa Fé. Even so, Dr. Bryce thinks it's serious, a very serious threat; and if Dr. Bryce thinks it's serious, I do too. Today he said something I've never heard him say before: 'Jim, we've got trouble.' And believe me, Senator, when Dr. Bryce says you've got trouble—well, by jiminy, you've got trouble.''

Again Reynard heard that voice in his head: *And now you are cursed from the ground . . . which has opened its mouth to receive your brother's blood. . . .* Aloud he muttered to himself, ''*Condor.*''

''I beg your pardon?'' asked Eldridge. ''I'm counting on you, Senator. I really am. Do you think we could meet and maybe talk about it further? See what we can do?''

''Give me your number,'' said Reynard abstractedly.

''Well, sure thing. Two-seven-one, four-three-three-four. But you'll call me soon?''

''What? Oh, yes. Yes, I'll call you tomorrow. Thank you very much for letting me know, Mr. . . .''

''Eldridge, Senator. Jim Eldridge.''

"Fine. Sure—Jim Eldridge. Thank you. And Rice, that's the name of the county medical examiner?"

"Bryce, sir."

"Right. Bryce with a 'B.' Very good, thank you. Good night."

There was anxiety on the other end of the line, a hesitant pause indicating that the senator hadn't been infused with the right degree of urgency. But without saying anything else, Reynard put down the receiver and sat tapping his teeth with the card on which he had written Jim Eldridge's number, deeply preoccupied. Surely, after all these years . . . surely it wasn't possible. Yet the words from the bible kept on sternly repeating themselves in his mind, and the name with which his deepest sin was identified kept on forming itself on his lips: "Condor."

It was polio wasn't it? A virulent kind of polio, just as they had told him. And the boy had contracted it near Conant's Acre. There was a terrifying irony of vengeance far greater than the usual course of human justice. Reynard felt as though he had been suddenly and belatedly judged by God—and found guilty.

Dick Elmwood poked his head in again. "I'm sorry to interrupt you, Senator, but Dean Farber is here. Do you want to come say hello?"

Reynard stared at him as though he didn't know who he was. Then he said, blurrily, "Whatever happened to Chiffon?"

Elmwood lowered his eyes. "You told me never to answer that question, Senator."

"Well, I didn't expect you to," said Reynard. "The question was rhetorical. But—there was no difficulty, was there?"

Elmwood said nothing. At last Reynard got up from his desk, and looked around and said, "Winter, that's all it is. Winter's coming. You can always tell, here in New Hampshire. You get a sense of fear."

"Yes, sir," said Dick Elmwood after a pause.

Much later Reynard excused himself from his meeting with Dean Farber and went upstairs to his bedroom. There, on his personal line, he put in a telephone call to a number in Anama City, West Florida. The number rang repeatedly, but Reynard was patient. He knew the man he was calling was very old and that he would probably take quite a time in getting to the phone.

At last a croaky voice said, "Hello? Ted Peale here."

"Ted? It's Reynard."

"Reynard? God almighty."

"Ted," said Reynard urgently, "I'm sorry to call you so late but I have to talk to you."

"Well, shoot. I was only having a drink out on the veranda before turning in. It's a real warm night—although I guess it isn't so warm up there where you are."

"Ted, can you get up to New Hampshire? I have to speak to you in person."

There was a sucking sound at the other end of the phone, as though Ted Peale had taken his dentures out. "Well, now," he said, "I really don't get around too much anymore. Thrombosis in the right leg. Doc says it could finish me off any time, without warning. Have to rest up a lot."

"Ted, it's about Condor. Something's happened."

"Condor? Come on, Reynard. I thought that was all dead and buried."

"So did I. But a young boy up here in Concord has contracted poliomyelitis."

There was a crackling silence. Then Peale said, "Aw, come on, Reynard. That's nothing to worry about. Kids are catching poliomyelitis nineteen to the dozen. That doesn't mean nothing."

"This isn't just ordinary poliomyelitis, Ted. I've just had the New Hampshire Commissioner for Health and

Welfare on the line. The Merrimack County medical examiner says it's something different, something special. Everybody's worried to hell about it.''

Ted Peale was silent for a while. Then he said, ''I really don't see how this could have anything to do with Condor, Reynard. I mean, we don't even know where that thing came down—or even if it came down at all.''

''It must have come down. You know that.''

''We never heard it come down.''

''You couldn't have heard anything in that storm,'' Reynard retorted.

''*I* would have heard it come down. Leastways I believe so.''

''I want you up here, Ted. I want to talk this over in a lot more detail.''

''I don't think I'm going to be able to make it, Reynard. I'd like to help out, really, but it's a long way to New Hampshire. Besides that, it's cold, and I'm not sure my heart's going to be able to take the cold, not at my time of life and the way it's been playing up lately.''

''Do you want me to send someone down to get you? I want you here, Ted.''

Another silence, longer this time. Then, ''I don't want to go back over those days, Reynard. Let sleeping dogs lie, that's what I say. We were all younger then. Different ideals. Different ways of looking at things. It was a different world then, Reynard. America wasn't the same as she is now. You know that, you're a politician. Things are different.''

''Ted—''

''I don't have anything useful to tell you, Reynard. I never saw it come down. Never heard it and never saw it. Maybe it overshot, who knows? It could have wound up anywhere from Turtle Town to Mast Yard forest.''

Reynard let out a sharp, exasperated breath. ''You heard

them on the radio though, didn't you? And Robert did too. You heard them saying they were in trouble.''

"That's what Robert told me. But who knows what he heard? And anyway, he's dead now. Dead these six years at least.''

"I know. Hilda wrote and told me.''

At last Ted Peale said, "There's no good in digging up old ghosts, Reynard. Best to leave them lie. Really. That's my advice. And I'm not coming up, not to New Hampshire. Lynn Haven is about the most I can manage these days.''

Reynard thought: he hasn't changed. Still the same old tight-minded Ted. Ignorant, prejudiced and as stubborn as a constipated mule. In those early days, in the 1940s, Ted's dogmatic approach to life had seemed like strength and certainty, especially at a time when everything was uncertain and no one seemed strong. But the passing years had shown him up for what he really was—a red-neck of the reddest hue. A tedious, small-minded, self-centered bigot.

"Ted," said Reynard, "I want you to think about what happened that night. I want you to go over the whole thing in your mind. I want you to *think*. Is there anything you might have left out? The slightest detail could help us. Is there anything you saw, or heard, or thought you might have seen?''

"Well, I'll think," said Ted. "I don't object to thinking.''

Reynard wished there were something more he could say, but there wasn't.

"Okay, Ted," he said. "I'm sorry I troubled you.''

"It's been over forty years," said Ted.

"Yes," Reynard concurred, although hearing Ted's voice made it feel much more immediate. Ted was one of those people who could make Reynard believe that time was merely a series of inconsequential pictures, only half-seen and less than half-understood. Goose-stepping marchers in Germany; the Japanese surrender on the *USS Missouri*; Ike and Dulles and the raging days of Nikita Khrushchev; Senator McCarthy and those "points of order"; Kent State and flowers in National Guard rifle barrels; LBJ hefting up his beagles by their ears; Watergate. Nothing more than a collection of images from some far-off land called America's Past.

All these things had happened since Condor. Some people had lived whole lifetimes since that night in 1944. Been born, grown up, married and died. But it had never gone away. Reynard had always harbored the terrible feeling that one day it would rise up from the ground again to haunt him. Every now and then he had woken up sweating, thinking of Condor and what he had done. And the worst thing was that he had never known what had happened to it, or where it was. It had vanished in that September storm, and nobody had ever discovered how, or where.

Ted had always maintained that it had lost its bearings and gone down in Winnipesaukee Lake. That was why the Winnipesaukee toxic-dump scandal had been so ironic. He had felt cursed, and he still felt cursed, even today. Condor had thrown a cloaklike shadow over his life from which he had never been able to escape.

Mind you, there was another memory. A sweeter, more fragile memory. These days it scarcely ever entered his conscious thoughts; he was almost afraid to allow it in the fear that, like a delicate piece of tapestry, it would grow faded from constant exposure.

It was because of that memory that he had first gone to Germany in the late 1930s, as a very young and very dashing young man. It was because of the memory that he had met some of the most high-ranking Nazis and grown attracted to their cause.

The memory was Ilse von Soltau, the Berlin actress with her blonde plaits and her gray eyes and her face as cold and Germanic and adamantly beautiful as a Rhine goddess. Reynard had met her when she was on tour in New York, then sailed on the *Berengaria* to see her in Germany. There had been dinners, parties, walks under the linden trees. There had been music, and lovemaking.

After his return to the United States, she had written to him saying she was expecting his baby. He had written back, pledging his love and begging her to come to America to join him. Three weeks later Hitler had invaded Poland and he had never heard from her again. But he had never forgotten her, not ever—even though he had no picture of her, nothing to remind him of the fiercest and the sweetest passion he had ever experienced.

Perhaps in Condor he had seen the possibility of his prewar romance returning to him, like the tearful ending to a Marlene Dietrich movie. But life wasn't like the movies, and Reynard had been left with nothing but regret.

He switched off the lights in the library and went back to the games room to rejoin Dean Farber and the others. A large board had been laid over the pool table and now it was spread with maps and diagrams and flowcharts. Dean Farber was an election specialist, probably the most efficient and technically experienced campaign manager Reynard had ever had. As Reynard walked into the room, his hands in his pockets, Dean Farber had just finished explaining how they were going to tackle the problem of white bitterness against the Democrats in Chicago.

Natalia Vanspronsen was sitting perched on the edge of a leather chesterfield on the far side of the room, wreathed in smoke from the small cigar she was lighting. She looked up and across at Reynard; the low-hung Tiffany lamp over the pool table shone through her pale pink blouse and softly revealed her bare breasts. Reynard eyed her boldly, then slowly and quite deliberately looked away.

Dean Farber raised his head too; the lamplight illuminated the brush of his blond, close-cropped hair. He had the milk-white face of a technocrat and the slightly protuberant eyes of a man who probably spends too much time in front of a PTS 6000.

"I have to tell you, Reynard, that on almost every count you have the positive edge. We've had some excellent responses from Democrats who voted for Carter in seventy-six but abstained in eighty because they didn't feel he had the eighty-four strength or the statesmanlike qualities they expected in a president. After 1984 people have had a stomachful of this economy, they see strength and statesmanlike quality in you. You're older, more experienced, more *comforting*. They know you've been involved in one or two scandals in the past, but at this distance in time they're not only prepared to forgive you, they're actually willing to see your involvement in those scandals as an asset. The voting public goes for a man who knows what he's doing, a man of the world."

Dean Farber looked around the table, one hand clasped on top of the other in a curiously boyish gesture. "That's the way I propose we present you in this campaign—as a politician of experience and acumen. As a candidate seasoned by time and experience, a man who not only cares for the welfare of the American people in every respect—financially, medically and socially—but a man strong enough and mature enough to deal with the Soviets nose to nose."

"You make me sound like an ancient relic," said Reynard dryly.

"Not at all, Senator," said Dean Farber. "Not in the slightest. An ancient relic you're certainly not. *You*, Senator—" and here he seized a sheet of paper with a dramatic flourish and unrolled it in front of everyone in the room. "*You, Senator, are A Man of the World.*"

Reynard looked for a long time at the blown-up photograph of himself with his hand resting possessively on his library globe. He had to admit it was one of the more flattering pictures he had seen lately, but he wondered whether the symbolism wasn't a little too obvious.

And he suddenly found himself thinking of a parody of the Nazi dictator. "Today . . . America. Tomorrow . . . *Die Welt*."

"I don't like it, Dean."

"I beg your pardon?" blinked Dean Farber.

"I said, I don't *like* it. Don't you understand English?"

Dean Farber glanced from left to right as though he were reassuring himself of where he was; that he was still in New Hampshire, still campaign manager for Reynard Kelly; that it was still 1988. Then he looked back at Reynard and said, "You will, Senator. Believe me, you will."

ELEVEN

Chiffon Trent opened one eye and tried to focus on that unfamiliar triangle of sunlight on the opposite wall. The sunlight never entered her bedroom, not first thing in the morning anyway. So maybe she had overslept; or perhaps she had had too much champagne and crashed out on the living-room sofa. She found it difficult to focus, and her brain felt like a large sponge filled with tepid water.

She opened the other eye. She was lying on a pillow, so she must be in bed. But why had she slept so late? She couldn't seem to remember what had happened the day before, or why she felt so weird. She hadn't been free-basing, had she? Piotr had brought over three ounces of really good coke yesterday (if it *was* yesterday), but she had never had a downer like this before.

She tried to turn over and discovered that she couldn't. Her wrists and ankles were tied up, not with ropes, but with bedsheets, or scarves. She struggled and twisted and managed to raise her head, but whoever had tied her up had made a professional job of it. Both of her wrists were knotted with red silk scarves to the brass head of the bed,

180

and presumably both of her ankles were similarly tied to the foot, although it was impossible for her to see them.

A feeling of deep, dark panic surged within her. Her fear was made all the more wrenching because she couldn't begin to remember how she had come to be here. She didn't scream; she uttered a queer, strangled sound, like a child too frightened to articulate. She struggled again, more desperately this time, but she succeeded only in tightening the scarves.

She lay still, letting her panic subside. She said to herself, think, think what happened. But her memory wouldn't, or couldn't, function. Jigsaws can't be put together without any pieces, and there were no pieces in her mind.

She began to feel chilled. It hadn't really struck her, since she always slept in the nude, but she was naked. Bound and naked in a room she had never seen before, with no memory of how she had gotten there. Maybe it had been the coke. Maybe her brain had dysfunctioned and she was lying in a mental hospital. But why would a mental hospital be furnished with this strange, tatty-rococo type of furniture—a white bureau with gilt handles and plastic curlicues? And there was another feeling too, one that Chiffon couldn't quite define. A feeling of being *elsewhere*—as though she weren't in New York, or Los Angeles, or any of the places she knew.

There was a different, elsewhere kind of sound outside her window: a distant swish of traffic, the sound of an airplane circling high up, a radio playing country-and-western.

If I should leave you in the rain in Klamath County . . .
If I should walk away and leave our love behind. . . ."

Chiffon suddenly thought of Reynard. She remembered Reynard saying they would have to stop seeing each other. She remembered the Palm Court at the Plaza, the piano music, the scraping violin. She remembered the face of

Reynard's henchmen as she walked away across the broad-patterned carpet. But that was all. After that, silence, invisibility, emptiness.

The triangle of sunlight moved across the wall. Chiffon closed her eyes, tried to get back inside herself, tried to persuade herself that she was really Chiffon Trent, not a dream or a character in a movie. If she were lost, or sick, or mad, then surely someone would come looking for her? Where was Piotr? He had been waiting for her in her hotel room. Surely he must have missed her. Where was Reynard? Where was anyone? She had been lying here for some time, and she hadn't seen or heard anything that suggested anyone else was in the building. Only that ceaseless noise of traffic and that endless twanging country and western music. But if there was music, *someone* must be listening to it.

More hours went by. The sun faded. The room grew colder, and the country and western music was switched off. Chiffon tried struggling at her bonds again, but now her wrists and ankles were so sore and swollen that she gave up. Her bladder was about to burst, but she hung on and refused to wet the bed because that would have meant she no longer had a chance of being released, of returning to her real life.

When it grew dark, she dozed; and when she dozed, the door of the room opened with a subtle clicking of lock tumblers. She became aware of someone standing by the bed only when a hand touched her, gently, like the hand of an alien touching a human for the first time.

She opened her eyes and said, "Wha—?" but a whispery voice immediately said, "Shh, don't get yourself excited."

She looked up, shivering. Her visitor was a large, bulky shouldered man in a light-gray, three-piece suit tailored for someone like a 1950s movie idol. He had chestnut-brown hair, waved in the style of the fifties, and a wide, bland face that was surprisingly young.

"Well, I'm sorry I couldn't get back to see you earlier." He smiled. "Unfortunately, I had an errand to run. You know errands. Always take longer than you think they're going to."

"Where the *hell* am I?" Chiffon demanded in a rush of fury. How could this man be so nonchalant when she had been tied up all day in this bedroom without a word of explanation, without food or water or even a chance to go to the bathroom? The whole situation was crazy, insulting and frightening, and this pale cinema specter needn't think he was going to get away with it.

"Calm down," said the man. He stood there regarding her idly. "You're lucky you're alive."

"What is that supposed to mean? Untie these damned knots, for beginners!"

"I *said*," the man repeated, quietly but insistently, "you're lucky to be alive. I mean, it's lucky for you that I recognized you. Otherwise, if you'd just been some dumb broad that somebody wanted disposed of. . . ."

Chiffon stared at him. "What are you talking about?" she demanded. "And will you please untie me? *Please.* I have to go to the bathroom."

"Well, I expect you do," said the man. He stared toward the window absentmindedly. "It's really only natural."

"You're crazy," said Chiffon. "Listen, I want you to untie me. I'll make it worth your while. I have money. I'll pay you anything you want. But please untie me."

The man smiled without looking at her. "Do you remember how you got here?" he asked.

She was silent for a moment. Then, in a hushed voice, she said, "No. I don't."

"It's the sodium pentathol," he told her. "It sometimes gives you a temporary loss of memory. But you'll remember.

Most of them don't, of course. Most of them never wake up. But it's lucky I recognized who you were.''

Chiffon said, ''I want you to tell me what's happened. Why am I here? What is this place? And who are you?''

The man took out a cigarette, tapped it on this thumbnail and lit it in a curiously old-fashioned way, with a match. He blew out the flame without taking the cigarette from his mouth. ''My name's Denzil Forbes,'' he said. ''You probably wouldn't have heard of me, not unless you were in at the dirty end of politics. But I come highly recommended. Jobs done, messages passed on, goods and services supplied, no questions asked, cash on the barrel head. *You*, you see—I was asked to deal with you. Senator Kelly's right-hand man asked me. Deal with this lady for me, he said, and make sure she's dealt with good. In other words, accidental demise, no embarrassing questions to be asked.''

Chiffon felt even colder. ''Reynard wanted you to *kill* me?'' she asked him. ''He actually hired you to—?''

Denzil Forbes smiled amiably. ''Lucky I recognized you. When they brought you in, I took one quick look at you and then I said, my gosh, Denzil—I was talking to myself, you understand—my gosh, Denzil, that is the well-known Chiffon Trent. I, uh, take a lot of interest in the movies, you understand. I always liked you a lot, especially in that made-for-TV movie—what was it, don't tell me. *Night Wind*. Was it *Night Wind*?''

Chiffon lowered her head back onto the pillow and she closed her eyes. She could hear Denzil Forbes talking as though he were on television, giving a chatty, unperturbed commentary on the way in which Reynard had tried to get rid of her. Actually have her *murdered* so she wouldn't cause him any more fuss.

''Fortunately for you, I just happened to be in New York. I could have been anywhere. Then the boys would have done what they were told to do and that would have been the end of it. But when Dick called us up from the Plaza, I decided to stay around, see what the boys brought in, and it was you, which was good luck for me, wasn't it? And for you, because you didn't wind up burning."

"Is that what you were going to do to me?"

"Aha," said Denzil Forbes. "That is what we have *already* done to you. Officially, of course. Look at this."

He walked around the bed, out of Chiffon's vision, and came back with a copy of the *New York Daily News*. On page three there was a photograph of a black, gutted sports car, and underneath, the headline, "Starlet Chiffon Trent Dies in Auto Blaze."

"You see that?" Denzil asked her, waving the paper in front of her nose. "You're dead. Charred to a crisp. But you know the way you used to drive. You never should have crossed that intersection on a red light, especially with that half-empty gas truck coming the other way. The truck driver was real lucky; he survived. In fact, he got scorched trying to pull you out of the wreck. He recognized your face at the window of the car, wasn't that fortunate? Here—listen to this: 'Right in front of my eyes that beautiful girl was burned beyond recognition. It was like watching it on television, except that I knew it was real.' "

Denzil Forbes tossed the paper aside. "Everybody has different realities. And reality can always be adjusted to suit your convenience. Wouldn't you say so? You're a movie actress; of course you know that. Makeup, trick camerawork. Stand-ins."

Chiffon said. "Who *was* that?"

"I'm sorry, who was who?"

"Who was that in my car?"

"Who *died*, you mean? Oh, nobody you need worry about. Just another girl that nobody had much use for. You know how it is. There are always plenty of girls around who know too much. It's not a very healthy thing, knowing too much. But now I'm beginning to sound like a gangster film.''

"Another girl died in my place?" insisted Chiffon.

"That's it. Right on the button."

"You burned another girl, *alive*?"

Denzil looked a little uncomfortable. "She was well-drugged. She wouldn't have felt anything. Besides, there was a whole lot of gasoline around. The heat, you know . . . you don't last for long in a situation like that."

Chiffon felt numb. She tried to relax but gradually the fragments of memory were beginning to come together in her mind—stray, multicolored pieces. And there were snatches of conversation too, and faces, and glimpses of street scenes. She could remember Piotr at the door, opening it and turning back to look at her and saying, "I'll see you at the Russian Tea Room . . ." and then opening the door again and turning back to look at her again, like a video loop that kept running over and over and over. "I'll see you at the Russian Tea Room."

Then almost immediately afterward, there was a knock at the door. Piotr coming back, she thought. He must have forgotten something. But then the door was slamming right back and two men in masks were jostling their way into the room and twisting her arm around and forcing her facedown on the bed.

Reynard, she thought. My God, what a bastard! Reynard, who said he loved me and cherished me and would have given me anything in the world. Reynard, who said he would die for me if I asked him to. Reynard actually took out a contract on my *life*!

Chiffon said, "I still have to go to the bathroom, you know."

"Yes," said Denzil. It was more of a question than a proper response. Chiffon wondered if he were tripping. His attention kept wandering in and out the doors of his eyes; it was as though he were leading three or four simultaneous and parallel lives. He seemed much more complicated when he looked, Denzil Forbes.

"I have to go," insisted Chiffon.

He went to the door and Chiffon heard him unlock it. There must have been someone standing right outside because no words were spoken, and the next thing Chiffon knew, someone was untying the scarves around her ankles. A woman, Chiffon guessed by the coolness and dexterity of the fingers. And when her wrists were untied, Chiffon looked up and saw that her guess had been right.

She was a blonde girl in her mid-twenties, with heavy makeup and a tight turquoise-blue mini dress. The kind of girl you saw only on Hollywood Boulevard, or Lexington Avenue in New York, or occasionally in small towns in Kansas—not at all a whore, but quite innocently anachronistic.

The girl lisped, "My name's Mae-Beth. I'll be taking care of you. Chiffon—that's a beautiful name. I always wanted a name like Chiffon. You know my mom was called Cleopatra? Isn't that a beautiful name? My grandfather got it from a book."

Mae-Beth wrapped the bedspread over Chiffon's shoulders and then helped her out the bedroom door and along the landing to the bathroom. The landing was bare, decorated with brown-and-yellow floral wallpaper that looked as though it hadn't been changed since 1955. A skylight at the far end was open, letting in the chill night air and the sound of traffic.

Chiffon said, "Where am I? I don't even know where I am."

Mae-Beth gave her an affectionate squeeze. "No place terrific, darling."

"But where? What city? This isn't New York, is it? Are we outside of New York? In White Plains?"

"I'm not s'posed to tell you nothing. But there was a

beer which made this place famous, and it kind of rhymes with . . . I don't know, bits. Or tits, I guess.''

Mae-Beth giggled. Chiffon stared at her and said, ''Milwaukee? We're in *Milwaukee*?''

''Don't say I told you. You're not supposed to know that.''

''But what am I doing in Milwaukee?'' protested Chiffon.

''The toilet's here,'' said Mae-Beth, opening the door. The bathoom was small, cold, white-tiled. ''I have to watch you. They don't want you going out the window.''

Chiffon was too relieved to worry. She sat and shivered while Mae-Beth primped in the cloudy mirror over the washbasin. Mae-Beth said, ''Denzil's in a funny kind of mood today, don't you think? He has his moods. But I think he likes you. He's a pretty good-hearted kind of guy usually. Very neat. That's what I like in a man. I'm not into that dirty-fingernail scene. Ugh.''

Chiffon asked, ''Who is he? I mean, what is he keeping me here for?''

''Oh, well, hasn't he told you? He's quite famous in his own field. He makes movies.''

''In Milwaukee?''

''I don't know. I never saw anything wrong with Milwaukee. Kind of blue-collar, I suppose. But you can't have everything.''

''I don't understand. Denzil makes movies? What kind of movies? For advertising or something?''

''He'll tell you,'' said Mae-Beth, pouting at herself. She turned to Chiffon and smiled. ''At least he likes you. God, if he didn't *like* you.''

''He burned a girl alive,'' said Chiffon.

''Well, that's right,'' agreed Mae-Beth.

''Doesn't that *scare* you?'' Chiffon asked.

''Of course it does. Denzil's a very scary person. But don't you think he has wonderful charisma? When you're around him, you know, it's the scariness that makes him so attractive. Then there's Billy Manzanetti. He's pretty scary too, but he's a professional, you know. And Eugene Rossi, he does the cameras and the lights."

"Two guys, that's all Denzil has?"

"Well, yes, I guess."

"How does he make movies with just two guys?" Chiffon wanted to know.

"They're only skin movies," said Mae-Beth. "They're not epics or anything like that."

"Skin movies? You have to be kidding. Denzil wants to put me in a skin movie? Who the hell does he think he is?"

"He was very pleased to get you. I mean, a skin movie with the name of Chiffon Trent on it has got to be worth a lot of money. He told me how pleased he was."

"I don't *believe* this," said Chiffon, but at that moment the bedroom door farther down the landing opened and Denzil appeared, smoking a cigarette.

"Aren't you girls through dolling yourselves up yet?" he asked. "I have to go see Dan Berman before nine."

Mae-Beth whispered to Chiffon, "For your own sake, please don't say nothing. For mine too. He'll flay me."

Chiffon glanced at her and saw at once that the girl meant it. She was tempted to push her away and make a run for it down the stairs, but she guessed that if Denzil had taken the precaution of tying her to the bed, he had probably made sure all the doors were locked. And where was she going to go at this time of night, in Milwaukee, with no clothes on? She would probably wind up raped.

"Come on, will you, for Pete's sake," urged Denzil. And so they came.

Piotr stepped out of the stage door of the O'Connor Theater, two French loaves under one arm and a scruffy script under the other. It was a cold, blustery day—only three days after Chiffon Trent had died in that auto accident on

93rd Street. Piotr felt depressed and a little drunk. He had finished half a bottle of Wodka Wyborowa with his breakfast that morning, not so much because Chiffon had died, but simply because it didn't seem to matter anymore whether he was drunk or sober, and so he might as well be drunk.

He hated the play he was rehearsing, and he particularly loathed his leading lady, who was French, smelled of Brie and never shaved her armpits. This morning's love scene between them had been a war of two overpowering cases of halitosis.

He crossed Sixth Avenue with the collar of his leather jacket turned up against the wind. Moscow could be perishing but only New York could scour your face with that particular mixture of grit, fumes and freezing-cold wind, along with that smell of bagels, subways and domestic cigars. He made his way along 36th Street, sniffling from time to time. His self-esteem had never been lower. After all the publicity he had received when he had first defected, and all the glamorous pictures that had appeared in *People* and *The National Enquirer* when he had dated Lois Brace, the actress wife of oil magnate George Brace III, to be walking unknown and hungover through Manhattan on a chilly Wednesday morning was far from uplifting.

He had almost reached the corner of Fifth Avenue when a shabby blue Buick Electra drew up beside him and one of the windows was rolled down. A sallow-faced man with heavy eyebrows and a gray hat leaned out the window and said, "Hey, Piotr Lissitzky, isn't it?"

Piotr ignored him and kept on walking. The Buick crept along beside him, its tires crushing discarded 7-Up cans, yogurt cartons and a scattering of broken pizza.

The man said, "I heard from your mother."

Piotr stopped where he was. "What do you want this time?" he asked sharply. This must be the sixth or seventh time the Russians had approached him with "messages from his family" or "kind greetings from the people of the

Soviet Socialist Republics.'' It was all pressure—anything
to prevent him from feeling he had broken his ties with his
mother country for good, anything to make him feel uncomfortable and alien. His defection had irritated the Russians a great deal, especially since he had by chance
defected when the Soviet ambassador had been making a
public announcement that freedom of movement and freedom of speech within the Soviet Union were ''cherished
and valued by all Russians.''

''I have a message from your mother, that's all,'' said
the man in the Buick.

Piotr glanced right and left in case he had to make a
quick escape. But since he was only twenty feet from Fifth
Avenue and there were plenty of people around, he didn't
feel he was in too much danger of a sudden abduction.

''What's the message?'' he asked.

''Get in the car. I'll tell you about it.''

''You can tell me right here and now.''

The man turned away and said something to the driver.
Then he leaned out the window again and said, ''Look,
it's personal. If you don't want to get in the car, let's talk
in that coffee shop right across the street. How about that?
We're not trying to kidnap you.''

Piotr hesitated, frowning across Fifth Avenue at the
Mucho Mocha. It looked pretty full; the man in the hat and
his unseen companion would have trouble if they tried to
start anything smart. There were two cops on the corner
too, talking to Con-Ed workers repairing cables. It seemed
to be safe enough.

''Okay,'' said Piotr. ''I'll meet you there.'' And with
that he walked away briskly, crossing Fifth Avenue and
pushing his way straight through the doors of the coffee
shop. He found a plastic-covered seat opposite the cashier,
disconcertingly close to a large rubber plant.

After a minute or two the man came in, carrying his hat
in his hands. He was almost bald but his remaining hairs

had been meticulously combed across his scalp. There was no sign of his companion. He sat down, unbuttoning the top button of his overcoat and setting his hat on the table.

"I must introduce myself," he said. His Russian accent was more pronounced now than it had been outside in the street. "Ilia Cerenkov. I work for Mr. Tamm, first deputy."

"What do you want?" Piotr asked aggressively.

"It is what *you* want that we must concern ourselves with."

"From you I want nothing," Piotr told him.

"Well, it's your mother," said Cerenkov. The waitress came across and he raised his hand. "Tea, please." Then he looked to Piotr and asked, "For two?"

"Coffee, black," said Piotr. He couldn't find a place to put his French bread so finally he propped it up in the one free chair, next to him. "I don't really think I'm going to believe anything you tell me," he said.

"This time I think you can," said Cerenkov. "Your mother sends you a message, or rather we are sending you a message on your mother's behalf. And you know we always do what we say."

"Go on."

Cerenkov took out a handkerchief and blew his nose. "The warmth after coming in from the cold," he explained. He folded the handkerchief, put it away, shifted his chair forward a little and said earnestly, "Your mother is about to be very ill."

"*About* to be?"

"Well, we both know that she is not particularly strong, don't we? Her heart has never been good. And if she is sent to Galic or Buj . . . it is a fairly safe assumption that she is about to be very ill."

"Why should she be sent to Galic or Buj? What has she done?"

"Ah, now, that's it," said Cerenkov. He rummaged around in one of his pockets and at last produced a crumpled letter. He held it up; on the front it was clearly marked for the attention of Piotr Lissitzky, c/o U.S. Embassy, Helsinki. "This is a letter from your mother to you, which fortunately was intercepted by a loyal Soviet citizen before it could reach its destination."

"Fortunately?" asked Piotr dully.

"Of course, because it contains all manner of lies and defamatory statements about the Soviet Union, and it would have been most unfortunate had they fallen into the hands of those who could and *would* have made propaganda out of them."

"Let me see that," snapped Piotr and tried to snatch the letter.

"Aha, I'm afraid not," said Cerenkov. "Because of its scurrilous content, this letter is now a prime exhibit in your mother's forthcoming trial. You know of course that it is an offense to defame the Soviet Union. You also know that the punishments can be severe."

Piotr said, "I don't believe any of this."

"That, of course, is your privilege," said Cerenkov. "You have, after all, washed your hands of your mother country, and washed your hands of your parents as well. I assure you, however, that your mother will be arrested and brought to trial. I can also assure you that the result of that trial is something of a foregone conclusion."

Cerenkov opened up the letter and squinted down at it as though he usually wore reading glasses. "Here," he said, "here she says that 'life in Moscow is worse than you can imagine . . . the food shortages are chronic, and we haven't tasted fresh meat in three weeks.' Well now, you and I both know what a slander that is, don't we, Piotr? Your mother is simply pandering to the prejudice of the Western media. What a story the American papers would make of this! 'Defected Actor's Mother Says She Is Starving in Moscow Food Shortage.' "

Piotr said, "My mother didn't write that letter. My

mother would never write anything like that. Whatever she is, whatever she was, she's not a fool."

Cerenkov tucked the letter back in his pocket and shrugged. "A state handwriting expert will conclusively prove the script is hers."

The waitress brought their tea and coffee. Piotr said, as an afterthought, "Please bring me a blueberry muffin."

"You have become very Americanized," Cerenkov remarked, sipping his tea.

"At least nobody threatens me here in America the way people are threatened in the Soviet Union."

"It is up to the people to support the state. The state is the people; anyone who slanders or betrays it slanders or betrays his fellow citizens. You don't think such a crime should be punished?"

"I want to know what this is all about," said Piotr. "Come on, Cerenkov, without the fudging and the phony evidence. The truth."

"The truth?" asked Cerenkov, raising his shaggy eyebrows. "Now you're asking for more than most people ever get in a lifetime. And over coffee you want it, in New York? But wait, I will tell you what we want; it is almost as important as the truth."

"Well?" asked Piotr.

Cerenkov leaned forward confidentially. "Something a little embarrassing is about to happen in Afghanistan. Well, I shouldn't tell you this, but it may help you to understand how serious we are. When this event occurs, many people in the West will, quite naturally, misunderstand the actions the Soviet Union will be obliged to take. We will, in all probability, get a very bad press."

"So what does that have to do with me?"

"It has everything to do with you. At the moment this event occurs, it will be announced that you have turned your back on the American way of life and that you are gladly and freely returning to live in the Soviet Union.

You will talk about the corrupt, misguided values of capitalism, and the laxness and immorality of the American people. You will divert media attention from Afghanistan and give us coverage that is entertaining, popular and supportive.''

Piotr poured sweetener into his coffee and stirred it. Cerenkov watched him, smiling.

"And, of course, if I don't agree . . ." said Piotr at last.

"We won't have any choice," nodded Cerenkov. "I'm sorry about her heart, but . . . as Turgenev said, 'Every man who prays, prays for a miracle.' Dear God, please grant me that twice two be not four!''

"Don't talk to me of God and prayers," said Piotr. "Not you. Not on this rat's errand. You're telling me to come back to the Soviet Union, and you're threatening to murder my mother if I don't. That's the beginning and the end of it, isn't it?''

"Do you want me to deny it?" asked Cerenkov.

"Should I call the police?" Piotr retorted.

An old, white-haired man came over and pointed to the chair on which Piotr's French bread was propped up. "Do you mind moving your groceries so an old man can sit down?" he asked.

"That seat is taken," said Cerenkov with a humorless smile.

"Two loaves of bread should occupy a seat?''

"Somebody's joining us," said Piotr as kindly as he could.

The old man shuffled off, grumbling. Cerenkov said, "You have plenty of time to think this over. But we would like to know within a day or so whether you're willing in principle to come back to the Soviet Union. You will be treated like a hero, you know—especially if you tell the Western media that you are tired of capitalism, tired of the emptiness of American greed and that you long for red-blooded Soviet life. You were brave to leave, we know that. But you will be even braver if you admit your mistake and come back.''

Piotr said, ''I'm not coming back.''

''I don't think that's very reasonable. Do you?''

''Cerenkov, you know New York. Would you go back if you had a choice?''

Cerenkov shrugged, smiled, stirred his tea. ''The question doesn't arise. But none of this will help your mother. And I'm afraid they're serious about it. If you don't come back, they will hold a trial and almost certainly find her guilty.''

Piotr covered his eyes with his hand and was silent for a long time. Cerenkov placidly sat and watched him, occasionally clearing his throat and once saying to a woman, ''I'm sorry. That seat's occupied.''

Piotr looked up. ''Do you think there's any chance of a deal?'' he asked.

''A *deal*? I shouldn't think so. What kind of a deal?''

''Well, the thing is, I have some quite interesting information. If you'd lay off my mother, and lay off me, maybe I could tell you.''

''Well . . . that doesn't sound like a very attractive proposition,'' said Cerenkov. ''I'm supposed to bring you back alive. You know? Big game hunt.''

Piotr said, ''You recall that I used to date Chiffon Trent? That actress who died three days ago?''

''Yes, that was very tragic,'' said Cerenkov. ''You have my condolences. But from what the newspapers said, she was always an impetuous driver. Not a girl to stop for red lights.''

''She was the mistress of Senator Reynard Kelly,'' said Piotr. ''When she was dating me, she was two-timing him. And she told me *all* about him. Very interesting information, some of it. And one piece of information in particular that was . . . well, dynamite.''

"Hmm."

"Come on, Cerenkov, don't be coy. You know as well as I do that Reynard Kelly stands every chance of being the next president of the United States . . . and if you had a really scandalous piece of inside information about him, wouldn't that help your masters in Moscow? Wouldn't that be worth something? Worth destroying that letter of yours maybe?"

"I don't think I have the authority. . . ."

Piotr beckoned Cerenkov to move closer. Cerenkov hesitated at first but eventually leaned his elbow on the table and bent his heavy head forward.

Piotr said, "If I tell you I have information that links Senator Reynard Kelly directly with Adolf Hitler . . . now, what would you think about that?"

Cerenkov sat back. "You're bluffing."

Piotr shook his head.

Cerenkov folded his arms. "I still say you're bluffing."

"Why should I bluff?" asked Piotr. "During the war Reynard Kelly had direct dealings with the Nazis. He told Chiffon all about it, I don't know why. He told her he'd never said a word about it to anyone else. Maybe he told her because he felt guilty. Maybe he was just trying to impress her. But whatever the reason, he told her, and *she* told me."

Cerenkov leaned back and eyed Piotr coldly. "I still don't believe you. Why should I believe you?"

"There were plenty of American politicians who didn't want to fight against the Germans, weren't there?"

"*Da.*"

"And there were plenty of American industrialists who didn't approve of the war?"

"*Da.*"

"So . . . Reynard Kelly was a young politician in those days, in the nineteen forties, with a father who had made a fortune in trading with Europe, particularly with Krupps,

Junkers and Horst . . . and Reynard Kelly was brought up with the sons and daughters of German industrialists and politicians. Don't you think perhaps it was natural for him to take quite kindly to Adolf Hitler and to consider that Germany made a better ally for the United States than Britain? Squalid, arrogant, cantankerous Britain? And Hitler all the time being so reasonable? And not only reasonable, but successful too.''

Cerenkov beckoned the waitress to bring more tea. "How do you know so much about this?" he asked Piotr. "All these things about Krupps and Junkers?"

"When Chiffon told me, I went to the public library and looked it up.''

"Why?''

"Because . . . I don't know. I suppose I was interested, and I didn't have anything better to do. And I suppose, in a way, I wanted to know something more about this man whose mistress I was taking to bed.''

"Jealous?''

"There's no point in that now, is there? She's dead.''

"And you're grieving?'' asked Cerenkov. "You don't look like a man who's grieving.''

"I don't know what to think,'' said Piotr. "Now I'm not so sure what I felt about her. I don't know whether I loved her or not.''

"No woman should be so unlucky as to have you for a lover,'' commented Cerenkov. "But still, tell me about this connection between Senator Kelly and Adolf Hitler.''

"I can't tell you any more until you guarantee that my mother won't be arrested,'' said Piotr. "And you must also guarantee not to make any more attempts to get me back to the Soviet Union and that from now on you will leave me alone.''

Cerenkov thought for a moment and then slowly shook his head. "I can't make you any guarantees like that.''

"Then you don't get the information.''

"Well . . . I shall certainly have to talk to my superiors."

"Then talk to your superiors. You know where to find me."

"You say Reynard Kelly had a direct connection with Adolf Hitler?"

"Direct," nodded Piotr. "They spoke to each other several times just before the war, and Chiffon said that Reynard was quite sentimental about him."

Cerenkov sat silent, drumming his fingers on the table so that his teacup rattled in its saucer. "It's hard to believe, this story of yours. I could have thought of five or six American politicians who might have sympathized with Hitler . . . but not one of them would have been a Democrat, and I certainly wouldn't have counted Reynard Kelly's name among them."

"Times change, Comrade Cerenkov, and people with them."

"Obviously. You too have changed."

"The women of famous men always know secrets," said Piotr. "I learned that in Hollywood. I also learned that the more secrets you know, the more influence you have. But most of the secrets I learned in Hollywood were simply who was going to bed with whom. Who was smoking dope, who was homosexual, who had money and who didn't. But the secret Chiffon Trent told me about Senator Reynard Kelly, that is a truly influential secret. An American politician making deals with the Nazis?"

"He made deals?" asked Cerenkov quickly.

Piotr shook his head. "I'm not going to say any more until you guarantee my mother's safety and my right to stay in the United States unmolested."

Cerenkov sipped his tea, then took out his handkerchief and dabbed at his lips. "Let me call you at home," he said.

"Of course. You know the number. I expect you have the phone tapped too."

Cerenkov gave a noncommittal wave of his hand. "You know how things are, comrade."

Piotr picked up his French bread and his script and stood up. "I'm not your comrade any longer, comrade. You ought to remember that. I'll wait to hear from you. *Da skorigh vstyrichi.*"

He left the Mucho Mocha and walked out into the street. Suddenly he realized that he liked New York very much, whether he were famous or not. Suddenly he realized that he would give up anything, and betray almost anyone, not to have to go back to the Soviet Union.

He began to walk uptown, against the wind. Cerenkov stood outside the coffee shop, blowing his nose and watching him go.

TWELVE

The epidemic broke out abruptly and unpredictably, and within the space of four hours on Wednesday afternoon Edmond had driven around to seven fatalities among his own patients and learned from Oscar and one of the county paramedics that other local doctors had attended five more.

Officially, of course, it still wasn't an epidemic. Just eleven unrelated domestic deaths caused by apparent asphyxiation. But on the three occasions when Edmond and Oscar met each other during the course of the afternoon, they exchanged looks of mutual understanding and arranged to meet again later to discuss their fears in private.

"You heard from Bryce?" Edmond asked Oscar as they stood outside a small house on North Curtisville Road, watching three sheeted figures as they were wheeled out to a waiting ambulance. Oscar wiped his forehead with the back of his arm and shook his head.

"Doesn't anybody understand what's *happening* here?" Edmond asked fifty minutes later at a tidy little house on Frost Road.

"It's not corelated yet," said Oscar with audible irony. "No matter how many people die, it isn't an epidemic until all their deaths have been corelated. Even the Black Death wasn't anything but twenty-five million individual fatalities. Or it might have been if the New Hampshire Health and Welfare Department had had anything to do with it.''

The deaths at Frost Road—the fifth, sixth and seventh of the day—were the first to make Edmond feel frightened. Suddenly something was happening beyond his control. And not only his patients were at high risk: *he* was too.

The family had still been lying on the sofa when he went into the house: a young couple in their mid-thirties, their eight-year-old daughter between them. The television had been tuned to "General Hospital." They could have been asleep, all of them, except that they were dead. A neighbor had looked in with a promised recipe for apple pandowdy and found them there.

"I saw them only this morning," she had said. "They were fine then, right as rain."

Edmond had given the neighbor an injection of Sabin-type vaccine, which was probably useless, a placebo for both of them. But it was all he could think of. His real fears now were that the virus would begin to spread quickly out of control and that he would contract it himself. He had already seen how inexorably it brought on paralysis of the respiratory system; the thought of struggling for breath and knowing as he struggled that his condition was incurable was a medical nightmare. He remembered slicing Arabelle's throat and couldn't keep the image out of his mind: the scarlet blood, the desperate struggle for breath. Perhaps this epidemic was God's revenge on him—so he would have to die just as Arabelle had died, gasping for air.

He called Christy at home and asked her if she had heard anything on the news about several deaths in Merrimack County, but she said no. There was nothing in the *Concord Herald* either, nor on WKXL. He began to feel that he and Oscar were fighting a disease that didn't even exist—a dream disease that haunted failed pediatricians and overworked pathologists, punishing them for having dared to set themselves up as medical gods.

"I had a call from Malcolm," Christy told him. "He said he might come up later this evening."

"I thought the party wasn't until Friday. Why does he have to come up tonight?"

"Because he's your brother. Besides, he's getting a ride from a friend of his who lives in Portland."

"I didn't think Malcolm had any friends."

"Darling, he's your *brother*."

"That's how I know what a total bastard he is."

He met with Oscar about eight o'clock that evening at the Cat'N'Fiddle on Manchester Street. He was drowning his fatigue and sterilizing his imaginary contagions in vodka and tonic, wondering whether he ought to send Christy to stay with friends in New York until the epidemic was under control. Or at least until his birthday party was over. Oscar walked into the bar with his coat slung over his shoulder, saying hi to everyone he knew. Then he pulled out a stool, and sat down next to Edmond and beckoned to the barkeep to bring him his usual—three fingers of Jack Daniel's on the rocks.

"Well," said Edmond.

"Well?" asked Oscar. "They can't say we didn't warn them."

"Still no word from Bryce?"

"Nothing. I tried to discuss it with him this afternoon after the first two fatalities—that couple at Bow Mills. But all he could say was that he was trying to get some action out of Eldridge. Well, you know what *that's* like, trying to get some action out of Eldridge. You might just as well try to get a rhinoceros to dance the fandango."

"Did you receive the autopsy report on the Osmans?"

"That was what I wanted to see you about," said

Oscar. His drink was served and he drank it in four larynx-bobbing gulps. He banged the glass on the counter and ordered another. "And another one here for my friend, the quack," he told the barkeep. "Vodka, forget the tonic."

Edmond said, "It's serious, isn't it? I mean, for no apparent reason, it seems to have broken out all over."

"Which is not at all usual in epidemics of poliomyelitis," said Oscar. "Poliomyelitis is generally transmitted hand to mouth. But this bug . . . well, it seems to have spread all over the locality without any particular pattern. In some cases there might have been contact, but in others there wasn't the slightest."

The barkeep set up two more drinks; Edmond called him back and asked him to top his glass with tonic. He was apprehensive about the epidemic and frightened of catching the virus himself, but he wasn't yet ready to drink himself into total unconsciousness.

Oscar opened a brown manila envelope and produced a sheaf of blurrily Xeroxed autopsy protocals. He licked his thumb and sorted through them until he found the page he wanted. "Here—take a look at this. It was impossible to tell whether Mr. Osman died as a result of asphyxiation by noxious fumes from smoldering furniture, from plain burning or from any other cause—simply because his remains were too severely charred. But when we come to *Mrs.* Osman, whose body was protected from the worst of the flames by a fallen closet door, we see that although she did in fact die from asphyxia, she most certainly had no trace in her lungs of smoke, carbon deposits or any of the chemical agents you would usually expect to find in the lungs of someone who had died in a house fire. So the conclusion is that she was dead *before* the fire took hold, or even before it started. She had already stopped breathing before the bedroom filled with smoke—hence no smoke in the lungs."

"Spinal fluid?" asked Edmond.

"Hard to tell exactly. It was pretty well simmered, to tell the truth. But there *were* signs of excess cells and a higher level of protein than normal, both of them symptoms of poliomyelitis."

"Any signs of the virus itself?"

"This is another reason I wanted to see you. We have a virus, yes, and it seems to have had a similar effect on the intercostal muscles as the virus that killed young Michael Osman. But it's changed quite considerably, not only in shape but also in its ability to dictate a faster rate of replication to the host cell. It seems to become successively more virulent, quite unlike other viruses. And if it continues replicating itself at this accelerated rate. . . ."

Edmond sat back and ran his hand through his hair. He could see himself and Oscar, captives in the dark, mottled mirror behind the bar. "What we *have* to know is where this virus originated," he said, "where it came from and why it broke out so suddenly, here in Concord and at this time of year. Young Michael Osman was the first, right? We have to discover where he picked it up and how it was passed on by the Osman family."

"We're going to have to quarantine the area," said Oscar. "There's no question about it. As soon as we've finished up here, I'll go call Dr. Bryce again. And if he still doesn't react, then damn it, I'll call up Eldridge personally. *And* the county commissioner. *And* the governor, if I have to."

"I'll call Harold Bunyan again," said Edmond. "That's about all the clout I've got."

"Well . . . I'm not so sure about good old H.B.," said Oscar.

"He was responsive when you showed him the Osman autopsy report?"

"Sure, but you know . . . I had the feeling he wasn't particularly inclined to do you any more favors."

"You didn't tell me that earlier."

"There didn't seem to be any need to. Not before this epidemic. You know—he wasn't exactly negative. He did promise to keep a watch on the situation. But he's not too keen on upsetting Bryce, especially now with elections in the wind. And he's definitely not too keen on having any kind of run-in with Eldridge."

Edmond drained his glass. "I see," he said. "We have the first signs of a wildfire epidemic on our hands and everybody's getting jittery about elections. Maybe I should call the mayor."

"The mayor will talk to Harold Bunyan, and Harold Bunyan will tell him that he's keeping a watch on the situation and not to panic. The mayor will then unquestionably decide to sit on his hands and smile. The winter tourist season is about to start. The last thing the mayor wants is to scare off half the tourist trade."

"Jesus, this sounds like *Jaws*," said Edmond. "A couple of guys discover a shark and nobody will admit it's there, let alone dangerous, just in case it hurts the tourist trade. We have exactly the same situation here in Concord with this damned virus."

"You've got to face it," Oscar told him. "We're just the dogfaces in the field, the medical infantry. And no general likes to take advice from his infantrymen. Not when it comes to strategy."

"Then let's talk to the media," said Edmond. "Let's talk to the newspapers and the television people. Let's tell them we think there's an epidemic on the way. Then Eldridge will *have* to act."

"I'm not sure," said Oscar. He waved to the barkeep to bring him another drink. "Give me twenty-four hours to see what I can get out of Bryce myself. The point is, if we go straight to the media, we're going to antagonize everybody: Bryce, Eldridge, the mayor. And Harold Bunyan will *definitely* disown us. They'll spend a lot of time and energy trying to show that we're overreacting, that we're just a couple of local troublemakers. In fact, they'll probably spend more time doing that than they will in coping with the epidemic.''

Edmond pressed his fingertips to his forehead. He had the dull beginnings of a headache. "Twenty-four hours, huh?" he asked.

"Well, sooner if I can, of course," Oscar replied.

"Oscar, I saw seven people dead today in four hours alone. You saw a dozen. And if you're sure about this virus becoming more virulent each time it replicates itself. . . ."

"I'm as sure as I can be. At least Dr. Corning is as sure as he can be. He still has a whole lot of work to do on it. But he says the virus shows an incredibly unusual twist in the way that its ribonucleic acid dictates the synthesis of new viral proteins. Instead of the RNA exactly replicating itself time after time, it progressively alters to improve itself, so that with every step it's much more active, much more infective and much more resistant to heat or solvents.''

"So it's rare, and it's highly contagious, and it's becoming more dangerous every time somebody passes it on. And you don't want to tell the media?"

"Not yet, E.C. What Dr. Corning is saying puts him so far out on a virological limb that Eldridge could easily produce another expert virologist who could legitimately say it's all wild-eyed nonsense and that no virus can possibly alter its genome. He could even claim that Dr. Corning must have cracked—all of which would hold us up even longer. E.C., listen, I'm as wound up about this as you are, but the name of the game is politics, and we're not going to get ourselves any official help unless we play the situation *their* way.''

Edmond said, "Meanwhile another twelve of my patients die. Maybe more.''

Oscar laid his hand on his shoulder. "I know it. But there's no other way. I've upset Bryce too many times already, and this time it has to be done by the book. The chain of command, that's one of Bryce's favorite phrases. 'Follow the chain of command, Dr. Ford.' "

"I still think we ought to bring in the media," said Edmond. "God, at least I'd feel as though we were *doing* something!"

"You go to the media, E.C.," said Oscar in his harshest voice, "and they'll ruin you. I mean that. They'll dump everything on you—everything—including the blame for the epidemic. You won't ever practice again."

"Oscar, for Christ's sake, people's *lives* are at stake here. People are going to die."

"Don't you think I know that? But there's nothing else we can do."

Edmond ordered another drink. He was halfway drunk already; he didn't think another one would make much difference. The barkeep winked at him and said, "Problems, huh?"

"Some," said Oscar. "Including a bartender who doesn't seem to be able to mind his own business."

"Just trying to be sociable," said the barkeep.

"Sociability is a disease," Oscar retorted. "Set me up another drink."

Edmond stirred the ice in his glass. He was beginning to feel very alone, very defeated.

"Do any other doctors feel the way I do?" he asked Oscar. "Dr. Redman had two patients die today, didn't he? And how about Dr. Krauss?"

"Well, they're being cautious," said Oscar. "They agree that we seem to have a form of poliomyelitis on our hands, but until they've seen the autopsy reports, they're not prepared to commit themselves too far."

"Not prepared to commit themselves, huh?"

"E.C., this whole epidemic could fizzle out into nothing. The virus could well be so fierce that it burns itself out after a couple of days."

"You don't believe that, do you?"

"No, not personally. But it's the way Dr. Redman and Dr. Krauss feel about it, and Dr. Clements too. They don't want to start flapping around like headless chickens until they can be sure of their ground. We've sent tissue and spinal-fluid samples from every one of their fatalities down to Dr. Corning. All we can do is pray that he's quick."

Edmond paused, then said, "I've been trying to analyze the way this infection has been spreading—at least among my own patients—and let's face it; I have the lion's share so far. But, you know, you're right—there doesn't seem to be any *pattern* to it. None of the people who died today were acquainted with the Osmans, although one of the families, the Perrins, were quite good friends of the Mayers, whose son Bernie was Michael Osman's best pal."

"You've checked on the Mayers in the past twenty-four hours?"

"I checked them about an hour ago, just before I left the hospital. They're all fine, fit and healthy."

"Maybe Bernie was simply a carrier," suggested Oscar. "It's possible that some people might naturally have an immunity to this virus, and Bernie could be one of them. It happens with poliomyelitis; children can be vaccinated and not catch polio themselves but quite freely pass it on to others."

"I don't know," said Edmond. "I'm still going to leave all the avenues open. But both Bernie and Michael were vaccinated with a standard Salk preparation at approximately the same age. If it didn't protect Michael, I can't on the face of it see any particular reason it should have protected Bernie. It might just have been chance. This virus seems to be so virulent, though, that I don't see how

Bernie could have contracted it or carried it without show-ing at least *some* symptoms.''

"Well, maybe you're right," said Oscar. "But Dr. Corning's still waiting for the full tests on Michael's virus samples; and I don't suppose we'll see the results of Mrs. Osman's virus tests for three or four days, and that's being optimistic. We won't know for sure until then.''

"There must be *some* connection, damn it," said Edmond. "And where did the damn thing come from in the first place? We don't have any known environmental health risks here. A few swamps around Turtle Pond, I suppose, and septic-tank sewerage in most of the houses. But noth-ing that could have been a breeding-ground for an unusual kind of poliomyelitis virus. Nothing like *this*. I mean, if Dr. Corning's right and this thing has a way of progres-sively altering the reproductive information passed on by its RNA—I mean, come on, Oscar. We're talking about a very rare bird here, not to mention a dangerous one.''

Oscar looked down at his whiskey, thought for a mo-ment and then tipped it down his throat. "Listen," he said, "I shouldn't be telling you this. I promised Dr. Corning I'd keep it to myself. But he has a strong private opinion about this virus, based on all the years he's been analyzing and studying viruses like polio, his particular speciality. *He* thinks—and I know this sounds crazy—but *he* thinks this virus was artificially bred.''

"He thinks *what*?"

"He thinks the virus was artificially bred. Genetically engineered. Developed by some scientist someplace for the specific purpose of infecting large numbers of people at an accelerating rate. Germ warfare, if that's what you want to call it.''

Edmond stared at Oscar's boiled-red face in disbelief. "What are you trying to tell me?" he asked. "That this is a *Russian* invasion or something? Or some kind of a leak from a germ-warfare factory?"

"I'm telling you what Dr. Corning thinks, that's all. And you know Dr. Corning—the world's driest and most unimaginative virologist."

"We don't *have* any germ-warfare centers near East Concord, do we?" asked Edmond. "There's that military area off Greeley Street in Sugar Ball . . . but they're not doing anything like that *there,* are they?"

"I don't think so," said Oscar. "But listen, E.C., you mustn't repeat any of this. Dr. Corning won't know for sure until he's run about a week's worth of tests, minimum. He promised to let me know as soon as he comes up with anything. Meanwhile, the best we can do is work on Bryce and Eldridge, convince them we're looking at an epidemic and see if we can get Concord quarantined. The whole of Merrimack County, if possible."

Edmond sat for a long time in silence. Then he said, "This could be it, couldn't it? It's quite within the bounds of possibility. This could be the start of World War Three."

Oscar looked at him seriously. "Not with a bang, but with a whimper, huh?"

"Are you afraid?" asked Edmond.

"Afraid?"

"Are you afraid of catching it? You've seen how quickly it kills, how fast it suffocates. You and me, we could pick it up at any time, just like that. We may have contracted it already."

Oscar beckoned to the barkeep for another drink. "You haven't lost your professional nerve, have you, E.C.?"

"I don't know. Maybe. I'm just beginning to think that if I have to die, I'd at least like to know what it was that killed me."

Just then the beeper in Oscar's pocket sounded off. He left his drink, went to the telephone at the end of the bar and dialed the county coroner's office.

When he came back, he said tersely, "Another family,

this one out on Sawmill Road near St. Paul's school. Five
of them—father, mother, three daughters. Looks like a
long, long night.''

"In that case," said Edmond, "let *me* call Bryce."

Oscar finished his drink and slapped bills on the bar.
"All right," he said. "But for the love of this world in
which we live, don't upset him."

"Take care, Oscar," said Edmond. He meant it.

Bernie spent the evening at home carefully putting together
a new plastic model kit of a Turbo Mustang. The model
had cost him ten dollars, partly financed by his pocket
money and partly financed by his sale at school of his
''secret obedience potion''—six glass phials of a clear
liquid, guaranteed when dropped into your parents' coffee
or cocktails to make them obey your demands to let you
stay up as late as you want and to eat as many cookies as
take your fancy. Each phial, eighty cents.

At first he had thought of keeping the phials. But the
truth was that he didn't understand why Michael had hidden them in the garage wall, and the more he took them
out and studied them, the more they irritated him. They
didn't even *do* anything. They were nothing more than
phials of water in a leather case. If they were filled up with
magic potion, that would be something. At least if they
were filled up with magic potion, he could get some
money for them. And that was how he had thought of
selling them; he had succeeded in disposing of the entire
six phials for four dollars and eighty cents.

His interest in finding out what had happened to Michael had met another setback when he had cycled down to
Conant's Acre on Monday after school and found that the
fence had been recently wound around with barbed wire.
Now it was almost impossible for anyone to walk across
the field, no matter how innocently. He had stood by the
wire, looking across at the woods. Well, suppose Michael

had managed to get as far as the woods and blaze his mark there? He couldn't have gone very much farther. Michael had never equaled Bernie's craft in tracking and hunting; he had never been as courageous as Bernie. A good sidekick, Michael. A good Tonto to Bernie's Lone Ranger. But that was all. The mark Bernie had seen on the tree was probably the only mark Michael had been brave enough to cut.

He carefully glued the suspension of his model Mustang together, his tongue protruding slightly. He heard the telephone ring downstairs and his mother answer it. The instructions said: "Glue wheel hub (23a) to wheel drum (27b) and leave to dry before affixing to axle (10)." His mother's footsteps came upstairs and his bedroom door opened.

"Bernie."

He looked up. In the light from the desk lamp, his mother's face looked oddly pale.

"Bernie, something terrible's happened."

He didn't move, the model car still held in his hands. Since a grown-up's idea of terrible wasn't always *his* idea of terrible, he waited to hear what it was that had brought his mother upstairs looking so white. Once, in tears, she had told him his Uncle Walter had died, and he had never been able to understand her grief. Uncle Walter, who smelled of tobacco and garlic and spat in the street? Why had his mother cried? And now she was saying that something terrible had happened.

"Jane Wyman died this afternoon. And her parents. They're all dead, the whole family."

Bernie stared at her and didn't realize that he was as white and cold as she was. "What?" he asked, but he wasn't conscious of asking it. Jane Wyman was one of his classmates; she sat two rows in front of him, two seats to the left. He had seen her only this morning, with the sun shining through the window and lighting up her bright auburn hair. Jane Wyman, one of the few girls he actually liked. But *dead*?

"They all caught some kind of disease. That's what Mrs. Downing told me. They found them all on the couch in front of the television. Oh, Bernie, I'm so sorry."

And it was then, straightaway, with the plastic parts of his car still in his hand, that Bernie connected the glass phials of "secret obedience potion" with the way in which Michael had died, and now Jane. Jane had bought one of his "secret obedience potions" the day before yesterday, Monday. And she had promised that she would try out the potion on her father when he came home from his business trip to Cleveland on Wednesday. She had wanted her father to let her stay up all evening and have a late dinner. But instead she had died, and her parents had died with her.

Bernie put down the model. His mother said, "Would you like something to drink? Your father brought root beer. Maybe some root beer and a pizza?"

"No," he said. Then, remembering his manners. "No, thanks, Mom."

"I hope you're not too upset, honey. But I had to tell you. I didn't want you to go to school tomorrow and find out by accident. I didn't want you to have a shock. Are you sure you don't want a root beer? Your father brought it specially for you, wasn't that kind?"

Talking brought the color back to Mrs. Mayer's cheeks. After all, she hadn't actually *known* the Wymans, and since Bernie didn't seem to be very upset, she felt a little easier.

Bernie sat and looked at the unfinished model. How could he finish it now—now that he knew how much it had really cost? The water in those phials must have been polluted: Michael had drunk some of it and died; then Jane Wyman had dripped it into her parents' food and they had

died too; and she had probably tasted it as well. All dead.
God! What was he going to do? He had sold every one of
those six phials at school; it meant that five other families
were still at risk. For all he knew, they might already be
dead. It might be too late to call and save them.

His mother left the room, leaving his door slightly ajar.
He stared into space. If I don't tell someone that all those
glass phials are poison, if I don't warn them, then think of
all the people who could die. Dennis Murphy, Clark Kounas,
Theresa Natti. . . . In his mind's eye he could picture his
classmates already white-faced and laid out in caskets,
their white-faced families all around them, a company of
corpses. God, I have to warn them! But then they're going
to know it was me who killed the Wyman family. I killed
an entire family. I *killed* them. For eighty cents I killed
Jane Wyman and her mother and father. I'll be locked up
in jail *forever*. Maybe they'll even send me to the chair.

He sat there holding his plastic construction kit, tears
welling in his eyes. He felt so rotten, so mean and selfish.
Those stupid glass phials. That stupid Michael. Because of
him, Bernie had ruined his whole life. Slowly, agonizingly,
he crushed the model Mustang to pieces, snapping the
suspension, twisting the roof and bending the windshield.

Then he buried his face in his hands and sobbed until his
throat ached.

Edmond crossed the parking lot, climbed into his Camaro
and started up the engine. But he didn't drive off immediately.
Instead he sat where he was, his head lowered, feeling
emotionally and physically shattered. Doctors should be
inured to death, he thought to himself: old ladies taken by
cancer, middle-aged men stricken by heart disease. But
this epidemic seemed to be more significant. It was a
challenge not only to his medical competence, but to his
ability to survive as a practicing doctor. He had only just
managed to survive the consequences of Arabelle's death.

Now it looked as though he were faced with a crisis even more difficult, even more challenging to his personal and professional honor.

He picked up the mobile phone and called his receptionist at the Merrimack Clinic.

"Lara? Dr. Chandler here. Any more emergencies?"

"Not so far, Doctor. A couple of minors. Sore throats, chills and one accidentally ingested Smurf."

"Can Dr. Colgan cope? I'd like to take a couple of hours off."

"Dr. Colgan's out at Pembroke. But I guess Dr. Wang can manage. Can I call you if things get too busy?"

"Just squeeze me a couple of hours, will you?"

A short silence. Then a quiet, sympathetic, "Okay." Lara knew what her doctors had to go through each and every day. She also knew that Edmond had attended seven deaths that afternoon, seven people he had liked and cared for. Even the hardest of doctors found death difficult. They were frightened of it not so much because of the pain and bereavement it brought, but because—unless it were dignified and natural—it represented failure, their personal failure. Death was a constant reminder that the medical profession was neither magic nor infallible.

Edmond drove home. There was a single soft light shining in the living-room window, and upstairs he saw Christy's shadow move across the blind. He wearily eased himself out of the car and walked to the front door, jingling his keys. The vodka had done nothing but give him a pounding hangover and a feeling of nausea in the pit of his stomach. He opened the door and called "Christy?"

There was no answer at first. He called "Christy?" again and began to mount the stairs. She appeared on the stairs landing, flushed, her hair awry, tying up the belt of her turquoise silk negligée. She had an extraordinary expression on her face that he had never seen before: fright, almost. Her eyes were wide and yet she didn't seem to be looking directly at him.

"Christy?" he asked her.

"You came back so early," she said, flustered. "I wasn't expecting you back till nine or ten."

"Is everything all right?"

"Well, sure, of course everything's all right. I was just taking a shower, that's all. I thought you were a burglar or something. You scared me."

He came a little way farther up the stairs. Christy stayed where she was, by the half-opened bedroom door.

"Has anybody else died since you called me?" she asked.

"I haven't heard. Death seems to have allowed me the evening off. I had a few drinks with Oscar, and now my head's thumping like a Cuban nightclub. I'm just going to get myself a couple of Alka-Seltzers."

"Well, no," said Christy. "Why don't you go downstairs and stretch out on the couch? I'll bring them down to you."

He came up to the landing and stood over her. She seemed ridiculously agitated, off balanced and upset. He took hold of her shoulders and through the thin, slippery silk of the negligée, he could feel her tremble.

"What's the matter? Are you *cold*?" he asked her.

"It's nothing. I don't know what it is. Just let me get you the Alka-Seltzer. I'll be okay. Go on, go downstairs and put your feet up."

"Christy, I'm quite capable of fixing my own Alka-Seltzer. Remember I'm a doctor."

"For once let me pamper you," she said. She was trying to be coaxing, trying to sound warm and sweet, but the words came out brittle and erratic.

Edmond glanced toward the half-opened bedroom door. The nausea and the weariness rose up inside him again, unbidden, and he could hardly identify the question he asked Christy next as his own.

"Is there someone in the bedroom?"

Christy didn't answer; she didn't have to. But for the first time she raised her head and looked him directly in the eyes; for the first time there was a challenge in her face, as well as guilt.

Edmond pushed her aside and went toward the bedroom. She shrilled *"Edmond!"* and for a second he hesitated.

"Edmond," she said, her voice quavering, "please don't."

"I think I have to," he told her.

She turned her face away. "You couldn't expect me to do anything else," she said. "Not after everything you've done to me. Not after all the women *you've* had."

He looked at the door. "Well, well," he said. "I thought all that was over and done with. I thought we'd left that kind of thinking behind in New York. It looks like I was being naive, doesn't it?"

"Edmond, don't go in there. Just take yourself out for a drive—ten minutes, half an hour. Go around the block. When you come back, he won't be here. You can just pretend it never happened."

"A total stranger just screwed my wife, in my bed, and I'm supposed to pretend it never happened? Just pretend? Christy, what the *hell* is going on inside your head?"

"Edmond—"

But his anger and his sickness were unstoppable now, and he threw back the bedroom door so hard it collided with the edge of the bureau and bounced back again. The bedroom was softly lamp-lit. The white woven bedspread was twisted and crumpled, the pillows in disarray. There was a smell of heat and perfume and sex in the air. Sitting up in bed, his attempt at a smile distorted by fear and tension, yet also strangely relieved, was Edmond's younger brother Malcolm—the one man in the entire world whom Edmond would never be able to forgive Christy for taking as a lover.

Malcolm said, "I guess you don't want me to come to your party now. Well, *c'est la vie*." He emitted a nervous chuckle and pulled up the sheets beneath his shaggy armpits.

Edmond stood for a long time staring at Malcolm in utter disbelief. Christy stood behind him, looking from one brother to the other, twisting the belt of her negligée around and around in her hands.

"Aren't you going to *say* something?" asked Malcolm. "Even if it's nothing more than 'Get the hell out of my bed?' "

Edmond opened his mouth, but at first no words came out. Then he said hoarsely, "How long has this been going on?"

"Oh, come *on* now," said Malcolm. "Of all the clichés. Don't we deserve better than that?"

"I want to know," insisted Edmond.

"So that you can judge how hard to hit me?" Malcolm asked. "Go on, hit me. Get it over with."

But Christy whispered, "Since New York."

Edmond stared at her. "Since New York? Since New *York*?"

"Since Arabelle, if you want to know the truth. Since the very beginning of you and Arabelle. You thought I didn't know, didn't you? All those late-night business meetings, all those medical conventions. Five conventions in a single month? And the whole time you were walking around as though there were flowers twined in your hair and birds singing around the top of your head."

She paused for a moment, and then she looked with great gentleness toward Malcolm and said, "Malcolm helped me through it. He didn't push me. He genuinely helped me. If it hadn't been for Malcolm, I don't think I would have survived. You never thought about anything *I* was going through, did you? Not once. But Malcolm helped me to stay alive at a time when you were slowly killing me.''

"At the expense of his own marriage, I suppose," said Edmond. "Not exactly the behavior of a great moralist."

"You know all about Dolores," Malcolm bit back. "Drunken, hysterical, falling to pieces."

"Not worth saving then?" asked Edmond coldly. "Trash, garbage. Unfit for a debonair man like you." The atmosphere in the bedroom was charged with the overwhelming voltage of sibling rivalry. Christy moved back almost as though she expected a devastating explosion of power to leap from one brother to the other. She had never seen two men look at each other with nothing on their faces but the all-consuming need to destroy. At that moment both men frightened her beyond excitement, beyond desire. Smoldering violence hummed and crackled between them.

Christy said, "Please, Edmond. This isn't the way."

"You don't want to face up to what you've done, is that it?" Edmond demanded. "You screwed my brother. God help you, you screwed my repulsive fat toad of a brother! And you can stand there and tell me this isn't the way. Well, the way is crystal clear to me, my dear. That way is divorce, on the grounds of your fornication with something that should have been aborted at eleven weeks. Of course there's still the small matter of Dolores, but what do either of you care about Dolores?"

"What did you ever care about *me*?" Christy screamed at him.

"I cared the whole damned world about you once, before you started judging my ethics. I made too much money in Manhattan, remember?"

"It wasn't the money you made, Edmond; it was the way you made it."

"Arabelle never cared about that."

"She should have. She might still be alive today."

Edmond swung out at Christy before he realized what he was doing. But she must have half-expected him to hit her because she instinctively flinched away; his hand caught her shoulder blade, sending her stumbling back against the bedroom chair.

"Don't you touch her again, you quack!" shouted Malcolm. He tugged back the bedcovers, jumping naked out of the bed in protective rage.

Edmond raised a hand to him, palm foward, warningly. "Get back, Malcolm. I don't want to have to knock you down."

"You bastard."

Edmond lowered his hand and turned away from his brother, his teeth clenched in a huge effort at self-control. He should have ripped Malcolm to pieces. He should have screamed and roared and torn the whole bedroom apart. He should have smashed mirrors, splattered makeup around, wrecked everything. Jesus Christ, Malcolm and Christy had been fornicating since *New York*. Three years of clandestine trysts, three years in which his brother had been anointing his wife's vagina with just as much enthusiasm as he himself had. The thought of it turned his stomach. He had always disliked Malcolm, even as a small boy. And as he had grown older, he had found Malcolm increasingly self-satisfied and obnoxious, an opinionated boor without a single original idea between one bloated temple and the other.

What made it worse, he had always found Malcolm physically repulsive. Malcolm had inherited the weakest of their parents' features: his mother's plumpness, his father's lack of grace. At grade school his classmates had called him Porpoise, and Edmond had led the taunting.

Maybe after all these years, this was Malcolm's revenge. Edmond, irrationally or not, had always believed in destiny, or at least in divine justice. Maybe his marriage to Christy had never been the strong and satisfying bond he had thought it to be. Maybe it had been nothing more than a sub-plot in some Shakespearean tragedy: Edmond and Christy, or What You Will, in which the despised younger brother cuckolds his older sibling in order to pay him back for years of childhood misery.

His marriage may not have been flourishing anymore; it may have been flawed, and at times uncertain. But as far as he was concerned, even after Arabelle it had been one of his major hopes for the furture. If only he had known, these past three years, how empty that hope was. It had been eaten away from the inside; only the shell remained.

Christy said, "Believe me, Edmond, I didn't want things to turn out like this. I tried so hard."

"Put some clothes on," Edmond told Malcolm. "You look disgusting."

"Not to Christy, old buddy."

"Christy never had too much taste," Edmond snapped.

"Oh, I see. Is that why she stuck with you?"

"Right now I don't know why the hell she stuck with me. Now get your clothes on and get the hell out of here."

Malcolm sat down on the edge of the bed. Edmond looked away from the thick black hair growing out of the cleft of his buttocks. Puffing a little, Malcolm pulled on a pair of Hawaiian-style undershorts, all sunsets and coconut palms, and a pair of pale-blue knit trousers.

"I have to tell you," he said, rummaging around under the bed for his socks, "that I'm not leaving unless I'm sure Christy's going to be safe. I'm telling you that now."

Christy said, "Edmond, please. Come downstairs. Let's at least try to talk about it."

"What the hell is there to talk about? You've been screwing my brother. There's nothing to talk about."

"Now let's be reasonable, Eddie," Malcolm began. But he didn't get the chance to finish his sentence. Edmond stalked forward, angry and jealous beyond control, seized his hair and punched him hard in the face. Malcolm grunted and fell backward onto the bed, his nose spattering blood on the white bedspread.

"Edmond, for God's sake!" screamed Christy.

"Shut up!" Edmond screeched back at her. His voice was so high and tight that he felt as though all the flesh were stripped from the inside of his throat. "I'm leaving. You can keep him. Keep him, fuck him all you like! Do whatever the hell you want!"

He stalked across to the bureau. On the bed, Malcolm was holding his nose and mumbling. Edmond opened the top two drawers, took out his spare watch, his insurance certificates, his cuff links. Then, losing the last shreds of patience and self-discipline that had been holding him together, he heaved out all the drawers, one by one, and threw them across the room, scattering handkerchiefs, underwear, socks and shirts.

"Edmond! You're a stupid, insensitive *bastard*!" Malcolm shouted, blood spraying out of his nose and down his chest.

Edmond looked around the room. He and Christy had shared love here, or so he had thought; shared emotions; shared hopes. But he would never come back here again. Whatever he and Christy might have had together—and it must have been something—it was gone for good.

He walked out of the room with the suddenness of a robot and ran quickly down the stairs, across the hall and out the front door. Before he knew it, he was speeding back toward Concord. Without thinking, he checked his pulse rate. Too fast, too angry, too crazy. But Christy with Malcolm? He felt like driving straight into the Merrimack River. Doctor Drowns in Death Plunge. But at least it would blot out the thought of that fat white belly on top of Christy all these years. At least he wouldn't have to think about Christy's fingers interlaced with that thick black body hair.

As he passed the Fort Eddy cloverleaf, there was a

discreet beep from his mobile phone. He ignored it until it beeped again; then he picked it up and said, "Dr. Chandler here."

"Dr. Chandler? This is Lara. You've had another emergency call, out on Hazen Drive. The Flanders family, number eleven-ninety-six."

Edmond didn't answer at first and Lara said, "Dr. Chandler? Can you hear me?"

"I hear you. I'll be on my way."

"Are you all right, Dr. Chandler? I called your home first and Mrs. Chandler said she didn't know where you were."

"That's right, Lara," said Edmond. "She doesn't."

Very much later that evening, only twenty minutes before midnight, Edmond sat in his room at the Brick Tower Motor Inn on South Main Street and telephoned Dr. Bryce at home. The Brick Tower's restaurant closed at 8:15, but the captain had brought him a club sandwich, nuts and two cans of beer. In one corner of the room the television flickered silently.

The phone rang for a long time before Dr. Bryce answered, and when he did, he sounded sleepy and irritable.

"Dr. Bryce? This is Edmond Chandler, from the Merrimack Clinic."

"Kind of late, isn't it, Dr. Chandler? Can't you call me back in the morning?"

"I'm sorry, sir, I'm afraid not. It's about this polio virus. I've been wroking with Oscar Ford, and it really seems as though—"

"I'm sorry, Dr. Chandler," Dr. Bryce interrupted, "but I've done everything necessary and everything possible as far as this particular incident is concerned, and I don't want to discuss it any further, not right now."

"What about Mr. Eldridge? What did he say?"

"Mr. Eldridge made a full report to the Health and

Welfare Department, to the governor's office and to Senator Reynard Kelly. He expressed some concern at the outbreak, just as I did, and he made specific requests for a county-wide quarantine and certain other measures, including vaccination and blood tests.''

"And?"

"I told you I don't want to discuss it right now," Dr. Bryce insisted. "Now, if you don't mind—"

"But what are you going to *do* about it?" Edmond demanded. "You have discussed it, you have agreed it's a problem, but what are you actually going to *do*?"

"For the time being, nothing," Dr. Bryce replied. "Watch and wait."

"Listen," said Edmond. "I have just come back from eleven-ninety-six Hazen Drive. The Flanders family, four of them, were patients of mine. They're all dead, and the indications are that they were killed by a virus."

"I'm very sorry to hear that," said Dr. Bryce. "Believe me, I'm doing everything I can."

"It's not enough, Dr. Bryce," Edmond insisted. "We've lost sixteen people—men, women and children—in less than a day. Tomorrow it's going to get worse. By the end of the week, half of New Hampshire could be wiped out."

"I think you're exaggerating a little, don't you, Dr. Chandler? I'm sure we can keep this business under control."

"It's not under control now. Haven't you seen the autopsy reports? The virus grows stronger every time it replicates."

"That's simply Dr. Corning's personal opinion."

"Well, what's *your* personal opinion?" Edmond demanded. "That we should let half the population suffocate to death because of paralyzed respiratory muscles? Is that what you think we should do?"

"Dr. Chandler, it's late and I'm tired and I have no wish to discuss this now. I'm doing as much as I can, but my hands are tied by the Department of Safety and the Department of Health and Welfare, not to mention the wishes of Senator Reynard Kelly.''

"Oh, yes? And what does Senator Reynard Kelly have to say about it?''

Dr. Bryce paused and then said quietly and in an unusually confiding tone, ''Mr. Eldridge spoke to Senator Kelly on three occasions. Each time Senator Kelly made it clear that the interests of New Hampshire could best be served by maintaining a low profile on this virus. Contain it, identify it and eradicate it, without making people hysterical.''

''And what do you think?'' asked Edmond carefully.

''What do *I* think? In this particular case, at this particular time, I'm reserving my judgment.''

''Dr. Bryce—''

''Listen, Dr. Chandler. I know you, and I know something about your record. If I were you, just at this moment I'd back off. There's a lot more to this outbreak than meets the eye.''

''Like what?'' Edmond demanded.

But Dr. Bryce refused to be interrogated. ''I've told you everything I'm going to for now. My advice is to back off. I'm not insensitive to what Dr. Ford has been saying, and I appreciate that this outbreak could get very much worse. But we're talking about political reality here as well as medicine, and one goes in hand with the other.''

''So I've learned,'' said Edmond bitterly.

''Well, you've learned something then,'' said Dr. Bryce and hung up.

Edmond didn't sleep that night. He was still looking out the window at the Boston & Maine Railroad yard when the sky began to leak away its darkness, like ink washed out of a cloth, and daylight appeared. At 6:30 he showered and shaved; by seven o'clock he was sitting in the inn's restaurant, waiting for his breakfast and reading the *Concord Journal*.

On page three, on the left-hand side, there was a story about "Hazen Drive Family Found Dead." Edmond read it twice, then folded up the newspaper and drank his coffee.

THIRTEEN

It was snowing in Raggarön when they arrived—thick, blurry clots of white that whirled and danced and then instantly dissolved into the sea. On their left, the Baltic was dark and green-gray, with visibility down to less than a hundred feet. Humphrey felt as though they were close to Valhalla, the dominion of the Norse gods—or at least close to the palace of the Snow Queen. In the past three days he had completely lost touch with reality. Derbyshire seemed like a memory. He had already missed his flight home by seventy-two hours, and he expected that by now his sister would have called the police. Unless, of course, Bill Bennett had somehow arranged for him to disappear, with no questions asked. And from what he had seen of Bill Bennett, that wouldn't have surprised him in the slightest.

He had asked him only yesterday morning, as they sat over a breakfast of ham and beer at a farmhouse near Edebo, "What if we *never* find him? What are we going to do then?"

But Bill had only smiled and cut himself more Emmenthal cheese, as though this whole expedition were nothing more than a game he had made up for his own amusement.

They had missed Klaus Hermann at Lingslätö. At first Bill hadn't believed Angelika and doubted that Hermann had ever been there, but after a thorough search of the small fishing cottage Angelika had said was a Soviet "safe house," they had found traces of cigarette ash and the white plastic cap of a tube of cream that Hermann used to ease the irritation of piles. Humphrey had waited outside while Bill searched the cottage. It had been a misty, mystical-seeming morning, and the ocean had beaten a drab message against the shore. He had wondered whether it was worth trying to make a run for it, but then he had imagined himself stumbling across the rocks, panting in his heavy overcoat, and Bill Bennett slowly raising his .38 and felling him. As a consequence, he had remained where he was, his hands clasped together in their gray knitted gloves, his polished shoes scuffed and dull after walking across the beach, accepting his age and his weakness with as much dignity as he could muster.

Bill had emerged from the cottage and called, "He's been here and gone. Angelika says he might be trying to get away farther up the coast."

Behind him Angelika Rangström had looked white, exhausted and cold. But Bill had taken her arm and led her back toward the car as warmly and as quickly as though she were a willing friend. Humphrey had followed them at a distance but close enough not to alert Bill's suspicions. It was possible that an opportunity for escape would present itself sooner or later, and when it did, he wanted it to be a complete surprise. At the moment, he very much wanted Bill to trust him.

They had driven northwest at first, on 76. Then they had turned sharp east to the small fishing port of Hargshamn, then northwest again to Osthammär. Bill had driven down every single side street, through every narrow lane and into every muddy farmyard, asking questions in Swedish, handing out cigarettes and money, smiling, chatting, laying his arm around the shoulders of plump, blonde fishwives and grizzled, toothless farmers. And always the same question: "Have you seen two men, one old and white-haired, one younger?" And all the time the weather had blown northwesterly from Gavleborgs Lán and grown colder.

Bill had assured Humphrey that Hermann was cornered, that the Swedish coastguard would be watching every passable port. It was just a question of scouring the local countryside and finding out where he was hiding. Angelika had sat in the back of the car humming tunes by Abba; Humphrey had stared at the endlessly wooded landscape. It had been a dream. Trees; wooden houses; dark, serrated horizons. And now, as they drove into Raggarön, the snow.

They drew up outside a wooden fishing cottage with a carved veranda. Bill said, "Stay here," and twisted around in his seat to pick up his hat in the back. Now that the windshield wipers had stopped, snow began to collect on the glass and Humphrey felt like they were being entombed alive. Angelika lit a cigarette and smoked it with her usual exaggerated gestures.

When Bill opened the car door to step out, the wind blew in with sharp ferocity. Humphrey and Angelika watched him struggle across to the fishing cottage, his head bowed against the blizzard. As usual, he had remembered to take the ignition keys with him. Humphrey knew it was possible to "hot-wire" a car, but he didn't have the faintest idea of how to do it himself. The few snowflakes Bill had admitted into the interior of the car melted on the vinyl upholstery.

Angelika said, "We are chasing a wild goose, don't you think?"

Humphrey shrugged.

"All this for one old man," she said. "And of what use will he be when we find him?"

"Do you think we actually will?"

"Your friend Mr. Bennett seems determined to."

"Determination isn't everything."

"No," said Angelika, "but he is also very ruthless . . . in a courteous sort of way."

"Well, that's the American Secret Service for you. Always polite. But too trigger-happy for my liking."

"I haven't forgotten that he killed my friend," said Angelika.

Humphrey looked at her and then sympathetically patted her hand. "I know. That was a dreadful thing to do. Completely unnecessary, not called for at all. Don't you worry, he's going to have to account for that one day soon."

There was a lengthy period of silence. The snow softly built up on the car's windows until they could no longer see out. Angelika crushed out her cigarette and began to rummage in her purse.

"Do you have a penknife?" she asked. "I left some loose thread in my purse and now it's all tangled up."

Humphrey reached into his inside pocket and produced a razor blade in a chrome holder. "This will probably do, won't it? I use it for cutting fishing line."

"Thank you," she said.

They waited for nearly five minutes more. Then the door of the car abruptly opened and Bill swung himself into the driver's seat, his hat clotted with white, his shoulders soaking.

"Didn't even ask me inside," he complained, peeling off his gloves and taking out his keys. "I guess he thought the weather was pretty mild for the time of year."

"Any news?" asked Humphrey.

Bill started up the engine. "As it happens, yes. Three hours ago two strangers came past in a blue Volvo and drove out to the far side of the island. There's a kind of an inlet there apparently."

"Three hours ago?" asked Humphrey. "Most probably they've been taken off by now if there was a boat waiting for them. We must have lost them."

"Let's go take a look, shall we?" Bill suggested and swung the Grand Prix sideways across the street, the tires whinnying and skating on the freshly fallen snow. "In this weather it would have been pretty difficult to bring a boat in through the islands, especially with the coastguard at Ellan on the alert. You never know your luck."

They drove between tightly shuttered weatherboard cottages, most of them deserted. When they reached the end of the road, where an outcropping of rock reared out of the sea, Bill cut the engine and the Grand Prix rolled to a silent stop. "Come on," he said, "let's get out and take a look around on foot."

"Not me," said Angelika. "I am too tired."

Bill hesitated for a second and then said, "Okay. But no funny business, you got it? You stay here and you keep quiet."

"Ich verstande, mein führer," Angelika nodded sarcastically.

Humphrey said, "I'd really rather not go either. This cold is far too much for me."

"You're coming and that's all there is to it," Bill told him. "You're the only one of us who can independently put the finger on Hermann, remember? I can't trust Fru Rangström here, much as I'd like to."

Humphrey started to protest, but Angelika touched his arm and said, "Go. It is necessary, you know that."

"Very well," said Humphrey. "But I don't like any of this one bit, and I don't mind saying so."

He heaved himself out of the car and into the snow. He almost slid and fell but he managed awkwardly to seize hold of the open car door and regain his balance. All the same, he painfully wrenched his shoulder.

"I'm not cut out for this kind of thing, you know," he told Bill, blinking against the snowflakes.

"Don't give me that. You're a pro," said Bill. "Come on, let's take a look past those rocks."

The northwest wind blew the teeming snow out toward the Baltic, where it was swallowed up. The ocean itself was so dark that it was almost invisible; unless Humphrey had heard the relentless splashing of waves against the rocks, he would almost have thought this was the edge of the world and there was nothing out there but blackness, hopelessly lost souls and wind-sculptured memorials to long-forgotten scenes of Nordic carnage.

"This way," Bill ordered. "And will you *please* try to keep it as silent as possible?"

"Well, I'll do my best," said Humphrey, climbing up a large stratified slab. "Oh, damn it. I've scraped my hand."

They made their way uphill and a little way inland, eventually managing to reach a large rock that overhung the inlet. Bill peered over, shielding his eyes against the snow with his hand. Almost immediately he tugged out his gun and waved at Humphrey to keep well back.

"Are they there?" panted Humphrey.

"Get down," Bill instructed him irritably. "If they see you, they'll run. For Christ's sake, get your head down. Your *head*."

Humphrey crouched uncomfortably on the rock. Bill lay flat on the ground and shouldered his way back to the edge of the rock, then motioned Humphrey forward with his gun.

"There," said Bill. "*Now* tell me that Hermann isn't important."

Humphrey strained his eyes against the gloom and the dancing snow. On the shoreline, distinguishable only by a faint and broken pattern of foam, he could just make out two men, both of them huddled with cold and fatigue. On the left, parked at an angle, was a bright blue Volvo, its dimmers still shining. The snow slanted over the scene like an endlessly falling curtain and gave it a peculiar air of theatricality.

"Look toward the inlet," said Bill. "Now—what can you see there?"

"In the sea, you mean?"

"That's right. Look, you can just make it out."

Humphrey took out his handkerchief and wiped the moisture from his face. Then he stared out to sea and at last managed to make out an extraordinary dark shape five or six hundred feet from the shoreline; it looked like the fin of a whale. Between this fin and the shoreline a small black-rubber dinghy was bobbing up and down on the water, making its way slowly toward the rocks.

"The wind's against them. That's good," said Bill. He cocked his .38 and lifted the barrel as though preparing for some heavy-duty shooting.

"You're not going to kill him," Humphrey insisted.

"We'll have to see what happens."

"I shall report you, you know, if you start firing indiscriminately."

"Humphrey," said Bill, "I'm *never* indiscriminate."

"Well, that's what *you* say, but—"

"*Never*. You understand me?"

Humphrey looked away, the snow stinging his cheeks. He felt annoyed and resentful but at the same time curiously excited. This was the first time in his life in which he had been involved in anything real. It was hard to believe that he was here—on this snowy night in eastern Sweden—lying on the ground beside a man with a loaded revolver. It was even harder to believe that he and Bill might actually succeed in capturing the men huddled on the shore.

"Submarine, I suppose," said Humphrey, nodding toward the distant fin.

"That's right. Soviet *Serpuchov*-class diesel vessel. Just like the Russians to name a submarine after a city that lies two hundred miles inland in any direction."

Despite his dislike of Bill's methods, Humphrey was extremely reluctant to see Hermann taken off by dinghy and transmitted safely back by submarine to the Soviet Union. Hermann, a Nazi war criminal, had been working against the West for over forty years, helping to build up Russia's stocks of noxious and infectious chemicals for use in war. Humphrey could still remember his father sitting in that brown brocade armchair by the parlor window at No. 49 Cavendish Street, talking about the gas attacks on the Ypres salient in 1915. "That gas shriveled everything it touched, both man and vegetation. I heard my old school chum Ronald screaming, even with a burned-out throat and incinerated lungs."

Bill said, "Follow me. But please, Humphrey, keep quiet. We don't want to alert them before we have to."

Quickly, moving crabwise, knees bent and head lowered, Bill led the way down the left-hand side of the rocks and then skirted around until he was no more than twenty or thirty feet from the two men standing on the shore. Humphrey came after him with as much agility as he could manage, but he barked his shins twice on the rocks and tore his trousers, and by the time he reached the inlet's bumpy beach, he felt sore and bruised, ready to give up.

From their new vantage point, the rubber dinghy appeared closer to shore, although it was making slow progress against the wind, and the Russian submarine's fin seemed to loom far higher over the snow-spotted ocean. Bill said, "Is that Hermann? The one on the left? For Christ's sake, Humphrey, look at him. Tell me that's Hermann."

Humphrey cleared his throat. "It's very hard to be sure."

"*Look* at him! Is that Hermann, or isn't it?"

Humphrey knew. He knew it was Hermann. He could tell by the shape of the head; he could tell by the stance. He had memorized so many pictures of the man—sketches by prisoners who had been in and out of Herbstwald, photographs by Jewish resistance workers and portraits made by students in Heidelberg before the war. Each of these pictures had helped him to form in his mind a holographic image of what Hermann actually looked like, and apart from underestimating Hermann's height and the exaggerated squareness of his jaw, that image had been startlingly accurate.

"Yes," said Humphrey. "I believe that's Hermann."

Bill lifted his revolver in both hands, but before he aimed it, he said, "If you push me, or touch me, or try to put me off my shot, then by God, I'm going to shoot you too. So be warned."

The snow pelted down on them. Bill held the revolver steady, squinting along the sights for what seemed like forever. Then he fired twice in quick succession, deafeningly loud shots. A man dropped from the rubber dinghy into the sea, quickly followed by another.

Hermann and his Russian bodyguard crouched immediately. Bill backed away, still doubled up, and detoured around the rocks until he was close to the shoreline on Humphrey's left, completely concealed by darkness and snow. Humphrey felt lonely and confused, and slowly he began to retreat, making sure to keep his head out of the firing line. God, he thought, a holiday in Sweden. What a holiday.

He waited for three or four minutes, huddled behind a jutting rock. Then he heard Bill calling, "Hermann! Klaus Hermann! My name's Bennett. I'm an agent of the United States government. I know who you are. Come out of there with your hands on top of your head. Otherwise you've got five and then I start shooting."

There was a long silence before a German-accented voice called back. "You're making a mistake, you know. That stupid Englishman!"

"He recognized you, Hermann," Bill called back. "He's an expert. Picking out Nazis is his job."

"I deny completely that I am Klaus Hermann."

"Angelika seems to disagree with you."

"Angelika?"

"We have her here, Hermann. She's sitting in the car, waiting for you. Better give yourself up, don't you think? That is, if you want to see her again."

"You're mistaken," Hermann repeated. His voice was off-key with cold and exhaustion. "You have the wrong fellow."

Just then there was a loud metallic sound from out at sea. Sparkling lights winked amidst the snow, and the next thing Humphrey knew, a burst of heavy machine-gun fire from the Russian submarine was howling and rattling around the rocks and moaning off into the night.

"Don't panic!" Bill called over to him. "They can't bring the submarine any closer in to shore. They're firing blind."

"It doesn't matter *how* they're firing if they hit us," Humphrey protested.

Without a word Bill raised himself up and fired a single shot into the darkness. Humphrey heard the light crack of a retaliatory pistol, then another. Bill fired a second time and then there was silence. He strained forward, wiping the snow from his eyes so he could see clearly. At last he called, "I got him, I think. I can see Hermann; he's down by the shore."

Humphrey waited for a moment and then clambered over the rocks to join Bill. "He may not be Hermann," he said.

"Of course he's Hermann, for God's sake."

"Well, if you're so sure about it, why did you want me to come along?"

Bill deftly reloaded his .38 and didn't answer. Apart from the gun in his hand, he was kneeling in exactly the pose as one of the adoring Magi.

Humphrey said, "I suppose you're going to kill him now."

"It depends."

"Well, I wash my hands of all this."

"Down," said Bill.

Humphrey immediately dropped his head. As he did so, a searchlight beam from the submarine's gun swept across the shoreline and probed up into the rocks.

It was then that they heard Hermann crying, *"Na pomahsch! Na pomahsch! Eedyeeti syuda!"*

Bill gave Humphrey a broad, self-satisfied wink. "He's calling for help. Sad, isn't it? They can't get near him."

Humphrey cautiously raised his head. "He's not trying to swim for it, is he?"

Bill looked quickly back toward the shoreline. "I hope not. Jesus, that water's freezing. An old guy like him wouldn't last longer than two or three minutes."

But sure enough, Hermann was already knee-deep in the icy surf and wading out toward the Russian submarine. He was still wearing his heavy overcoat and his arms were raised in supplication. The searchlight from the submarine's fin abruptly lanced over and illuminated him, his white hair shining like a crown.

From the submarine an amplified voice bellowed, *"Stoy! Stoy! Ahpahsnah!"*

Bill said to Humphrey, "Wait here," and vaulted over the rocks. Humphrey could see his silhouette against the floodlight as he ran across the beach, shoulders hunkered down, and straight into the water. The Russians didn't fire at him—but then of course they were afraid of hitting

Hermann. They kept their searchlight on both of them, however, as Bill plunged waist-deep through the waves and tackled Hermann just as he was about to launch himself into a breast stroke.

"Na pomahsch!" shrieked Hermann. Bill seized his coat collar and dragged him around and back toward the shore. There was a brief flurry of spray and fists as Hermann struck out at his assailant, but then Bill twisted the old man's arm behind his back and half-shoved, half-carried him back to the rocks.

Humphrey stayed where he was. He didn't want the Russians picking *him* off out of pique. After a minute or two, however, Bill and Hermann came panting and struggling around the outcropping and collapsed side by side, each shivering and soaked.

"Well, well, it's you again," said Hermann. "I might have guessed. I learned in the war that the English could never be trusted to do as they are told."

"You're lucky you weren't killed," Humphrey retorted petulantly. "If this fellow hadn't shot you, you certainly would have drowned."

"I see," said Hermann. His face was luminously white and his teeth were chattering. "I'm supposed to thank you both for saving my life."

"You're supposed to keep quiet and do as you're told," said Bill. He looked up over the rocks to make sure the Russians hadn't dispatched another dinghy. "I want to get you back to Stockholm as fast as possible, before your Russian friends really understand what's going on."

"I hope you realize you are making a grotesque mistake," said Hermann. "I played a few games with this English gentleman here, pretending that I was something sinister. But what would you do if someone followed you home the way he followed me? And now of course he seems to assume that I am someone other than myself. I have heard of Hermann, naturally, but I can absolutely assure you that I am not he."

Bill tucked away his gun and snorted seawater out of his nose. "What do you think, Humphrey?" he asked. "Is this our man, or isn't it? Because if it isn't, I think I'm going to blow his head off and then bill him for dry-cleaning my coat."

Humphrey scrutinized the German closely. There was no question about it; there never had been as far as he was concerned. The nose, the skull, the set of the jaw—they were Hermann's, identifications as distinctive as though he had been wearing a badge saying, "Klaus Hermann, Nazi War Criminals Convention."

Unhappily Humphrey said, "This is Klaus Hermann. No mistake. But I must insist that you not shoot him."

"He was trying to escape," said Bill with a smile.

"I still insist," Humphrey repeated. "He may have behaved like a monster, but he must have a trial."

"I don't really think that's going to be possible. There are too many influential people in the United States who would rather he didn't."

"So for the sake of those influential people, you're going to execute a man in cold blood? I shall report you, you know."

"In that case, I'll have to dispose of you too."

"You wouldn't dare," Humphrey cried, aghast.

"You don't think so?"

"No," said Humphrey slowly. "I don't think so. There's been enough of a disturbance here without a British national being shot. Especially since Major Milner knows what's going on."

Hermann interrupted. "Gentlemen, I'm very cold. If you have a car, perhaps we can go back to it."

Bill Bennett glanced toward the shore and then said, "Okay. I think I'm going to have to take some advice on this. Let's make our way back. Up the rock there and

along the overhang. The Russians will still be watching
us.''

Hermann said to Humphrey, stretching out his hand,
"Will you help me, please? I am very cold."

Humphrey looked at Bill and then back at Hermann.
"No," Bill said simply. Then Humphrey began to climb
unsteadily up and away through the thick of the snowstorm,
catching his hands on the rocks, feeling tired and dull and
sick with everything that history did to people and people
did to themselves. Behind him he heard Bill and Hermann
speak to each other quickly in German, and as he reached
the ledge, he saw Hermann feebly scaling the rocks behind
him, Bill pushing him on.

They were almost out of sight of the inlet when they
heard a loud clacking sound. Humphrey turned around,
bewildered. He thought for a moment that the Russian
submarine was shooting at them again. But then Bill waved
toward the north, through the slanting snow, and from the
direction of the Ormön inlet Humphrey saw a helicopter
approaching, shining a dazzling white floodlight on the
ocean below it. It was an SH-2 Seasprite of the Swedish
Navy, and it was quickly followed by another, and another.
The three copters gathered around the Russian submarine,
illuminating it so brightly that it resembled a model constructed for a stage set. The entire surrounding inlet was
theatrically brilliant.

"What you are now witnessing is an international incident in the making," smiled Bill. "And all thanks to
young Hermann here."

"I am not Hermann," insisted the old man. "Now, please.
I am dying from the cold."

Humphrey asked, "What will they do?"

"The Swedes?" asked Bill. "It's up to them. But this is
the second submarine incursion into Swedish waters in
four weeks."

They continued on their way back to the car as the

Seasprites danced and wove around the surfaced submarine.
Suddenly there was a deafening roar, as though a huge
furnace door had been opened, and a Sidewinder missile
curved downward from one of the helicopters and struck
the Russian submarine directly on the side of its fin.

"Time we left," said Bill and hurried them on until
they were out of sight of the inlet and almost to the car.

Behind them there was a shattering explosion. Humphrey felt it on the back of his head—a wall of compressed
air and then a wave of heat. Bill said, "Come on," but
Humphrey had to turn around and look, and what he saw
were chunks of fiery metal turning and turning in the air
amidst the snow, and gouts of flame, and then a sharp,
abrasive crackle as hundreds of rounds of machine-gun
ammunition went off.

"Tomorrow's headlines," said Bill. "Come on, Humphrey, let's hustle. I want us out of here quick."

The helicopters were still waltzing and roaring around as
Bill swerved the Grand Prix away from the shoreline and
drove at high speed back through Roggarön. He had pushed
Hermann into the front passenger seat, while Humphrey
had clambered into the back with Angelika.

"This is *ein Alpdrücken*," Hermann garbled. "I am not
the man."

The sky was still lit with orange fire as they drove
across the causeway to the island of Tvärnö. Angelika
must have fallen asleep for she nodded and bounced against
Humphrey with every bump in the road. The darkness
closed in again; soon they could see nothing through the
windshield but snow and the vague white curves of the
road. But Bill drove through the tumbling flakes with his
foot hard on the floor, skating the car through bends and
turns and over the last blinded bridge to the mainland and
back to Stockholm.

Humphrey relaxed a bit, feeling oddly deflated now that
their search for Hermann was over. Looking back on it, he

saw that it had held for him the extraordinarily wild excitement of a dangerous expedition in a strange land. He felt an urge to go on to Gavleborgs Län, and Västernorrlands Län and eventually to Lapland. But now here he was, driving through the snowy night—a boring three-hour motor-car journey with a silent American, an elderly German and a Swedish actress who was determinedly asleep. The helicopter attack had been so exciting, but it was over too quickly. The missiles and the explosions had all been discharged in a matter of seconds. Humphrey could hardly believe it had actually happened.

"*Ein Alpdrücken*," Hermann repeated.

"What does that mean?" asked Humphrey.

"A nightmare," Bill translated.

"Ah. How long before we get back to Stockholm?"

"Two, two and a half hours. It depends on the weather."

Humphrey looked out the window. Nothing but the night; snowy fields and dark rows of trees. "Do you think they sank that submarine?" he asked.

"I doubt it. Damaged it more likely. Just enough to keep it on the surface while they make an official complaint to the Soviet ambassador."

"I see. It looked very dramatic."

"It was dramatic. It was probably the beginning of World War Three."

Hermann shifted around in his seat and looked first at Angelika and then at Humphrey.

"She's asleep?"

"She's exhausted," said Humphrey.

"Well, it is my fault," said Hermann. "I have put her through hell."

"That seems to be your vocation in life," commented Bill.

They drove through Brollsta. Hermann dozed for a while, his heavy head resting on his chest. Humphrey found it impossible to rest; his mind felt as though it were tumbling over and over like a child's kaleidoscope.

"You know, I don't understand you at all," he said to Bill.

"Do you find it necessary to understand me?"

"I don't know. I'm half-afraid of what I might discover if I did."

"I'm a professional cleaner-upper, that's all," said Bill. "An international janitor."

"No, you're not that at all. I can't make out whether you enjoy what you're doing or not. I keep thinking to myself that you seem to be intelligent, almost witty at times. Yet you shoot people as though they were flies."

Bill was silent for a few miles. Then he said, "You forget that I went through Viet Nam."

"Was it really that bad?"

"For some. But it had an effect on almost all of us. It introduced us to our own innate brutality. The trouble is," and here his eyes flicked up to the rear-view mirror and regarded Humphrey steadily, "once you've discovered that Mr. Hyde inside of yourself, he refuses to go back into concealment."

"I'm not sure I understand what you mean."

"I was trained to kill people, and I actually killed them, all in the line of military duty, that's what I mean. But killing people is one of those strange things you can get a taste for. That's partly why I do this job. If the urge comes over me, at least I'll be killing with official permission. Better to kill a Soviet agent than an innocent bystander."

"You don't think that woman Birgitta was an innocent bystander?" Humphrey demanded.

"She was involved."

"And was that sufficient justification for killing her?"

Bill's eyes returned to the road. "Just be thankful I haven't climbed up any tall buildings and started picking off people at random."

"Thankful?" Humphrey found Bill's psychology completely impossible to follow.

"Killing's a drug," Bill commented. "Unfortunately, I happen to be an addict."

At that moment Angelika Rangström slid sideways and her head struck Humphrey's knee. He attempted to raise her up again but then he realized that she was very cold and very heavy. He struggled to push her into a sitting position, and as he did so, he found that his hands were covered with something cold and sticky and dark.

"My God," he said.

"What's up?" asked Bill.

"For God's sake, she's dead!"

"What do you mean, she's dead?"

"For God's sake, stop the car! She's dead. She's cut her wrists. The whole car's full of blood."

Bill steered the Grand Prix into the side of the highway and switched off the engine. Hermann woke up and lifted his head. *"Was ist los?"* he asked. He looked quizzically at Bill and then turned around in his seat to stare at Humphrey. Humphrey was holding up his hands, crimson with blood.

"Seine Händer," frowned Hermann. *"Sie haben roten Händer."*

"It's Fru Rangström," said Humphrey, desperately upset. "I'm afraid there's been an accident."

There was no option now but to call the police. The woman's blood had saturated the car's upholstery, and in daylight the vehicle would resemble a slaughter site. They stayed by the side of the highway with their hazard lights flashing, the snow tumbling down around them. They laid Angelika on a piece of carpet in the snow and Klaus Hermann stood over her, weeping freely and every now and then letting out a long, shivering sob.

Bill paced up and down, quite patient, quite resigned. He had learned years and years ago that this was a far-from-perfect world.

FOURTEEN

Natalia Vanspronsen was typing up her notes for next week's media campaign in Connecticut when the telephone rang. She picked up the receiver, tucked it under her chin and continued typing.

"I wanted to speak to Senator Reynard Kelly," said a man's voice.

"I'm sorry, Senator Kelly isn't here right now. This is Natalia Vanspronsen, his media assistant. Can I help you?"

"Well, I don't think so. I have to speak to the senator personally. Do you know where I can get ahold of him?"

"He and Mrs. Kelly are on their way back to Washington at the moment. You could try his office at the Senate. Do you have the number?"

"Damn it," said the man. Then, "I'm sorry, I had hoped to speak to him face-to-face."

"He's quite busy right now. I guess you know he's declared himself a candidate for the presidential nomination."

"I read about it in the paper. Listen—does he have an assistant, someone with whom I can discuss a serious problem?"

Natalia stopped typing. She took the telephone out from

under her chin and held it in her hand. "It depends on what kind of problem," she said. Something in the man's voice had alerted her seventh sense to trouble. "Can you tell me who you are? Perhaps I can do something to help."

"Dr. Edmond Chandler. I'm a pediatrician at the Merrimack Clinic. The point is that I believe we have the beginnings of a polio epidemic here in Concord, and yet it seems as though there's been some kind of cover-up going on. Well, when I say cover-up, I don't exactly mean Watergate. But the impression I get is that for some reason Senator Kelly has directed that everybody should keep it under wraps."

Natalia looked toward the window. Outside there was autumn sunlight and a view of the Colonnades' fruit orchards, the pear trees naked now, and pruned for winter. "I'd like to know who gave you that impression," she said. Then, "A *polio* epidemic? I haven't heard anything about it on the news. And nothing's come to the senator's desk."

"Believe me, the senator knows about it. The medical examiner has sent him a note and so has the Commissioner for Health and Welfare."

"Well, how serious is it?"

"As of right now we've had nineteen deaths. Is that serious enough? I attended one about an hour ago and that's why I'm calling. If I can't talk to the senator and find out what's going on here, I'm going to go straight to the media."

"Have you talked to the medical examiner?" asked Natalie. Quickly, worriedly, she jotted down notes on her pad.

"No response at all. He says he's aware of the situation, intends to keep a watch on it, and that's as far as he's prepared to go. But I can tell you something: that isn't enough. There's a cover-up here of some sort and if I can't get anything done about it, I intend to blow the whistle."

"Dr. Chandler," said Natalia in her softest and most persuasive voice, "can I please ask you not to contact the media until we've had a chance to check this out? I can't believe for a moment that anything as serious as a polio epidemic would be covered up, especially not by Senator Kelly. As you know, he's a strong advocate of public medicine."

"I'm not going to wait all day," said Edmond. "My patients are dying, and I want something done."

"But please don't go to the media just yet. Not until I've had a word with the senator himself. There could be a very good reason why this outbreak is being kept under wraps, and if you go to the media without consultation— well, it could have a negative effect. Panic, for instance, or people leaving the county and spreading it around indiscriminately."

Edmond said testily, "I don't think I need a media assistant to tell me the consequences of letting this epidemic get out of control. Now, how long are you going to be?"

"I'm going to contact the senator right away."

"And then what?"

"Well—where can I reach you?"

"Either at the Merrimack Clinic or my private office in East Concord. Or the Brick Tower Motor Inn. I'm at the clinic right now."

"The Brick Tower Motor Inn?" asked Natalia, raising an eyebrow.

"That's what I said. South Main Street, two-two-four, nine-five-six-five."

"I'll call right back."

Natalia put down the phone and immediately punched out Len Gieves' number, but Gieves didn't answer. He must have left for Stamford already. She tried Dick Elmwood's phone, but he had gone too. She tossed back her hair tensely and looked for Reynard's number in Washington.

It was while she was punching out this number that there was a rap at the door and Walt Seabrook put his head in. "Hi. Oh, I'm sorry. I didn't realize you were on the phone."

"That's okay. Come in."

Walt went to the window and looked out over the orchard. "Some place here, isn't it? It would make a terrific country club."

Natalia got through to Washington. The nasal voice of Reynard's personal secretary reported, "I'm sorry, the senator hasn't arrived at the office yet."

"Tell him Natalia Vanspronsen called and it's about a crisis."

"A crisis?" asked Walt as Natalia put down the phone.

"I'm not really sure yet," she said, standing up. "Listen, Walt, you're a doctor. Do you know anything at all about a polio epidemic in Concord?"

"A polio epidemic?" Walt frowned. "Not a thing. You're not serious, are you? Oh, come on, we haven't had a polio epidemic in the continental United States since nineteen fifty-four. Polio doesn't even rate as a percentile cause of death these days, not in the selective mortality statistics. It comes under 'all other diseases.' "

"I just spoke with a doctor on the phone who says there's the beginning of a polio epidemic in Concord. He says nineteen people have already died. Worse than that, he's kind of suggesting that Reynard already knows about it and has been trying to keep it quiet."

Walt stared at Natalia in bewilderment. "Reynard knows about an epidemic and hasn't told anyone?"

"That's what this doctor's saying."

"Who is he?"

"Edmond Chandler, a pediatrician at the Merrimack Clinic."

Walt said, "Listen, we'd better talk to this man. If I'm going to be Assistant Secretary for Health, the last thing I want to have on my record is a covered-up epidemic."

"I think we'd better talk to Reynard first."

"Reynard won't get to Washington for another three or four hours yet. We have to talk to this joker before he starts making any more accusations."

Natalia thought for a second and then said, "Okay. I'll get my jacket."

"A polio epidemic," Walt repeated. "Listen, it has to be a put-on."

"It didn't sound like it," she said as she donned her tweed jacket. She tucked her spectacles into her hair and packed her notebook into her purse.

"He hasn't talked to the media yet?" asked Walt.

"Not so far. But he will, he says, unless we do something positive."

"This is all I need. I was going to play golf with the hospital superintendent today. We haven't played together in six years."

"You're worried about golf? If this turns out to be as bad as I think it might, you're going to be worrying about the future of human life."

They walked side by side down the wide, sweeping staircase. Walt said testily, "Greta's right, you know. He's incapable of doing anything straight. He's a natural twister. He wouldn't know the truth if it came up to him and punched him on the nose."

Eunice was walking across the hallway as they came downstairs. "You're going out, Miss Vanspronsen? Dr. Seabrook?"

"We shouldn't be much longer than an hour or so."

"Can I say where you are if anyone calls?"

"The Merrimack Clinic, okay? Talking to Dr. Chandler."

They crossed the driveway to the old white-painted stables where the cars were garaged. The day was sharp and sunny, and as far as Natalia could see, the hills and fields were bright with the colors of fall—red maples, yellow larches, and birches like showers of coins. They climbed into her silver BMW and drove out toward Concord.

Walt said, as they passed through the gates of the Colonnades, "You know something? I have a very bad feeling about this."

Denzil Forbes was seated at a corner table in the bar of the Marquette Hotel in Wauwatosa when the red-jacketed waitress came over with a telephone and said, "You're Mr. Hope?"

"That's right. Thanks," said Denzil and reached into his pocket for his billfold to tip the girl a dollar. Then he picked up the phone and said, "Mr. Hope here."

The voice on the other end of the line sounded small and far away; there was a long-distance twanging on the line. Most of the black, vinyl-covered banquettes around Denzil were empty; it was almost midnight, after all. But the jukebox was still playing and he had to put his finger in his ear to shut out the sound of the Bee Gees.

"I got your message," said the voice. "I've talked to the principals involved and they're very interested. They're not sure about the price though. The price you're asking is steep."

"They think so? Well, that's too bad."

"They want to see the finished product first, before they put up any money."

"I'm sorry, Mr. Billings. It's cash up front or nothing. This isn't something I can do twice, you know."

There was a pause on the other end of the line. Then the voice said, "You won't come down from a million-one?"

"That's the price. Come on, Mr. Billings; this is Chiffon Trent we're talking about. You've seen the Polaroids. You know this is on the level."

"There's a lot of risk involved."

"Are you telling *me*? Listen—either you want in on the movie or I go to the Chinaman. You want me to go to the Chinaman?"

"Of course not, Mr. Hope. But this is a lot of lettuce we're talking about here, and supposing you skip? That's what the principals are worried about. With that much lettuce, you could disappear and never resurface."

Denzil beckoned to the waitress to bring him another drink. Into the phone he said, "Are they stupid or something? I've got a fifteen-percent royalty in perpetuity. That's going to make me a million-one fifty times over. Why should I skip?"

Another pause. Then, "Okay . . . but they want to know how you're going to do it. You haven't even sent down an outline."

"You think we're making *War and Peace*?"

"Listen, Mr. Hope, they're probably willing to put up the money, but they want to know how you're going to do it."

"All right," Denzil agreed impatiently. "Roughly what we're going to do is this. We'll make six regular one-hour videos over the next three days, then bring in four or five guys for the final torture scenario."

"The principals don't want phony."

"They won't get phony. They'll get whatever they want."

There was an even longer pause. "This is an open line, right?"

"Don't worry about it. I'm in a bar. I've never been here before and I'll never come here again."

"You're not taping any of this?"

"Mr. Billings, do you want me to hang up?"

"We're careful, that's all. It doesn't seem to us like *you're* being too careful."

"I'm as careful as I need to be. You want me to wear a mask and speak through a handkerchief? Just remember this girl's already officially dead and buried. It's not like there's anybody looking for her.''

''All right,'' said the voice reluctantly. There was a moment's conversation on the other end of the phone with someone else. Then, ''They just want to know how you're going to do it. You know, the denouement.''

''They've got a choice. I suggest a burning. Seems kind of appropriate in the circumstances.''

Two or three minutes' silence. Denzil waited patiently, examining his fingernails and smiling at the waitress when she brought him a fresh frozen daiquiri. ''Business, business, business,'' he told her and she smiled back at him.

Eventually the voice on the other end of the line said, ''They like the burning. What are we talking about, gasoline?''

''I have a warehouse where I can do it.''

''Okay then. They'll put the money where you asked for it, no later than tomorrow afternoon.''

''Sooner if you can. I'm not shooting one single inch of tape until it's there.''

''All right, Mr. Hope. I think we understand where you're coming from. My principals just want to say that for a million-one they expect the best, you understand me?''

''They'll get their money's worth. Not a cent more, not a cent less.''

''Good evening, Mr. Hope.''

''Same to you, Mr. Billings.''

Denzil sat for a long time finishing his drink before signalling to the waitress. ''What's your name, honey?''

''Sally, sir. Why?''

A noisy, impromptu party was already in progress at the Georgetown apartment of Reynard's younger brother Lincoln when Reynard and Greta arrived from the airport. There was Dom Perignon champagne and Iranian caviar and five or six of those stunning, toothy girls who always seemed to hover around Lincoln like a cloud of butterflies. His "cheerleaders," he called them. His wife called them his "ego masseuses."

Senator Willard Pearson of Alabama was there, the fat and powerful chairman of the Committee for Banking, Housing and Urban Affairs. So was Senator Pete Kolaski, the hardheaded northern Democrat whom Reynard was considering as his attorney-general designate. The noisiness of the crowd was swelled by Robert Trump, the liberal novelist, and Phil Weston, the young movie actor who had made *All of Our Days*, the controversial film about the Viet Nam generation.

Lincoln came over, hugged Reynard and slapped him on the back. Most of the party cheered.

"What a declaration speech!" he enthused. "That was a declaration speech with *everything*: timing, relevance, dignity and warmth. Did you see what your opponents had to say about it?"

Reynard smiled, a little cagily. "You can't blame them, I suppose."

"And *Greta*, how are you? It seems like it's been forever," said Lincoln, kissing her on both cheeks. Greta was looking exceptionally stylish in a gray Bill Blass suit and a diamond spray brooch of impressive size. Lincoln took her arm and led her into his white-carpeted apartment, where politicians, campaign supporters and newspeople sprawled on the white-leather furniture, sat on the white-railed stairs or tangled in the white-cushioned conversation pit.

Reynard shook a few hands, accepted a few congratulations and spent a few minutes talking to Senator Pearson about campaign finances; then he excused himself and called Lincoln across to the side of the room. "Listen," he said, "something's come up. Sort of a hiccup."

"A hiccup?" asked Lincoln. He smiled and raised his

champagne glass to a passing acquaintance. He was leaner and sharper-looking than Reynard, although his hair was whiter and his face was always dark orange from too much sunlamping. He looked closely at his brother and said, "What do you mean by a hiccup?"

"Come into the study," said Reynard.

"And leave the party?"

"Just for a minute."

"Well, okay. But don't you just adore that redhead in the corner? The one in blue? I found her in Macon, Georgia, of all places. She votes with her *poitrine*."

Reynard impatiently took Lincoln through to the study, which was equally stark and white, with Italian stainless-steel lamps and leather chairs that looked like enormous white catchers' mitts.

"I thought everything was all systems go," said Lincoln. "Dick Elmwood was on the phone this morning and he said you were almost certain to clean up in New England, especially since New Hampshire is your home turf and votes first."

"Something's come up," said Reynard edgily. "It's an epidemic of sorts."

"An *epidemic*? You mean a political epidemic or a disease-type epidemic?"

"A disease. A kind of polio."

"Where? I haven't heard anything about it."

"In Concord. So far, I don't know, fifteen or twenty people have died."

Lincoln drained his champagne and went across to the bar for another bottle. "I thought more or less everyone was vaccinated against polio."

"Not against this polio, they're not. It's very swift, very fast-breeding, and it can kill you in a couple of hours. Apparently it suffocates you by paralyzing your respiratory system."

Lincoln eased the cork out of the narrow neck of the

Dom Perignon. "I don't really see why you're so worried. I mean, you could actually make some capital out of it, couldn't you? Presidential candidate urges epidemic relief. They could take some shots of you weeping by some poor kid's bedside. You think you can manage some real tears?"

The cork came out with a satisfying pop and Lincoln poured each of them another glassful. He looked at Reynard intently as he was doing so and said, "Show the media you know how to cope in a crisis. Come January you'll be off and running and not even your strongest opponent will be able to catch you."

"You're not listening to me, Linc," said Reynard. "This epidemic is very, very serious. The virus is virtually unstoppable. By next week the whole of Merrimack County could be dead or dying. The virus gains strength with every regeneration. By next month there may not even be anyone left in New England to vote for me."

Lincoln said nothing at first, but then he sat down in one of the catcher's-mitt chairs, crossed his legs and stared at Reynard acutely. "There's *more* to this, too, isn't there? Am I right? It's not just the epidemic you're worried about."

"You're right. The point is, the disease spread from *my* land. It came from my estate. So in a way I'm partly responsible. In fact, a great many people may say later that I'm wholly responsible."

"The disease spread from your land? How? What are you talking about?"

"I can't explain any more than that, Linc. But take it from me, if any of this comes out, we're finished."

"*We're* finished."

Reynard turned around and jabbed a finger at his brother with all the abruptness of a street-fighter. "Don't forget who you are and why you're so successful in politics."

"Are you threatening me or what?" Lincoln demanded.

"First of all, you come out with some half-assed story about an epidemic—"

"There's nothing half-assed about this particular epidemic, I can assure you," Reynard interrupted him. "It comes from something that we were doing on the estate during the war. That's all I can tell you."

"What was it, some kind of experiment? Nobody ever told *me*. Jesus, Reynard."

"You were too young. You wouldn't have understood. Besides, it had to be kept a total secret."

"Look, you're asking me for help and yet you won't tell me what's going on. Well, Reynard, you listen to this: unless you explain *exactly* what it is that you're so damn worried about, unless you fill me in completely, you can *forget* any help, now or ever. I've had just about enough of this big brother 'I-know-better-than-you' stuff; I've heard it ever since I was knee-high."

Reynard was about to bark something but pressed his mouth shut instead and took a deep, flaring breath to control himself. The truth was that he was in a state of completely unprecedented panic. He had managed to keep Eldridge quiet, at least for the time being, but he knew that Eldridge was a determined and responsible man who wouldn't be silenced for very long—not unless Reynard could come up with some real hard and fast reasons why. He also knew that any one of the doctors or pathologists in Concord who were having to deal with the epidemic might take it into his head to contact the newspapers or the television channels at any moment. The only lever he had was a mucky little piece of political scandal he could use against the state's attorney general, but if he stooped to that, he would gain himself nothing more than a day or two—maybe only an hour or so—and in return he would certainly lose forever the support of some of New Hampshire's key government executives.

Usually Reynard had an unerring talent for formulating

a comprehensive political game plan to deal with almost any crisis that came his way. Now, however, he felt as though he were in a devastating spin. If he tried to keep the epidemic under wraps for much longer, he would almost certainly be accused of deliberately playing down a vicious sickness for the sake of protecting the business interests of his home town. If, on the other hand, he publicly announced there was a polio outbreak, there would be confusion, recrimination and mass chaos—and he would be held responsible for all of it.

Even worse, the Health and Welfare Department would quickly send in trained medical researchers, and how long would it be before one of them was able to trace the virus back to its source? And when *that* happened. . . .

Reynard felt as though everything for which he had worked during forty-four years of politics, everything for which he had lived his life, was teetering beneath him, on the edge of collapse.

He remembered that night in 1944 as though it were the night before last. To establish his personal alibi, he had been dining and dancing that evening at the PeeWee Club in Manhattan with Lydia Jennings, the beautiful wife of Congressman Richard Jennings. It was typical of Reynard's thinking that he had chosen to create an alibi that itself was slightly scandalous. If he said he was dating another man's wife, why, he *must* be telling the truth. Anyone else would have said he was visiting his mother, going to confession or reading to the sick at Havenwood.

The barman had called him over to the telephone. Ted Peale's voice had said, croakily, "Is it storming down there in New York?"

"I don't think so," Reynard had told him. "I haven't been outside in three hours. Why, is it storming up there?"

"It's Hades up here, let me tell you. Absolute Hades."

"And?"

"Well, we think it came in."

"You *think* it came in? What do you mean, you *think* it came in?"

"I don't know. Maybe we heard it and maybe we didn't. Robert swore it came right overhead. But I don't know. We don't have any radio contact now. I'd say that it's probably gone down over Snap Town, or Penacook."

"You mean crashed?"

"That's about the size of it."

"Jesus Christ!"

And then he'd had to dance the rest of the evening with Lydia Jennings, cheek-to-cheek, trying not to sweat, trying not to show that he was worried, waiting all the time for the phone call that never came, the phone call that would have told him everything was all right, that Condor was down, that he didn't have to worry any longer.

And the band had been playing "Blue Baby". . . .

Blue baby, don't say you're sad,
Tell me that you'll always stick around.

Lincoln said now, more soberly, "If this really *is* serious, Reynard. . . ."

Reynard went to the window and looked out over the gray curve of the Potomac and the dim outline of Theodore Roosevelt Island. "You know something?" he said. "The world changes and the public mood changes every couple of months, and if you really believe in something consistently and strongly—well, you sure can get . . . you know . . . taken by surprise. During the war, things were different. Oh, sure, we tell the revised version these days. How everybody supported the war effort, how we all wanted to crush Hitler. . . . But that wasn't the way it was, not at all. In forty-three and forty-four there were still millions of Americans who believed in what Germany was doing. A strong, unified Europe would have given us a powerful counterbalance to the U.S. economy, helped us to get over the hill. We would have had none of this recession, none

of this NATO business, none of this weakness in the face
of the Soviets.''

"What are you trying to tell me, Reynard?'' Lincoln
asked. "I don't understand.''

"Well, I don't understand it either, not now. History
turned out differently. But it needn't have. Just imagine
what the world would have been like today had Hitler been
allowed to stay in charge of Europe. That kind of thinking
seems pretty old-fashioned these days, doesn't it? But in
those days there were plenty of young American politicians who believed in what Hitler was doing.''

"In Auschwitz? And Belsen? You believed in that?''

"We didn't *know*, Linc. We just didn't know. And if
Hitler had been allowed to stay in charge, well, who can
say? The whole problem would have sorted itself out in
time. A lot of people died in that war, Linc. Nearly three
hundred thousand Americans died in battle. It was a global
war, the result of economic and social turmoil. The world
develops, changes; people become casualties. But go
ahead—you ask anyone today if he would trade the world
he has now for the world he had in nineteen forty-two. I
guarantee you that no one would say yes.''

"Reynard,'' Lincoln chided gently, "Reynard, you're
rambling. I don't know what this is all about, but you're
rambling.''

"I'm trying to *explain*, Linc. I'm trying to make you
understand why we did it.''

"Did *what*, Reynard? I mean—does all this have something to do with this virus? You cooked up this virus in
forty-four? I mean, for what? What did you do? I can't
help you unless you tell me.''

Reynard sat down and slowly massaged his face with his
hands. "You're going to judge me, Lincoln. You're going
to weigh me in the scales and you're going to find me
wanting.''

He looked up. "I'm a hero, do you know that? One of

the great hero figures of the twentieth century. When they come to write the political history of the nineteen seventies and eighties, my name's going to be up there along with the best of them. Reynard Kelly. The man who carried the work of Jack Kennedy into the eighties and beyond—the one man who kept the faith.''

He was silent for a long moment and then said pleadingly, "The thing is, you're going to have to help me, Linc. Otherwise this administration is over before it begins. I have everything it takes to be president, Linc, but you must help me.''

Lincoln poured himself more champagne. This was his sixth glass; but although his face had turned even more violently orange, he was still extremely sober. He had never seen his brother like this before, and he had certainly never heard him talk this way, even at his drunkest.

Reynard said, "I've had to carry this cross now for forty-four years. How about a toast—forty-four years, my cross and me. *Skol!*''

"Reynard—'' said Lincoln.

"No, no, no. Don't 'Reynard' me, Linc, whatever you do. Let me tell you something. In the spring of forty-four, after I'd been out boating with a girl on Lake Massebesic, I was approached by a man who said his name was Johnson. I could pick him out today if you showed him to me. Small spectacles, big nose and a ridiculous laugh. This man Johnson said I could help to end the war if I wanted to; naturally I listened to what he had to say.''

"A man came up to you after a boating trip and said you could help to end the war? And you believed him?''

Reynard raised a hand. "Those were much more innocent times. People took more on face value then than they do today. A man's expression was his guarantee, and for most people that was enough.''

"Must have been *great* times,'' said Lincoln sarcastically.

"You can mock, but they were,'' retorted Reynard.

"Did you ever know what it was like driving through Mine La Motte, Missouri, in a Chrysler Saratoga convertible—two years old, of course, because we stopped car production in forty-two. But do you know what that *felt* like? You were only a kid in those days, but they were great days."

"Reynard," said Lincoln worriedly, "Reynard, why don't I get you some coffee? Come on, you're not making too much sense here. Really."

Reynard stared at the floor for a long time. Then he said, "God, Linc, I don't know what to do. This one . . . I can't figure how to handle it. We've got to talk this over, get it all straightened out before the media get their hands on it—and there're twenty people dead already. Twenty. And all those bodies are laid at my door, Linc. All those people were *my* responsibility."

"So some virus escaped from your property? Or somebody stole it? Is that it, somebody stole it? Was it in a test tube or something? How can you blame yourself? How can *anyone* blame you? It wasn't your fault; we can produce patent proof of that."

Reynard said dully, "They'll find out how old the virus is, and how it was developed. Have you seen the forensic equipment they use these days? I've already read the preliminary virology reports from HEW. Well, half the stuff I couldn't understand, but the virologist made it quite clear that he believed the virus had been artificially developed and that it was growing stronger every time it infected someone, and that as yet there was no known antidote."

Lincoln said, "You'd better tell me the whole story, Reynard. This way I can't help you at all."

Reynard finished his champagne and looked down into the bottom of the glass. "I'm not drunk, you know," he told his brother.

"I know. But carry on. Tell me what happened."

"Well," said Reynard wearily, "you may or may not

know it, but during the war, the Germans had one plane that was capable of flying the Atlantic nonstop. It was the Focke-Wulf Two-hundred, and it was mostly used to harass the merchant fleets that supplied Britain with food and armaments after Dunkirk. Tremendous airplane, way ahead of its time. Churchill called it the 'scourge of the Atlantic.' It went out of active service in forty-four because it was actually designed as nothing more than an airliner, and it couldn't stand up to the rigors of combat duty or attacks by British fighter patrols. But Hitler several times considered sending one of these planes to drop bombs on New York as a show of strength, and one of them flew the Atlantic and actually dropped a bomb on Glace Bay, Nova Scotia, just to prove that an attack on New York was feasible.''

Lincoln said nothing. By now, however, he was quite convinced that the strain of preparing and declaring his candidacy had tired his brother to the point of semi-breakdown and that he was going to have to usher everybody discreetly out of the party and call for Dr. Lansing.

But Reynard was too preoccupied to be aware of Lincoln's reservations about his sanity, and he continued to drink, pacing up and down and relating disjointedly the story behind the six glass phials that Michael Osman had found in the woods at Conant's Acre.

''This man Johnson met me at the old Parkway Motel on Manchester Street and told me that Hitler had already drawn up plans for the invasion of the United States. Hitler had apparently decided that a full-scale military assault was out of the question. At that stage of war he had neither the finances nor the resources to meet the United States head-on. Apart from that, he knew he already had millions of sympathizers within the United States and that it would probably take only a single strong move to force a United States truce. Six Wall Street banks had pledged him support if he could pull it off, and the list of major industrial-

ists who said they would go along with him would be
worth a fortune if you could find it today.''

Lincoln said, a little testily, ''You believed all this?''

''Johnson showed me his credentials. Papers, copies of
letters, notes from American financiers. But what really
convinced me was a letter from Henry Weidman, and I
recognized Weidman's initials.''

''But you weren't a Nazi,'' said Lincoln. ''Why did you
even listen to this man Johnson?''

''You're looking at this thing with modern eyes,'' Reynard told him. ''In those days, before we knew what the
outcome of the war would be, there were still plenty of
people within the United States who felt that by fighting
against Germany, we were fighting our friends. And what
did we care about some power struggle in Europe? It was
much better to let the best country win and leave it at that.
Americans weren't very internationally minded then, Linc.
Besides, whatever you say, we didn't know anything about
Auschwitz or Ravensbruck. We just didn't *know*.''

''But you weren't *politically* a Nazi.''

''I was a nationalist; I still am. I sympathized with many
of the Nazi ideas. Lots of us did. I've changed since those
days of course. The war, and the bomb, and the nineteen
fifties—they changed us all. It was finding out about the
Holocaust that changed me more than anything else. I
could understand persecution, particularly at a time when
Germany was struggling for its survival, but I could never
understand genocide.''

''So where does this airplane fit in?'' asked Lincoln.
''This Focke-Wulf Two-hundred or whatever you call it.
And what does this epidemic have to do with it?''

After a pause Reynard at last sat down and loosened his
tie. ''Don't judge me, all right? Remember, the times were
different, more uncertain. I was thinking of the family's
future. I never guessed—well, I never guessed. Let's leave
it at that.''

"More champagne?" asked Lincoln but Reynard ignored him.

Slowly, precisely, in a more collected voice, he continued. "I met Johnson three times. On the third occasion he made it clear that in any kind of treaty between Germany and the United States, I would play a powerful political role. I suppose I actually believed I was doing something great, something of international importance. Anyway, the plan was that the Germans should fly into the United States six phials of a newly developed virus—a very potent piece of microbiological warfare that one of their leading doctors had developed in the nineteen thirties. The plane was supposed to land at the Colonnades, which was well within the limits of its range if it took off from Paris. Johnson and his agents would take the virus and distribute five phials of it around the United States—at military centers in San Francisco, Fort Mead, Fort Rucker and a couple of other places I forget."

"You were going to spread an epidemic among the U.S. forces?" asked Lincoln incredulously.

Reynard shook his head. "There was no serious intention of actually releasing the virus. Once the phials were distributed, we were simply going to contact President Roosevelt and his cabinet and tell them that Hitler was very interested in a truce between our two nations, that it would be much more reasonable of the president to comply than to carry on the fighting. The Focke-Wulf airplane would be shown to the president as proof that the mission had actually been carried out, and the one remaining phial of virus would be given to the Pentagon for analysis so they would understand fully the pressure they were under."

"You were prepared to blackmail the entire country? Your own country, to which you had pledged complete loyalty and allegiance? You were actually prepared to be a traitor? Jesus God, Reynard, what the hell were you *thinking* about?"

"I keep telling you, things were different then," Reynard growled at him. "If everything had gone according to plan, this family could have been the wealthiest and most influential dynasty in America. Don't you believe in the Kellys even that much?"

"I don't know what the hell to believe in."

"Anyway," said Reynard, breathing heavily, "the question doesn't arise. The plane arrived at New Hampshire in a heavy electrical storm, and just before landing, we lost contact with it. It crashed somewhere; we searched but we never found it. You know how thick some of those woods are. Even an airplane that size could have vanished, and of course I didn't dare send anyone out to look for it who wasn't involved in the plan."

"How many people knew about it?" asked Lincoln. "More pertinently, how many of those people are still alive?"

"Only three people knew, including myself, and the Germans of course. Robert Rearden, our groundsman, and Ted Peale. Rearden's dead now but Peale's still alive. He lives in Florida."

"Do you think there's any chance he would talk?"

Reynard gave Lincoln an odd sideways look he couldn't quite understand. "I don't think so."

"And you never told anyone else before me?"

Reynard shook his head. "I once told Chiffon Trent that I'd had contact with the Nazis during the war."

"What the hell did you do that for?"

"I don't know. There was a television program on CBS about Hitler and she wanted to know something about the war. She was so young, you know, that none of the old wartime figures seemed like real people to her. She was amazed that I'd actually met Churchill. Then she asked me if I'd ever met any real Nazis. I don't know why I told her; I'd never told anyone else. But it doesn't really matter too much now, does it? Not now that she's dead."

"Let's pray she didn't pass the information on to any-one else."

"Chiffon?" For a moment Reynard looked almost wistful, and haunted as well. Then he took a mouthful of Dom Perignon, shook his head and said, "No. Not Chiffon. She was too loyal. She wouldn't have talked."

"Okay," said Lincoln, "if only you and Ted Peale know where this virus came from, what are you so worried about?"

"They'll track it down, Linc. You know that as well as I do. If that virus has gotten loose, it means that someone's found the six glass phials, and if he's found the phials, he'll find the plane, or what's left of it. I daren't set up a search myself; it would cause too much suspicion. And supposing the health department finds the plane first and knows that I've been searching? Instant incrimination."

Lincoln said, "Well, well. The Nazi skeleton in good old Reynard's closet. And I thought that toxic-dump affair had been a scandal."

"You have to help me, Linc. You have to think of some way out of this."

"To begin with," said Lincoln, "you simply have to deny all knowledge of it; that's if they *do* find the plane."

"But meanwhile all these people are dying. The longer I keep quiet about it, the more people are going to die. There are *children* dying, Linc. And what do you think is going to happen to me if they eventually discover what I did, especially after several thousand people have already been wiped out? I've got twenty on my conscience already."

"You never had too much conscience before."

"Don't be cruel."

"Well, Jesus, Reynard, what the hell do you *expect*? Either you're going to be ruthless or you're not. If you can't be ruthless, you're not fit to be president. We can't have a man in the White House who's going to hesitate to push the nuclear button because he's worried about all the people he'll have on his conscience.''

Reynard raged back, "Nuclear war is fantasy, pure theory. These people are real, and they're already dead.''

"What do you mean, nuclear war is fantasy?''

"Well, do you seriously believe that if we were truly capable of grasping what would happen if we used those weapons, we'd use them?''

"Reynard," said Lincoln, "I think I'd better get you a doctor.''

"I don't *need* a doctor.''

"You're going out of your mind! First you tell me all this Nazi stuff and then you start sounding off like a peace freak.''

"I've killed people, Linc. Can't you understand that? New Hampshire people. Concord people. And there's something even worse than that.''

Reynard raised his head; there were tears in his eyes. Not genuine tears of grief—he was incapable of those—but tears of sentimental regret, and tears of bitterness at himself for being what he was.

"I killed Chiffon too.''

Lincoln stared at his brother for a long time. Then he picked up the phone and said, "Dean? I need you in here, right now. That's it. The library. Something's come up.''

Dean Farber came in holding a glass of orange juice, his pale face as blank and innocent as a child's. There was a brief burble of laughter and conversation from the living room as he opened and closed the door.

Reynard was sitting with his head in his hands. Lincoln had his back to the door. Farber's smile gradually diminished. "Is anything *wrong*?" he asked cautiously.

"Yes," said Lincoln. "Reynard's announcing his withdrawal from the presidential race as of now. His doctor's just told him that to continue would be detrimental to his health.''

"Doctor?" asked Dean Farber in astonishment. "What doctor?"

"Doctor Death," said Reynard in a harsh voice. "Linc— pour me some more champagne."

Later that morning, near Anama City, Florida, Ted Peale was sitting on his veranda, wearing his bright Hawaiian shirt and his ill-fitting Bermudas. He was cleaning and repairing his fishing tackle when his wife called, "Ted, there's a telephone call for you."

He laid down his tackle and walked slowly into the house. His wife had been baking and there was a smell of apple pie in the air. He picked up the phone and asked, "Yes, who is it?"

"A friend, Mr. Peale," whispered a hoarse Chicano voice. "Somebody from New Hampshire sent me."

"Well, I told my friend I couldn't make it up to New Hampshire. I'm sorry."

"Your friend understands that. But your friend says he should maybe pay you a little something . . . just to make sure you say nothing to anybody about the little business you had together."

Ted Peale sniffed. "He wants to pay me money?"

"A little something for your trouble."

"Well, he can do that if he wants to."

"Unfortunately, not at your house, Mr. Peale. Too suspicious. But come down to the intersection of George and St. Andrews in fifteen minutes and park behind a green Chevy you'll see there, with Florida plates. Get into the back seat of the Chevy and I'll be there to pay you the cash."

"How much cash?" asked Ted Peale warily.

"I think twenty-five."

"Twenty-five *thousand*?"

"I think."

"I'll see you in fifteen minutes."

Under a glaring noonday sun, Ted Peale backed his '66 Impala out of the creeper-lined parking space at the back of his bungalow, giving his wife a good-bye toot on the horn. She had asked him to bring back some cinnamon since he was going out. He had put on his green eyeshade against the glare. He could have been any other Florida geriatric trundling down to the market for groceries; it gives the old boy something to do, running a few errands for the wife.

He parked, badly, behind the rusting green Chevrolet. Leaving his engine running, he approached the car and bent down so he could see who was inside. Two young Chicanos, both with mirror sunglasses and greased-back pompadours. One of them was sitting in the driver's seat, smiling, a thin wrist with a flashy gold wristwatch resting casually on the steering wheel; the other was sitting in the back, holding a large brown-paper parcel on his lap.

"How you doing, Granpa? Get in," said the one in the back.

"Can't you just pass it to me out the window?"

"People going to see us," the boy insisted.

"Well, okay," said Ted Peale. He opened the rear door of the car and eased himself onto the sticky green-vinyl seat.

"You don't have to worry about nothing," grinned the boy. "It's all here, twenty-five g's."

"How come my friend sent you two?" asked Ted Peale. "You don't look like his usual style."

"Different jobs, different styles," said the youth in the driver's seat. "For this job he wanted somebody real glamorous." And he emitted a high-pitched giggle.

"Like your shirt, man," said the other boy, fingering the sleeve of Ted Peale's Hawaiian top. "That would suit me, something with pineapples on it."

Ted Peale gave an uneasy nod. "You don't want a

receipt or nothing?'' he asked. ''Then I guess I'll just take the money and go.''

''Oh—wait a second, man,'' said the boy sitting next to him, and he plunged a foot-long, double-edged bayonet right up to the handle into Ted Peale's stomach.

Ted Peale gasped with shock as the cold steel pierced him. He stared at the boy, then down at the bayonet handle, then back at the boy again. ''What did you do that for?'' he asked.

''Yes, man, what did you do that for?'' mimicked the boy in the driver's seat. ''You just ruined the damned shirt.''

Ted Peale was about to open his mouth and scream, but the shock was already too much for him. His heart stopped and he died within less than a minute.

''Let's go,'' said the boy in the back seat.

''Old man Freiburg ready for him?''

''You bet.''

The Chevrolet lurched away from the curb and began the long trip to Bonita Springs in Lee County, just west of the Corkscrew Swamp Sanctuary. There, at Freiburg's Marvel Gardens & Alligator Farm, Ted Peale's body, like so many others before him, would be dismembered and fed to old man Freiburg's thirty fully grown alligators. A great tourist attraction, old man Freiburg's alligators, although some of his neighbors could never understand how he prospered so well on the proceeds of $2.50 tickets.

''What a way to end up, huh?'' said one of the Chicano boys rhetorically. ''Alligator shit.'' He nudged Ted Peale's body and said, ''You hear that, Granpa? Alligator shit.''

FIFTEEN

Piotr was changing into his jockstrap and tights at the O'Connor Theater when Billy Manzanetti walked in, carrying a large grocery bag full of sausages, cheeses and fresh fruit, and smoking a smelly French cigarette. Piotr had worked with Billy in an off-off-Broadway satire that had consisted mostly of jokes about herpes.

"How are you doing, Rasputin?" Billy asked.

"Billy, hi. I'm doing fine as a matter of fact. Well, at least I'm working. How are you doing?"

"Oh, bad, good; here, there; up, down. You know how it is. You want an apple?"

"Thanks."

"You want a sausage? Bologna, they're the best."

"Mmm, no, thanks. My whole childhood was sausages, remember? A sea of sausages. How's Trixi?"

"Pixi? Oh, good, bad. You know. Actually as a matter of fact, pretty indifferent."

Piotr bit into an apple. "You got something on your mind?"

Billy nodded. Smoke wafted up the left side of his face and he coughed out of the right side of his mouth.

"You remember I told you I knew a guy who was big in porno movies?"

Piotr looked at him suspiciously. "I remember."

"Well, apparently, and I got this from Jack Bigelow himself—you know, the guy they call the Mighty Salami— apparently there's a real big picture going down. One of the classics of all time, that's what the word is, and they're paying big big money for the right guys. Guys who can screw like mules and keep their mouths shut. But I mean big money."

"What are you telling *me* for?" Piotr asked.

"Well, this could be your big chance to break into the skin business. A famous young exile like you. They're offering twenty grand for each of the male parts, and I say parts advisedly."

"Billy," Piotr protested, "I'm a serious actor."

"A lot of actors are serious actors but they still do porno. Come on, what have you got to lose? Twenty big ones, all in cash; IRS-exempt."

"You sound like you're recruiting," said Piotr.

"Well, I guess I am, really. I'm supposed to come up with five guys. And they're all supposed to be exceptional. I get an extra ten-percent commission."

"Hmm," said Piotr. Twenty thousand dollars sounded tempting, he had to admit. The theater production hadn't paid him for two weeks now, and he was a month behind with his rent. To his Russian mind, pornography was an anathema, the lowest of the low; but he was a free citizen now, wasn't he? If he wanted to act in a sex movie, who was to stop him? And his agent didn't have to know about it; nor would he ever be likely to find out, as respectable a man as he was.

"You want to give me some details?" Piotr asked, trying to sound offhanded.

"They start shooting on Monday; it'll be a selection of videos. Then they'll do a big s-and-m production."

"S-and-m?"

"Spaghetti and meatballs."

"What?"

"I'm kidding. It means sado-masochism. You know, tying the girl up, pretending to rape her, that kind of thing. You'll love it."

"They won't put the movie into general release?"

"Oh, no, nothing like that. It's for private distribution only. Clubs, private parties, mail-order sales. Nobody who sees it will even know it's you; and even if they guess, I don't think they'll mind, as long as you keep it up."

"I don't know," said Piotr reluctantly.

"Well, make your mind up by tomorrow. Then call me. Here—don't use my home number, call me at this one. You have to make up your mind by tomorrow because the filming's out of town and I have to book tickets."

"How much out of town?" asked Piotr. "Not New Jersey? I went there once; never again."

Billy pinched the stub of his cigarette out from between his lips and spat a shred of tobacco. "Nope. You ever heard of Wisconsin?"

"Wisconsin? But that's not out of town. That's the midwest!"

Billy winked. "I knew you'd like the idea. Call me tomorrow. And remember, twenty big ones, all for you."

Piotr sat in the dressing room for five or ten minutes after Billy left. He had to admit that the idea of appearing in a sex movie quite aroused him. To make love to a girl in front of other people, and to be paid for it too. And if the first movie was good, there might be others and he could earn himself a steady income, enabling him to hold out for bigger and more satisfying roles on the stage.

It makes sense, he told himself . . . and what, after all, is immoral about it if the girl is getting paid too?

*   *   *

Edmond escorted Natalia Vanspronsen and Walt Seabrook from the Merrimack Clinic and over to the Hot Cookie Coffee Shop across the street. The day had suddenly grown dull, and a chilly wind scudded in from the northwest, scattering red and yellow leaves across the sidewalk. They found a corner table and ordered coffee. Edmond asked for a lemon Danish because he hadn't yet had breakfast.

"I might as well tell you why I'm living at the Brick Tower," he said. "My wife and I just parted."

"I'm sorry," said Natalia.

"Don't worry," put in Walt. "You're better off without her. I left my wife on our sixth anniversary. I told her, 'For six years I've been listening to you talking about things you know nothing about. For six years I've been wondering whether I ought to tell you that your face gives me chronic dyspepsia. That's it. Now I'm going to live a life of silence and certainty, with a settled stomach.' "

They laughed but soon grew serious again. For each of them, the epidemic and its consequences were crucial.

"I haven't had any further reports of hyper-polio since earlier this morning," said Edmond, "but I have no doubt at all that it's going to spread. In the last few cases we've attended, death was very rapid indeed, and although we haven't been able to determine how the epidemic started, or why, we're now beginning to trace chains of contact from one family to another. The most alarming part about it, though, is that each time the virus seems to take less time to infect its new hosts. In other words, the rate of new infection is accelerating as well as the speed with which the virus kills."

Natalia said, "I don't want to change the subject, Dr. Chandler, but have you any idea of why Senator Kelly might have wanted to keep news of this epidemic under wraps? Is there any medical reason?"

"I thought you were on his staff. I was expecting you to tell *me* the answer to that," said Edmond.

Walt Seabrook gave a lemony little smile. "Well . . . Dr. Chandler . . . a politician like Senator Kelly doesn't always take everyone into his confidence. All we're trying to discover here is how serious this epidemic might be, and what you consider the most effective way of dealing with it."

Edmond glanced from Natalia to Walt and back again. He felt refreshed and collected this morning. Surprisingly, he had slept better at the inn than he had slept in years; he had debated with his reflection as he shaved whether his marriage to Christy hadn't been giving way piece by piece from the moment they had walked out of the Stamford Episcopal Church. He had thought at various times that he loved her overwhelmingly, but he had decided this morning that he really loved only those women who were just beyond his reach. Now that he had left her, he felt a deep sense of relief and purpose. While he knew it might not be anything more substantial than the euphoria that often follows any kind of important break in a person's life, he felt it was far more than that.

"There is no medical reason I can think of for suppressing the news of this epidemic," he told Natalia. "There may be an *administrative* reason. It may be that Senator Kelly is concerned lest there be widespread panic and more people killed or injured as a result of a wholesale exodus. After all, we have thirty-five thousand people here in Concord, and if they were all to try and leave the area at once. . . ."

Walt nodded toward the file of reports Edmond had laid on the table. "Those are the autopsy protocols?"

"That's right. Take a look if you want to. Dr. Corning is quite emphatic. We have a fast-regenerating, highly infective, polio-type virus here, with certain unusual characteristics in the way its RNA behaves. It's very dangerous, and I for one would have gone to the media a couple of days ago, although not all my colleagues agree with me. Some of them say it hasn't technically reached epidemic proportions yet and that we still have a massive amount of detailed research to do, and that if we break up the community by stampeding everyone, we may jeopardize our chances of discovering how the virus spreads.''

''And what's your argument against that?'' asked Natalia, looking at Edmond steadily. Despite the gravity of the problem, she was conscious that she found him attractive.

''My argument against that is simple. Every time the virus spreads, it kills someone. If we fail to alert the community, we're guilty of treating people as human guinea pigs. We may even be guilty of something worse than that.''

Walt asked, ''What does Carroll Bryce think?''

''You know Dr. Bryce?''

''Sure, we play golf together. What's his view? I mean, I'll speak to him later, but first I want to find out what kind of response you guys in the field are getting from HQ.''

''Well . . . ambiguous,'' said Edmond. ''I get the feeling that Dr. Bryce is very anxious about the situation. At the same time, I get the feeling that he's doing what he's told. He's a stickler for protocol, as you know, and he's not likely to go against direct instructions from above.''

''From Senator Kelly?'' Walt suggested.

''Senator Kelly may well be president next year,'' Edmond pointed out.

''Precisely,'' said Natalia.

At that moment Edmond's beeper sounded. He said, ''Excuse me,'' and went to the coffee-shop telephone. He came back and announced, ''Another one. A family out at Swenson Avenue. I'm afraid I'm going to have to leave you. Would you mind picking up the check for the coffee?''

''You go right ahead,'' said Walt.

When Edmond had gone, Natalia and Walt sat and looked at each other questioningly.

"Something doesn't fit here," she said. "There's something about this epidemic that smells, and it doesn't just smell of dead bodies."

"My view exactly," agreed Walt. "One of the first procedures in the outbreak of any dangerous infection is to immediately inform the local populace through the media. It's been almost a week since the initial case of hyperpolio, and so far there's hardly been a squeak. Dr. Chandler is prepared to speak out, but I get the feeling he's a little reserved. Maybe he has a skeleton in his closet. Carroll Bryce is usually outspoken; I certainly would have thought *he* would have said something official by now. Then there's Eldridge at the New Hampshire Department of Health and Welfare. Why doesn't *he* make an announcement?"

"Reynard asked them not to. Well, more than asked them, I shouldn't wonder. Coerced them. But why?"

"Natalia," said Walt, "if Reynard finds it expedient to cover up the existence of an epidemic, there's only one reason why. In some way he must be connected with it."

"How could he possibly be? A *disease*?"

"They don't know where it came from yet, do they? But suppose the cattle on Reynard's land are diseased and people have been given contaminated milk . . . simply because Reynard has ignored proper pasteurizing procedures. Or suppose a sewer on Reynard's property has cracked and raw sewage has been leaking into Concord's drinking water. That's highly possible, especially when you consider that the polio virus is usually passed from excrement to mouth."

"But how can we find out?"

"We can ask Reynard."

"But suppose it *is* something like that—diseased cattle or something? That's going to be disastrous for his candidacy. Nineteen people dead just because he couldn't be bothered to keep his property or his livestock in good condition?"

Walt paid the check and they walked out on to Pleasant Street. The autumn wind blew Natalia's hair. Walt said, "I don't know about you, Natalia, but it means a very great deal to me, Reynard Kelly being elected president."

Natalia looked at him narrowly.

"I'm an excellent administrative doctor," he said. "I'm chairman of the hospital committee, senior gynecological consultant, and I attend more health-service finance and administration meetings than there are days in the week. I'm supporting Reynard because I'm what you might call a friend of the family. But, more important, I'm supporting him because I want to be the Assistant Secretary for Health. I'll never get another chance at it. It's my medical and political goal in life. I want to make an impression on this country's health services, and with Reynard's help, I can do it."

They had reached Natalia's Porsche. She took the keys out of her purse and opened the doors.

"And you?" Walt asked her. "What's your reason for being here?"

"I'm here because it's my job," she said. She didn't look at him. "I'm here because I was asked to be here."

"Is that all?"

Natalia started up the engine. "Of course it's not all, damn it. I'm here because opportunities like this come only once in a lifetime and if you throw them away, you're crazy."

Natalia's hand was on the gearshift. Walt put his hand on top of it and looked at her closely. "Let's agree that we're both ambitious then, shall we? And let's agree that if Dr. Chandler is even halfway right about this epidemic, Reynard could be in serious trouble. So let's agree to call Reynard and see what we can do."

Natalia waited without moving or speaking until Walt

took his hand away. Then abruptly she shifted the Porsche into gear and screeched away from the curb.

Greta had already expressed her opinion about Reynard's suggested withdrawal from the presidential race by hurling her champagne glass at the wall.

"I thought you had courage, damn it! I didn't think you had much else. Maybe a certain brutish charisma. Maybe a kind of macho, cuff-tugging, soap-opera masculinity. But certainly *courage*!"

Lincoln said defensively, "We don't have a courage difficulty here, Greta. We have an historical political problem that is threatening to bring this whole family crashing into ruin, you included."

"I can hardly believe it," snapped Greta. "You did some grubby little deal with the Germans in nineteen forty-four, some ridiculous comic-opera arrangement for which you didn't even get paid. . . ."

"You're wrong about that," Reynard interrupted.

"What do you mean? The Germans *paid* you?" asked Dean Farber. He looked paler than ever.

Reynard nodded. "Six million dollars in gold bullion. Well, I got only half of it. The rest was due on completion."

Lincoln pressed his knuckles to his forehead and let out a sigh of total resignation. "This is it," he said. "This is the absolute finish. The Nazis paid you three million dollars in gold for blackmailing Roosevelt? And you accepted it? You *banked* it?"

"It was all banked in Switzerland. It was still there after the war. Just how do you think this family remained so prosperous when everyone else was feeling the pinch? How do you think we were able to keep the Colonnades up to such a high standard of excellence?"

Lincoln asked, "Did Father know about any of this?"

"No. I told him the money came from a deal I'd made in South America."

"Well, thank God for small mercies. At least he went to his grave still believing you were decent."

Greta snapped her fingers at Dean Farber. "Find me some more champagne, will you? I can't even begin to think about any of this without a drink. And let's stop moaning and moralizing, shall we, Lincoln? What on earth does it matter if your father knew or not? The most important thing we can do now is to decide on how we're going to maneuver our way out of all this. We have several important points in our favor. The strongest is that no one has yet connected the epidemic with those glass phials—even supposing that anyone has found them. It's more than likely they've been thrown away by now.

"The second point is that even if the outbreak *is* connected with your land and the medical people start searching it for a possible cause, what do you seriously think they're going to come up with? You're panicking, Reynard. If *you* haven't come across that airplane in forty-four years, do you honestly believe for one moment that a few off-duty policemen are going to stumble into it?"

"But the plane must be *somewhere* there," Reynard told her. "The first few victims of the epidemic lived around the southern part of the estate—Conant's Acre and the Middle Meadow. Logically that must have been where the phials were found. I've had the place wired off and I've taken a cursory look around there myself, but the trouble is that I wouldn't trust either of my groundsmen to keep quiet if they actually found it."

"Good God, Reynard, you can plead complete ignorance of the whole thing," put in Greta.

"While more and more people die of this disease, I can pretend not to know anything about it? Is that what you're suggesting?"

"You were in New York when the plane came in, weren't you?" Greta insisted. "And you've told us already that only two other people knew about it, and one of those is dead. The other man could be paid off, couldn't he? Or, I don't know, faced with a little friendly persuasion? Even if the health people *do* trace the phials and *do* find the plane, all you have to do is act completely surprised.''

Reynard stood up and went to pour himself another drink. Lincoln moved forward to stop him, but he lowered his head in that way Lincoln recognized from boyhood as a signal that was completely adamant.

"Maybe you're right, Greta,'' said Reynard with studied graciousness. "Maybe I *did* panic to begin with. But I think you all know what this bid for the presidency means to me and what it means to this family; it has to be one-hundred percent. This is my last possible shot at the White House and if anything goes wrong, or if anything is likely to go wrong, I'd rather back off. We have the name of Kelly to think about too. You say the likelihood of anyone's tracing those phials or connecting them with me is remote. Well, that may be the case, but we don't know for sure, and believe me: as this epidemic gets worse, which it will, the Health Department's efforts to discover where it came from are going to grow increasingly intensive and increasingly thorough. If that plane is there to be found, which I believe it is, in the end they'll find it.''

"But for God's sake, all you have to do is stare at it as though you've never seen it before,'' Greta protested.

"Greta,'' said Reynard gently, "you're living in an unreal world. What do you think would happen if a nineteen-forty-four Focke-Wulf Condor were to be discovered on the New Hampshire estate of one of the leading candidates for the Democratic presidential nomination? It would be one of the sensations of the century—politically, historically, aeronautically. That airplane would be stripped down to the very last bolt—reassembled, photographed and identified—and every research historian in the whole world with the slightest interest in World War Two would want to know what it was doing there. Eventually—in weeks or maybe months—they'd find out. The Germans kept meticulous logs of all their Condor flights; you don't think a special flight like this one would have gone unrecorded? I was worried enough when they dug up those so-called Hitler diaries in case there was any mention of Condor. There's bound to be a memorandum about it somewhere, believe me.''

The telephone rang. Dean Farber picked it up. ''Congressman Kelly's residence.'' Then, ''You wanted *Senator* Kelly? Okay, just hold one moment and I'll see if he's still here. What's that? I see. Okay, well, hold on, please.''

He covered the receiver with his hand and said to Reynard, ''It's Mr. Eldridge from the New Hampshire Health and Welfare Department. He wants to talk to you.''

''Of course he wants to talk to me. What does he want to say?''

''He wants to say that twenty-six more cases of hyperpolio have been identified in the past two hours and that he intends to declare Merrimack County a quarantine area, regardless of any personal consequences.''

Reynard said, ''Give me the phone.''

Eldridge sounded calm. He said, ''Your aide gave you the message, I gather. From right now, what we have here is officially an epidemic.''

''Mr. Eldridge,'' said Reynard. ''I specifically asked you to keep this under wraps, didn't I? For the sake of the people of New Hampshire. This outbreak still hasn't reached truly epidemic proportions, has it? You're creating a public panic without any justifiable cause.''

''That's my responsibility,'' replied Eldridge shortly. ''If I'm wrong, I'm prepared to take the blame. I've carried quite a few cans back in my time; I'm not frightened to do it now. People are dying here, Senator, and I have to say that I'm surprised at your attitude. You won't be getting any vote from me, I can assure you.''

Reynard could think of all kinds of absurdly chastening

things to say, like "I'll break you, Eldridge," or "You'll never work in government again." But as it was, he simply said, "All right, Mr. Eldridge, if that's the way you want to do it," and hung up.

They were all watching him, their faces serious. Greta, Lincoln, Dean Farber—they could have been mourners at a child's funeral.

"That's it," said Reynard. "Lincoln's right. I'm going to have to withdraw. There's no other way we're going to get out of this with our reputations in one piece; even then we'll have a lot of difficult questions to answer."

"You will *not* withdraw," said Greta. "You will stay in the race, and you will win it."

"Greta, it's too risky. Too many people have died already. We have to call a halt somewhere. Besides, think of the international repercussions of this if it's discovered *after* I'm elected president."

"Think of the repercussions if I announce to the media that we've been living apart for the past few months and that you bribed me to pretend we were still happily married."

Lincoln and Dean Farber stared at each other.

"Is this *true*?" asked Lincoln. "I knew you hadn't been seeing too much of each other, but that happens to all congressmen and their wives. Reynard, is Greta telling me what I think she's telling me?"

"We had a temporary marital glitch, that's all," said Reynard dismissively. "We've settled it now."

"Let me tell you how temporary it was," retorted Greta, a sharp smile on her face. "All my clothes have been moved down to Newport. Reynard is paying me a separate allowance. And I have a new man in my life who makes Reynard seem like Attila the Hun. Oh—I beg your pardon, I forgot that it was bad taste to mention Germans around here."

Lincoln raised his hands. "Now I've heard everything," he said. "Jesus, Reynard, do you know how much money we've invested in this campaign, how hard people have been working to arrange tours and media appearances and rallies? And all the time you have a Nazi warplane in your back garden, a fortune founded on Nazi gold and a First Lady-to-be who doesn't even *like* you, let alone live with you."

Reynard cleared his throat and drummed his fingers on the back of one of the catcher's-mitt chairs. "It seems as though I've miscalculated, doesn't it?"

"I think 'miscalculated' is the understatement of all time," said Lincoln. "Do you know something, Reynard? I always thought you were strong. I always thought you were self-confident. But all of that strength, all of that self-confidence, do you know what that was? Nothing more than the dining-out suit of a character completely devoid of any kind of moral judgment whatever."

He paused and then said, "If it's any consolation, I think you're ideal presidential material."

Dean Farber had been making notes on his clipboard. He raised his hand as though he were in class and said, "Excuse me. I think we're all forgetting something here. Something essential. The epidemic."

"What about it?" barked Reynard. "There's nothing more we can do now. Eldridge is going to declare a state of quarantine."

"But you said it was unstoppable. You said it couldn't be cured. That means that if no one finds an antidote, or at least some kind of preventive treatment, the entire population of Merrimack County might die. The last census figure I have here for Merrimack County is over eighty-five thousand. And in all probability the epidemic will spread even beyond that. Some people may already have carried the virus out of the state."

Reynard looked around the room. "Well," he said at last, "there *was* a treatment . . . as far as I know. Johnson said that the doctors who developed the virus had also found a way of keeping it in check. But this was all of forty-four years ago. Those doctors are probably dead by now. It would take months to discover who they were and whether they'd left any notes about it.''

"What I'm trying to say here is that regardless of our political or personal problems, we still have an epidemic on our hands,'' said Farber.

"Well, we *know* that,'' said Greta obtusely.

"You're missing my point.''

"I wasn't aware that you were making one,'' Greta retorted.

Farber set his clipboard down on the desk as though it were a point in itself. ''The point is that whenever you have a disadvantageous political situation, instead of trying to run away from it, or withdraw, or even argue about it, you should *take charge of it*. Senator Kelly by his present actions is only attracting suspicion. What he should do is to call Mr. Eldridge, and regardless of the fact that Mr. Eldridge has already announced a state of quarantine in Merrimack County, he should *demand* a state of quarantine in Merrimack County; and then he should go to the media and make the official announcement that Concord has been struck by a mystery disease while—let me finish, please—while at the same time making a pledge to pour thousands of dollars of his own money into setting up an epidemic-research laboratory to find out where the virus came from.

"Then he will not only have regained the political initiative and all the credit that goes with it, but also total control over any laboratory tests that have to be made. Most important of all, he will have diverted suspicion from his own estates and his own unfortunate involvement in all of this—maybe long enough for a few of us to make a fresh search, come up with that Nazi plane and destroy it.''

Reynard looked across the room at Lincoln. ''Where did you find this guy?'' he asked. ''He's good.''

Greta said icily, "Perhaps *he* ought to be running for president. I think personally I'd feel safer about the future of the world."

Later that day it was announced on network television news that an epidemic of a disease called "hyper-polio" had broken out in Concord, the capital of New Hampshire, and that thirty people had already died from it. The true figure was nearer fifty, but some cases had yet to be discovered and others were waiting on slabs for examination by pathologists.

Edmond would always remember it as the day chaos finally broke loose. After meeting Natalia Vanspronsen and Walt Seabrook, he had gone straight to attend a young family who had died in the most *Saturday Evening Post* of circumstances: Mom in the kitchen, halfway through frosting a chocolate fudge cake; Dad and one of the younger boys lying in the yard, curled among the leaves they had been raking. And in the bedroom, a little girl of only eighteen months, one hand still clutching her teddy bear. A young paramedic who had already seen five other deaths that day had turned away and wept.

During the afternoon and into the evening, the epidemic spread wider and wider, like a forest fire leaping from treetop to treetop. But instead of a conflagration, there was a rustling undercurrent of fear and anxiety; the roar of cars starting up, loaded with people and possessions; the banging of shutters as homes were locked up and garage doors closed. Lawnmowers were left abandoned on half-trimmed suburban lawns.

For six or seven hours the highways from Concord out to Keene, Manchester and Laconia were blocked with lines of steady traffic. Some people were bolder and took complicated detours, but every highway and rural lane was barred by police, and the signs were up: "QUARANTINE AREA." The cars, trucks and vans were jammed so solidly that many drivers simply switched off their engines, engaged neutral and went to sleep where they were, awakening only for the slow-nudging tide of traffic to bear them along.

The news was out. Senator Reynard Kelly had made an official announcement on television news at five o'clock, appearing serious and drawn—the new Democratic candidate for the presidential nomination who had already upstaged all his competitors.

"This outbreak is both tragic and alarming. I mourn the deaths of those who have already been taken and grieve with their bereaved. We don't know yet what caused this epidemic, what triggered it, but we intend to find out. And I am personally financing an emergency research laboratory, to be staffed by some of the finest neurologists and virologists in the country as well as a team of medical researchers from New Hampshire's Department of Health and Welfare—all working in a concerted effort to bring this terrible epidemic under control."

There were fresh cases reported around the nation—in Los Angeles, in Denver, in Seattle—as visitors to New Hampshire unknowingly took the virus back with them. In Lincoln, Nebraska, fifteen students at Wesleyan University died at a party in the small hours of the following day. In South Portland, Maine, a family of three were found drowned in their indoor swimming pool, suffocated by hyper-polio. A couple died at their table at a restaurant in Atlanta, Georgia.

Outbreaks were still sporadic, however, and because so many cases went unrecognized at first—the couple at the restaurant were mistaken for over twenty-four hours as choking victims—no immediate connection was made between the epidemic in Concord and the sudden asphyxiations around the country. But coroners, medical examiners and pathologists from Maine to California found they were working through the night; it would be only a matter of hours before the Department of Health in Washington realized it faced the beginning of a devastating national epidemic.

Edmond was called to eleven more cases before Thursday dawned. After the panicked exodus of the previous evening, Concord was now unnaturally silent and most of the cars on the streets were police cars, looking for would-be looters. A large fire was burning over at the New Hampshire Technical Institute—huge, roiling orange flames with thick, black smoke. Somewhere to the west there was another, fiercer blaze, as though a car or a light aircraft were aflame.

Oscar Ford was already in attendance when Edmond arrived at his tenth case, this one on Shawmut Avenue in East Concord. Oscar looked tired and sweaty, and he blew his nose loudly as two paramedics carried the first of the family out of the house.

"Did you know them well?" Oscar asked Edmond.

Edmond nodded. "Nice family, well-behaved kids."

"Nice people are going down all over," said Oscar. "Nice people, with well-behaved kids."

"Some surprise party, huh?"

Oscar patted his arm. "This is what they call a disaster, E.C. You know, on television, when they show those movies about fires and earthquakes and stuff like that? Well, this time we're living it for real."

"You know that it's going to get one of us next. Or both of us."

Oscar pulled a face. "We pathologists don't think about things like that. When you have to spend your working days probing around inside half-rotten stiffs, you block out of your mind the inevitability that one day you're going to be a stiff yourself."

"What's that? Dr. Ford's profound thought for the day?"

Oscar tapped his forehead. "Just a way of staying alive, inside here."

The paramedics brought out the last victim, a boy of six. The red blanket didn't quite cover his tousled hair, and Oscar stepped forward and tugged it over.

"By the way," he said to Edmond, reaching into his pocket, "what do you make of this?"

He passed Edmond a glassine envelope containing an empty clear glass phial. Edmond turned the envelope over in his fingers and then held it up to the spotlight on top of the ambulance. A tiny quantity of colorless liquid lay at the bottom of the phial, and there were whitish translucent blobs around the neck of it, as though it had once been sealed with wax.

"Where did you find this?" he asked.

"In the house there, down the back of the sofa. I always shove my hand down the backs of sofas. You'd be amazed at what you find down there. Force of habit, I guess. I once found a twenty-dollar bill down the back of my mother-in-law's couch; I thought it a small but just recompense for all the bullet-hard cookies of hers I'd ever had to eat."

"This is German," said Edmond. "Look, there's a German name engraved on the side of it."

Oscar leaned over and frowned at the envelope. "I don't have my glasses," he said. "Here—take it out of the envelope if you want to, but hold it at either end. I want to have it checked for prints when I get back."

Edmond opened the envelope and carefully extracted the phial. He had a magnifying glass in his bag in the car; he took the phial over to examine it. Oscar waited beside him, his hands in his pockets, sniffing from time to time. "I bet I caught that stupid Moretti's cold," he remarked.

"Here, it's quite clear," said Edmond. "Oberhausen Glasfabrik, and then a serial number."

"Could it have contained some kind of drug?" Oscar suggested.

"We can soon find out, can't we? There's enough liquid

in the bottom for analysis. I'd be interested to know what it is.''

"Well, I'll pass it over to Lim Kim. He's our mysterious-substance expert. The only analysis that's had him licked so far is the main ingredient of my mother-in-law's cookies. We both agree that the principal constituent is cement, but we're still arguing over the granite and the deadly nightshade.''

Edmond knew that Oscar was bantering only because he was frightened. He handed back the glass phial, then gave him a slap on the back and said, ''I hope I don't see you later, okay?''

"Forty-seven so far,'' said Oscar.

"At least Eldridge has ordered a quarantine.''

"Bryce said they should have done it earlier—much earlier, when we first suggested it.''

"Bryce said that?''

"Bryce may be a stickler for protocol but he's a good doctor.''

They drove off in their different ways, Oscar following the ambulance to the hospital, Edmond heading toward the Brick Tower Motor Inn. Edmond was exhausted now, and sticky with sweat. All he wanted was a hot shower, a cup of coffee and an hour's sleep. It was almost dawn; a streak of gray light was spreading on the horizon behind the darkened brow of Taylor State Forest. The radio was tuned to the news, but the only mention of the epidemic was a message from the governor that Edmond had heard twice already, appealing to the citizens of Concord and Merrimack County to ''remain calm, don't panic, and observe the quarantine.'' The governor then gave five emergency telephone numbers to call ''should you feel unwell or experience any untoward difficulty in breathing.'' One of the numbers was Edmond's. He expected that Lara was tearing her hair out back at the clinic, trying to answer all the calls. The governor should have given his own damned number.

Edmond had just joined the Frederick E. Everett Highway when there was a beep on his car phone. He picked it up and said, "How's it going, Lara? Chaotic?"

"I think the switchboard's going to melt," she told him. "But I'm okay. I've had one of my roommates in to help. We take turns and answer twenty calls each."

"I'm going to try to catch an hour's sleep and a cup of coffee," said Edmond. "We haven't had any more emergencies, have we?"

"Only one, and Dr. Pryor's dealing with it."

"God bless Dr. Pryor. Anything else?"

"Well, if you're still anywhere near East Concord, we had a call from the Mayer family—you know, young Bernie Mayer? Apparently Bernie's not feeling too well, although they don't think he's actually contracted hyper-polio."

Edmond said, "Tell them to give him a junior aspirin and send him to bed."

"Okay," sighed Lara.

Edmond rubbed his eyes. God, he felt tired. But supposing young Bernie had caught hyper-polio? "On second thought, I'll go around there," he told Lara. "Maybe I'll be able to catch someone who's only just caught the disease. So far all I've seen are corpses."

"Whatever you say, Doctor."

He turned off the highway at the Fort Eddy cloverleaf. The fires at the technical institute had died down now, although there still lingered a pall of heavy black smoke through which a tracery of skeletal fires flickered like a prehistoric encampment. A police car was parked halfway across the turn-off ramp to Sugar Ball, and the officer waved him to the side of the road, but as soon as Edmond showed his doctor's ID, the man told him to carry on.

"We're just watching for looters, you know? We caught a family coming through here with a trunkful of garden furniture. People are dying, and all they can think of is garden furniture."

Edmond arrived outside the Mayer's house and parked his car. It was light now; a solitary bird was chirping and fluttering on a small tree in the center of the lawn. Mrs. Mayer opened the front door when Edmond was only halfway up the path and beckoned him inside.

"I know how busy you are, Doctor, what with this epidemic. But Bernie's in a terrible state. He won't speak to us; he won't eat. He keeps crying all the time. And if we ask him how he's feeling, he tells us we won't understand."

"Hi, Doctor," said Mr. Mayer, coming out of the kitchen. "Sorry to call you out like this, but we're *worried*. Especially after what happened to Michael."

"Would you like some coffee?" asked Mrs. Mayer.

"You never said a more enticing word," Edmond replied.

He went upstairs to Bernie's bedroom. The drapes were still drawn and Bernie was huddled in a corner in his pajamas, his face in his hands. Edmond drew up a chair, turned it around and straddled it. He looked at Bernie for a long time before he spoke.

"Your mom and pop tell me you're not feeling too good."

Bernie didn't answer.

"They say you're not talking; not eating. They say you keep crying all the time."

Still no answer. But Bernie opened his fingers just a crack, and Edmond could see one glittering eye examining him carefully.

Edmond ran his fingers through his hair. "Is it something to do with Michael?" he asked. "I told you before that you'd have real feelings of sadness for him."

"No," Bernie croaked.

"It's not about Michael?"

"It was Michael's fault."

"What was Michael's fault? That he died and left you?"

"Uh-uh. It was Michael's fault that all these people got sick."

Edmond frowned. "It wasn't his *fault*, Bernie. He got sick too. It's just one of those tragic things that happen sometimes."

"It wasn't me. I didn't know what was in them. But now everybody's going to think it was my fault when it was Michael's. It wasn't me at all. I swear it and hope to die. I didn't know."

Edmond got up and went over to sit on the side of the bed, where he reached out and laid a hand on Bernie's knee. "Listen, Bernie, I'm not sure I understand any of this. What wasn't your fault?"

Bernie was trembling. Although he kept his hands pressed to his face, a single sparkling tear oozed out between his fingers and ran down to his wrist.

"Bernie," Edmond urged him, "I'm a doctor. Do you know what that means? It means that no matter what you say to me, no matter what you've done, I'm not allowed to tell anybody else about it, not unless you want me to. When I became a doctor, I had to take an oath of professional secrecy, and I've never broken it."

Bernie parted his fingers a little. "You mean that? You've never told anybody anything? What if I said I was a murderer?"

"Well, I'd probably try to persuade you to give yourself up. But I wouldn't go to the cops."

"It wasn't my fault," Bernie repeated. "It really wasn't, honest."

Edmond was silent for a moment. Then he said gently, "Tell me."

"It must have been the bottles."

"Bottles?"

Bernie took his hands away from his red, tear-stained face and held his index finger and his thumb about four inches apart. "Six little glass bottles, in a leather case. I found them in our secret hiding place in Michael's garage. I didn't know what they were. I got, I don't know, kind of *angry* about them because Michael was dead and couldn't tell me. In the end I got tired of taking them out and looking at them, so I took them to school and sold them. I told everybody they were secret obedience potions, and if you gave some of the potion to your mom and dad, they'd do anything you wanted them to."

Edmond said in a quiet and controlled voice, "Can you remember the names of the people you sold them to?"

Bernie nodded.

"Let me tell you who they were," said Edmond; he recited a list of six family names, ending with the family at Shawmut Avenue whose house he had just left.

Bernie stared at him in amazement. His eyelashes were stuck together with tears. "How did you know that?" he asked.

"Because all those families have a child at your school, Bernie, and all of them are dead."

Bernie looked down at the bedspread. Two more tears ran from his eyes and down his cheeks.

"Will they lock me up?" he asked.

Edmond put his arm around Bernie's shoulders. "No, they won't lock you up, Bernie. Maybe you should have come out and said something sooner, but I think everyone will understand why you didn't. It takes a whole lot of courage to admit that you've been foolish, especially when the consequences are as serious as this. People much older than you have done far less tragic things and been scared to admit it."

Bernie clung to Edmond tightly and wept. Edmond patted his back and calmed him down. At last he said, "Do you have any idea where Michael might have found those bottles?"

Bernie sniffled and nodded. "I think so. When I was

out at my music lesson that day, he went to Conant's Acre, right by Webster Crescent, and I think he explored the woods on the far side there. I went across myself and I saw Michael's mark on one of the trees. We had a secret trail-blazing mark, but I couldn't find out where the trail went because a man came along and told me to go away."

Edmond stood up. "Listen, Bernie," he said, "I'm going to use your mom's phone. While I'm phoning, I want you to get dressed. Jeans and a sweatshirt, something warm. Then I think you ought to take me over to Conant's Acre and show me just where you saw Michael's mark. Do you think you can do that?"

"Yes, sir."

"Okay, then. Quick as you can, you got it?"

Edmond went downstairs. Mr. and Mrs. Mayer were waiting for him in the hallway. "Is he all right?" asked Mrs. Mayer. "He doesn't have polio, does he?"

Edmond shook his head. "Physically, he's fine."

"What are you trying to tell us, that mentally he's not?" Mr. Mayer asked.

"Mentally, Mr. Mayer, he's just a little worried. But I think we're going to clear that up pretty fast. Do you mind if I use your telephone?"

"Go ahead," said Mr. Mayer, obviously bewildered.

Edmond put in a call to Dr. Oscar Ford, who had only just reached his office. He sounded tired and irritable.

"Oscar, it's Edmond. Listen—I've had a real breakthrough. I want you to come down to East Concord as fast as you can make it."

"E.C., that's *impossible*. I've got bodies backed up to the parking lot; it's seven-thirty; I haven't slept all night. And I have nine autopsies to finish before I get to bed. *Nine*, E.C. So don't ask me."

"Oscar, I think I may be close to finding where the virus has been coming from."

Oscar was silent for a long ruminative moment. "You're sure about that?"

"As sure as I can be. That glass phial you found at the Harrington place—it was one of six. Young Bernie Mayer discovered them in a secret hiding place at Michael Osman's house after Michael died. Bernie kept them for a while, then sold them to some of his school friends. And those school friends' names tally with the death list."

"For Christ's sake!" said Oscar. "Where did Michael get them?"

"Bernie thinks Michael might have found them on Conant's Acre someplace. He went up there a couple of days ago and saw marks that Michael had blazed on some of the trees. He wasn't able to follow them because one of Senator Kelly's men told him to clear off, but he seems to be pretty sure that Michael must have found the phials somewhere around there. The two kids were bosom buddies and always told each other everything. So if Michael had been blazing marks on trees, he must have done it on that one afternoon when Bernie wasn't with him—the afternoon he died. He never had a chance to tell Bernie what it was he'd found."

"I've already sent the phial down to Lim Kim for analysis. I don't think he gets into the lab until nine-thirty; we should have some results by lunchtime."

"Oscar, just get down here, will you? Let the dead wait for now."

Oscar cupped his hand over the telephone for a moment; Edmond could hear him speaking in a muffled voice to someone else. Then he said, "All right, E.C. I'll be with you in ten minutes. Give me the address, will you?"

SIXTEEN

At almost the same time, Chiffon Trent was given her first
taste of Denzil's creative moviemaking.

He had awakened her at dawn by screaming in her ear at
the top of his voice. She had screamed back at him in
terror and twisted against her bonds. But Denzil had just
stood there, his hands in his pockets, and laughed at her.
He had been smartly dressed in a pearl-gray 1940s-style
suit and a wide tie with a purple palm tree painted on it.

"Scared you, didn't I? It's dawn."

"Dawn?" she had asked him blurrily.

"Didn't you know that all great directors get up at
dawn? That's when the stars are at their freshest and most
vulnerable. You—well, my love, you look especially,
superbly vulnerable."

"You're not going to—you're not going to make a
movie? Not *now*?"

"Now, pronto, *immediatement*."

"You're crazy. I'm not going to—"

Denzil laughed. Not a very humorous laugh—more like
the laugh of a carny clown or a sideshow busker. "You're
dead, remember? Such a tragedy. Even more tragic that

once you're dead, you're not entitled to have opinions anymore. How can you call me crazy when you're dead? How can you object to starring in a couple of little movies when you're dead? You're *dead*, Miss Trent. Deader'n mutton. So if anything should happen to you—you know, if you should start getting ideas about *protesting*—well, just remember that nobody's going to come looking for you and nobody's going to care. You're already beyond care, my love. Understand me, young lady: if you don't do as you're told, you're going to regret it. And I mean really regret it.''

He had quickly snapped free the scarves that bound her and then ushered her naked down the corridor, soft carpet on bare feet; down a narrow, carpeted flight of stairs; along another corridor lined with framed prints by P. Buckley Moss, spindly people in spindly landscapes, until he suddenly slammed open a door and there it was: the studio. Dazzlingly lit, it was a large, high-ceilinged room that had originally been a body shop. Denzil had painted the brick walls a photographic mat-black, and at one end he had erected a three-sided plasterboard wall, decorated with gold-flocked wallpaper and hung with mock-Regency paintings—a suitably rococo background for the orgy-sized, ornate bed that stood in center-stage, carefully made as though by a hotel chambermaid, with plumped-up pillows and neatly turned-down sheets.

It was not the bed that immediately caught Chiffon's attention, however. It was the sight of the two naked men who stood on the opposite side of the studio, arms folded, sharing a joint. One was black, one was white. Each was well over six feet tall, and built like a football player, with deep muscular chest, narrow waist, and sinewy thighs like Kentucky hams. They were speaking carelessly in random phrases, as though they were standing in line for a job at an Illinois meat-packing plant. Men who had come to service whatever girls had been arranged for them. Did you see the Giants last night? What about that eleven-yard rush? That was *bad*.

"Here she is, boys," said Denzil. "Our star."

The men glanced at Chiffon quickly and then turned back to each other. Chiffon had the feeling they were almost embarrassed to look at her, although she couldn't think why. If they were skin-flick actors, why should they be embarrassed?

"Come on over," said Denzil. "Introduce yourselves. You ought to be *introduced*, at least. I'll go see what's happened to Rossi."

Chiffon stood where she was, close to the end of the bed. The men shrugged to each other, then walked across and stood at either side of her, their muscular arms folded.

The black man was the taller by two or three inches. He was utterly bald, his scalp so polished it had the sheen of a Washington Red apple. He said, "If you want to call me anything at all, you can call me Pisco. That's what my friends call me."

The white man was blond, with tangled blond curls and a small blond mustache. He did nothing but grin shyly and say, "I'm John. How're you doing?"

Chiffon said, "I never did anything like this before."

"Well, sure, everybody has to start somewhere," said John with an absent grin. "You'll probably take to it, you know. It's good money for easy work. Well, I mean, it's easier for a girl than it is for a guy. I mean, a guy has to keep it solid all the time, and that takes a special kind of talent, you know? You have to think about something else, like second-hand auto prices. I'm in second-hand autos myself when I'm not doing this. John's High-Class Heaps."

"Shut up, man," put in Pisco. He sucked at the roach before pinching it out with his fingers.

Just then Denzil returned, with Mae-Beth strutting close behind him, wearing a salmon-pink crocheted mini dress, and his cameraman, Eugene Rossi, shuffling a few paces after, carrying a heavy tripod. Rossi wore a red baseball cap, and sneakers that sounded as though they were three sizes too large. He didn't even look at Chiffon as he set up the video camera.

Mae-Beth came over, put her arm around Chiffon and said, "Don't worry about this one, honey. This one is just a straight half-hour porno film." She smiled, kissed Chiffon's cheek and said, "I know these two guys. They'll treat you good, I promise. Won't you, guys?"

"Sure, Mae-Beth," said Pisco laconically. "Good as gold."

Denzil coughed into his hand and said, "Are we going to get this together or what? Let's have you people on the bed—Chiffon in the middle. We'll start with lots of foreplay, okay?"

Chiffon lay down between them, smelling the coconut oil on Pisco, the plain sweat on John, and she shivered because she was half-frightened and half-aroused. The feeling that her own free will had been taken away from her disturbed her the most, the feeling that she no longer existed as a person. She was nothing more than a nameless, naked woman whom any man could use exactly as he wanted—because no one was ever going to come to rescue her and the only way she could survive from day to day was by doing exactly as these men demanded.

"Chiffon, this is going to be a fantasy sequence, right?" said Denzil, strutting in front of the camera, his hands in his pockets. "Later on we're going to slot this into a longer movie, you understand, but we're also going to market it as a short video. You've fallen asleep; you've been having a dream about these two guys; all of a sudden you believe you're actually living it."

Chiffon was trembling. In a choked voice she asked Denzil, "I don't know what to *do*."

"Just respond, okay? You know how to *respond*, don't you?"

"I don't know whether I can."

"Well, for Christ's sake, you're going to have to."

"I don't know. I don't know. I *can't*."

But then Pisco turned over and murmured to her, "Don't panic. You understand me? We're not going to hurt you. Take it easy. Be cool. Just close your eyes and think of somebody you love. You can do that much, can't you?"

Chiffon swallowed, and nodded. The next twenty minutes or so seemed like a lifetime—her terror and feeling of shame evidently achieved the effect Denzil wanted, because he proceeded to ignore her and merely directed her two partners. Afterward she remembered only part of what had happened. She remembered both of them thrusting into her at once—two slick, muscular, sweaty bodies, one underneath her, one bearing down on her from above.

Denzil watched it all without blinking more than twenty or thirty times, smoking a cigarette. He had seen it scores of times before; he would see it scores of times again. Raw pornography. The gradual stripping-away of a woman's pride and identity and sense of herself until she was willing to do anything for anybody and not even care if she were being paid for it, or even if it meant the difference between living and dying. When the final scenes were filmed—the shootings or the stranglings or whatever it was the client had requested—the girls were almost always ready for it: a last cleansing agony, a sexual martyrdom. Ordinary people didn't understand. It frightened them. But Denzil knew how close this lay beneath the skin of ordinary men and women, and that was why it didn't frighten him at all. Violent orgasm and violent death shared the same basic ingredients.

"Two minutes," he remarked to Rossi, watching with complete detachment as Pisco climaxed spectacularly.

Mae-Beth said, "It seems like a shame, you know?"

"*Life* is a shame," replied Denzil.

Rossi stepped back at a three-quarter angle from the bed

to record John's climax, then abruptly raised the video camera and said, "That's it, that's a wrap." As suddenly as it had begun, it was all over.

Chiffon lay where she was, staring up at the black-painted ceiling. Mae-Beth went over and sat on the edge of the bed with a box of Kleenex.

"Are you all right, honey?"

Chiffon looked at her blankly, as though she didn't understand what was happening. Mae-Beth dabbed at her with a Kleenex and said, "It's a shame, the whole thing, but what can you do? It's supply and demand, you know? People want something, other people are prepared to pay good money for it. That's it."

"All right, Mae-Beth," said Denzil coldly. "Just get her back to her room, will you?"

Chiffon was led away like a woman hypnotized. Pisco meanwhile pulled on a black-leather supporter and opened a can of V-8; John sat naked on the end of the bed with his knees together and painstakingly rolled another joint. Denzil went around switching off lights so the studio grew dimmer.

A door at the side of the studio opened and three young men walked in. One of them went straight up to Denzil, held out his hand and said, "Hello, Mr. Forbes. How're things?"

"Oh, you," said Denzil without shaking hands. "Who are these bozos?"

"Two of the best studs in the business. Actors too. Professional actors."

"Any experience?" Denzil asked them.

"Some," said one of the young men, a tough-looking Hispanic in yellow jeans.

"You?" Denzil asked the other one.

"I am a professional actor, just as Mr. Manzanetti said. You want me to do something and I will do it."

"What are you, Polish?"

"Russian," the young man told him.

"Russian? Well, well. *Rad pazhnakomitsah*."

"You speak Russian?" Piotr asked him warily.

"Oh, boy, I know lots of things," grinned Denzil. "Keep it up for as long as those Soyuz space stations and we're in business. Did you get a look at that last session we shot? Isn't that girl something? That's the girl you'll be working with."

Piotr nodded and tried to smile, but he didn't answer. He was still shocked by what he had just witnessed from the studio's upstairs balcony. Chiffon, of all the girls in the world! Chiffon, over whom he had grieved so bitterly. Alive, as provocative as ever—and making sex movies in the midwest. He felt such an explosion of emotion over seeing her that he didn't know what to say, or even what to think. Relief at seeing her alive, but revulsion at seeing her filmed with two strange men, and ultimately anger at having been taken for a dupe. She must have decided to break with him, to break with Reynard and to break with that failing movie career of hers—to strike out on her own as a porno queen. Then what? A new life under a new name? Piotr neither knew nor wanted to care. It had been difficult enough for him to decide to come to Milwaukee and make himself some money as a hired stud. Then to find the girl he was most fond of in the whole of the United States was already here and making sex movies. . . . He tasted bile in the back of his mouth, and the hot smell of movie lights and electrical equipment began to suffocate him.

"I must get some air," he told Billy Manzanetti.

"You're not sick? You look kind of pallid."

"I'm okay, just tired."

"You'd better not be sick. You can't make sex movies when you're sick."

"I'm not sick, all right? I just need some air."

Billy Manzanetti reached into his jeans pocket and brought out a set of Avis keys with a red-and-white plastic tag.

"Take the car. Go down to that store we saw on the corner and buy us a couple of bottles of Chardonnay. You need some money?"

"Okay. I'll be back in ten minutes."

Piotr left the large, scabby-looking building on West Good Hope Road and walked out to the parking lot. The white Pinto they had rented at the airport was parked next to Denzil's huge, sagging Imperial Le Baron. It was nearly eight o'clock in the morning. The sky was light, with a high cloud cover, and the air was chilly. A typical fall morning close to Lake Michigan. Piotr rubbed his hands together to warm them up; for some reason he felt for the first time in years like a Russian, a compromised stranger in an uncompromising land.

He drove down to the store on the corner and parked. He climbed out of the car, crossed in front of the store and picked up one of the outside telephones. He said, breathily, "I want to make a collect call to a number in New York, please."

It was almost three minutes before the call was cleared. Then a sharp voice answered, "Yes? This is Cerenkov."

"I'm in Milwaukee," said Piotr.

"So I understand. I'm paying for this call, remember."

"Listen, I've found the girl. She's still alive."

"What girl?"

"Chiffon Trent. It must have been a trick of some kind. Chiffon Trent is alive, and she's here. She can tell you everything you want to know about Reynard Kelly firsthand. She knows more than I do."

"Give me your address."

"No, not before I have a promise from you that my mother will be left alone."

"Oh, come on now, Piotr. You could be making all of this up. It said in the newspapers that the girl was dead, and now you have made her alive again?"

"It's true."

Cerenkov was silent for a while. Then he said, "We may be able to come to some arrangement if it is really her."

"It really is."

"Well, it's most suspicious."

"Cerenkov, it's true. I can hardly believe it myself. One minute we were lovers, the next minute she was gone; and then I heard she was killed. Now I come to Milwaukee and quite by accident find that she is here. But it is true."

"I'm not sure, Piotr. Your mother has been guilty of many serious offenses."

"Leave her alone, Cerenkov, and I will tell you where you can find Chiffon Trent. I won't consider any other arrangement."

"Hmm," said Cerenkov.

A chilly breeze blew a center section of *The Milwaukee Journal* across the parking lot, followed by the front page. The headline read "Mystery Polio Hits Milwaukee?"

Cerenkov at last said, "All right. I think I believe you. I guarantee I will send instructions to Moscow to let your mother go. Now, tell me where you are."

Piotr told him. Then he hung up the phone and stood in the wind for a while, his arms crossed over his chest as though he were ill. At last he pushed his way into the store and looked around for the liquor cabinet.

SEVENTEEN

Edmond had borrowed a pair of wire clippers from Bernie's father; it took them only three or four minutes to snip away enough of the barbed wire to clear an access. Oscar said, "I hope you know what you're doing, E.C. Senator Kelly isn't known for his sense of humor."

Oscar didn't really mean it; it was nothing more than a way of concealing his nervousness. He was very tired now. He had been up all night, and like everybody at the hospital, he was frayed and edgy and almost at the point of breaking down. Edmond tugged away the last length of barbed wire and said, "I'm not asking anybody to *laugh*, Oscar. Heaven forbid."

Bernie stood a little way off with his mother. He said, "It's over there, by that big tree. A triangle with a circle in the middle."

Edmond looked at Oscar meaningfully, although Oscar didn't really care or understand why. This was the first time Bernie had ever divulged his and Michael's secret blazemark to anyone else. Edmond thought: thank God that people can still keep confidences, that intimate secrets can still be held safe. Poor Bernie. He had suffered so much because of the bond he had had with Michael—strong even after Michael's death. Edmond hoped that God and whatever guardian angels there were would keep the boy safe from hyper-polio.

"We'll go ahead on our own now," said Edmond. "I think it's wiser. But we'll tell you straightaway if we find anything."

"Okay," said Bernie.

"And what do you *say*?" demanded his mother.

"Thank you," Bernie told Edmond. He was embarrassed, but Edmond could tell that he meant it.

"That's okay," Edmond acknowledged. "If I'd ever had a boy, I would have wanted him to be just like you. You got me? Secret Agent X-Seventeen, over and out."

Bernie joined in the game and saluted. Oscar pulled a face and asked, "What is this? The 'Gangbusters' fan club?"

"Don't show your age," retorted Edmond.

He and Oscar climbed over the fence and jumped down heavily into the plowed soil of Conant's Acre. In the distance, over the trees, a flock of crows rose into the early morning sky like a sprinkling of cloves. It was a cold morning; winter wasn't far away. They trudged over the furrows, their shoes making a brittle, crumbling sound in the earth.

"Do you have any idea of what we're looking for?" asked Oscar, sniffling.

"Do you?" asked Edmond. "Where could a leather case full of virus-infected liquid have come from? The *glass* is made in Germany but that doesn't mean anything."

"Lim Kim said the phial looked old-fashioned. He hadn't seen one like it for twenty years."

"Did he have any preliminary opinions about the liquid?"

"He's going to run every test known to man on it. Do you know what he said though? There's an old Chinese saying: 'Truth comes in bottles, but out of old bottles come old truths.' Not bad, huh?''

Edmond wiped sweat from his forehead with his handkerchief. "I don't think I've ever believed in old sayings, except never trust a woman, and keep your powder dry."

They were almost halfway across the field. Oscar said, "You're still staying away from home, huh?"

"What would you do if you found your brother screwing your wife?"

Oscar took out his handkerchief and trumpeted his nose. "I think I'd probably shake him by the hand and nominate him for a Congressional Medal of Honor."

Edmond smiled wryly, then laughed. "You're a stupid bastard," he said affectionately.

They reached the woods. At first they couldn't find Michael's blazemarks, and they walked up and down for fifty yards in each direction, north and south. Oscar called, "I hope young Bernie was telling the truth. I'd hate to think I did all this exercise for nothing." But then he suddenly said, "Here it is. Is this it? The triangle with a circle inside it?"

They strode noisily through the undergrowth and examined the mark carved into the bark of the tree. Edmond touched it with his fingertips. If only young Michael had known what was in store for him when he had cut that mark. "This is it," he nodded to Oscar, and they trod farther into the woods, stepping carefully and looking out for more marks.

They found another, and another. The fourth one was way off to the right. "If you ask me, he got scared 'round about here, didn't want to go too deep," Oscar commented.

Edmond listened to the silence of the woods. There was a strange eeriness to the air. The dry leaves fell soundlessly on the crisp, carpeted floor. Up above, the clouds were as still as a painting. No wind blew. "There's another mark here," said Oscar.

They came across the Condor undramatically, almost expecting it, as though this strange specter was the inevitable source of a malevolent sickness like a hyper-polio. The excavation was exactly as Michael had left it when he ran away. Edmond and Oscar approached the plane in awe, neither of them shocked by the sight of a corpse but both silenced by the sight of an entire airliner cockpit buried in the leaves and the loam of a New Hampshire woods.

"Jesus Christ!" said Oscar, hunkering down.

Edmond carefully slid over the edge of the diggings and brushed loose soil and leaves from the plane's roof. He peered inside the broken windows and said, "There are two bodies in there. Well, what's left of them."

"Look at that flying jacket," said Oscar. "It looks like something from the fifties, maybe even earlier. Did you ever see a flying jacket like that?"

Edmond said, "We have to get into that cockpit somehow. Maybe there's a door a little farther back along the fuselage."

"But how did it *get* here?" asked Oscar. "How does anybody bury an entire airliner in a woods? I can hardly believe what I'm seeing."

Edmond stood up and shaded his eyes against the gray morning glare. He pointed to the southeast and said, "Supposing it was trying to make an emergency landing on Conant's Acre . . . I mean, Conant's Acre would make quite a reasonable airfield for a large plane like this."

"Then what?"

"Well, suppose the pilot misjudged his approach. He could have hit the bank on the other side of the woods there and gone straight in. The ground's very soft and boggy around here, and it's even softer down there."

"Are you kidding?"

"Not at all. There was an article in the newspaper six or seven months ago about an historical society in England that goes around locating and excavating old World War

Two fighters and bombers that were shot down during the Battle of Britain. Whole Dornier bombers, buried in fields in Kent. Spitfires and Hurricanes and what have you, complete with the pilot still inside. Twenty feet deep, some of them. They dug up an entire B-Seventeen too.''

Oscar rested his hands on his hips and looked down at the half-buried cockpit of the Condor. "But *here*?" he asked. "You think this plane hit the bank down at the bottom there and pushed its way right in under the woods?"

"I don't see how else it could have gotten here. It wasn't buried deliberately. Look at the way those tree roots are tangled around it, and most of those trees must be a lot older than the plane."

Oscar said, "Let's dig a bit more, see if we can't find a door."

They found a couple of strong sticks and began to hack away at the damp, crumbling soil. After five minutes or so, Oscar took off his coat and rolled up his sleeves. They were silent as they dug. Both of them felt unreal, as though they were participating in an extraordinary nightmare; the stillness of the woods served only to heighten the sense of unreality. A squirrel watched them from high in a nearby tree, and birds chittered excitedly every time the plane's aluminum frame resounded with a blow.

At last, a few feet back from the cockpit windows, they came across the lip of an access door. The aluminum skin of the airliner was corroded and leprous, and as cold as a metal coffin. With the point of his stick, Edmond cleared the dirt out of the sides of the door and chivvied a bowl-shaped lump of impacted mud out of the recess that housed the handle.

"There's some lettering here," said Oscar, wiping the aluminum with his hand.

Edmond took a look. The words were painted in black, scratched and faded but unmistakable. *"Hier öffnen."*

"German," he said quietly. "It's a wartime German bomber."

"It can't be," said Oscar.

"I don't know whether it can or it can't be, it *is*," Edmond insisted.

"Did the Nazis have planes that could fly the Atlantic?"

"I don't know. Well—they must have. Here it is. QED."

"Maybe it was an airliner from the nineteen thirties, made in Germany," Oscar suggested.

"There's only one way to tell for sure. Help me get this door open."

"Maybe we should go back and tell someone before we start tampering with it. We don't want to do any damage, mess up any clues or anything."

"Oscar, we don't have the time. If that virus came from this airplane, I want to know how and I want to know why. The quickest way of identifying it is by discovering who synthesized it. If we can do that, we may learn how to vaccinate people against it."

"If this is a German bomber, E.C., the guy who synthesized it is very likely dead by now. Long dead."

"Let's just get this door open."

They took turns wrestling with the corroded handle. They broke three sticks in trying to lever it downward, and they were about to give up when Edmond picked up the stone Michael had used to break open the cockpit windows and gave the handle six or seven heavy whacks. Gradually, a fraction at a time, the handle budged downward until at last Edmond could ease it free. He gave one last pull and the door of the Condor rattled open.

Cautiously they climbed inside. There was a choking smell of earth and decay. A little light streamed down the airplane's interior corridor from the broken cockpit windows up front, but the main body of the fuselage was pitch dark.

"I want to take a look in the cockpit first," said Edmond.

They made their way forward between gray aluminum walls dripping with moisture and scaly with corrosion. The first body they came to was that of the navigator—a headless heap of bones in a black flying jacket hunched over a chart table. The map in front of him was mildewed and spotted with damp, but there was no mistaking what it was. A chart of New England and Nova Scotia, folded in half, with vectors drawn on Concord, New Hampshire. The map was marked *Nordöstliche Vereinigte Staaten* (Hamburg, 1942). As Edmond carefully eased it out from beneath the navigator's skeletal hand, Oscar edged forward a little and dislodged something on the floor; it rolled away noisily down the dark length of the plane's body.

"What the hell was that?" Edmond asked as the object reached the unseen tail end of the plane with a hollow clonk.

"Sorry. The navigator's skull," said Oscar. "Guy was careless enough to leave it on the floor. No wonder he flew his buddies into this woods."

They went forward, into the main body of the cockpit. There they found the pilot and co-pilot: the pilot leaning sideways with his head half out the broken window, the co-pilot sitting stiff and mummified at the controls. Behind the pilot's seat, doubled into a fetal position as though bracing itself for a crash, was a yellow-skinned semi-skeleton in a green raincoat. It was wearing an old-fashioned trilby hat and round, horn-rimmed spectacles, and among the scattered bones of the left hand there was a gold wedding band.

Edmond distastefully opened the skeleton's raincoat and reached into the inside pocket. Between finger and thumb he carefully drew out a brown-leather wallet and took it over to the navigation table.

Inside the wallet there was five hundred dollars in U.S. bills; a folded receipt for cleaning at Zur Wäscherin, 71 Neukirchstrasse, Minden; a small black-and-white photograph of a plain-looking woman with dark, braided hair, sitting on a bicycle; two torn-off theater-ticket stubs, each priced at two reichsmarks; and an ID card issued by the OKW, the German Supreme Command, naming the mummy in the trilby hat as Dr. Wilhelm Eckhardt. There was a curled-up photograph of a round-faced man with short black hair.

"What do you think?" asked Oscar.

"I don't know. I don't know what to think. But this is a German wartime plane all right, and for some reason it was flown here to New Hampshire sometime during the war. Late nineteen forty-four, I'd say—look at the date on the laundry bill. They obviously *meant* to fly here, to Concord, because the flight's all worked out there on the map. In fact, they meant to land exactly here, on Conant's Acre."

"*On* it rather than *in* it," Oscar commented. "But what the hell were they doing here?"

"Maybe they were bringing the virus over to infect the population of the United States," suggested Edmond. "Maybe they thought they'd never win the war by military force so they'd try something else, something more subtle."

"I don't call hyper-polio subtle," said Oscar harshly.

They poked around the cockpit a while longer, but apart from code books and flying charts, they found nothing else of interest.

"What do we do now?" Oscar asked.

"What we do now is what we should have done way back at the very beginning. We go to the media and tell them what we've discovered. We show them the maps, the wallet, the leather case and as many of those glass phials as we can find. We put the whole thing in front of the public and hope that somebody out there will know enough about World War Two to be able to help us, and to help us quickly."

"You're going to upset a whole lot of people, including

some of our friends. I misjudged Bryce, you know: he's really been pulling for us on this one. Why don't we take the whole lot to him?''

"Because it's too late for protocol, Oscar; and something else has been rattling around in the back of my mind. Why did Senator Kelly try to keep this epidemic under wraps? Do you think he might have *known* about this airplane and what was in it?''

Oscar led the way back along the plane's corridor and grunted his way out of the hatch. "I don't see how he could have known. I mean, if he'd known about it and wanted to keep it quiet, all he had to do was destroy it. And the virus too—if it *is* the virus. We'll have to wait and see what the lab has to say about it.''

Edmond climbed out the hatch and scaled the side of the rough excavation, holding on to tree roots to pull himself up. "What do *you* think it is?''

"I think it's the virus, but I'd prefer to know for sure.''

"How long is it going to take?''

"A couple of hours. They may even know by now.''

Edmond dusted off the maps and the wallet. "All right. Let's go back to the hospital and wait until the lab can tell us for sure. Then we're going straight to the *Concord Journal* and WKXL.''

They retraced their steps through the woods and crossed Conant's Acre until they reached the fence. Edmond twisted some of the barbed wire back together again with the pliers so it wouldn't immediately be obvious that someone had broken through.

Oscar looked back across the field. "You know something," he said. "I almost wish we'd never found that thing.''

"I don't see why. Not if it's going to help us save lives.''

"Oh, I know that. It's just that I don't think I'm ever going to feel happy about flying again.''

Edmond's car phone was beeping when he opened the door. He sat sideways on the seat, picked up the receiver and said, "Dr. Chandler here."

It was Lara. She said, "We've had seven more cases reported, Doctor. And there's one that's special."

"Special? What's special about it?"

There was a long pause and a crackling on the wire. Then Lara said in a strained voice, "It's Mrs. Chandler, Doctor."

They sat in a bare, cream-painted room at the American Embassy in Stockholm's Diplomatstaden, looking out through barred French windows over the embassy courtyard. It was an unexpectedly bright and sunny afternoon, with sunshine streaming through the bars and casting striped shadows of imprisonment across Klaus Hermann's face and shoulders.

Bill Bennett stood with his arms folded, watching the man proprietorially. He wore sharply pressed gray slacks and a red *Montana State University* sweatshirt.

Humphrey sat in a corner on a tubular-steel chair. The Swedish authorities had allowed him to go back to his hotel and collect his clothes—which had been crammed untidily into his suitcase and left in the lost-property closet. Now, however, they wanted him to remain in Stockholm for two or three more days in order to complete his formal identification of Klaus Hermann and to assist with their lengthy investigation into the circumstances of his capture. Because several people had died, the Swedish police and intelligence services were anxious to have all the formalities properly dealt with.

Klaus Hermann himself seemed a little sad, a little tired, but philosophical about his fate. He commented to Humphrey that "it was a day of terrible destiny, wasn't it, when I sat in that café next to you?" Humphrey had shrugged and said, "Yes, I suppose it was."

Today they had been running through Hermann's version of what he had been doing since 1945. He claimed that he had been working as a clerk for the Vsevolosk chemical factory, nothing more. "Do you think they would have entrusted a German, a Nazi, with anything more important?" But neither Bill nor Humphrey believed him for a moment, and it was clear from the flat way in which he spoke that he didn't expect them to. He was simply making it clear to them that they would get nothing more out of him.

Bill said, "Tell me something about Angelika Rangström."

"What can I tell you?" asked Hermann. "She's dead."

"All the same."

"I loved her. She died for me. What else do you need to know?"

"You tell me. Did she ever visit you in Russia? Did she sympathize with the Soviet Union?"

"Sympathize? What kind of a question is that?" asked Hermann. "How can anyone sympathize with the Soviet Union? The Soviet Union is not a sympathetic nation; it never pretends to be. Sentimental, yes. Gloomy and magnificent. But not sympathetic."

They sat again in silence. Humphrey wasn't sure of the purpose of these sessions or why Bill Bennett expected him to stay there. He had already formally identified Klaus Hermann six times to six different officials, including a taciturn colonel of the Swedish security services and a young Israeli woman. Bill appeared to be making no serious attempt to interrogate Hermann, and quite often they had sat together without saying a word for more than twenty minutes.

Humphrey said after a while, "Do you think we might all have some tea?"

"Tea?" asked Bill. "Yes, of course."

Klaus Hermann shifted his position on his chair. "It was

with tea that the British won the war, you know. If there were any secret weapons in nineteen forty-five, tea was the greatest. Dr. Mengele used to say that an Englishman can endure anything—any torture, any privation—as long as you give him nine cups of tea every day, with sugar. He had quite a sense of humor, you know, Josef."

Bill went out of the room to call the embassy secretary who had been detailed to look after them. He left the door ajar.

Humphrey said, "This really does seem to be taking an awfully long time, doesn't it?"

Klaus Hermann shrugged. "It is the way of every great bureaucracy to move with infinite slowness. You will probably find that all manner of complicated negotiations are taking place in order to have me extradited. And of course several different nations will be laying a claim to the right to try me, and to hang me. As long as the Israelis don't get me, I don't think I really care very much."

"Aren't you frightened?"

"I don't know. A little, I suppose. Everyone will say I killed so many innocent people without compunction during the war that I have no right to be frightened for my own life. But, yes, I am—just as all those unfortunate Jews were."

Humphrey looked at Hermann for a long time. Then he asked, "Do you feel guilty about what you did? Have you *ever* felt guilty?"

"It is difficult for me to describe what I feel. Regret was useless, there were so many of them. I felt no regret. But sometime during the nineteen fifties, about ten years after it was all over, I felt strangely *haunted*, as though the ghosts of all those Jews trailed after me like an invisible cloak, a cloak that grew heavier and heavier as the years went by. I decided that whether you feel guilty or not, the souls of the people you kill cling to you; they never leave you."

Humphrey stood up and walked to the window. The sun had retreated behind a heavy bank of clouds and the shadows of the bars had faded. "I believe in fate," he said. "I came here to Sweden because fate dictated it. My first holiday alone for years and years! And I should meet you."

Klaus Hermann said, "Well . . ." in a philosophical voice. Then, quite suddenly, "Have you heard the news from America?"

"What?"

"I was listening to the radio this morning. I have a radio in my room upstairs. They say that America has been struck by an epidemic."

"Yes, so I understand. Quite serious too. The British government is insisting that all visitors from America have polio vaccinations."

"Yes, quite so."

Humphrey turned around. "What made you think of it?"

"I beg your pardon?"

"Just now. The epidemic. What made you think of it?"

"Well," said Hermann, rubbing his hands together, "the open door made me think of it. Or rather, the idea of being able to walk out of the open door."

"I don't understand."

"Ah, Mr. Browne, then let me make it clear. This is a delicate matter, you see. I have to phrase it correctly or you might possibly get the wrong idea. You are a fair man, I think. You are rather different from your friend, Mr. Bennett."

"He's not my friend, you know. I didn't go with him voluntarily. I'm not here voluntarily, even now."

"I understand that," said Hermann. "But nonetheless Mr. Bennett needs you because you lend some legitimacy to what he is doing. He badly wants to see me dead, but he must be careful."

"What does the epidemic have to do with any of this?"

"I believe—although I am not yet completely sure—that I am the cause of the epidemic."

"*You*? How?"

Hermann looked down at the floor. He spoke quickly and quietly, as though he were reading from a book. "During the war I was commissioned to breed a strain of virus capable of decimating the population of the United States. Hitler had spoken again and again of how the wealth and power of the United States would bring about his downfall unless some way were found either to persuade Roosevelt to withdraw his support for Britain or to cripple the United States so that she would have to withdraw from the conflict."

"Germ warfare; that was the answer, was it?"

Hermann shrugged. "We didn't exactly call it that. *Biokrieg* was the phrase we used at the laboratory at Herbstwald. There were twenty-nine of us there—research chemists and biophysicists and virologists, the best in the country—and I was in charge. They gave us unlimited money, you know, and the finest facilities you could dream of. And of course we had all those human guinea pigs on which to test our various preparations. We made huge strides in biochemistry and biophysics, even by the standards of today. We discovered so much that sometimes we used to laugh out loud in the laboratory, just as though we were drunk! And then—in nineteen forty-three—on one hot summer afternoon, we made the final breakthrough that allowed us to develop a strain of poliomyelitis virus almost completely impervious to the usual methods of immunization and cure. Also, as the virus was passed from one human being to another, it would grow in strength and virulence until it could cut swathes through millions of people in the space of a few weeks."

Humphrey said, "I don't know whether to believe you or not. It sounds so dreadful."

"Dreadful, yes! That's the very word to describe it. We called it Pest Ninety-one simply because that was the number of the culture in which we first developed it. But dreadful, certainly; and also very difficult to breed and handle. In the end we managed to suspend the virus in a liquid solution that would preserve it, we hoped, for several months. But we were able to produce only six small phials of this liquid in time for Hitler's proposed biological attack on the United States."

Hermann took out his handkerchief and blew his nose loudly. Then, folding up his handkerchief again, he said, "The plan was for one of our team to fly to the United States in a Focke-Wulf Condor. That was the only aircraft we had which was capable of crossing the Atlantic without refueling. There our man would make contact with some Americans who were sympathetic to the Nazi cause—*now* you can talk about sympathy!—and five of the phials would be distributed to German agents the length and breadth of the United States. The sixth phial would openly be shown to the American government, as would the airplane itself. Roosevelt would be threatened that unless he withdrew immediately from the European theater of war, the virus would be released and millions would die."

"I've never heard a word about this," said Humphrey. "You're inventing it."

"No, my dear Mr. Browne. I regret not. *Now* I can talk about regret! The Condor set off for the United States —and disappeared. Perhaps at sea, we don't know. Our friends in America swore they heard it pass over the landing site. But wherever it came down, it vanished completely. And inside it, of course, were the six phials of Pest Ninety-one. On the radio they call it hyper-polio."

Humphrey asked, "Why are you telling me this? I don't understand."

"My reason is this, Mr. Browne. You are the only

person who can rescue me. You are the only person who will even contemplate helping me escape."

"I won't do anything of the kind! Just because I've held all along that even a beggar such as you deserves a fair trial—well, good gracious, man, that doesn't mean I'm going to help you get away. You're a mass murderer. You've as much as admitted it. And worse, if this story of yours is true, about the epidemic . . . good God, you're still killing people, even today!"

"*Listen,*" insisted Hermann. "The Americans are determined to silence me. After the war, when I was first working for the Russians, I was involved in a great many business deals between arms manufacturers and drug suppliers, both in America and the Soviet Union. I know far too much for the comfort of far too many American industrialists. You've heard of Mr. Walter Ridgefield—of Ridgefield Petroleum? Yes, he is one of those honorable gentlemen who would do anything to have me disposed of. And there are many more. You remember what embarrassment Klaus Barbie caused among the good people of Lyons? I can wreak far more havoc should I survive. But of course your friend Mr. Bennett will make sure I don't."

"But this virus—"

"This virus, my dear Mr. Browne, is my key to freedom—my only key. And the reason is that all my wartime colleagues are now dead; all my records are safely stored in the Soviet Union. The only person in the Western hemisphere who knows how to stop that virus from wiping out sixty percent of the population of the United States by Christmastime is me."

"There *is* an antidote?"

"Oh, yes. But it isn't at all conventional. If an American scientist manages to work out what it is in time to save the last few percent of his countrymen, I shall regard it as a miracle."

"*Now* I understand you," said Humphrey, outraged.

"*Now* I understand what you are. Once a Nazi, always a Nazi!"

Hermann gave a faintly rueful smile. "You are probably quite right, Mr. Browne. Hitler instilled in us a deep and everlasting hatred that never seems to completely leave one's mind or one's body. He always used to say that freedom could be achieved only by pride, and willpower, and hate, and hate, and once again, hate."

Humphrey said, "You'd better tell Mr. Bennett what this antidote is so he can pass it on to the proper authorities."

"Are you mad, Mr. Browne?"

Humphrey flushed. "You can't let thousands of people die when you know perfectly well how to save them!"

"Oh, I can. Why should I care? I'm old, I will die soon in any event—if Mr. Bennett doesn't blow off my head first."

"This is insane."

"No, Mr. Browne, not insane. It is nothing but the ruthless bargaining of an elderly man who wishes to stay alive. Now listen to me. They will be taking me away soon, and disposing of me. There can't be many more opportunities remaining for you to help me escape. You must go and speak to a man called Bendix. He has a house on Ostermalmsgatan. Tell him where I am and what is going to happen to me. Tell him also that you will try to get me out of the embassy at some unforeseen time of the day or night and that he is always to have a man ready to whisk me away."

"Herr Hermann, this is preposterous. You're under guard! I'll never be able to get you out of here!"

"You don't think so? Well, perhaps it will be difficult. But while you go to speak to Bendix, I will do my best to think of a way."

"And in return for your freedom, you'll tell Mr. Bennett what the antidote to this virus is?"

Hermann shook his head. "I'll tell *you*. I'll write it down sometime today, and when you have managed to get me out of the building, I will give it to you. If I don't keep my part of the bargain, you will have a chance to cry out for help, and I might still be caught. So you see, you have some guarantee.''

"Supposing you just write down something completely worthless? And how do I know there really *is* an antidote to this virus?''

"Mr. Browne, if I escape, I scarcely wish to live on a planet where Pest Ninety-one is loose. You have my word that there is an antidote and that I will give it to you when I am free.''

Humphrey said, "I've a good mind to tell Mr. Bennett all about this, right away.''

"And what good would that do you? I will deny everything you say. And I can assure you that even under torture I will not reveal the antidote. If you hurt or kill me, you will all come to hell with me, you and Mr. Bennett and the entire population of the world.''

There was a staring, fanatical look in Klaus Hermann's eyes and Humphrey involuntarily shivered.

"I'm going to have to think this over," he said solemnly. "I'm not the treacherous type, you know. I worked very hard for the war effort, trying to catch up with chaps like you. This does rather fly in the face of all that.''

Bill Bennett walked back in again, smoking the last of a cigarette. "Tea will be here in a couple of minutes," he said, breathing smoke out of his nostrils. He went over to the corner of the room and stood where he had been standing for most of the morning.

"Perhaps we should have a game of cards," suggested Hermann.

Bill stared at him without a word.

"Well, it was only an idea. Something to pass the time.''

Humphrey said, "They don't have any biscuits, do they? I'm afraid my stomach's rumbling rather a lot."

Bill didn't answer. Silence fell between them again. Humphrey went back to his tubular-steel chair and sat down.

He didn't dare look at Hermann, but the man's proposition was churning around in his head. No one would need to know it was he who had released Hermann; he could always pretend that Hermann had forced him—with a knife perhaps, or a broken bottle. And when he produced the antidote for the virus, think of the fame and the recognition he would receive. Fifty times more than any of the credit he would get for having identified an old ex-Nazi. He would be seen as the man who had single-handedly saved the world. He would mix with royalty, film stars and heads of state.

Bill said to him sharply, "Something on your mind, Humphrey?"

"What? Oh, no. Not particularly. I was just wondering whether I might be allowed out to do some shopping this afternoon."

"I'm going to need you back here at four. I've got two guys coming over from Finland."

"Well, of course. I'll be back whenever you say."

"That's very cooperative of you all of a sudden."

Humphrey attempted a smile. "We're all on the same side, aren't we? Special relationship and all that. And, well, now that we've caught Hermann, there's not much more to worry about, is there?"

"If you say not."

Malcolm was downstairs in the living room, already half-drunk. Edmond walked in and stood looking at him without speaking.

"I didn't think it could be so sudden," said Malcolm in

a hoarse voice. "One minute she said she couldn't breathe properly. The next. . . ."

Edmond said, "You realize that you may now be infected too?"

"Huh?" said Malcolm. "Yes. It had crossed my mind."

"As far as we can ascertain, the virus is passed through the digestive tract just like the usual polio virus. Since you and Christy have been having sex together, the possibility of a virus having passed between you is relatively high."

Malcolm opened his mouth and then closed it again.

Edmond went on. "As yet, we have no way of curing it. If you have contracted hyper-polio, you're going to die."

"I see," said Malcolm. He let out an uneven laugh. "The wrath of God, huh, for taking my brother's wife in adultery?"

"Maybe."

"Oh, 'maybe.' Listen to you, you priggish bastard. You screwed around more than anyone I ever knew. And now *I* get punished for it? Whoever punished *you*?"

"You did," said Edmond quietly. "You punished me when you slept with Christy. The fact of the matter is that I did love her."

"You don't know the meaning of the word."

Edmond said, "Have another drink. You might as well. It won't feel so painful if you're smashed."

Malcolm swayed and then suddenly sat down on the arm of the sofa, splashing whiskey over his wrist.

"You're serious," he said. "You really don't have any kind of cure for this?"

"Have you heard the news? It's broken out all over the country now, and there's nothing that anybody can do to stop it. The government's sending up a special team of biophysicists from UCLA tomorrow morning and a whole regiment of assorted specialists from every germ-warfare center in the country. Eighteen hundred dead already."

"Edmond, if I really have caught this thing—" Suddenly there were tears in Malcolm's eyes.

Edmond said, "Don't plead with me, Malcolm. If I had a cure, I'd give it to you. But don't plead, because there isn't one. And for God's sake, don't tell me you're sorry."

Malcolm raised his hands in a gesture of helpless despair. Tears ran down his cheeks.

"Go on, finish the bottle," said Edmond. "Knowing your luck, you probably haven't caught it anyway."

He left Malcolm and went upstairs to the bedroom. Christy was lying on the bed, fully dressed in a turquoise woolen suit, very white in the face. Edmond approached the bed slowly and stared down at her as though he expected her to open her eyes at any moment and smile at him. He felt almost foolish for not greeting her.

So this is where it ends, he thought. All those years together. All those arguments, all those problems, all that loving. For this we met and courted and married. For this we went on vacation to South Carolina. He looked over at the wardrobe with its white louvred doors and wondered whether it was worth taking her clothes out, and sorting her jewelry. But then he thought to himself, what's the point? It's finished. All her possessions are as dead now as she is.

He thought: it's strange, but I don't feel like crying.

There was a soft knock at the door behind him. Oscar stood there. He said, "You okay, E.C.?"

Edmond nodded. "I think so. Maybe the shock will hit me later."

"Do you still want to go talk to the press?"

"I want to do that right now."

"I'll drive you down there, huh? Stacey and Killigan can take care of Christy for you, and I'll make sure they lock up the house."

"Don't worry about that. My brother's here."

"You mean the dark-haired guy who pushed past me in

the hallway? No, he's not. He went out the door and took off like a rabbit."

Edmond glanced toward Christy. "He may have contracted hyper-polio."

Oscar said, "You told him?"

"Yes."

"Well then," said Oscar, "you did get back at him after all, didn't you?"

By mid-afternoon the president had declared a nationwide state of emergency. The National Guard was mobilized in every state, and contingents of regular soldiers were sent out to guard every hospital, clinic and medical warehouse. All police leave was canceled except in Alaska, and a curfew of seven o'clock was imposed on everyone except those performing essential services.

"I may be accused of overreacting," the president had said gravely on network television news, "but I have to take serious account of the fact that more than two thousand Americans have already died from the effects of hyper-polio and that so far the epidemic shows no sign of abating. We must do whatever we can to minimize the spread of this deadly and indiscriminate disease. I ask you to remain calm, to avoid traveling whenever possible, and to be constantly vigilant. Be assured that we have already set hundreds of highly qualified scientists the urgent task of finding a cure for hyper-polio and that we shall soon be successful. A special government fund is being set up to finance the vaccination of every man, woman and child in the United States as soon as an antidote is discovered that will halt hyper-polio in its tracks. We can lick this disease, but we need your help. So stay at home. Stay alert. And stay safe."

It was impossible for the economic survival of the nation for the administration to impose a total ban on travel; but medical students were drafted from hospitals and colleges all over the country and given the job of checking passengers at airports, harbors, bus terminals and railroad stations. They were told to check for redness at the back of the throat, shortness of breath, cramps, stiffness and shivering.

The nation was unusually calm and quiet. A newspaper reporter wrote that he drove all the way from Salinas to Ventura and didn't pass a single car on the road. There were some fragmented outbursts of hysteria. Hundreds of would-be emigrants clashed with Canadian customs officers at the border station of Blaine, Washington; an elderly man was fatally shot when he tried to ram the barrier in his station wagon. His two-year-old granddaughter was found cowering in the back seat. And at Tijuana, CBS news cameras filmed the jarring spectacle of Mexican police and customs officials using truncheons and rifle butts to push back scores of screaming Californian refugees, many of whom were brandishing diamond necklaces and hundred-dollar-bills, and even paintings, just to be allowed to escape from the United States and make their way south to Brazil or Uruguay.

A family of five were shot dead as they walked across the border at Sasabe, Arizona; their bodies lay in the sun for three hours, their blood drying in the dust, before U.S. officials were allowed to come across and take them away.

But mostly there was an extraordinary quiet over America, from the shoreline at Kill Devil Hills to the beach at Punta Gorda, through the suburbs of Baltimore and Chicago to the Creole quarter of New Orleans. Silence and stillness, as though the whole nation was afraid to draw a breath in case the air might be infected.

Reynard Kelly sat in his Colonial house at English Village, Maryland, and watched the president's announcement with a stony expression. Then he turned off the set by remote control and sat back in his large, buttoned armchair, one hand clasping a goblet of white wine, the other masking the lower part of his face.

He had been thinking all afternoon of his prewar days in Germany. Daydreaming of Ilse and those dances where the only way in which it had been possible to tell the men from the women was that the men were often prettier. Strange, heady, perverse days; as alluring in his memory as they had been in reality. And he could almost hear, even today, the moist, soft click of Ilse's lips parting to kiss him.

He had been in love then. Yet his love had come back to destroy him. Perhaps men who sought political greatness should never fall in love, he thought to himself. And he remembered with terrible vividness the way Goebbels had shook his hand, nodded and said, "You have the face of a dreamer, Mr. Kelly."

On the far side of the room, Natalia Vanspronsen observed him. She wore sharply creased white slacks and a dark-blue linen blouse. Her figure was reflected in the highly burnished oak flooring: a white and immaculate image of professional femininity.

"Well?" she asked.

Reynard didn't even look at her. He had decided since her arrival in Washington that he didn't like her anymore. Perhaps it was because she made it quite obvious that she wouldn't go to bed with him, and obvious not just to him but to everyone else. He couldn't even intimate that they were lovers. That, for Reynard, was something of a small defeat.

"Well," he said, clearing his throat, "they'll find an antidote, that's for sure. They must. With dozens of the best scientists in the United States working on it, how long can it take? A week, maybe two weeks, not longer."

"Do you think that will absolve you?" she asked.

"Absolve me? From what?" Now he shifted around to look at her.

"From guilt. From responsibility. It was you who brought the virus into the country, after all. Every one of those two thousand deaths is your responsibility in the final analysis. Or don't you think so?"

"Do I pay you to provoke me?" he asked.

"You don't pay me at all. My fees are met by the Democrats for Reynard Kelly."

"But *I'm* Reynard Kelly."

"Yes. And right at this moment I expect you wish you weren't."

Reynard drank his wine. He looked at Natalia, at her fine-boned face. "You're a bitch of a kind," he told her.

"That's why I was chosen to represent you. Or didn't you know that?"

"You and that wife of mine, both bitches."

"Well, so we may be—to you," said Natalia, airy and dismissive.

"What was your suggestion again?" asked Reynard, abruptly changing the subject. He didn't feel in the mood for mental fencing, especially with a woman whose mind was as sharp as her looks. He could cope with women who were sexual: women who cooed and teased and draped themselves around him. But women like Natalia Vanspronsen made him unhappy. He was too old for cutting critiques and smart, creative talents. He wanted women around him who would remind him of how radiantly his charisma still glowed, women who would caress his vanity, if not his penis.

"My suggestion was simply that the best form of defense is attack," said Natalia. "Dean Farber is basically right. You should deny any knowledge of the virus and the plane that brought it over. So what if they *do* find it on your property? Nobody else knows about it, except you and me and your immediate political family. And since you've already set up this research laboratory, you can take the whole thing a step farther and develop the scenario that

Walt Seabrook and I worked out between us on the way down. The laboratory could 'discover' that the virus came from the Merrimack River—a freak pollution that affected one boy, just by accident, and then was passed on from person to person, growing more infectious all the time.''

''Just how is the laboratory going to 'discover' that?'' asked Reynard coldly.

''Very easily. Walt can take a virus culture from one of the hyper-polio victims and inject it into a sample of Merrimack River water.''

''Are you really that unscrupulous?''

''Aren't you?''

''I'm not sure,'' he said.

''You're not *sure*? Listen, Senator, over two thousand people have already died. You *have* to be sure. Otherwise we're all going to go to the political abattoir together.''

Reynard looked at her narrowly. ''I don't believe you're sincere about this,'' he said.

''You don't expect a woman to suggest anything so unsympathetic?''

''I don't believe you're sincere, that's all. I don't trust you. Is that blunt enough?''

''So what's your alternative? To sit here and quake like a bowl of jelly, hoping something will turn up?''

''You're fired.''

''Don't be ridiculous. You can't fire me, not now. I'll be straight out the door and down to the *Washington Post* before you can cough.''

''Blackmail?''

''Mutuality.''

''Mutuality, my ass,'' Reynard growled. He drank more wine. He wasn't as angry as he appeared to be, but he felt a terrible sense of political bad fortune all around him, reminiscent of Macbeth, or King Lear. He couldn't shake it off, and Natalia Vanspronsen didn't make him feel any less doomed, in spite of her bright and crooked suggestions.

He had learned long ago that trickery always brought its own hideous revenge, with bells on. Condor was the supreme example. After forty-four years, the specter of his past had risen out of the ground and blighted his future, and it was far too late to make amends.

Over two thousand Americans had already died; thousands more were inevitably going to follow them. And Chiffon, for God's sake. He had ordered Chiffon's death like a man ordering a meal. And in the end, that was what had broken him. That was what had brought him to understand what kind of man he actually was.

"You say Walt Seabrook can mock up a sample of polluted river water?" he asked in an offhand tone.

"That's what he says."

"He wants to be the Assistant Secretary for Health that bad, huh?"

Natalia nodded. "I believe so."

"And you want to be there when they elect me president?"

"Mutuality," she said.

There was a brisk knock at the door and Dick Elmwood came hurrying in. "Mr. Senator," he said as a courtesy, but without saying anything else, he picked up the remote control next to Reynard's chair and switched on the television again. They heard the voice first—a voice Natalia recognized at once. Then they saw the face—Edmond Chandler, with Dr. Oscar Ford in the background.

"—from a Nazi bomber?"

"That's right. We found it buried in the woods at a place called Conant's Acre, which is in the southern section of Senator Reynard Kelly's estate."

"You mean to say that this Nazi bomber had crashed on Senator Kelly's property at some time during World War Two?"

"Yes. Exactly that. It isn't very common knowledge, but aircraft can sometimes bury themselves deep into the soil when they crash, especially when at high speeds, and disappear almost without a trace.''

"And you think the hyper-polio virus was brought over by this bomber in World War Two?''

"We're sure of it.''

"Well, we already have our roving-camera team out at Conant's Acre, and . . . just a minute, yes, here's the first report. Hello, Marcus; have you located anything yet? Can you hear me?''

"Hello, Dave. Yes, we've found it, and let me tell you here and now that this is a most spectacular find. We've located the front section of a huge buried airliner here, and—most gruesome of all—if you look here, you'll see hanging out the window the skull of the pilot who flew this plane here in the nineteen forties; he's still wearing his flying helmet and black-leather flying jacket. There isn't any question at all that this is a genuine find; this whole airliner is absolutely buried here in the woods, tree roots still clinging around it, and we have our aeronautical expert here, Kenny Freo. Kenny, you work for the Smithsonian, isn't that right? What do you judge this plane to be?''

"Well, there's no doubt about it, Marcus. This is the nose section of a Focke-Wulf Two-hundred, the Condor, which was an airliner built to fly nonstop from Berlin to New York in the late nineteen thirties, but it was later used to attack British convoys across the Atlantic because of its exceptionally long range.''

"And how would you rate the discovery of one of these Condors buried in a woods here in New Hampshire after all these years?''

"Well, momentous, that's the only word for it. Although Condor was supposed to have made a bombing run on Nova Scotia during the war, it was never proved; but here we have an entire airplane that conclusively establishes the fact that the Nazis did try to reach the United

States during World War Two and did actually succeed, which just goes to show how close we were to having World War Two fought on our own soil.''

"In our studio, Dr. Edmond Chandler of Concord, New Hampshire, believes that World War Two has actually caught up with us in the form of the hyper-polio epidemic sweeping the nation from East to West. . . .''

Reynard switched off the television with the remote control and sat tense and hunched without saying a word.

"That was the doctor who spoke to us in Concord,'' said Natalia.

"Him?'' asked Dick Elmwood. "Dr. Edward Chandler?''

"Edmond. Edmond Chandler.''

"How did those people get on to my land?'' asked Reynard dully.

"Does it matter?'' asked Natalia.

"Obviously it doesn't,'' said Reynard. "That's the whole trouble with this world today. Everyone thinks he has a right to intrude. Everybody thinks he can go wherever he wants, regardless of other people's property. They found it, damn it. The damn thing was buried. Buried! How the hell did they find it? Forty-four years I've looked for that plane!''

"Senator,'' said Dick Elmwood soothingly, "there isn't any future in getting upset.''

"There isn't any future at all,'' said Reynard. "They've found the damned plane. Use your brains, Dick. Don't you think there were maps on the plane, showing where it was supposed to land? A navigator's log? Maybe even instructions from the German Supreme Command.''

"You *deny* it,'' Dick insisted. "You deny all knowledge. You never saw or heard of that airplane before in your life.''

"But for God's sake, Dick. They found it on my land. More than two thousand people have died because of that plane. Do you think I can live with that? Do you think I want to?''

"Senator," warned Dick, "you have to ride this thing out, one way or another. I mean, think about the alternatives. You were involved with the Nazis during the war? What do you think that's going to do to you? You took money from the Hitler regime? And then Greta's going to say that you rented her services as First Lady-designate even after you'd separated and she was living with another man? We're talking about the finish here, Senator. We're probably talking about a jail sentence. Watergate isn't going to have anything on this. And what other skeletons do you think are going to be exposed when some of your trusty aides start plea-bargaining? Chiffon Trent? Ted Peale? Senator, you have to keep on going, because if you don't, you're sunk.''

Reynard smothered his face with his hands and sat silent for whole minutes on end. Then he looked up and said, "What can I do? Go on, tell me. What can I do?''

"You have to be cool, first of all," said Dick. "You have to stop feeling guilty. You have to tell yourself this epidemic was all an unfortunate accident, because it was, wasn't it? You didn't *want* it to happen. That's the first point. Then you have to say to yourself, this Dr. Edmond Chandler is probably being vindictive, right at the start of my election campaign. He happens to have stumbled across an old German airplane buried in my woods—a plane I knew nothing about—and in some ridiculous way he's trying to connect it with the epidemic. How *could* it be connected? It's all nonsense. There were several attempted Nazi flights to America; one of them happened to go astray and crash on my property. That's not my fault. Besides, I've already spent thousands of dollars of my own money to set up a research clinic to determine how this epidemic can be beaten. So what do you say to that?''

Reynard said, "It's no good, you know, Dick.''

"It's no good because you're feeling depressed and guilty. For God's sake, have some confidence! All you have to do is to *deny* everything, rock solid, over and over again. In the end they'll believe you. And if your clinic can actually come up with some kind of antidote, you'll be right on top."

Just then Walt Seabrook came in. "Hope I'm not interrupting," he said, "but I've been talking on the phone to some of the medical people in Concord. They're furious, of course, because Dr. Chandler has gone right over their heads, straight to the media. And the guy most furious of all is Harold Bunyan on the Health Committee."

"Well?" Reynard demanded.

"Well, it seems like the redoubtable Dr. Chandler doesn't have such a good reputation. He moved to Concord from Manhattan because he killed his girlfriend by attempting a tracheotomy with a restaurant carving knife. The Medical Association was going to bounce him apparently, but he called in a few markers, especially with Harold Bunyan, and in the end they allowed him to set up in practice near Concord, attached to the Merrimack Clinic."

Reynard sat up straighter. "What are you saying, Dr. Seabrook? That he's a *killer*?"

"He cut his girlfriend's throat."

"Would you say as much on television?"

"It's true. Why shouldn't I say it?"

Reynard clapped his hands. "We've got him then! If he's a killer, we've got him! Who's going to believe the word of a killer? A doctor who slits people's throats?"

Natalia said, "You'll ruin him, you know that?"

"My dear, that's the whole idea. What do you think he's trying to do to me?"

"I don't know. Nothing. It seems to me like he's trying to put a stop to this epidemic."

"Well, first things first. And the first thing to do is to

get Dr. Seabrook here on network television, denouncing Dr. Chandler as a killer and a phony.''

''Do you know something?'' said Natalia. ''I came here today prepared to help you get out of a difficult and dangerous situation. I knew you had done wrong, but I thought it was one of those long-forgotten things that didn't mean too much. Now I think I made a mistake. You supported the Nazis during the war and you haven't really changed, have you, for all of your talk about Medicare and sharing the wealth and helping the poor. Deep down, Senator Kelly, you have nothing in your heart but utter contempt for everyone around you. No wonder you supported Hitler. You're an empty, arrogant, careless and brutal man. And worst of all, you have the gall to sit there and denounce a man who *does* care.''

Dick Elmwood looked across at Reynard with an expression that obviously meant, what are we going to do with *her*?

But Reynard seemed scarcely to have heard Natalia. He said to Dick, ''Make the media arrangements, will you? Get Dr. Seabrook on the first prime-time news this evening. Let's show these people what we're made of.''

''Slugs and snails and puppy-dogs' tails,'' said Natalia. She collected her purse and her notes and stalked out.

''You're going to let her go?'' asked Dick. ''She knows all about Condor. She could ruin everything.''

Reynard's left eye twitched involuntarily. ''Yes, well, you're right. Make sure you . . . well, just don't tell me about it. But make sure. I don't want any repercussions— not with all this other business to take care of. Now, Dr. Seabrook, what were you saying about this doctor? What did he do? Cut somebody's throat?''

Walt Seabrook looked anxious. ''You're not going to do anything to Natalia, are you? I mean, I get the feeling that you're thinking of—''

''What?'' asked Reynard. He focused on Walt as though

he were drunk, gazing from one eye at a time. "You get the feeling that we're thinking of *what*?"

"I don't know," said Walt uneasily. And it was then that he understood for the first time just how far out of his league he had strayed and that he was now among players who were prepared to give up everything rather than lose. Who would kill to win.

"I don't know," he repeated. "I must have—misunderstood."

EIGHTEEN

Natalia survived by acting swiftly. Instead of going back to her room to collect her overnight case, she walked straight out the front door, across the cobbled courtyard, climbed into her rented Zephyr and drove out through the gates of Reynard's house with a quick squitter of tires. One of Reynard's men was at the gate, but Dick Elmwood hadn't yet had time to warn him, and he smiled and saluted as she sped past.

She drove out through English Village and headed northeast for Wisconsin Boulevard, turning southeast through Chevy Chase and into the outskirts of Washington itself. She felt utter fright as she drove and kept checking her rear-view mirror to see whether any of the cars from Reynard Kelly's house were following her.

It was an unnaturally dark afternoon. A heavy bank of clouds had moved in from the west, and even though the sky over the city itself was still bright and the Capitol shone like some exotic Oriental palace, most of the traffic was driving with dimmers on. She joined the anonymous river of cars flowing along Massachusetts Avenue toward the center of the city.

Natalia was not certain of why she had felt the need to escape from Reynard's house so urgently. But all her life she had been extra-sensitive to atmospheres, to undercurrents of fear, and even when she and Walt Seabrook had first arrived there, she had sensed almost at once that something was wrong. She had remarked to Walt that the house had the same dreadful electricity as Hitler's bunker, or the White House during the last days of Watergate. There was a closeted, hysterical feeling, with the staff rushing around in ever more hopeless circles while, at the epicenter of the tragedy, the once-grand leader sat inert—unwilling and unable to carry on.

They had come down to Washington to present Reynard with their plan to blame the epidemic of hyper-polio on pollution of the Merrimack River—faked up, as she had explained—but even before they had begun to really discuss it, she had realized it was all too late. The epidemic had spread much more quickly than Walt Seabrook had expected, and the irreversible fact was that Reynard had given up. There was murder in the air, actual fresh-blooded murder, and Natalia wanted out, fast.

She checked the rear-view mirror again. Off to the left, a dark-blue Thunderbird with a tan roof was keeping pace with her, although it was impossible to tell in the late-afternoon gloom whether it was the same Thunderbird that had been parked outside Reynard's house. She changed lanes and the Thunderbird changed lanes behind her. Maybe the driver was just taking advantage of the gap she had left in the flow of traffic. Or maybe he was following her.

When she had first arrived at Reynard's house, she had looked around at Reynard's senior staff—Dick Elmwood, Dean Farber and all the others—and she had seen for herself why Greta had once called them the Snake Pit. Wherever she had gone, one of them always seemed to be there, watching coldly, giving her a reptilian smile, more unsettling than no smile at all.

Greta herself had spent most of the day shut up in her bedroom, talking on the telephone to her lawyers, her real-estate managers and as many of her friends in New England as she could reach. When Natalia had seen her at lunch, she had seemed distracted, almost haunted, although her mood had improved later, after she had spent some time with Walt Seabrook. Natalia suspected they had either been snorting, making love or both.

All the same, it was extraordinary and disturbing to see how many of the people around Reynard Kelly seemed to be winding down and malfunctioning, as though they were automata who had depended on Reynard for their power. Natalia could understand it in a way. Reynard *was* power. He had money, influence and position—when it wasn't all threatened by Condor.

But now it was no longer possible for Reynard to escape blame for what he had done; the burden of responsibility he had to bear was too crushing even for a man as unscrupulous as he was. Natalia's hopes of fame and glory for herself had died the moment she had seen Reynard's face today—shifty-eyed, gray and somehow bloated, as though all the lies he had ever told had decayed within him.

She took a sudden right off Massachusetts Avenue, heading south down 23rd Street. Two cars followed her, but the blue Thunderbird carried straight on. She pulled over to the side of the road and waited until at least a dozen cars had overtaken her. Then she drew out into the traffic again and carried on south, crossing the Potomac over the Arlington Memorial Bridge and making for the airport along the Mt. Vernon Memorial Highway. Planes rumbled overhead, rising from the airport runway with lights flashing and wings catching the last of the sun.

It would soon be curfew time, and without her permit papers—left behind in her room at Reynard's house—Natalia was going to find it difficult to travel. But at least she had her airline tickets, where she had carelessly left them in the Zephyr's glove box. She thanked God for her one principal personality flaw, her untidiness.

She parked the car outside the terminal building and left it there. She didn't think she would be coming back to Washington for a very long time, if ever. Not as long as Reynard Kelly still lived. She went straight to the shuttle desk and found there was one last shuttle to Boston, leaving in ten minutes. The girl behind the desk didn't even ask to see her ID.

She went to the telephone and put through a collect call to Dr. Edmond Chandler in Concord. While she waited to be connected, she kept her eye on the terminal entrance in case she saw anyone she recognized as from the Reynard entourage. The last thing she wanted to do was to end her life in an airport phone booth.

"Edmond Chandler," said his voice at last, just when she was about to give up and make a run for the plane.

"Dr. Chandler, it's Natalia Vanspronsen. I don't have long, I'm running for a plane. I'm flying back up to New Hampshire and I'll see you later tonight. The most important thing I have to say to you is this: Dr. Walt Seabrook is probably going to denounce you on late-afternoon television as a fraud. Something about a fatal tracheotomy you once performed. Well, never mind now. But be warned that's what they're going to do. And also be careful. Reynard Kelly is very desperate, and I'm worried he's going to stop at absolutely nothing to keep this business under wraps."

Edmond said, "You sound kind of strained. Are you okay?"

"Well, let's just say that I got out from under as quick as I could."

"Call me as soon as you get into Concord Airport. I'll come by and pick you up."

"I'll see you later, Dr. Chandler."

"Take care, Miss Vanspronsen."

Natalia hung up. Her flight was being called. She walked quickly across the concourse and through the gate.

Denzil Forbes switched on the lights in the warehouse one by one. It was a huge, dry, airy place, once used for the storage of grain and sugar. Now, however, it was Denzil's special movie location: the studio where he could film the ultimate in eroticism and the worst in human agony. In the center of the floor a large carpet had been laid out and heaped with dozens of pillows and cushions, and all around this makeshift set there were clusters of lights, and two movie cameras had been set up on tripods.

What wasn't yet in view was the large can of gasoline Denzil intended to use in the final moments of his moviemaking. Nor was the fire-extinguisher with which he could prolong the agony at will, dousing and relighting the fire again and again.

The five young men who followed Denzil into the warehouse were barefooted and dressed in a variety of robes and towels; they looked like a sorry collection of bathers from a cheap Eastern-seaboard hotel. Piotr wasn't among them: he had made an excuse to an irritated Billy Manzanetti about a bad stomach and borrowed his fare back to New York. Denzil looked the young men over, tightening his necktie as he did so, and said, "Not exactly the greatest team of studs I've ever laid eyes on, but I guess you'll have to do."

"Hey, is there any chance of getting something to eat?" asked one of the young men. "I'm starved."

"We'll send out for some burgers later," said Denzil.

"Charbroiled, huh?" giggled one of the young men nervously.

Denzil gave him a stare that could have frozen Lake Muskego. He was in a state of high tension himself, but when he was taut like this, he preferred to stay tense until everything was over. He didn't appreciate wisecracks.

"I just want to say one thing," said Denzil. "You boys know what we're doing here. You've been paid big money to do as you're told and to say nothing when it's finished. Just remember who you're doing business with—not some half-assed Hollywood outfit trying to make a few extra bucks. You're doing business with big people, people who can reach out and get you no matter where you go. So do me a first-class job today, then go away and forget about it forever. You understand me? *Comprendo*?"

A door at the far end of the warehouse opened and Mae-Beth came in, leading Chiffon by the hand.

"Hey, she's *nice*!" said one of the young men.

"Jesus," said another, thinking with excitement and dread about what they were going to do to her.

Obediently Chiffon went over to the heaps of pillows, and there Mae-Beth helped her take off the loose white caftan she was wearing. She stood where she was, unmoving, staring blankly. This was her seventh movie in three days, and at some stage during those seven movies her mind seemed to have switched itself off so that she did nothing more than eat and sleep and wake up and do as she was told. Denzil had taken away her will and replaced it with a set of instructions for survival. At least he had told her it was a set of instructions for survival, and she had believed him simply because there was nothing else for her to believe.

Denzil's cameraman came in, wiping his wet hands on the back of his jeans. "Don't you have towels in your john?" he demanded and then finished drying his hands on one of the boys' flannel bathrobes. "Is she ready?" he asked.

Chiffon was standing in front of the cameras, meek and nude, her eyes fixed on a point somewhere between infinity and utter forgetfulness. She was startlingly beautiful this morning, regardless of what had been happening to her and regardless of her unseeing stare.

"Let's do it, shall we?" suggested the cameraman, unconsciously repeating the death-house words of Gary Gilmore. He switched on the movie lights, and the heaps of pillows were transformed into a brightly illuminated arena.

"Off with the robes, *muchachos*," said Denzil. He was deliberately needling the one Hispanic among them, a sallow boy with an incipient black mustache. The young men stripped off their robes and shuffled around uneasily.

They filmed for an hour. The young men were awkward and bashful at first, but as the heat from the lights became more intense, as Chiffon responded to them with all the sighs and moans and writhings that Denzil required of her, they began to grow more lustful and thrusting, thrilling to the total sexual license Denzil had given them to ravish this pretty girl in any way they wanted to.

As the hour came to a close, Denzil laid his hand on the cameraman's back, which was a signal for him to cut; it was time to prepare for the climax. The final torture, the final conflagration.

"Take a break now," said Denzil. "Let's get ourselves into shape for the big exit, huh?"

The boys climbed up sweaty and panting from the pillows.

Denzil moved away, and as he did so, he heard a door open somewhere on the opposite side of the warehouse, and he began to turn back again. There was a shuffling, scuffling sound, like soft-soled feet dashing quickly across the concrete floor. Then a sharp snap.

To everyone's amazement, Denzil's head blew apart. The shoulders of his smart gray suit were suddenly dark with gore, and he dropped to the pillows as abruptly as though he were a large marionette whose strings someone had decided to snip.

The five young men turned this way and that in bewilderment. But it was only when there was a rattling burst of submachine-gun fire that they understood.

"Oh, God!" one of them cried out, but those were the only words spoken. Mae-Beth dropped to the floor, patterned with red; and then there was a long spasm of fire that brought down three of the five young men. The Hispanic boy almost made it to the door before he was hit in the back again and again and again, his flesh torn to shreds.

Denzil's cameraman, more experienced in making quick getaways, dodged and ducked and rolled himself across to the opposite side of the warehouse. A burst of six or seven bullets hammered on the partition wall beside him, and a fragment hit him in the muscle of his upper arm, but he managed to tuck himself down beside a tea chest full of rubbish and sawdust, and the next hail of bullets that came after him failed to penetrate. Cautiously he raised his head, just in time to see a man in a gray-green combat suit and a gray ski mask run quickly across the warehouse floor.

"Listen!" he called out. "I give up, okay? I surrender. This had nothing to do with me. I was just hired to take pictures. I didn't even know what they had in mind."

There were more sounds of softly running feet. The cameraman guessed they were trying to surround him.

"I'll surrender, okay?" he called out again.

"*Idyiti syuda,*" a voice nearby instructed, although the cameraman wasn't sure they were talking to him.

He glanced to his left and saw a door that led out to the parking lot. If he could only manage to get it open and roll out of it, he would have a chance. The problem was that there were four or five feet of open, exposed space between him and the door. They would shoot him down as soon as he appeared.

Then he turned to his right and saw the gasoline can Denzil had brought along for the movie's blazing denouement. That was metal, right? Probably thick enough to deflect a couple of bullets. If he could hold the can up in front of him, he might be able to get out the door before he was hit. At least it was better than lying here all crouched up, waiting for them to move in and execute him.

He shuffled backward until he could feel the large, cold can of gasoline against his back. Then he reached behind, grasped the handle and shifted it slowly forward until it was beside him. Now all he had to do was to hold the can in his arms as though it were an oversized, overweight baby, keep his head well down behind it and make a dive for the door.

A voice, even nearer, said, *"Stoy."*

But the cameraman lifted himself up on to one knee, embraced the gasoline can, hefted it up a little higher so his head was protected, and lunged toward the door. There was a crackle of firing. A shower of bullets boomed and pinged against the side of the can, and a ricochet shattered the small window in the middle of the door. The cameraman almost lost his balance and lurched against the wall, but he managed to reach out and seize the doorknob and wrench it open.

As he tried to duck into the doorway, however, there was a heavier, louder shot—a round from an AK47, with a muzzle velocity of 2,350 feet per second. It burst into the gasoline can, which exploded with a breathy and fearsome *whoosh*! The can fell. The cameraman shrieked. And for one moment he was framed in the doorway, his head and shoulders a mass of flames, his hair sizzling, his hands raised like torches. Then he dropped sideways out of sight.

One of the men in combat suits walked cautiously forward, his Czechoslovakian Skorpion machine-pistol raised in his left hand. He looked down at the burning cameraman for a while, then turned back toward his three colleagues and said, *"Prinyistyi mnyeh devushka."*

Chiffon, shivering, shocked, was brought across the warehouse, one of the terry-cloth robes wrapped around her to hide her nakedness. She stared at the man with vacant eyes.

He said carefully and slowly, "You have been rescued. Do you understand me? We have rescued you from these people."

Chiffon stared at his faceless ski mask and then past him to the doorway, where the cameraman's body was still guttering like a fatty candle.

"You will come with us; we will give you clothes and medication," said the man.

"You sound like Piotr," said Chiffon weakly.

"I sound like Piotr because I am Russian. Do you understand me? You are safe now."

Chiffon nodded almost imperceptibly. "Yes," she repeated. "Yes, I understand . . . I am safe."

The clock in the embassy hallway struck three as Humphrey opened the door and cautiously looked around. The hallway was deserted; its polished black-and-white tiles reflected the cold Swedish daylight. His heart pumped violently and his hands were sweating, but he had made up his mind to do what he believed to be right. "This way," he said to Klaus Hermann, who was standing close behind him, gray-faced.

They tiptoed across the hallway, two old men with creaking shoes and creaking joints. Humphrey opened the door that led through to the kitchens, listened for a moment and then whispered, "Come on."

They went through and Humphrey closed the door behind them. "Now, follow me," he said. "And for goodness' sake, if we're challenged, just say that you felt unwell and I was going to get you a glass of water."

"All right. I understand."

They crossed the large, old-fashioned kitchen with its blue-and-white painted furniture and its rows of gleaming tiles. A row of big, shining carving knives hung on hooks along the wall, and there were fish kettles and saucepans and asparagus steamers shining in every glass-fronted cupboard.

Humphrey unlocked the back door and they stepped out into the sharp fresh air of the embassy garden.

"If only I could have brought my coat," said Hermann with a wry smile. "It's cold."

They walked around the side of the building, keeping close to the wall when they passed the windows of the duty officer's room; and then they went through the wrought-iron gate that led to the embassy courtyard.

Humphrey said quickly, "That white Skoda across the road. All you have to do is walk across, tap on the window, and the driver will let you in."

Hermann took Humphrey's hand. "It is difficult for me to express how I feel for what you have done," he said. "I know it was not an easy decision for you to have made. But during the war I always thought that the British were— what did they call it?—pukka."

"Well, yes, pukka," said Humphrey anxiously.

"And now I fulfill my part of the bargain," Hermann told him. From his cuff he produced a ruled sheet of paper he had torn from an embassy notebook. It was filled with neat, tiny writing, all in German, and three biochemical formulae. He thrust it toward Humphrey with a trembling hand.

"I want your promise that this is genuine," said Humphrey.

Hermann nodded. "I think to have been at mortal risk for the first time in my life has led me to understand that life is a precious thing," he said. "I have killed too many people in my career; let this be an end to it."

He held Humphrey close, hugged him and said, *"Auf wiedersehen,* Mr. Browne. In other circumstances you and I perhaps could have been the best of friends."

Humphrey watched Hermann limp steadfastly toward the embassy gate. The uniformed guard looked around at him incuriously and then went back to staring out at Strandvägen. The guard was conditioned to prevent unwanted visitors from coming in, not to prevent people from leaving. By the time he realized it was Klaus Hermann who had walked past him, it would be too late. Beyond the embassy gate lay diplomatic immunity.

Hermann reached the gate. He walked right through it. Now he was out on the sidewalk of Strandvägen, looking left and right to cross the road; the white Skoda started up its engine. Humphrey watched Hermann reach the crown of the road and his fists were clenched with tension. Hermann was almost there. The Skoda driver had reached behind and unlatched the rear door.

It was at that moment that Bill Bennett stepped out from where he had been waiting behind a tree in the Nobelpark on the other side of Strandvägen. Klaus Hermann didn't even notice him—he was too intent on reaching the Skoda—but Humphrey did. He watched in hypnotized fascination as Bill Bennett raised both hands and fired three silenced shots at Hermann, one of which hit him in the face, the next in the chest and the third in the hip as he fell.

The Skoda driver revved up the engine and the car began to pull away. But Bill Bennett simply swung his upraised arms around and fired one more shot; it shattered the car's back window and hit the driver in the back of the neck. The car swerved, bounced against the curb, and the engine died.

Humphrey walked slowly out into the road.

"You've got the formula?" asked Bill. He pushed the revolver back into his putty-colored anorak.

"Yes," said Humphrey thickly. Then he cleared his throat and repeated, "Yes."

Bill looked down at Klaus Hermann, sprawled with his mouth open against the red tarmac of the road.

"You know he was going to be executed, one way or another?"

"I suppose so."

"You did the right thing. Saved him some agony."

They heard the braying of Swedish police sirens. Hermann's blood began to trickle across the road, following the depressions in the surfacing. Humphrey couldn't take his eyes off him. To think that only a few seconds ago he had been embracing this man, holding him close.

He looked away, through the trees of the Nobelpark to the dull gray water of Djürgardsbrunnsviken. His eyes watered in the wind and he thought he must be growing old. His sister would probably bake a Madeira cake for him when he got home, by way of a celebration.

Bill said, "The formula?"—and Humphrey handed it over.

"You'll be rewarded for this," said Bill. "A whole lot of very important people in the United States are going to be very thankful over what happened here today."

Humphrey cleared his throat again. "I don't think I want a reward, thank you."

Natalia was awakened by a hand on her shoulder. She opened her eyes to see Edmond looking down at her gravely, holding in his other hand a cup of black coffee. The room was dim; the drapes were still drawn, but there was a sharp chink of sunlight in the far corner that told Natalia today would be one of those bright New Hampshire days when the sky is as blue as paint and the trees are as vivid as gold.

"What time is it?" she asked. She was naked underneath the blanket and she drew it up to her chin.

"Eight o'clock."

"My God, I wanted to be up at six."

"It's this couch. It's more comfortable than it looks. Besides, you probably needed the sleep."

"Have you heard the news yet?" she asked.

"The epidemic's worse," he told her. He drew a chair

over so he could balance her coffee cup on it. "Well over two hundred dead in Merrimack County alone."

"And nationwide?"

He went over to the window and drew back the drapes. Natalia shielded her eyes from the brightness with her hand.

"Six, maybe seven thousand. And it seems to be moving faster all the time, just like Dr. Corning said it would."

"Aren't you going in to the clinic?"

He shook his head. "First thing this morning, your friend Dr. Walt Seabrook made an announcement from Washington, as the newly appointed man in charge of Senator Reynard Kelly's hyper-polio research unit. He told everyone it was scandal-mongering for me to suggest that the virus had originated from the German plane on Senator Kelly's land and that Senator Kelly had been as surprised as anyone else when the plane was discovered. He said it was a sheer fluke. The Germans must have made several attempted landings in America during World War Two, he said, and this time they had crashed on his property, and that was all. Can you believe that?"

"Knowing just how much Reynard was implicated, it makes me *retch*."

"Well," said Edmond, "this'll make you feel even sicker. Reynard's already cordoned off his property to keep away sightseers and television reporters, and he's said he's going to commission a properly supervised archeological expedition to salvage the plane. This, he says, could take weeks, maybe months. And all the time people are going to be dying of hyper-polio—just to save his neck. Not even that. Just to save his damned *career*."

Natalia said nothing but sipped at her coffee.

Edmond went on. "One more little stab, of course, was that Dr. Seabrook reported that I was a dangerous quack; he produced medical records to prove that I performed an unsuccessful tracheotomy in a New York restaurant. He produced medical examiner's photographs too, showing the girl's neck wounds, just in case people didn't get the point. About an hour ago I had a call from Mr. Eldridge of the New Hampshire Health and Welfare Department, telling me not to bother to practice medicine in New Hampshire anymore, or words to that effect.''

Natalia sat up, wrapping the blanket tightly around herself. "But that's *criminal*!"

"Yes, it's criminal. But not as criminal as the fact that Senator Kelly is allowing thousands of innocent people to die for no other purpose than to save his candidacy for the White House."

Natalia said, "I think he no longer knows what he's doing. At every meeting they had down there in Washington, everything was all so unreal. Reynard and Dick Elmwood and the rest of them—they kept talking about 'sorting people out,' as though they were intent on murdering half the political population of the District of Columbia."

"Do you really think they would have tried to kill you?"

She put down her cup. "I wasn't going to stick around to find out, thanks very much. This is good coffee."

"Blue Mountain."

Natalia ran her hand through her hair. "I guess I'm going to have to stand up and be counted. Go to the media and tell them everything I know."

"Kelly will deny it all, of course," said Edmond. "And if you have any skeletons in any closets, he'll dig them out and try to ruin you. But—if you can stand that. . . ."

"I can stand anything to stop more people from dying. I had an abortion once. I think that's about the worst thing I was ever guilty of."

"You didn't have to tell me that. I wasn't prying."

"I'm not ashamed of it."

Edmond came over and sat down beside her. "I hope

we survive this," he said. "Both of us. After this nightmare is over. . . ."

"I'm not sure you're the right kind of man to get close to, Dr. Chandler. One lady dead from a throat operation, the next dead of disease."

If she had said it in anything other than a teasing tone of voice, it was the kind of comment that could have been tasteless and crass. But the way she looked at him and the way she put her head a little to one side, provocative and questioning, and with the smallest smile touching the side of her mouth—all these things redeemed it, gave it a different and intimate meaning. She liked men who were prepared to stand up for what they believed in, far more than she liked winners. Maybe that was why she and Reynard Kelly, even if Condor hadn't come to light, would never have worked smoothly together. Reynard was a winner, but he didn't believe in anything.

Edmond said, "Everyone's entitled to one or two mistakes."

Natalia touched his wrist with the tip of her finger, a gentle touch that asked forgiveness. "You're hurting, aren't you?"

"I don't have anyone to blame but myself. But when you love people so much that they mean everything to you, and you hurt them and can't seem to stop hurting them, no matter how hard you try . . . well, that's when you begin to wonder whether you're any good at love."

Natalia couldn't help smiling. "Don't you know that it happens to everybody? You're a doctor, you should know that."

"I'm not qualified in the repair of broken hearts."

"Don't ask too much of yourself," she said. "You can't be perfect; you can't accept all the blame for everything."

The telephone rang. Edmond reached across the back of

the couch and picked it up. "Dr. Chandler," he said, tucking the receiver under his chin.

It was Oscar. He sounded tired, and his voice was rough. "E.C.? Sorry, but I've got some bad personal news for you."

"Not Malcolm," said Edmond.

"I'm sorry," Oscar told him.

Natalia laid her hand on Edmond's shoulder. "What's happened?" she asked.

Oscar said, "He went off the bridge about an hour ago. Right off Manchester Street into the river. The police say he was probably doing seventy-five, maybe eighty."

Edmond took the phone out from under his chin and held it in his hand. "Was it instant?"

"Must have been. Broke his neck as soon as he hit the water."

"Oh, Christ."

"Don't blame yourself," Oscar said. "I ran a test and he definitely showed signs of hyper-polio. He would have died anyway."

"You're not just saying that to make me feel less guilty?"

"Come and look at the autopsy report yourself. You think I'd do anything to make a quack like you feel less guilty?"

"Okay, Oscar. Thanks."

"I'll drop by when I can. Meanwhile, you know, fight the good fight."

Edmond put down the phone.

"Do you want to talk about it?" Natalia asked.

"I don't know," he replied. "In a while. I think I need a drink first."

The call came for Reynard Kelly at six that evening. By then, hyper-polio had spread so far across the United States, and so many people had died, that the president was considering putting the entire continent under quarantine. The government's special biochemical task force had failed again and again to make any inroads on the vitality of the virus, despite having tried the gamut of lipid solvents, from ether to termazine, and having bombarded it with X rays and ultraviolet.

Reynard Kelly had been listening hourly to news of the epidemic, sitting in front of the television in his drawing room with the drapes drawn and the lights dimmed. He was seeing no visitors apart from Dick Elmwood and his immediate staff, and taking only the most critical of phone calls. He refused to talk to Greta but he also refused to let her out of the house; she and Walt Seabrook had spent the evening together in the library, tense and wound-up and clean out of cocaine.

Dick Elmwood came into the room on silent feet and leaned close to Reynard as though he were imparting a forbidden secret. "There's a call for you, Senator."

"I'm not taking any more calls today, Dick. I think I've taken enough calls for one day, don't you? I've done enough."

"This call, sir, I think you ought to take."

Reynard looked up. His eyes reflected the flickering light from the television. "Well?" he said.

"It's from someone who says he has proof that what Dr. Chandler was saying on television is true."

"Someone's been talking to that Natalia woman, that's it, isn't it? You let her go, for Christ's sake, and now she's been opening her mouth to anybody she can get to listen."

"We know where she is, sir. She's with Chandler, in Concord. But we don't think she's been talking to anybody, at least not yet. There haven't been any more reports on television about Condor, and nothing in the newspapers either."

Reynard nodded toward the telephone. "Then who's this on the line?"

"I don't know, sir. But it sounds genuine."

"Pick up the extension, listen in," Reynard told him. Then he lifted the receiver and said impatiently, "Yes, this is Senator Kelly speaking. Who is this?"

There was a crackling pause before an accented voice said, "Good evening, Senator. I have some good news for you. Tremendous news."

"What tremendous news? Who are you?"

"My name is Cerenkov; I'm calling from New York. I'm happy to be the first to tell you that your friend is still alive. Not very well, admittedly, but still alive."

"What the hell are you talking about?" Reynard demanded. "Is this some kind of joke?"

"Not at all, sir. You remember Miss Chiffon Trent, surely?"

"Chiffon Trent? Don't be so damned disrespectful! Miss Trent was a dear and close friend of mine, and now she's dead."

"Oh, no, Senator. Chiffon Trent isn't dead. Chiffon Trent is here with me now, at Five-fifty-five Madison Avenue. Whoever died in that car wreck, it wasn't her. We found her in Milwaukee, Wisconsin, where she was being forced to star in what I believe you Americans call a 'snuff movie.' Fortunately we arrived in time to save her from the 'snuff.' "

Dick Elmwood glanced across at Reynard uneasily. Reynard was ashen, his knuckles showing white where he clenched the phone.

"What do you want?" Reynard demanded.

"*Want*? My dear senator, we don't *want* anything. Except, perhaps, to inform you that Miss Trent will always be prepared to testify to what you told her about your cooperating with the Nazis during the war, and that if you are fortunate enough to survive this present scandal—and it actually seems as if you might—then we shall always be here, ready with our testimony in case you are as aggressive and as uncooperative toward the Soviet Union as were some of your predecessors. Of course I'm not personally in a position of sufficient influence to be able to say what we might ask from you at a later date, but it could well be something to do with the withdrawal from Europe of cruise missiles, or perhaps with less interference in Central America.''

Reynard, without warning, banged down the phone. Then he picked it up again, tore it out of the wall, threw it onto the carpet and stamped on it until it was smashed.

Dick said, ''Senator Kelly, I have to tell you that I had no idea Miss Trent was still alive. I commissioned people in whom I had every reason to be confident . . . I mean, this comes as just as big a shock to me as it does to you.''

Reynard stared at him, his face shuddering, saliva spraying from his lips. ''It's Condor,'' he raged. ''The whole thing started with that damned airplane. Well, that's the only solid evidence they've got. If we get rid of the solid evidence, if we get rid of that evidence once and for all, then, by jiminy, they won't have any way of proving what happened, no way at all. So I'm telling you what we're going to do. We're going to fly back to Concord tonight, Dick, that's what we're going to do, and we're going to blow the whole damn plane right out of the ground, and then we're going to blow it into miniature pieces, and then we're going to blow the miniature pieces into miniature pieces.''

''Senator, listen—''

''Don't tell me to listen!'' Reynard screamed. ''I've listened long enough! None of this would have happened if it hadn't have been for you and the rest of the morons who spend all their time taking my money and sucking my brains and treating this whole damned campaign like a carnival! I want explosives, that's what I want. Where can we get explosives?''

''Senator, please—''

"Where can we get explosives?" Reynard shrieked at him. "Where? I want explosives!"

"Well, sir, there's a demolition contractor in Washington who might be persuaded to help. He was a friend of someone I knew in Seattle, and—"

"I don't want your goddamned life history," Reynard raged. "I want explosives. Do you understand me? And I want a man who knows how to use them. Got that? Got that, Dick? And I want them now. And we're going to fly them up to Concord, and we're going to—"

"Senator, we're going to have to charter a jet. We won't be able to take explosives on board a commercial airliner."

"I've got my own jet, damn it."

"Sir, that's in Concord, undergoing—"

"Then just get one, for Christ's sake. Do I have to think of every damned stupid little pusillanimous detail around here?"

"No, sir."

"And I want to leave tonight. You with me? Tonight."

"There is a curfew, sir."

"Damn it, Dick, I'm Reynard Kelly. I'm the man who started the damned disease! It's because of me they've got themselves a curfew in the first place."

"Yes, sir."

"Yes, sir," Reynard mimicked.

Dick Elmwood left the room. He didn't close the door behind him, and when Reynard looked across at it in annoyance, he suddenly saw why. It was Greta, in an emerald-green cocktail dress, standing there watching him, silhouetted by the light from the hallway. Her hair shone; she wore diamonds. He could smell her perfume even from the other side of the room. Eau de Joy. Some joy, he thought.

"What do you want?" he demanded with undisguised impatience.

"I just wanted to see you." Her voice was low.

"I'm busy. I don't have any time for talking now."

"Oh, I didn't want to *talk* to you. I just wanted to *see* you. I just wanted to see how a great man can bring himself down to absolute ruin merely by failing to recognize the needs and hopes of the people around him. No one can be great on his own, Reynard. You could have been great had you looked at other people a little more closely, a little less selfishly. But you didn't have it in you, did you? Personality problems. In some people, you know, being selfish is an affliction. You make it a way of life."

Reynard turned his back on her and examined the draped window intently. "Have you finished gloating?" he asked.

"I don't think I ever will, not quite," she told him. He hated the amused malice in her voice.

"I'm flying back to Concord," he told her. "I'm going back to do something I should have done sooner. I'm going to destroy that plane, blow it up."

"Are you mad? That won't solve anything. What do you think the media will say if you do that?"

"I don't care what they say. It's their only piece of solid evidence."

"But, Reynard—"

He whirled around and glared at her in fury. "You're all the same, all of you. Full of rotten, weak-kneed, clumsy advice. And for all these years I've been stupid enough to listen to it and act on it, and look at where the hell it got me."

"You betrayed your country long before you ever met me."

Reynard shouted, "*Agh!*" in inarticulate rage. He seized the bodice of her dress and tore it away, leaving her with deep scratches across her half-bared chest.

"You bastard!" she screamed at him. "You ineffectual bastard!"

Reynard grunted, seized her again and slapped her open-handed across the side of the face and then, with the back of his hand, across the other side. Her pearls broke and poured on to the carpet. Reynard's heavy rings cut and bruised her nose, and her right eye swelled up almost at once.

Screaming, Greta tore at him with her fingernails. He slapped her again, then again, and she fell back against the couch. She tried to get up but he had the upper hand now, and every time she raised herself, he hit her.

When his temper died down finally, he turned his back on her, breathing heavily. "After all these years," he said obscurely.

Greta could do nothing but weep. She tried to stand up but she couldn't, and so she knelt on the floor and wept.

"After all these goddamned *years*," Reynard repeated.

Edmond was almost asleep when the telephone warbled. He groped around in the dark before he found it and picked it up.

"Dr. Chandler."

"Dr. Edmond Chandler?"

"That's right. Who's speaking?"

"This is Greta Kelly, Reynard Kelly's wife."

Edmond sat up in bed and fumbled for the light. "How did you get my number?" he asked.

"It's in the Concord directory, Dr. Chandler. It wasn't difficult."

"Well, what can I do for you? Are you all right? You sound—I don't mean to be personal, but—"

"My husband just beat me, Dr. Chandler. He beat me and then he left Washington to fly back to Concord."

"I see. Well, as a matter of fact, I *don't* see. What does that have to do with me?"

"Dr. Chandler, he's crazy. He's gone hysterically crazy. He's rented a jet and he's flying up to Concord with a whole cargo full of high explosives. He says he's going to blow up that Nazi plane and destroy the evidence against him.''

Edmond rubbed his eyes. ''Then what I guessed about the plane is true?''

''Fundamentally, yes. But you've got to stop him, Dr. Chandler. He's going to end up killing somebody unless you stop him.''

''Mrs. Kelly, I don't really see what I can possibly—''

''Please, Dr. Chandler, do something. He'll be arriving at the Colonnades in less than a half-hour.''

Natalia came to the bedroom door. The sound of Edmond's voice had awakened her. ''Is something wrong?'' she asked.

Edmond put down the phone. ''The world has just happened to lose its last remaining marble,'' he said. ''That was Greta Kelly, telling me that your erstwhile employer is flying up to Concord with the intention of blowing that Nazi plane to bits.''

''Is he mad or what?''

Edmond tugged on a pair of slacks and took a shirt from his wardrobe. ''Let's put it this way. I think the strain of hiding this secret for forty-four years has finally proved too much for him.''

''What are you going to do?''

''I don't really know what the hell I *can* do. The first thing I'm going to do is to call Oscar. After that, who knows?''

It took Oscar almost five minutes to answer the phone. When at last he did, he sounded as though he were still dreaming. Edmond told him about the call from Greta Kelly.

Oscar said, ''The answer's easy.''

''What do you mean, the answer's easy?''

''The answer is, we prevent him from landing on his own property—force him to divert to Concord Airport or someplace else. Then we immediately alert the cops so they can pick him up wherever he lands.''

"Why not just call the cops straightaway and tell them what he's up to?''

"Because Senator Kelly is Senator Kelly, my dear friend, and because the chief is not going to risk sending a dozen of Concord's finest to beat their way across Senator Kelly's private land without a warrant and without reasonable grounds.''

Edmond said in exasperation, ''How the hell do we prevent him from landing?''

The LearJet whistled low over the Merrimack River and began its turn toward East Concord. It was three o'clock in the morning; the sky was clear and cold. Reynard peered out the window, watching the familiar landmarks pass underneath—the Soucook River, Horse Corner, Loudon Road and, off to the left, the winking lights of Concord Airport.

Dick Elmwood sat next to him, chewing nervously at his lip. He had taken almost everything into account in his career with Reynard—except the possibility that the man might one day break down and behave as he was tonight. The fact that they were carrying nearly fifteen hundred rounds of high explosives in the back of the plane didn't do much to relax him either.

The pilot said, ''Fasten seat belts, please, Senator.''

Reynard looked up, frowned and said, ''What?''

"Your seat belt,'' Dick repeated.

"Ah,'' said Reynard.

In the seat behind, a crop-haired man in a checked shirt sat glumly looking down at Concord through binoculars. This was the explosives expert whom Dick had managed to persuade to fly north with them to deal with the Condor. He had finally agreed to lose a night's sleep on the promise of ten thousand dollars, cash.

The LearJet lowered its undercarriage and sank below the tree line. The tarmac runway at the Colonnades was on the northeast side of the house. When he had bought his first jet, nine years ago, Reynard had arranged for the land to be specially drained and a full-length tarmac runway constructed. The grassy surface of Conant's Acre had been too rough for jets, and in any case, it was more profitable under the plow.

Reynard could see the house now, symmetrical and white. "Home," he said to Dick, who nodded and gave an unintelligible grunt of acknowledgment.

They waited until the last moment, their cars hidden side by side in the long grass of the orchard. Edmond and Natalia sat in one of the cars, Oscar in the other. They maintained radio silence lest their short-wave frequency be picked up by anyone in the house; instead they signaled to each other with prearranged waves of their hands. One wave meant I see the jet; two waves meant go like hell; three meant let's get out of here.

About ten minutes earlier the bright, parallel lines of lights along the runway had been switched on, and through the rows of pear trees they had seen lights go on in the house. Natalia had said, "It must be any moment. The servants are getting ready to welcome their homecoming lord."

Edmond had said nothing. He wasn't convinced that preventing Reynard's landing was a good idea. He wasn't even sure it was necessary to stop him from blowing up the Condor. They hadn't finished examining the plane yet and there could well be vital evidence left inside it; but there wasn't any doubt in Edmond's mind that if Reynard blew the craft to pieces, he would be doing nothing more than confirming his guilt. And what was he going to do with the pieces? Bury them again? Grind them up and scatter them over the sea?

He remembered what Greta had said—*"He's hysterically crazy"*—and if that were true, Reynard was probably capable of doing anything to anybody, including blowing himself up along with the plane. In the dreariest sense of the word, Edmond supposed he had a duty toward Reynard, and to the city of Concord itself, to try to prevent him. He was still a doctor, after all.

They heard the LearJet before they saw it. A low whistling, coming from the southeast. Then suddenly, much lower and from a different direction than Edmond had expected, they saw the blinking lights of the plane itself. Oscar's hand waved; they switched on their headlights, and with a skidding of tires on wet grass, they roared and bounced out of the orchard toward the runway. Natalia said, "Oh, God, I hope the plane can pull up now. It seems incredibly close."

Its suspension jolting, Edmond's car reached the tarmac itself. He spun the wheel, floored the gas pedal and drove head-on down the runway toward the descending jet. Oscar's car was only a few feet behind, off to the left.

"It can't pull up!" screamed Natalia. *"Edmond, for God's sake!"*

Edmond saw the LearJet's lights, the silhouette of its wings. It seemed to fill the entire windshield, and he had no doubt in his mind they were going to collide head-on. Natalia covered her face and bent double, too terrified even to scream. The whole world was drowned out with the thunder of jet engines and a shrieking noise that hurt the eardrums.

Then, through the deafening clamor, Edmond realized that the plane had climbed over them and was still climbing, at full throttle. They had reached the end of the tarmac, and the LearJet was climbing, climbing, trying to clear the tall trees at the far end of the meadow, turning off to starboard.

People were running out of the house toward them, but

they stopped their cars, both of them, climbed out and stood in the breezy morning air watching the LearJet climbing and turning against the pale eastern sky, listening to the aching thunder of its engines as it struggled to gain height.

"It's okay," said Oscar hoarsely. "It's okay, he's going to make it."

But almost as soon as he said it, there was a faltering note in the engines that penetrated Edmond's very stomach, and the jet seemed to drop sideways. They saw its wing tip catch a tree, and then it suddenly spun and hurtled to the ground.

There was a dull thumping sound, oddly subdued. Some of the staff began to run toward the plane, not shouting, not calling out, quite silent. But then there was a massive and overwhelming explosion, one and a half thousand pounds of high explosives detonating at once—a roar that blotted out all conscious thought and made Edmond's ears sing with pain. A lurid orange fireball roiled up into the sky and vanished, a sudden genie. Then, one by one, like a flock of birds that had died in the sky, the pieces of plane began to fall around them, rustling through the orchard, clattering onto the tarmac. Among those pieces was Senator Reynard Kelly.

Oscar turned away at once and began to walk back to his car. Edmond and Natalia stayed where they were. Edmond couldn't take his eyes off the blazing wreckage. Natalia held him close and tugged the lapel of his jacket across his chest to keep him warm.

The following morning, a few minutes after eight, Piotr was eating a breakfast of cold cereal and black tea when there was a buzz at the doorbell. Wiping his mouth with the back of his hand, he went to the door calling, "Who is it?"

"It's Chiffon."

He unlocked the door and opened it. She was standing in the gloomy hallway in a red belted coat with a scarf tied around her head. Both of her eyes were bruised and there were crimson marks around her mouth and on her neck. She wore impenetrable dark glasses.

"Chiffon," he said, so quietly she could hardly hear him.

"I only came by to say thank you," she said. "They told me it was you who called them. The Russians, I mean. Mr. Cerenkov."

"They didn't hurt you?"

She shook her head. "They took good care of me. I was a valuable asset, after all. You know, considering what I knew about Reynard."

"But they let you go?"

"Haven't you heard the news this morning?"

"Not yet. My television's in for repair."

"Well, Reynard's dead. He was flying back to New Hampshire and his plane crashed. Reynard and that other creep, Dick Elmwood. Both of them were killed."

"You'd better come inside," Piotr suggested.

"No, I won't stay."

"At least have a cup of tea."

"Well . . . for a moment."

She stepped into his tiny, sparse apartment with its severe black-and-white photographs of Russia and its framed sketches of theatrical costumes. The morning sun shone on the bare, polished floorboards. He guided her through to the kitchen by her elbow, scarcely touching her.

She said, "You saved my life, you know. They almost killed me."

"Do you know what I was doing there in Milwaukee?"

"Cerenkov told me that too. It doesn't matter. I'm a little too far gone to worry about things like that. I'm a little too far gone to worry about any kind of relationship with anybody."

"Are you . . . ?" he began to ask her, but he knew the question was more than either of them could endure. Are you hurt, was what he meant. Are you damaged, traumatized, shocked? She wouldn't sit down. Instead, she stood beside the table in that ill-fitting red coat, twisting the ends of the belt around and around in her bruised and swollen fingers.

"I called Dr. Emery first thing," she said. "He couldn't believe it was me, not at first. Well, of course he thought I was dead. But when I told him about the last examination he did on me, he believed me then. He said maybe I needed a hospital. You know, just for a while."

"Yes," said Piotr. He looked down at his half-eaten breakfast. "I only hope you understand how sorry I am."

"It wasn't your fault. I got caught up in something that was bigger than I was, that's all. Just like you. When the elephants do battle, the mice get smashed, isn't that right? Didn't somebody once say that? Shakespeare?"

"I don't know. It doesn't sound like Shakespeare."

"Well, whoever," said Chiffon.

Piotr said, after a while, "I find it hard to believe that Reynard's actually dead. A plane crash? I suppose it was quick."

"Quick, slow, who cares?"

They stood side by side in silence for almost a minute. Then Chiffon said, "I won't have any tea, if it's all the same to you."

Piotr frowned as though he had never mentioned tea. But then he nodded and said, "Ah, well."

"You look terrible," Chiffon told him. "You haven't been sick, have you?"

"Well," he said, "I had some delayed bad news."

"You didn't get the Olsen part?"

"No, no. From Russia." He held up an airmail letter and then dropped it back on the table. "They censor mail, you know, and so it always takes such a long time to get here. This letter was mailed in Moscow on May fifth—almost six months ago.''

Chiffon stared at him without speaking. He tried to smile at her, but in the end he couldn't manage anything except a shrug of emotional acceptance. ''My mother died in April. In April! She had pleurisy. They cremated her two days later, and that was it. No word, no ashes. All I received was this.''

He gently shook the envelope and out fell a small lock of fair hair, bound with faded blue ribbon.

''That was mine,'' he said, tears in his eyes. ''I remember the day my mother cut it. She was baking on that day—*Pozharsky*-style patties and bread. I remember the smell. And when she cut my hair, someone in the yard outside started to slaughter a piglet. The squeals! You wouldn't believe them.''

Chiffon raised a hand toward him and touched his sleeve. Then she withdrew it.

''I'm sorry,'' she said, ''I have to go now. I have a friend waiting for me downstairs. I only came to say thank you.''

''You have nothing to thank me for. Our fates were all twisted up together.''

She left the apartment and he stood by the door as she walked quickly down the stairs to the street. He heard the door bang, and then there was silence.

''Da svedahniya,'' he told her softly.

The press was already waiting for Greta as she was hurried out of the house and across to the long, white limousine, which seemed incongruously festive for carrying a woman who was only a few hours widowed. There was a sustained flicker of electronic flash, like autumn lightning, and the *meep-meep-meep* of self-winding cameras. Four Secret Servicemen—all shoulders, tight expressions and bulging jackets—kept the reporters and jostlers away from

her, but before she was able to climb into the car, one of
the *Times* reporters managed to struggle forward and shout
out, "How do you feel, Mrs. Kelly?"

Greta's eyes glittered through the black lace of her veil,
and she gave him a look that would appear time and time
again as the face of the year, the grieving politician's
widow. "I'm devastated," she said. "Reynard Kelly was
America's last hero."

Almost immediately afterward Walt Seabrook came hurrying out of the house, his face half-hidden by his upraised
raincoat. He climbed into the Cadillac next to Greta, and
one of the Secret Service officers slammed the door. "Jesus
Christ," Walt blasphemed, "I didn't think I was going to
make it. Did you see those *crowds*?"

Greta laid a black-gloved hand on his wrist. "It's over
now. One way or another."

"Hmm," said Walt, "—until someone's behind with
his rent and decides to sell the whole story to the *Washington
Post*."

"Oh, we can take care of that. Reynard always did. Did
you ever read a bad word about Reynard in the papers?"

"Did you ever read a *good* word about Reynard in the
papers?"

"They can't do anything to harm us now," said Greta,
taking hold of his arm. "Every grieving widow is entitled
to seek some conciliatory company."

Walt sat back in his seat as the limousine bounced out of
the driveway, crept slowly through the crowds and then
abruptly squealed away toward the airport.

"I've learned one thing," Walt remarked as they sped
along Bradley Boulevard through Bethesda.

"What was that?"

"Play in your own league. Reynard was too heavy-
weight for me. My league is the state legislature; Department of Health and Welfare. No higher. I don't have the
head for it."

"You'll make it one day," Greta told him. "You just wait and see."

"Uh-uh, not me. I'll stick with what I know."

"You've lost your ambition because of what happened to Reynard?"

Walt shook his head wryly. "Let's just say I've seen for myself what I really am, and what I'm really not."

"Coward," she teased.

"No," he said. "Realist."

"Well," said Greta after a while, "maybe Reynard should have learned that lesson too. He certainly wasn't in Herr Hitler's league, was he? After all these years, Hitler finally caught up with him."

"Maybe," Walt replied. "Maybe Reynard finally caught up with himself."

They watched the suburbs of Washington unravel past them, a flat and dusty diorama. Then Greta said with self-betraying uneasiness, "You'll stay with me, won't you?"

"You think I wouldn't?"

"I don't know. Tell me. Go on, reassure me."

"All right. I'll stay with you."

She clasped his hand, so tightly that her diamond rings cut into his skin.

"Well," said Walt, "maybe we both turned out to be weaker than we'd imagined ourselves to be. It doesn't do anyone any harm to recognize his limitations."

"It's the foolishness of it that embarrasses me so much."

"Foolish? You shouldn't think you were foolish. You called Dr. Chandler, didn't you, and that wasn't foolish."

"It wasn't heroic either."

"Standing up for what you believe in is always heroic, no matter how late in the day you do it."

Greta said nothing for a long time, but at last she leaned her head against his shoulder and said, "I feel like a child,

Walt. Either a child or a very old woman. Help me, Walt; just through this part of it."

He nodded and kissed her head, and that was all Greta needed.

Humphrey awkwardly maneuvered his new green-vinyl suitcase out the doors of the bus and set it down on the wet sidewalk while he made a performance of turning up the collar of his coat, unfurling his umbrella and tugging on his string-and-vinyl gloves. Beside him the bus clashed its gears, closed its doors and bellowed off on the Bakewell road, giving one last pneumatic wheeze before it disappeared behind the higgledy-piggledy stone houses and overhanging oaks.

The rain came down in that soft, persistent curtain that characterizes the Derbyshire Dales in autumn. Low gray clouds moved silently eastward over the glistening rooftops, a procession of depressing and indeterminate dreams; the puddles in the roadway were pocked by raindrops.

Across the triangular green, beyond the stone war memorial, was the terrace of houses where Humphrey and his sister lived. He stood under his umbrella staring at it; he was surprised at how it seemed to have shrunk in only a few weeks, and at how dingy it was. The guttering at the front was still broken, and he thought of the old house on Pilogatan where Klaus Hermann had first led him. The front garden gate was still hanging off its hinges; the grass was bright and overgrown. His sister hadn't got out the mower then. Maybe in her heart of hearts she had always suspected he would come back.

He was about to pick up his suitcase when he saw the front door of the house open and his sister emerge wearing a transparent plastic rainhood and a maroon raincoat. She put up her umbrella, walked through the front gate and made her way toward the Corner Shop & Post Office, carrying her bright-yellow, polyethylene shopping bag.

Humphrey watched her in unhappy fascination. He saw her reach the shop; he even heard the tinkle of the bell as she opened the shop door. He stayed where he was, with the rain pattering on his umbrella, unable to move, paralyzed by what he had seen and lived through, unable to take the first step that would enable him to rejoin his everyday life.

How could he tell his sister what had happened to him in Sweden? How could he explain what he had felt when Bill Bennett had shot Birgitta? Or when Angelika Rangström had cut her wrists with his fishing blade? What would his sister possibly understand about pain, and blood, and the terrible embrace he had been given by a man who had killed three thousand people?

He waited and waited in the rain. In the west, toward Longstone Moor, the sky began to lighten a little, a yellowish smear of autumnal sunshine. And just then, its roof reflecting that sunshine as though it were a sign from the angels, the Chesterfield bus appeared over the brow of the hill, heading back in the direction from which Humphrey had come. Without thinking, his heart tight, Humphrey picked up his suitcase and walked across the road to the bus shelter, where he stood in line behind two old men in wet tweed caps and a ruddy-faced young woman with a squalling child and a folding buggy.

Humphrey mounted the wet brown steps of the bus and fumbled around in his coat pocket for his fare. He wrestled his suitcase onto the rack. Then he sat down beside a fat woman who smelled of saddle soap and onions. He didn't look back.

Just as the bus was pulling away from the curb, he saw his sister come out of the corner shop. He thought to himself: good-bye, my dear. You will have to believe that your brother Humphrey is dead, and perhaps that will be all for the best. Live out your small, diminished life; enjoy your church bazaars and your craft sales—and your mints

at Holy Communion. A new life is waiting for me somewhere in the rain, somewhere out beyond Chesterfield's
twisted spire, out there in the wide and vicious world.

The next shop was Nether End. The bus drew into the
side of the road, and the other driver waited patiently
while a very old lady was helped up the steps. The doors
were open and Humphrey could smell the rain and the
dales. He looked at the fat woman sitting next to him. She
stared back at him unsmiling, very Derbyshire. He got up
out of his seat, struggled toward the front of the bus and
retrieved his suitcase.

"Getting off, chum?" the driver asked. "You're paid as
far as Chesterfield bus station."

"I—ahem," replied Humphrey indistinctly. He manhan-
dled his suitcase off the bus and stood back, turning up his
coat collar again. All the passengers stared at him out the
rain-beaded windows as the bus drove off. In a minute it
was gone, leaving no trace behind it of Humphrey's imaginary future but tire tracks on the muddy verge and the
smell of diesel.

Humphrey suddenly realized he had left his umbrella on
the bus.

He changed his suitcase from his right hand to his left
and began the long walk back home. The rain was lighter
now but still steady enough to soak his shoulders and cling
to his eyelashes.

As he walked, he remembered the line in *Lolita* that
describes why twelve-year-old Dolores Haze crept back
into the arms of her middle-aged lover (yes, covertly
Humphrey had read *Lolita*): "You see, she had absolutely
nowhere else to go."

And as he walked, and as he remembered that line,
Humphrey had to lift his suitcase so he could wipe his eyes
with the back of his hand in case anyone realized his
cheeks were not wet with rain, but with tears.

* * *

Bill Bennett was sitting at the bar of the Sheraton, drinking dry martinis and nibbling peanuts, when the small, narrow-chested man in a gray suit came across and sat down next to him. There was no hesitation, no apology, despite the fact that there were plenty of other empty bar stools.

"Well, well," said Bill, taking another small handful of peanuts. "I was wondering when someone was going to get in touch."

The man took off his horn-rimmed glasses and wiped them with one of the paper coasters. He stared at Bill with protuberant, unfocused eyes and then put his glasses on again. "We didn't meet in Haiti?" he asked. "In nineteen seventy-one, when Baby Doc took over? At the Toussaint Hotel?"

"Not me, pal," said Bill. "Are you going to buy me a drink?"

"Sure. My name's Welby. As in Marcus, M.D."

"Nice to know you."

Welby reached inside his coat pocket and produced a long white envelope that he passed over as though it were a gift. "Your check," he said. "Also your assignment papers."

Bill tucked the envelope into his windbreaker.

"Aren't you going to open it?" asked Welby.

"And let you see how much I make?"

"I know how much you make."

"Well then, I still don't need to open it, do I?"

Welby beckoned the bartender over and said, "My friend here will have another martini, please. I'll have a beer. Lätøl."

"You drink that piss?" Bill asked.

Welby ignored the question and said, "Don't you want to know where you've been posted?"

"Why should I? They promised me a stateside posting, and if it isn't a stateside posting, I'm going to quit."

"I don't think they'd like it very much if you quit."

"They promised me a stateside posting, that's all; and if they're not going to keep their promises, I'm not interested."

Welby coughed. Then he said, "You know how things are. Times change, policies differ."

"What does that mean?" Bill demanded.

"It means we have to be circumspect."

"And circumspect means I don't get the job they promised me? Is that it?"

"Well . . . there are problems. The Swedish security people complained to the State Department. And—well, you know. The can has to be carried back by someone."

Bill said sharply, "I did as I was told. I did what I was instructed to do, and I did it within the parameters of my authority."

"I know, yes," said Welby soothingly. "But all the same, there was kind of a mess. We're not blaming you personally, but like I said, someone has to carry the can back—and be seen doing it."

"Meaning me."

"Well, you were the agent in the field, after all. And the last thing we want to do is to upset the Swedes."

The bartender brought their drinks. Bill prodded at his olive, then fished it out and ate it.

"Where are they sending me?" he asked at last.

"You have a choice."

"What kind of a choice?"

"Costa Rica."

"That's the choice? Costa Rica?"

"Do you want it or don't you? We think Gulderhof could be there."

Bill said, "The choice is either I go to Costa Rica or I don't go to Costa Rica?"

"Well, yes."

He sipped his drink. Then he turned to Welby and said, "Gulderhof?"

"We've had a tip-off."

Bill shook his head. "I don't think I want to go to Costa Rica, okay?"

"That's your privilege."

"And that's all?"

"What else do you want?"

"Well, I don't know—maybe some other kind of assignment."

Welby said, "I'm sorry. Costa Rica is all we have."

"Can I change my mind?" Bill asked.

"You mean, can you change your mind and accept?"

"Yes."

"If you want to."

Bill hesitated and then said, "No. I don't think I want to go to Costa Rica."

"Again, that's your privilege."

"That's all then?" Bill asked.

"That's all."

They drank in silence. Then Bill excused himself and went up to his room. He stood with his back to the door and tore open the long white envelope. It contained a certified check for $62,500 and a note on plain paper saying simply, DEP ARLANDA 11.00 HRS: ARR SAN JOSE COSTA RICA 15.45 LOCAL.

He crumpled up the paper and tossed it across the room. Then he went to the bathroom mirror and stared at himself. Was this it? The end of his whole career? Squeezed out of the service like a teardrop from a cynical eye? No fuss, no argument. Just occluded from the world of secrets and sudden death as though he had never existed—as though that world had never been?

He suddenly felt very ordinary. He felt as though, somehow, Humphrey's mundaneness had rubbed off on him, tarnished his personal glamour, scuffed his ego. He had a strong urge to call him up and speak to him—either to shout angrily at him or to tell him that all the time, *he*, Humphrey, had been right about everything, and particularly about betrayal.

He drew back his jacket and looked at the butt of his holstered .38. He thought to himself: this is it. This is the instrument of betrayal. And if killing is a way of life, maybe it's a way of relief too. Quick, black, silent. What more could anybody wish for? Killing was almost better than love. . . .

Except that he was too much of a soldier, too much of an egotist, and, in the final analysis, too much of a coward. That was the worst thing Humphrey had done to him. Humphrey had shown him that he wasn't brave.

There was a knock at the door. It was the chambermaid, asking if she could make up his room.

"I'm leaving," he told her, and of course he was.

Two days later, under a warrant issued by the Supreme Court of New Hampshire, police, pathologists and forensic examiners came with shovels, picks and hoisting gear and began to excavate the carcass of the Condor. It rained all day, a fine drizzle that silvered the grass and clung in teardrops to the brims of their hats.

One of the first important finds was within the rear part of the Condor's fuselage. Neither Edmond nor Oscar were there to see it because they were still undergoing questioning at police headquarters, but Greta had flown up to Concord early that morning, and an officer was sent to the house to ask her if she would care to visit the site.

Young Bernie was there too, with his bicycle and chewing gum, unnoticed by the sodden crowd of diggers, scientists and officials.

They sheltered the discovery under a plastic awning so its peculiar fragility wouldn't be damaged by the rain.

Greta came forward and stood and stared at it for a very long time.

It was the mummified body of a young woman in a coat that must once have been maroon-colored. She wore black fur-lined boots, presumably against the cold during her long flight, and a black-feathered hat. In her arms she still clutched a wizened little creature in a faded and tattered blue suit. It was the mummy of a child, perhaps four or five years old, although it had shrunk so much it was difficult to tell.

In the woman's luggage they discovered a letter from Reynard Kelly, telling her how much he loved her and that he hoped one day to see her again. Ilse, my dearest.

Greta said to the police officer standing next to her, "That was my husband's first mistress."

The officer looked embarrassed and glanced back toward his sergeant for reassurance. The sergeant shrugged. Who cared? Let her ramble.

"And that child," added Greta, "if this plane had landed safely, and if its mission had been successfully accomplished—that child might very well have grown up to be the first führer of the United States."

HYPER-POLIO Ko'd BY K-SOLVENT

Hyper-polio can now be brought under swift and effective control, thanks to the discovery of "K-Solvent," which wipes out the virus with one hundred-percent effectiveness.

Assistant Secretary of Health David R. Snoman said in Washington today that the Federal government is financing urgent and widespread treatment of hyper-polio victims and the immunization of everyone within affected areas in the country.

The miracle breakthrough was effected by the government's special biochemical research team with the assistance of information on viral behavior received from Germany.

Mr. Snoman said, "We are confident that this terrible epidemic will soon be nothing more than a nightmarish memory."

GRAHAM MASTERTON

BESTSELLING BOOKS FROM TOR

☐ 58725-1 *Gardens of Stone* by Nicholas Proffitt $3.95
  58726-X Canada $4.50

☐ 51650-8 *Incarnate* by Ramsey Campbell $3.95
  51651-6 Canada $4.50

☐ 51050-X *Kahawa* by Donald E. Westlake $3.95
  51051-8 Canada $4.50

☐ 52750-X *A Manhattan Ghost Story* by T.M. Wright
  $3.95
  52751-8 Canada $4.50

☐ 52191-9 *Ikon* by Graham Masterton $3.95
  52192-7 Canada $4.50

☐ 54550-8 *Prince Ombra* by Roderick MacLeish $3.50
  54551-6 Canada $3.95

☐ 50284-1 *The Vietnam Legacy* by Brian Freemantle
  $3.50
  50285-X Canada $3.95

☐ 50487-9 *Siskiyou* by Richard Hoyt $3.50
  50488-7 Canada $3.95

Buy them at your local bookstore or use this handy coupon:
Clip and mail this page with your order

TOR BOOKS—Reader Service Dept.
P.O. Box 690, Rockville Centre, N.Y. 11571

**Please send me the book(s) I have checked above. I am enclosing
$_____ (please add $1.00 to cover postage and handling).
Send check or money order only—no cash or C.O.D.'s.**

Mr./Mrs./Miss _____

Address _____.

City _____ State/Zip _____

**Please allow six weeks for delivery. Prices subject to change without
notice.**